RT Book Reviews raves about Cindy Dees

Cl

"Dees blen
in this character-d
keeping readers en
is unveiled and t

Night Rescue

"Dees's exciting, action-packed story speeds along on all cylinders, with a smoking-hot pair at the center of it all. Your fingers will get exercise as they rapidly turn the pages of this compulsively readable tale."

Flash of Death

"Dees brings readers into an action-packed world, with superhuman operatives. Add to that a sympathetic heroine and a sizzling romance, and this is a book you can't put down."

Deadly Sight

"Dees crafts the perfect blend of romance and suspense with her latest story featuring members of the special ops group Code X. A solid, suspenseful plot, tormented, vulnerable characters and beautiful, compelling writing will keep you turning the pages."

The 9-Month Bodyguard

"There's action and hot attraction galore in this addition to the Love in 60 Seconds series. Dees does a terrific job of advancing the overall series while lending her unique talent to her vibrant individual contribution."

Also available from
Cindy Dees
and Harlequin HQN

Close Pursuit
Take the Bait

CINDY DEES

HOT INTENT

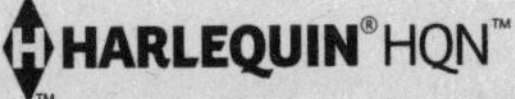

ISBN-13: 978-0-373-77889-8

HOT INTENT

This edition published by arrangement with Harlequin Books S.A.

For questions and comments about the quality of this book, please contact us at CustomerService@Harlequin.com.

HARLEQUIN®
www.Harlequin.com

Printed in U.S.A.

This book is for you, dear reader.
You, who enthusiastically pick up books and throw yourself headfirst into stories, who let your imagination soar and who grant me the privilege of taking you on a journey of thrills, chills, laughter and love. The storytelling process would not be complete without you.
Thank you for being here, and enjoy the ride!

CHAPTER ONE

KATIE MCCLOUD STARTED as the front door's elaborate electronic locks buzzed to indicate they were disengaging. Her heart leaped in eager anticipation. He was home. Finally. After nearly a year away.

She'd been head over heels for Alex Peters when he was sucked into some supersecret CIA training program last year. He'd been yanked away from her just as they were really getting to know each other. But now he was back, and their life together could resume where it left off.

Their relationship had been forged in danger as they'd fled forces intent on killing them and the infant girl they'd rescued together. Alex, a trauma surgeon by training, had been in the remote central Asian country of Zaghastan illegally delivering babies, and she'd been there as his translator and babysitter. Although who'd watched whom was still open to debate.

His CIA handler, André Fortinay, had briefed her not to assume anything about her relationship with him when he got home. To let Alex set the tone and pace of the reunion. Almost as if they'd broken him in some way while he was gone. What exactly had they done to him in his training, anyway?

Alex stepped into the living room, and her heart gave a lurch. God, he was more beautiful than she remembered. Tall. Dark. And even more dangerous than before. His coffee-dark hair was a little lighter, his skin darkly bronzed. He was leaner through the waist and bigger across the shoulders. But those changes weren't what really arrested her.

Something intangible had changed about him. His natural confidence had been replaced by something else, something more…powerful. Now it came across as utter belief in himself. He'd always had a lethal quality to him, but it had a new focus about it now, a cold reserve that oozed don't-screw-with-me-in-a-dark-alley.

She realized she'd risen to her feet after the fact. Crud. She'd planned to stay seated, arranged sexily on his white leather sofa. Oh, well. So much for pretending to be calm, cool and sophisticated. She was a hot mess and would always be a hot mess. To heck with André Fortinay's do's and don'ts for Alex's homecoming.

"Alex!" she cried joyfully. She started forward and managed to catch the edge of the flokati area rug with her heel, slam her shin into the glass coffee table and pitch headlong into Alex's arms as he dived forward to catch her.

"Been working on your coordination in my absence?" he murmured as he drew her up against his body. His mouth closed on hers and the wild magic exploded between them like it always did. His lips slashed across hers as her mouth opened eagerly. Their tongues collided, and he inhaled her like he couldn't get enough of her. At least that hadn't changed about him. Relief crept through her nervousness.

Her arms slid around his waist. He was more muscular, harder, than before. But then, so was she. She'd been working out like crazy while he was gone. Some of it had been boredom, and some frankly had been a remedy for horniness. And a little of it had been insecurity over how a girl like her was ever going to hold the attention of a man like him. He was James Bond, and she was the girl next door.

He came up for air long enough to murmur, "Where's Dawn?"

"Asleep. Would you like to peek into her room and see her, though?"

He smiled and the warmth reached all the way to his eyes. "Yes."

Keeping her plastered against his side, he strode across the sleek living room of his penthouse condo and down the hall to the nursery where their adopted daughter, who recently turned one year old, slept.

He cracked the door open and crossed the floor to the crib. "My God, she's grown so much," he breathed.

A wedge of light from the doorway fell upon her blond curls and chubby cheeks. She slept on her tummy, her knees tucked up under herself and her diaper poking up under the pink blanket. Adorable didn't begin to cover her angelic cuteness.

"I thought they taught you in medical school that growing is what babies do."

He snorted without taking his gaze off the sleeping baby. “She’s gorgeous.”

“Did you ever get a good look at her birth mother before she died? The girl was stunning. Our Dawn’s going to keep you hopping in about thirteen years when the boys start sniffing around.”

“There will be no sniffing,” he said firmly.

She laughed under her breath. “Good luck with that.”

He backed out of the doorway and headed toward the white quartz bar in the corner of the living room. He poured himself a shot of expensive Russian vodka neat and tossed it down. He made a sound of appreciation.

“Missed the good stuff?” she asked.

“You have no idea.”

“Tell me about it. What was your training like?” André had told her not to ask any questions, but he could get over it. Alex would think something weird was up if she didn’t display at least a little curiosity.

His eyes shuttered instantly and completely. “Rough.” And that was obviously all he planned to say about it. Great. He was back to minimal communication punctuated by long silences.

“Fair enough. Glad to be home?”

He looked around the condo, his sharp gaze probing the corners carefully. “Thanks for house-sitting.”

She laughed. “It was a real hardship, living in all this luxury for free.” She added more seriously, “Actually, it helped me feel a little closer to you while you were gone. I missed you.”

He bit out grimly, "I missed you, too."

She knew him well enough not to take it personally that he sounded supremely unhappy about that development. He'd been raised by his spy father to believe that all human emotions were weaknesses in need of expunging from his heart and mind.

"André said you might want some time by yourself to decompress after your training. I've talked with my parents, and they've invited Dawn and me to come hang out at their place for a while and give you some space."

"No," he replied sharply. "Stay."

"Are you sure?"

"You're safest here."

He wasn't kidding. She'd spent the past year learning the security features of his fortresslike home and they were daunting. Like him. The place was elegant and gorgeous on the inside, hard and impenetrable on the outside.

"You haven't lived with a toddler before. Dawn will totally destroy your grand solitude. Chaos is the normal state of affairs around here," she warned him in all seriousness. Not to mention, she was concerned about his reflexive responses to a baby. Who knew what knee-jerk reactions had been hardwired into him this year? Were she and Dawn even safe around him? After seeing the icy detachment in his eyes, she wasn't a hundred percent sure.

"I insist."

Big words. Still, she worried about how he would react to Dawn and her. He'd lived alone basically his entire life, and the transition to having an overnight family was not going to be easy for him. No way would she even consider staying here like this were it not for the threat his father posed to them all.

"I had an intercom system installed while you were away, Alex. I hope you don't mind. It's just that the apartment's so big I can't hear Dawn if she's in her room and I'm in—" She broke off. How to describe the master bedroom? Was it still just his room? Their room? It had been her room for the past year.

"Good call on an intercom," he remarked.

"Are you hungry? Tired? It's late. Have you traveled a long way to get here? Oops. Strike that last one. But you do look tired."

He actually looked more than tired. Up close, she spied lavender shadows beneath his eyes, and a certain haggard quality clung to him. He looked bone-deep exhausted. She could imagine the kind of stuff the CIA trained its field operatives to do, and he probably had good cause to look wiped out.

She murmured, "Let me check on Dawn, and then I'll be back to welcome you home more thoroughly."

His gray, intelligent gaze went alert and predatory. Her tummy fluttered excitedly in response. Who'd have guessed she was still such an adrenaline junkie after a year of sedate parenthood?

"I'll be waiting," he murmured.

Now why did that sound like a threat? Was it just his habitual economy of expression, or was it more? Either way, her heart leaped in anticipation.

Hah. And André had hinted broadly that Alex

might not want to have a romantic relationship with her when he got home. He'd been home five minutes and already laid a smoking-hot kiss on her and was now moving things to the bedroom. Along with her triumph, a dose of abject gratitude flowed through her.

He was still hers. Brilliant, tortured Alex Peters—genius, surgeon and now spy—still wanted her. Part of her—okay, a scarily big part of her—worried that it was too good to be true. That he was going through the motions now because he thought she expected him to. That the past year's worth of training had forced him to revert to form and shut down emotionally. That he would ultimately push her out of his life.

Worried, she leaned over the crib in the nursery. Sweet Dawn, the best baby ever, settled in under her blanket without waking up. If the way she kicked off blankets was any indication, she was on her way to being a great soccer player.

Li'l munchkin had been through a lot in her short life. She'd been born into a war zone and her mother had died in childbirth despite Alex's heroic efforts to save the girl. Her entire village had been massacred and the three of them had barely made it out with their lives.

But thanks to the trust fund Alex had set up, the legalities his lawyer had sorted out to give Alex and her permanent custody of Dawn and, of course, the roof Alex had put over both of their heads, it was nothing but smooth sailing for Dawn now. For all of them. No more running around being chased by bad guys out to kill them. Katie tiptoed out of the nursery and down the hall to Alex's bedroom.

ALEX STOOD IN the darkness of his bedroom absorbing the familiarity of its dark shapes, noting the differences Katie had brought to the space. He could do this. He could pretend to be a normal man. Living a normal life. He could experience pleasure. Family. Love. He would not break.

Nothing would break him.

They'd tortured him and screwed with his head and made him kill. But in spite of it all, he had not broken. And to think, he'd once believed his father a bastard for training him like a spy. If only he'd known just how easy his old man had taken it on him.

Alex pulled his shirt off over his head, not bothering to unbutton it. Cool air blew lightly across his skin causing goose bumps on his chest, back and arms. He kicked off his shoes and stripped off his pants and socks. Naked, he stood stock-still in the middle of his bedroom. Nothing but darkness clothed him.

Memories rolled over him then. Remembered tortures that made him tremble even now. They'd begun like this, too. Exposed skin, cool breath upon his flesh. Then pain. Exquisite, fiery pain.

And in his agony, all the demons from his past had come calling, singing to him like sirens, calling him home. It would have been so easy to lose himself in them. Then check out of the prolonged agony and go to that other place inside his soul.

But he'd chosen the pain. He'd stayed present. Suffered the agonies of hell. Only then had he been sure he was still alive.

Even now, especially now, he wondered if any of this was real. It was so mundane. His house. Katie. The baby.

Was this the cruelest torture of all? Were they going to let him get comfortable and then rip it all away from him? If he knew what was good for him, he would reject it all. He would find the pain and live there.

But that welcome-home kiss…

He swore violently. Kissing Katie might just be worth going to hell for.

KATIE STEPPED INTO the darkness of the master bedroom and screamed a little as strong arms came out of nowhere to sweep her up against a hard body. "Gotcha. I win," Alex announced. "You are the worst spy ever."

"Mmm, but I'm the softest and sexiest and love you the best."

"True," he agreed as his mouth closed over hers.

The explosive attraction that had simmered between them before erupted, crackling like chain lightning across her skin, striking further and further inside her as their kiss deepened. Craving twisted her innards into tight knots of desire. She could never seem to get enough of him.

Her clothes went every which way as the passion overtook them, and frantic urgency spurred them onward. Naked and devouring each other, they fell onto his bed. She'd have laughed, except he speared his hand into her hair and pulled her head back so he could plunder her neck and shoulder with teeth and tongue, and the laugh became a gasp of pleasure instead.

He took control tonight, demanding ever more response from her as he kissed and stroked and nipped his way across her flesh. Where she was cold, he was hot. Where she was soft, he was hard. And where she was hungry, he starved her for more.

With hands and mouth, he played her body, using his knowledge of her pleasures and desires to drive her into a frenzy of blind lust. She needed to have him crushing her into the mattress, to fill her body with his, to feel his power and desire as he pounded into her…oh, yes. She needed all of that in the worst way.

But frustratingly, he withheld it from her tonight. Instead, he kissed his way down her body until she gasped with need. His tongue circled her most sensitive bud, wet and hot and maddening until a climax started to claw its way out of her belly. And then his mouth withdrew.

"Tell me something, Katie. How bad do you want this?"

Oh, no. "Um, bad enough to beg?"

"Is that all?" he murmured in disappointment.

"Bad enough to do anything you want?" she tried.

"You'll do that anyway," he replied dismissively.

True. She never could say no to him. "Bad enough to cry?"

His thoughtful silence was encouraging. Although on second thought, she wasn't sure she wanted to find out how he would make her cry. He'd warned her before that his sexual tastes could run pretty dark at times. And he'd just come off a year of pretty dark, violent training, if she had to guess.

Before he could act on her ill-considered offer, she added, "Bad enough to say 'please?'"

He rose up over her on powerfully muscled arms. "Say it."

"Please, Alex." When he didn't move, she continued. "Please give us both an orgasm. Or ten. I want you so much I can't stand it. Now. Take me now. *Please.*"

In typical Alex fashion, he continued to stare down at her, letting her frustration and desperation build until she thought she might die.

"Will you beg me to stop, too?" he growled.

"Never."

He made a skeptical sound. Cynical mood he was in tonight.

He waited until she all but sobbed with need. The pleasure she knew he could give her hovered just out of reach like a tantalizing piece of candy dangling on a string. Why did he insist on playing these wicked games with her? He knew how he made her feel. He knew how deeply she lusted after him. And still, he made her wait. And suffer. As if he was punishing her for making him feel the same way she did.

She knew why he did it, of course. He hated love. But it didn't make this cruel game of his any easier to bear.

Her entire body throbbed with unfulfilled desire for the sex that was right there. So close, and yet so totally out of her control. If she could only get him to actually make love to her, his emotional barriers would crumble the way they always did. But for now, he fought it. So hard, he struggled to hold himself apart from her. From everyone.

Tonight his fight was worse than ever. His features pulled into a macabre rictus of suffering half-lost in shadows. It was hard for her to look at. What had they done to him?

She put her hands on either side of his face and tried silently to reach past the suffering to the man beneath. But he was lost. His eyes were black hollows. All she saw in them was pain, and more pain.

"Come back to me, Alex," she whispered.

His hands went around her neck. They were big and capable and strong. He could snap her neck quickly or choke her to death slowly if he so chose. Soul-chilling terror flashed through her, along with instinctive *knowing.*

They'd turned him into a killer.

She spoke slowly and clearly into the hush while he debated ending her life. "Do it, Alex. If it will heal your soul, do it."

"Gah!" He flung her back against the pillows and grabbed her hips, shoving her thighs wide. If he'd thought to scare her, he failed. She'd decided long ago that she trusted him with her life. Giving him her body was kid stuff by comparison. She arched her chest up toward him in invitation.

The fight played itself out on the beautiful, dark features of his face above her. He hated her for how she made him *feel,* and yet he craved those feelings with every ounce of his being. He wanted with his entire soul not to give in to her, to what she represented. Enough that he'd seriously considered killing her. He was physically shaking with the effort of withholding himself from her.

She truly wished love didn't hurt him so much. But she also knew he needed it. Needed this. He'd been gone a year. That was a long time not to feel anything nor to let down his emotional walls. If she knew the CIA, his training had only reinforced his belief that feelings equaled weakness.

He plunged into her without warning, hard and deep, his capitulation not quite painful as her body stretched to accommodate him. It had been a year for her, too, and he was not a small man. Oh, how he wanted to hurt her. It was right there in his eyes. But he couldn't quite bring himself to do it, and she trusted him not to.

He might hate the fact that he had feelings for another human being, but he did have them for her. Dawn and her—his Achilles' heels and greatest weaknesses. The two of them had snuck past his guard and forced him to join the human race, like it or not. Most of the time, he did not like.

Tonight, he definitely did not like. Rage and self-loathing flashed across his face. Someone who knew him less well might not have seen them. But she'd greedily memorized every nuance of him in their brief time together last year. And she hadn't forgotten anything. Sadness washed over her for the lonely child who had grown into this isolated, injured man.

He withdrew most of the way from her body. She braced herself, and sure enough, he slammed into her again. But this time, a faint shudder passed through him. *Thank God. He was starting to crack.* She opened her body and soul completely to him, allowing him to take whatever he needed. Offering herself up on the altar of his hatred and love.

He groaned his surrender and the terrible tension left his body. She exhaled in relief. One of these times, his walls would not break down. What then? She didn't want to be around when that happened. She suspected his capacity for love would be exceeded only by his capacity for cruelty.

She wrapped her arms and heart around him, drawing him into her as his arms collapsed. His weight crushed her the way she'd wished for, and he pounded into her with all the desperation she could have hoped for. She locked her legs around his hips and rode the storm, meeting it with abandon, glorying in the power of it as the two of them flung themselves into the maelstrom and were swept away.

The sex was hot and slippery, with heavy breathing and hair stuck in the sweat on her face, and bite marks on her neck and scratches on his back, bodies straining urgently toward each other until where she stopped and he began blurred and disappeared. And through it all, he poured his soul into her and she refilled the empty places in his heart with her unconditional love.

Gradually, gradually, the sex changed. Grew more languid. Sensual. Personal. He propped himself on his elbows and pushed her hair back from her face. He found a slow, gliding stroke that her body matched with easy undulations born of exhaustion and relief. It was sultry and sexy and made her breath catch in her throat. He wasn't entirely gone, after all, her Alex. The killer hadn't quite won out. Not yet.

Finally, at long last, the massive, emotional orgasm that had been clawing for escape inside her broke free, ripping her apart with its power as she lurched up against Alex and cried out wordlessly. With a drawn-out groan of his own, he found his release, and she fell back to the bed panting.

His forehead rested on hers, and she lazily counted his heartbeats pulsing against her breast. He might win when it came to sneaking up on her in the dark, but she always won this battle of wills.

So far.

Normally she slept like a baby after making love with Alex. He demanded everything she had to give physically and emotionally, usually leaving her drained, but peaceful. Tonight, though, she found herself lying awake, staring at the flickering shadows on the ceiling from the swimming pool outside, worrying about him. About them.

He was fundamentally different than before. Changed.

What had they done to him? Was she an idiot to trust him? She knew in the depths of her soul that he would never do anything intentionally to hurt Dawn. But at the end of the day, could she say the same thing about herself? There'd been a moment there when she thought he'd slipped away from her into a very dark and violent place.

It was all well and good for him to insist that she and Dawn stay here with him and play house. But she didn't kid herself that he was in an emotional place to let go of his past. If anything, the past year of training had driven him deeper into that locked-down part of himself. Sex with him—heck, *life* with him—had the potential to be very scary if she ever failed to break through his rage.

If only there was a way to exorcise the demons from his past. The biggest one of all being the one he never spoke of.

His mother. The woman who'd left when he was an infant, never to be seen or heard from again. She'd abandoned him with his father—a Russian spy who used Alex as a cover to infiltrate the United States and who brutally trained his son to be a spy just like him. Alex didn't even know his mother's name. No doubt, her abandonment was the source of his rage toward all women. If only she could find his mother for him—

Uncle Charlie, a deputy director of Plans at the CIA, *did* owe her a huge favor for getting Alex to agree to work for the agency. Oh, technically, he'd gone to work for Doctors Unlimited, but they all knew it was a CIA front.

With all the CIA resources her uncle could bring to bear on the problem, could Alex's mother be found? Could she lay his demons to rest for him once and for all?

It was worth a shot. She had nothing to lose by trying, right?

Excited at the prospect of how surprised—and potentially healed—Alex would be if she could present his mother to him, she rolled over and went to sleep, eager for morning to come.

IT WAS NEARLY NOON, though, before showers, breakfast and playtime with Dawn wound down. Katie watched Alex like a hawk with the baby, but he showed no violent tendencies with the toddler. In fact, she thought she glimpsed moments of genuine pleasure on his face as he flew Dawn around the living room to the accompaniment of baby squeals of laughter.

Alex offered to take the baby out for a walk so Katie could run the errands she'd mentioned over breakfast. As Alex and Dawn headed for the local park, she went the other direction down the sidewalk toward a shopping area bound to have cabs loitering nearby.

Alex's insurance company had delivered a new BMW to replace his wrecked one, but Katie was leery of driving the German sports car. She hadn't gotten around to buying a car of her own yet. Alex had sent word to her to feel free to use his checking account for anything at all in his absence, but she'd felt hinky about buying something as expensive as a car with his money. Yes, the account had enough money to buy ten cars in it, but still. She was a McCloud, and McClouds had their pride.

Besides, Washington, D.C., had great public transportation, and a train ran daily from D.C. to her hometown in Pennsylvania.

She'd been home often in the past year to visit her

folks. Dawn officially had all five of her uncles and both grandparents wrapped around her tiny pinkie finger. Katie shook her head. She hated to see how bad they were all going to spoil her as she got older.

After seeing the emotional condition Alex was in last night, she probably ought to consider making a quick trip with Dawn to Pennsylvania to let him decompress a little more by himself. But memory of the pain on his face as he fought his demons made Katie long to stay and comfort him. *Grr.* No one had warned her that the demands of being a parent and a lover could conflict so badly.

Her thoughts jerked back to the present as the taxi stopped at the guard shack in front of CIA headquarters. She climbed out and the vehicle pulled away quickly. She could relate to the driver's nervousness. A sinister vibe did radiate off the sprawling building. After showing proper ID to the guard, she walked across the visitors' parking lot and through the main entrance.

It was ballsy to show up unannounced at Charlie's work like this, but she figured the man could stand a reminder of just how much he owed her.

She was duly checked out in the agency's computers at the reception desk and given a visitor's badge. An escort, a perky coed girl no older than Katie, took her up to see Charlie. Her uncle was a deputy director of Plans and had a plush office with a nice view of the woods outside.

"Katie! What brings you here today? Is everything okay?"

Which she supposed was spy-speak for *Alex hasn't gone off the reservation already, has he?* "Yup. Everything's great. Thanks again for sending in the cavalry to rescue us from that hit squad and for arranging Alex's training."

He leaned back in his chair and pursed his lips. When he spoke, his low-country Southern drawl was a little thicker than usual. "Oh, I don't know that my crew did that much to help last year. You and Alex had things well under control by the time we arrived."

It was a lie, but she wasn't interested in arguing about it today. "I have a favor to ask of you, Uncle Charlie." She cursed herself silently for using that little-girl tone of voice with him. She was done acting like the baby of the whole damned family. She'd grown up a lot in the past year, and her clan could just get used to it. Although *she* probably was the first person who had to get used to it.

"Do tell." His expression went bland and unreadable, his blue eyes oddly opaque all of a sudden. He'd dropped into master spy mode. Alex did the exact same thing.

"You said you'd owe me one if I brought Alex to you. And I did. He's completed his training, and he has agreed to work for Doctors Unlimited."

"He's been out of training for one day. And you're already calling your chit in? So soon?"

"Yes," she replied firmly. "I've had a year to think about it, and seeing Alex last night only confirmed my decision. I need to find out who Alex's mother is. The circumstances of his conception, birth and her leaving. Not knowing anything tortures him. I figure it's the least we all can do for him after what we've put him through."

"Did he talk to you about his training?" Charlie asked quickly.

She frowned. "No. He didn't." But why did Charlie react that way after she used the phrase *after what we've put him through?* What on earth did they do to him during his year of training with them?

Charlie leaned back in his leather desk chair. "And what makes you think we know anything about his mother?" Obviously, he didn't want her to ask any more questions about Alex's training. She went along with the change of subject.

She shrugged. "You're the CIA. You can find out anything."

He steepled his fingers together thoughtfully but didn't deny the truth of her words. "And then we'll be even?" he asked.

"Correct. Give me Alex's mother, and we're good."

He didn't say yes or no exactly, but she got the impression that he was going to look into it. She supposed that was the most she could hope for out of a spy like him. She'd learned that much around Alex. Spies were hesitant to answer questions directly or commit themselves to anything.

As another intern walked her out of the CIA building, it belatedly occurred to Katie that her uncle hadn't put up much of a fight at the notion of being able to find Alex's mother. What did he know that he wasn't telling? Had the CIA already found the woman? It would make sense that in vetting Alex to become an asset for them they'd looked into his mysterious, missing parent. Why, then, hadn't they shared what they'd found with him out of general principles?

Suspicion blossomed in her gut that there was more to the story of Alex's mother than Charlie was letting on. Why did it feel like she'd just cracked open the lid of Pandora's box? Maybe she should slam the thing back shut and put a big, fat lock on it.

Memory of the rage and desperation in Alex's eyes last night as he fought off his impulse to kill her flashed into her mind. Nope. Whatever evils hid in Pandora's stupid box, it was high time to let them out and deal with them.

CHAPTER TWO

ALEX LOOKED AROUND reflexively, checking for tails or suspicious individuals, as he reached the playground a few blocks from the house. No one who didn't belong in the area was obvious. If they were out there, they were good enough at their work to stay hidden. Which meant he didn't have to kill anyone today. Relief trickled into his awareness. He wondered idly if he did something like that in front of Dawn, would she remember it? Would it traumatize her or was she too young to register such violence? He supposed babies and murder didn't mix. He pushed the stroller deeper into the park.

The sheer normalcy of this place was a shock to his system. After the past year, it was hard to believe that this other world existed…filled with people who were so clueless. So naive. So completely unaware of the dangerous, parallel world that existed alongside this boring, safe, average existence of theirs. Spies and criminals, watchers and killers, were out here. Wolves among the lambs. And he was one of the biggest and baddest wolves now.

Dawn squealed, jerking his attention back to her. She wasn't old enough to play on the climbing fort or swing in the swings, but she smiled up at the sunshine and waved her arms excitedly whenever other children laughed or shouted nearby. She would undoubtedly spend many happy childhood hours here.

He silently vowed to make sure her life was nothing like his. He'd spent his youth in a virtual boot camp being turned into a future master spy by Peter Koronov. He only hoped that Dawn would never learn to hate him the way he hated his father when he bothered to feel anything at all for the man.

Although after the past year, he was starting to wonder if Peter had been holding back more than Alex realized as a kid. Was it possible that his father wasn't quite the villain he'd always painted him to be in his own mind?

He reached into the stroller and adjusted Dawn's hoodie sweatshirt up a little higher around her ears. She smiled up at him and his heart melted at the trust in her dark eyes. He smiled back at her.

His phone rang and he fished it out of his pocket. The unidentified caller's number was long and began with a foreign exit code and the country code number for the United States. His jaw clenched. Only one person could be calling him from overseas. He knew better than to ignore the call.

"Hello, Peter," he said grimly.

"Son. How are you doing after your training?"

"Fine. Why are you calling me?"

"To thank you at long last."

"For what?" Alex asked with long-suffering patience. He'd learned long ago that the best way to get rid of Peter was to play along and not fight him. Peter made people pay when they pushed back against him.

"I was able to warn the foreign minister and president of our country to expect that call from the American president last spring."

Our country? Russia was not *his* country. But Peter steadfastly refused to acknowledge that. The man was convinced that, one day, the prodigal son would come home to Mother Russia. *Never,* Alex silently swore to himself.

Alex turned the rest of his father's comment over in his mind. His father must have won a lot of political points for being first to warn the Russian leadership that the Americans had discovered the Russian shenanigans in Zaghastan last year. Competition was fierce between Russia's FSB, military intelligence and a few other assorted secret agencies to see who brought in the best information first.

"They asked me to pass on their thanks to you, my son."

Peter had given *him* credit for delivering that intel? What the hell? Was his father pretending to his bosses that Alex was an active FSB asset?

Deep unease rippled down his spine, an unpleasant reminder of how dangerous a man his father was. What game was Peter playing at now?

His father was speaking again. "I hear you have accepted long-term employment with Doctors Unlimited."

Alex looked around the park in panic. How in the world did his father know that? He'd only officially been assigned to the aid organization a few days ago, and he'd been in various CIA training facilities and out of sight before that.

Not that it should surprise him that there were moles inside the CIA. But still. It was alarming to receive incontrovertible proof of it. Was Doctors Unlimited itself penetrated? He'd thought that was what Peter had wanted *him* to do. Was getting inside D.U. a test, then? Any intel Alex passed on to his father would be vetted against intel from the other mole in the organization?

It was a neat way to trap him. Alex would have no choice but to pass on real information. Which would constitute treason. Which would make him dead meat if the U.S. government found out. Which meant Alex would have no choice but to throw in his hat with the FSB and accept his father's protection and patronage.

Peter must be desperate if he was showing his cards this openly.

In the millisecond it took all of this to pass through his mind, the sun passed behind a cloud, casting the park in an abruptly dim and shadowed light. "Your intel is correct, Father. I did take a job with Doctors Unlimited."

"You will get me that list of employee names and where the organization's members are posted abroad, yes?"

He thought fast. *Was it worth endangering the lives of dozens of doctors, nurses and translators to throw his old man off the scent?* He answered smoothly, "Of course. Because of all my training, I haven't had anopportunity to get the list. But D.U. is open for business in its repaired offices now. I should be able to get you the list quite easily."

Who in D.U. was the mole? To whom did he dare talk about his dilemma? If he gave a false list of staffers and their postings to hot spots around the world—ostensibly to render medical aid and unofficially to observe and gather intelligence—his father would know him for the traitor to Mother Russia that he was. *Not that the United States of America trusted him any farther than Uncle Sam could throw him.*

But if he gave away the real list, his colleagues' lives could be in terrible danger.

"I shall await the list with great eagerness, Alexei."

He'd bet. The damned list potentially represented his first step down the slippery slope to treason. And the bastard couldn't wait to push him the rest of the way down that hill.

He disconnected the phone call, careful not to show any physical or facial reaction to the call. Knowing his old man, Peter was watching him on a satellite this very minute for a reaction. Too tense to sit still for long, though, he stood and pushed the pram a lap around the paved path outlining the park. He nodded and smiled at a few mothers with strollers and an elderly man with a pair of hairy little dogs that looked like mops.

Leisurely, he headed back toward the condo.

As if they'd been monitoring his phone calls, a new call vibrated his phone on cue, this time his boss, André Fortinay. The man had put his life on the line for him, Katie and Dawn last year, and had supposedly been a big advocate of bringing Alex all the way into the CIA fold, but did he dare trust the man?

He took the call. "Hello, André. How are you today?"

"I'm fine. You?"

"Good. What can I do for you, sir?"

"Any chance you could come into the office in the next day or two? I'd like to talk over possible postings for you. We have too few doctors and too many crises around the globe where people are desperately in need of medical care."

Not to mention he was a trauma surgeon who could handle the sorts of terrible combat wounds that few physicians were trained to treat. The same sorts of wounds he'd spent the past year learning how to inflict.

"What's a good time for you, André?"

"Now, if you're not busy."

"I've got the baby with me."

"Bring her along."

"I can be there in, say, a half hour?"

"Perfect."

Alex flagged down a cab and pulled up in front of the D.U. office—a restored mansion on embassy row—in more like twenty minutes. However, it took him nearly ten minutes to get past a phalanx of cooing secretaries and nurses with Dawn to André's door. He left the baby and a bottle with the man's secretary. She was in transports of ecstasy at getting to feed Dawn.

He stepped inside Fortinay's office and threw a harried look at his boss.

"Now you know why your old man used you as a cover," André observed dryly. "Nobody can resist a cute baby."

Alex scowled and dropped into the chair in front of his boss's desk.

"Adapting to parenthood all right?" the man asked.

"Dawn's great. Family life is…relaxing." When he wasn't quietly flipped out over whether or not any of it was real, that was.

"So. Let's talk about what you'll do and where you'll go next."

"That sounds like a plan. I'm not the type to sit around the house staring at my toes." While he talked, Alex reached across Fortinay's desk, picked up a pen and scrawled the words "White noise generator?" on a sticky pad.

Fortinay nodded and held up a finger. "I hear you. Inactivity makes me lose my mind in short order." He opened a desk drawer and pulled out a gadget about the size of an old-fashioned cassette tape recorder and set it on his desk.

"All right. White noise in place. What's up, Alex?"

"My father phoned me this morning."

"Did he, now? The man's not wasting any time calling in the favor he earned by saving your life."

"He claimed it wasn't him who gave the order not to kill me last year."

Fortinay leaned back hard in his chair at that. "Is he still sticking with that line?"

"It didn't come up today. But as far as I know, he's standing by the assertion. Not that I'd know with him if it's true or not. Best liar I've ever seen. No tells at all."

"Duly noted—never play poker with the man. Or his son, the way I hear it."

Alex shrugged. He'd made millions gambling at the tables in Vegas and Atlantic City. High-stakes poker had been one of his more profitable endeavors, in fact. It hadn't all been about being a good liar, though. His eidetic memory and master's degree in cryptography had helped.

"Your training reports are pretty impressive, Alex."

"I had a head start on the other kids."

"It's more than that, and you know it. You have a gift for black ops."

This wasn't news to him, but it didn't mean he had to like being told he was a natural monster.

"Why did your father call you, then?"

"He wants me to hand over a list of D.U. staffers and where they're posted."

"I'm sure he does."

"Tell me, André. Are you going to be my handler?"

The man studied him intently, weighing both him and the question. Alex mentally gave the man credit for catching the nuance behind the seemingly straightforward question. Alex was laying out the ground rules for their working relationship going forward. He didn't want any fake niceties where they all pretended he was a good guy doing honorable deeds for altruistic reasons. They'd turned him into a killer, and that was how he wanted his boss to deal with him.

"I'll be handling you for the most part," André answered blandly.

Crap. So. They were going to pass him around from department to department within the agency to do their dirty work for them.

Alex supposed he ought to be grateful for the man's honesty. In return, he took a deep breath and did a difficult thing. He extended tentative trust to his boss. "Peter indicated that he already has a mole inside Doctors Unlimited. Besides me."

André leaned forward hard, staring. "Who?"

"No idea. But he'll vet any information I pass him against this other mole's intel."

"Sonofabitch."

The two men stared at each other in grim silence. Eventually Alex asked, "Have you picked up any new employees recently?"

"You mean besides you and Katie?"

"Could it be someone in the wider government umbrella?" Which was a delicate way of asking if D.U.'s handlers at the CIA were infiltrated. Doctors Unlimited, technically a nongovernment aid organization, covertly reported to the CIA what its staff observed overseas.

"Possibly. I picked everyone for this outfit by hand. It's my operation."

Alex frowned. "Has someone done deep background checks on your staff recently?" He added lightly, "Someone impartial?"

André swore under his breath. "Who do I pick for the job? What if I pick the mole?"

Alex understood the man's dilemma. The hardest thing to do as a spy was to find someone, anyone, to trust. It was a world built upon lies within lies within lies.

"Will you do it?" André asked abruptly.

"You have no way of knowing if I'm a mole or not at this point. For all you know, I am working for my father."

"You're a known risk. Everyone else here is now officially an unknown."

Alex blinked, startled. André had just put him on notice not to trust anyone else at D.U. "How do you want to handle the list for my father?"

"Give me a day to review where everyone is placed right now. Based on where our assets are at the moment, we might be able to hand over a snapshot list."

Alex nodded. "Let me know when you're ready, and I'll hack into your system and pull a copy of it."

"Our computer security's pretty tight around here."

Alex just smiled gently.

"Has anyone ever told you you're a scary bastard?" André blurted.

"Once or twice." His first week in prison at the ripe old age of twenty-four, he'd all but killed three Russian-mob strongmen to make the point to the rest of the inmates that he was not to be messed with. For the remaining four years of his DUI incarceration—and more to the point, avoiding recruitment into the FSB by his father—not another soul had laid a finger on him. His father had been a proponent of shock-and-awe since long before it was an official strategy of war. Yes, indeed. Peter had taught his son well how to instill fear in those around him.

Except for Katie. None of his tactics had ever worked on her. For some inexplicable reason, she insisted on loving him in spite of all his worst behavior. God, he hoped that never changed.

It went without saying that his investigation of Doctors Unlimited would be entirely off-book. Which meant he needed to head home to begin his work. He collected Dawn and left, already planning his approach.

When he opened the condo's front door, loud, off-key singing emanated from the kitchen. He smiled indulgently. Katie had a lot of wonderful qualities, but perfect pitch was not one of them. "We're home!" he called out.

Katie rushed into the living room, most of her shirt dusted in flour. She planted a light kiss on Dawn's cheek and a rather more carnal one on his mouth. "You're just in time to taste-test the first edible batch of cookies. C'mon. I need your opinion. More chips or not?"

"Ahh. So that's the slightly burned smell coming from my kitchen."

"Be nice. Your oven runs hot and I had to figure out how to set the oven on the first pan of cookies."

Suppressing a burst of what he would label amusement if he allowed himself to feel such things, he trailed after her as she hurried back to the kitchen, all energy and laughter and golden hair. He took the proffered cookie, which turned out to be as warm and sweet and gooey as its creator.

"I see what all the fuss is about. That's tasty," he admitted.

"Have you never had a warm chocolate chip cookie fresh out of the oven before?" she demanded.

"Never. My father and I didn't cook."

"You poor, deprived man!"

She stood on tiptoe to plant a chocolate-flavored kiss on his mouth. She smelled of vanilla and joy. What must it have been like to grow up in her family? A blade of jealousy sliced into his heart for an instant. "I have some work to do. If you could take the baby…"

"Of course." She scooped Dawn out of his arms. "What kind of work?"

"The kind I can't talk about."

Her bright blue eyes clouded over, but to her credit, she didn't pry. He'd explained to her that he was accustomed to secrecy and that she couldn't expect him to share every aspect of his life with her all the time. But he felt bad as he retreated to his office. What the hell was she doing to him? Since when did he want to spill every detail of his existence with anyone?

Furthermore, since when did he have feelings toward any other human being? His father had taught him well that feelings were the greatest weakness any spy could fall prey to. God knew, the past year of CIA training had only reinforced that message.

He'd thought he'd purged all deep feelings from his heart in that CIA training facility. But apparently not. Dammit. He had to find a way to isolate and contain these warm feelings he was having toward Katie.

Setting aside the problem of Katie McCloud, he locked himself in his office and got to work.

Mentally shaking his head, he broke into D.U.'s personnel files with a few casual keystrokes. Actually, it wasn't that easy. He'd worked for months in jail developing and perfecting the decryption algorithm he used today.

He printed a hard copy of the entire employee roster of Doctors Unlimited and went to work. Financials were the easiest place to spot a turned spy. Mounting debt, illicit spending on a personal vice, an illness in the family—all the symptoms of a spy vulnerable to bribery or coercion—showed up most readily on bank statements. So, that was where he concentrated his search. He figured André would have done a thorough job vetting his people's distant past and extended families, so he skipped looking at personal histories for now.

But after an entire afternoon of work and nearly a dozen of Katie's irresistible cookies, nobody was leaping out at him as a candidate to be his father's mole. Frowning, he went for a stroll around the terrace garden that had been his father's pride and joy. He had to admit, Peter had a good eye for texture and color. The contrast of the stark cacti with softer, greener plant material was striking.

Contrast.

Maybe he'd been looking for the wrong thing. He'd been looking for a big change in someone's spending habits. Instead, maybe he ought to be looking for a long-term pattern of expenditures that, in comparison to other D.U. employees, contrasted with the other people's in the organization.

He went back to his computer to run a position-by-position spending comparison on D.U.'s staff. But that, too, turned up nothing.

Katie brought him a salad at some point and he ate it absently. Food had been optional often in the past year and was not something that held his attention anymore.

It grew dark outside, and he continued to poke and prod at the D.U. staff. But no matter how he examined them, nobody stood out as a mole. Which meant one of two things. Either there was no mole and his father was bluffing, or the mole was very, very good. He strongly suspected the latter was the case.

He leaned back frowning. If he were infiltrating Doctors Unlimited, how would he go about it? The aid organization placed physicians and nurses around the world in dangerous hot spots where regular aid organizations refused to send their people. The staff of D.U. was dedicated, passionate and a little crazy. Money wouldn't be high on their personal priority lists. Ideals would be, though.

He ran a quick search of political affiliations. And that was when he got a hit. Dmitri Churzov. D.U.'s I.T. guy—responsible not only for its in-house computers, but also the all-important interface with the CIA's computers—had been flagged by the FBI for attending several Communist Party rallies in college.

Alex winced. God, it was so cliché. The kid even had a Russian name.

He frowned. In point of fact, the guy was a little too cliché. His father was emphatically not the type to recruit so obvious a target. Were he Peter, Dmitri would be the one guy he would *not* recruit to work for the FSB.

Decisively, Alex crossed Dmitri off his list of suspects. *Who, then?* The problem with an organization like Doctors Unlimited was that it used its legitimate work to passively collect intelligence on the side. André reported what his people observed. Nothing more. It wasn't like anyone at D.U. besides André would know about, let alone get involved with, any high-profile, active ops. Why would anybody bother to infiltrate such a low-level group? Especially with a live mole who would be expensive to recruit and compensate, and who would be high maintenance to run?

André had allowed that the mole could be someone who merely interacted with D.U. at CIA headquarters. Maybe that was where his father's mole was placed.

The agency's computers would be significantly more difficult for Alex to hack than the D.U. system, particularly if he didn't want to cause all sorts of alarms to go off and a black ops team to show up at his door. But it was by no means impossible.

Rather than make a direct attack, he instead went after André's home computer. It took him nearly an hour, but eventually he lifted most of his boss's passwords from his other accounts. Armed with those,

Alex attempted a straight-up log-in to the CIA's system as if he were André himself.

Tsk. Tsk. The same password that logged the guy into his daughter's school grades got Alex into the CIA mainframe.

He unashamedly browsed his boss's correspondence with his CIA superiors. If he'd once had any sense of ethics and morals about privacy, they'd been stripped out of him this past year.

It was mostly desultory reports and the occasional debrief on a concluded overseas mission by one of the D.U. medical teams. Even the intelligence reports were predictable, though. Troop emplacements, supply routes, casualty numbers, the usual stuff. But then a phrase jumped out at him.

Cold Intent. Major intelligence and military operations were given two-word names, a random adjective/noun combination. Some of them became well-known: Rolling Thunder. Desert Storm.

What major op could an unassuming, passive intel collection outfit like Doctors Unlimited be involved in?

The whole message read, *Cold Intent is on track. The asset is in place and unaware.* It was dated right about the time he and Katie were sent overseas last year.

He stared at the words on his screen with foreboding. *The asset is in place and unaware.* Unaware of what? What asset? Why did he get a sick feeling in his gut that the message had something to do with him?

Cold Intent. He typed the phrase into the CIA

search engine. Immediately, a screen popped up announcing that André did not have access to that information. If it was above André's pay grade, then why was the man aware of it and referring to it in a message?

Frowning, Alex turned his attention to the recipient of the message. There was no name, merely a series of random numbers and letters belonging to an IP address—a location designated somewhere on the internet to receive messages without being attached to any one email account or identity.

He initiated a deep system trace on the location of the IP address. He might not be able to find out *who* the recipient was, but he could find out *where* the recipient was.

The message had bounced off seven of the thirteen nodes that all internet traffic passed through and his system was painstakingly searching back to an eighth node when everything went crazy. Attack warnings flashed on his screen. Automated notifications that his antihacking software had been activated flashed up. Lines of code scrolled too fast to read, and then his computer screen went blank. A silent, blue screen of doom glowed at him.

What the hell?

"Are you coming to bed soon?" Katie asked from the doorway.

He looked up, startled. To bed with her? So she could smash through his emotional defenses with the shocking ease she always did? A frisson of dismay whispered through him. "No. Go on without me."

Social norms dictated that he should probably kiss her good-night or in some other way act affectionate and social. He really owed it to her to at least pretend normalcy, but he just couldn't bring himself to do it. He felt bad about not being able to show her simple affection, but he just couldn't. He really ought to be riveted on how his computer had just been shut down. And *why.*

Katie retreated silently, disappointment darkening her blue eyes, and he turned his attention back to his dead computer.

What—who—was Cold Intent? Why did the mere act of tracing an IP address send an attack at him that had triggered a tactical nuclear meltdown of his computer?

He was shocked at the amount of damage the attack had done to his normally intensely secure computer. He ended up more or less wiping out every file on the hard drive, restoring it to the factory defaults and starting over from scratch reloading and rebooting the entire system from his backup files.

He was still working hours later when he heard Dawn stirring in her room over the intercom and went in to rock her back to sleep. He sat down with her in the rocking chair in her room and let the deep peace of the night and her sweet baby smell pass over him. How could something so innocent exist in the evil world he knew it to be? How was he ever going to manage to keep her safe from it all? The weight of the responsibility pressed down on him until he struggled to breathe. He laid the sleeping baby in her crib and went back to work grimly.

He took a break to doze on the leather sofa in his office while some particularly large files uploaded. But he lurched awake as an alarm sounded abruptly. He raced over to his computer and was stunned to see a warning that one of his bank accounts had just recorded an attempted hack-in. He sat down and typed quickly, locking down the account and his other accounts while he was at it.

He'd barely finished before the phone on his desk rang. What the hell? It was 4:00 a.m.

"Go," he snapped.

"Mr. Peters? This is Advanced Security Systems. I'm sorry to disturb you at this hour. But we've just gotten notification on our internet server that there has been an attempt to break in to your house's alarm protocols. A note on your file said you wanted to be notified immediately of any such incidents."

Sonofabitch. Who was coming after him like this? Surely, it had something to do with Cold Intent. "Thanks. Lock it down for now. I'll be in touch in a few hours with further instructions."

"Will do, sir."

He grabbed a jacket and headed out of the condo. Time to get the hell away from his home and his family to continue this search. He headed for an internet café, but not just any café. The Flaming Frog catered to hackers specifically. The firewalls and other protections in the café made its systems nearly impossible to trace. And even if a hack was traced, the café kept no records of who'd sat at which terminal. The FBI and NSA hated the place, but so far had failed to shut it down despite repeated visits to local courts on various trumped-up charges.

"Hey, dude. Haven't seen you in a while." The night manager waved cheerfully at him. Store policy: no names got used. Ever. He waved back at the girl, who looked about twelve but was probably closer to thirty. She was also a top-notch hacker.

"Hey, Blondie," he murmured across the counter. "Feel like taking on one of the big boys?"

"Sure. Which alphabet agency we goin' after?"

"I've got a name. I need more on it."

Her face fell. "Just a vanilla research job, huh?"

"An aggressively defended name," he corrected. "Nearly killed my home system earlier."

She perked up. "Well, then. That's better. Let's have this name."

"Cold Intent."

"What the hell is that?" Blondie demanded.

"That's what I'm trying to find out," he retorted.

"Race ya," she challenged.

"The bet?"

"Loser buys me a tattoo."

He grinned. "What if I win?"

"You ain't gonna win, old man."

"If I do, I want a copy of the algorithm you used to hack the IRS last year."

She sucked in a sharp breath, but she eventually shrugged. "You're gonna lose, so what the hell. Deal."

He threaded past a half dozen people staring at

computer screens and sat down at a terminal in the back where no one could look over his shoulder. He started to type. *Come to papa, Cold Intent.*

CHAPTER THREE

KATIE WOKE UP SLOWLY. The sun was shining in around the edges of the heavy curtains too brightly. She lurched up out of bed and raced down the hall to Dawn's bedroom. The baby was still asleep. Wow. Nearly 7:00 a.m.

She tiptoed down the hall to Alex's office. What on earth had he been working on so hard yesterday? She poked her head in the door to ask—

Huh. He wasn't there. She backed out and headed for the kitchen. His car keys were gone from the hook on the wall. That was weird. Where would he go this early? Particularly without telling her?

Alarmed, she headed back to his office. His computer was running some sort of diagnostic that she probably couldn't interrupt. She spied a legal pad on his desk. What looked like rows of random numbers covered it. Although knowing Alex and his huge background in math, the numbers weren't random at all. The rows of digits were interrupted by a single pair of words tucked off to one side of the pad. *Cold Intent.* What was that?

She heard the front door unlocking and moved out of his office before he could catch her snooping. She greeted Alex. "You look exhausted. Have you been working all night?"

He made an affirmative sound.

"Coffee or sleep?" she asked sympathetically.

"Sleep."

"By all means." She'd heard that doctors' spouses had to get used to some weird working hours. Not that Alex had hinted in any way about marriage, of course. The poor guy was barely getting used to the idea of having a girlfriend, let alone a daughter. Of course , the obvious question—exactly how long was she planning to wait for him to get used to having a family—lingered in the back of her mind, a grenade without a pin in it. But for now, she kept her fingers wrapped around the handle and the bomb deactivated.

She heard Alex's shower running while she dressed Dawn and fed her breakfast. The baby was starting to feed herself, which entailed much hilarity with flying food and lots of cleaning up. After breakfast, Dawn settled down to play with a pile of stuffed animals in need of chewing and tossing while Katie flipped on the television to check out the news. Ever since she'd hooked up with a spy, she paid much closer attention to world events than before.

Not that she was exactly sure what Alex was anymore. Supposedly, now that his training was finished, he would go back to work as a humanitarian aid doctor.

The morning news focused mostly on a hurricane entering the Caribbean. It was forecasted to grow into a major storm. Current storm tracks had it pointed at

Cuba. Too bad. The impoverished nation needed a natural disaster like it needed a hole in the head. The news moved on to a shooting in a shopping mall somewhere on the west coast, and Dawn squalled. Katie picked her up quickly and shushed her lest she wake Alex. Sensing a bout of baby squeals and babble coming on, she bundled Dawn up and took her out onto the terrace for some fresh air.

Dawn bounced up and down excitedly in her walker, and Katie pulled out her cell phone to check her texts and email. Nothing much was happening with her friends or family. Bored, she pulled up a search engine and typed in the phrase she'd seen on Alex's desk.

Her phone took a long time doing the search, and when the results finally flashed up on the small screen, they were worthless. Every hit had both of the words in it, but not together. It was a bust. She would have to wait until Alex woke up to ask him what it meant. She shrugged and strolled along behind Dawn, enjoying the early-springtime sun. Winter in Washington, D.C., was a gray, wet affair, and she was ready for some decent weather.

After nearly an hour outside, Dawn caught one of the wheels of her walker on a pavement joint, and without warning the whole thing started to tip over. Katie dived for the baby and walker just as the waist-high ceramic planter beside her exploded. Black dirt flew everywhere. What the heck? The baby started and let out a howl while Katie brushed dirt off both of them.

"Get inside," Alex barked from the sliding glass door to his bedroom.

Katie looked up, shocked to see the blunt shape of a pistol in his fist. Keeping her head down, she raced through the door behind him. Dawn started to cry in earnest, no doubt sensing Katie's panic. Alex slipped outside, closing the door behind him, while Katie tried to calm the baby. But Dawn was having no part of it.

Had the sharp warm-up overnight caused the cold ceramic to crack? Alex was going to be annoyed if that was what woke him up. He was so jumpy since he got back. Was he going to whip out a gun at every loud noise?

The outside door slid open, and she tensed. Okay, so she was jumpy, too. Hard not to be after all the crap last year. A bunch of people had made a good-faith effort to kill the three of them and nearly succeeded. And for the first time, they were all back together.

"Shooter's gone," Alex bit out.

"It was just a big pot cracking—"

He dropped something small and irregular on the bedspread. It looked like a pebble. She picked it up to examine it.

"Medium caliber slug," he said tersely.

"You're saying someone shot at you out there?"

"No. Someone shot at *you.* I dug that out of the dirt from the big planter that broke right beside you."

She lurched. "Are we under attack? Do I need to get Dawn to the safe room?"

He shook his head briefly in the negative. "Shooter's fled the area. We're clear." His syllables were clipped but stripped of any actual emotion.

Wasn't he the slightest bit freaked out that someone had just *shot* at her? "Who was it?"

He shrugged. "I got no visual. I've called Langley, though, to have them pull satellite telemetry."

"Now what?" she asked nervously. "What do we do?"

"Do? Nothing. It's over. You're safe. I'll investigate who shot at you. When I know the source of the threat, I'll eliminate it."

God, not even a bump of emotion entered his voice as he casually talked about killing someone. A chill rattled across her skin. Who *was* this man? What had they turned him into? She stared at him in dismay. "But I thought we were done with all of that. The people who came after us before are all dead or in custody. It's finished. They told me it was all over. And no one's tried to kill me and Dawn since you left. Why now? If someone wants to kill me, why wait until the person who can best protect me comes home?"

He exhaled hard. "I kicked a hornet's nest yesterday. This is my fault."

She stared at him, wide-eyed. He hadn't been the only one kicking at hornets. Yesterday, she'd asked for information on his mother from the CIA. Had *that* provoked someone to take a potshot at her? If so, *who?* And why? What was the big deal about his mother?

"What kind of hornets did you kick?" she asked him.

"Can't say," he bit out.

Dammit. She'd forgotten how fiercely he guarded his secrets. She should have known he'd be worse than ever about not sharing when he got home.

"I'm sorry, Katie," he murmured, gathering her and Dawn close in a protective hug. "I swear, I won't let anything bad happen to either one of you."

She ought to tell him about the hornet's nest of her own that she'd kicked. Let him off the guilt hook. But she'd really been hoping to surprise him with the information on his mother. The moment passed when it wouldn't have been awkward to say anything. Great. Now she was keeping secrets from him, too. The guy's bad habit of not sharing was contagious apparently.

"The windows are all bullet resistant and coated so heat-seeking equipment can't see through them. The walls are treated the same way. Stay in here while I close the blinds throughout the house. And then you should be safe to move around inside the condo."

As if that solved everything! Who'd just shot at her? And why?

Alex came back to report that the blinds were closed, and then he retreated to his office and closed the door. How could he go in there and poke at his laptop like someone hadn't just narrowly missed killing her? She was completely freaked out! Were it not for Dawn already being upset, she would march in there and give him a piece of her mind.

Was he napping on the sofa or maybe doing something with Cold Intent and all those numbers on his computer? Curiosity would be the death of her yet.

Speaking of which, she called Uncle Charlie's cell

phone number and left a message in his voice mail asking if there'd been any progress on her request. She added that there had been some interest shown in her query this afternoon.

Trapped in the house by possible snipers outside, she plopped down in front of the television. She was intrigued that Alex hadn't attempted to give chase to the shooter or in some way report the guy to the police. Were such occurrences so commonplace in his world they didn't even register as worthy of response?

Although now that she thought about it, if she'd just taken a shot at someone, she would leave the area quickly so she didn't get caught. Alex must have figured the shooter had too big a head start in fleeing to make a chase worthwhile. Still. What a lousy way to live. Was this what she had to look forward to for the next fifty years or so?

Despair washed over her. She'd thought they'd left all this stuff behind last year. How in the world were they supposed to raise a child in this insanity?

She vaguely heard Alex's cell phone ring.

Maybe ten seconds passed before his office door burst open. "Turn on the news, Katie. Now."

He sounded strange. Tense. She turned on the TV and asked him quickly, "Local, national or international?"

"Local."

He moved to stand behind the sofa, and she swiveled around to stare at him. "What's happened?"

"Someone has been murdered."

"Who?"

"Hacker. I don't know her real name. She was young, late twenties. It would likely be associated with something innocuous, like the theft of computer equipment. Have you seen anything like that today?" he asked urgently.

"No. Nothing," she replied, alarmed. "They haven't reported on any women being murdered or dying in some sort of accident. They're talking mostly about the hurricane heading into the Caribbean."

He swore under his breath.

"What's going on? Who was she? You're scaring me."

"They're covering up her death. Which speaks volumes about who killed her."

They *who?* What wasn't he telling her? "Volumes about who?" she demanded.

"They're powerful. Connected. Probably government."

"Our government? You're saying an American citizen was killed right here in Washington by our government and it's being covered up?" *Holy crap.*

"You really have to get over the whole Mom and apple pie thing when it comes to the United States, Katie. All governments work for their own best interest by whatever means they have at their disposal. *None* of them are nice about it."

Sometimes she forgot what a cynic he was. The uncomfortable thing was that he might be right. Still, her patriotic upbringing ran deep. "Hey. You work for the U.S., too."

He scowled and muttered, "Don't remind me."

True alarm speared through her. He was having second thoughts about hitching his fate to the CIA and not to his father's FSB? She shuddered to think what hell would be unleashed at them if he changed his mind about working for Uncle Sam at this late date. No way was she raising Dawn in Moscow.

Alex was speaking again. "…need to leave town before whoever shot at you tries again. Stay inside for now." He continued. "I have a few things to take care of before I can go. They'll take me about an hour. Can you and Dawn be ready to leave in that amount of time?"

"Of course."

The threat to Dawn's safety rubbed at her psyche until she felt raw and exposed. If they were back in the crosshairs, the baby needed to get away from her and Alex. Again.

Failure burned in her gut like acid as she packed. What kind of mother was she if she couldn't even keep their baby out of mortal danger? Where were they taking Dawn, anyway? She needed to know so she could pack the right kinds of clothes for them both. She headed for Alex's office and knocked on the door.

"Come in."

He swiveled in his desk to face her. A glance over his shoulder revealed his right hand closing his laptop screen. He was hiding whatever he was working on from her. *Why?* The question exploded across her brain, rife with suspicion.

"If you don't have any better idea, I was thinking

we could take Dawn to stay with my folks until we figure out who's shooting at us."

Alex's eyes clouded with what looked like genuine regret. It was genuine, right? God, it sucked not knowing if she could trust him or not. If only she could shake the feeling he was up to no good.

Although, truth be told, she was working behind his back, too.

He nodded once, grimly. "Sure. We can drive up to Pittsburgh tonight." He looked impatient, and she took the hint, merely nodding and backing out of his office.

Anxiety prodded her. In the past, when he got all secretive like this, his father had had something to do with it. What was Peter Koronov up to now? The man just couldn't leave his only son alone. It was an obsession between the two of them. They were locked in some sort of mortal struggle that neither one would let go of. So unlike her big, happy-go-lucky family.

She made a call to her mother, who was delighted to take Dawn for a few days while she and Alex took care of a few things. Not that she thought her mother was fooled for a second that there wasn't some sort of problem. The woman had raised five soldiers and cops. She could smell trouble from a mile away. She just knew not to ask about it. Her kids would tell her what was going on in their own time. Strong woman, her mother.

Katie busied herself packing the copious gear a well-spoiled baby required for any self-respecting road trip. It took the full hour Alex had given her to make trips to the underground parking garage and cram the BMW's trunk to the gills.

Just as she finished, he emerged from his office, grabbed a prepacked bag, for which she hated him a little, and was ready to go.

Traffic was heavy until they cleared the Washington suburbs, and then they made good time to Pittsburgh. It was about a two-hundred-fifty-mile trip and took a little over four hours. But by halftime of the Monday Night Football game, they'd arrived at her folks' house. In time-honored ritual, her brothers and dad were gathered in front of the large-screen TV in the family room yelling at one another and armchair-coaching.

Alex joined the men, but sat off to one side sipping at the beer her father poured for him. He looked misplaced among her burly brothers, although he had more in common with them than most people would guess at a glance. They were all lethal men who took care of their own. Dawn would be perfectly safe ensconced among the McCloud men.

Katie was just retreating to the kitchen for some girl talk with her mother when her cell phone rang. She was lifting it to her ear when Alex's went off, as well. Their gazes met grimly as they took the calls.

"Hi, this Ashley Osborne at D.U."

André Fortinay's admin assistant? What did she want?

"Are you up for an emergency deployment, Katie?"

"Where to?"

"Miami, for now."

"I thought D.U. didn't work in the United States. What happened to all the doctors in Florida?"

"We're prepositioning a team to insert into Cuba after Hurricane Giselle strikes it."

She frowned. "It's going to get that bad?" Her knee-jerk reaction was to say no and hang up the phone. She and Alex were done with dangerous missions to deadly places, right?

"We're being told this will be a major storm with heavy damage. A lot of casualties," André's assistant explained persuasively.

"Huh. Who all's going?"

"Just you two. Obviously, we're hoping to send you and Alex together."

What was so obvious about her and Alex going together? Was it her job to keep an eye on him? Make sure he didn't stray off the CIA reservation? After all, she wasn't even a nurse, let alone a physician. Sure, she'd taken a first-aid class in the past year while she waited out Alex's training, but what she knew how to treat didn't amount to anything when stacked up against a natural disaster.

Ashley was speaking again, a little more urgently. "Can you be ready to leave first thing in the morning?"

Come to think of it, why was a low-level admin type calling to send her on this mission that everyone knew she wouldn't want to go on? Katie's antennae went up and started to wiggle. In her years of working with children, she'd learned to sense a lie or evasion, and she was getting one now.

"I'm not in D.C., actually. I can't really give you an answer tonight."

The girl's reply was perky. A smidge too pushy. "No problem. You can fly out of the airport nearest to wherever you are now."

Alarm exploded in her chest. No! She couldn't just drop everything and race off to parts unknown on a dangerous adventure! She had a baby to take care of. A fragile relationship with Alex to nurture into something more stable and permanent. For all she knew, she needed to talk him down off whatever emotional bridge the CIA had forced him to climb this year. The last thing she needed was to dive headlong into life-threatening danger.

She asked cautiously, "Is someone talking to Alex now?"

"André's on the phone with him."

Katie glanced across the family room. Alex had turned his back on everyone and was in the corner having a quiet, intense-looking conversation with his boss. And it was taking longer than, "Hey, Alex. You wanna go to Cuba?"

Dammit, what were they whispering about? Alex turned slightly, and she caught sight of his face. It was more alive than it had been in weeks. His eyes were bright, his entire body vibrating with tension. Excitement.

Dismay crushed her. She'd known as soon as he got home that Alex had been changed by the past year, but there had been more to it than just that. Something had been missing from him, but she hadn't been able to put her finger on it. Not until now. Not until this dangerous, electric side of him awoke and showed itself. *This* was what had been absent.

Was the prospect of domestic bliss with her and Dawn so stifling, then? Apparently so. Who was she trying to kid? She would never tame the tiger within him. Not without killing that part of him. He would never be happy without living on the edge. Heck, he'd spent his entire life walking a high wire without a net. What made her think that clumping around in the mud of average life with her would be enough for him?

Racing off to a dangerous place like Cuba was more than what Alex did. It defined who he was. If she gave half a damn about him, she wouldn't stand in his way. Except she wasn't ready to let go of him yet. Even if her dream of a life with him was doomed.

All that was left for them was a swan song. One last adventure. How, when it was over, would she ever find a way to let him go?

"Lemme talk with Alex," she mumbled into her phone. "We'll let you know."

Ashley replied too brightly, "Send me your location, and I'll set up your itinerary and flight reservations."

Were they not being given any choice in the matter, then? Was that what was taking so long between Alex and André? She ended her call, frowning.

Cuba, huh? She flopped down beside the brother everyone in the family thought was an intelligence officer for the SEALs. "Hey, Mikey. Whaddya know about Cuba?"

"That I can talk about with you?" he retorted.

"Duh."

She listened intently as he and several of her brothers pitched in to bring her up to speed on the political and military situation with the island nation. The only big, unpleasant surprise to her was how active the Russians still were in Cuba.

No wonder André was all hot and bothered to get Alex down there on any pretense he could. Alex possibly knew more about Russian intelligence practices than just about any other person at the CIA. After all, he'd been raised by a master KGB spy and carefully trained to follow in Daddy's footsteps.

At long last, Alex disconnected his phone. "You up for a trip?" he asked her tersely.

"Not particularly. I'm not crazy about leaving Dawn, and frankly, I could do without being shot at again."

"I won't let you get shot at."

"You can't promise me that," she retorted.

Alex frowned. "I need to go."

"Why?"

He glanced at her brothers, who were unabashedly taking in the exchange. "We'll need to discuss that in private."

"Aw, c'mon," Mike complained. "We're family."

Katie sympathized with the pained look on Alex's face. He wasn't used to dealing with a big, nosy family like this. She took pity and nodded toward the back porch. "Let's go outside."

Her brothers protested, but they could get over it. This was between her and Alex.

He pointedly turned his back on the picture windows. Good call. A couple of the McCloud men could read lips. "There's more to this trip than just treating hurricane victims."

"There always is, isn't there?" she replied rhetorically.

He merely rolled his eyes at her.

When he didn't speak, she demanded, "You're not seriously going to put your neck on the line again, are you? I thought we agreed this stuff was over. For both of us."

He sighed and moved toward the edge of the big deck. "Things have changed. My…role has changed."

She wanted to shout at him that his role was to be Dawn's dad and her lover and eventual husband. But she bit the words back. She'd known going into this relationship what his priorities were. But she'd thought she could change him. Or at least change his priorities. Foolish her. Yup, that was her heart cracking just a little bit more in her chest. How long until it shattered completely?

He continued. "Cargo ships have been seen making unscheduled stops in small ports along the east coast of Cuba. No off-loads or on-loads have been observed. We've been asked to poke around. Talk with the locals. See if they know something about any smuggling that might be going on."

"What kind of smuggling?"

"No idea. Could be drugs, weapons, human trafficking…hell, it could be cigars for all I know."

She snorted. "If the CIA wants to send us in to have a look, they think it's more serious than cigars."

He exhaled hard. "You always have been too smart for your own good."

She took a step closer to him, to where he stared out at the woods. "It's not our problem anymore. Other people with a death wish can go check it out."

"But I'm uniquely qualified—" he started.

"Why? Because you're practically a Russian agent yourself?"

He spun to face her. Something dark and cold emanated from him. This was the side of James Bond the movies never portrayed. They might get the fun and games right, but the movies mostly ignored what it meant to be a trained killer. A couple of her brothers were trained killers. She knew the signs of it in the way Alex held himself now. In how he watched everything and everyone, in the way he moved, always coiled, always ready to spring. He was a living, breathing hair trigger.

Alex spoke low and hard. "My father's telling the powers-that-be in his government that I'm working for him. I can use that against him. I ought to be able to use his name to move around with impunity."

"Until they get wind of you working for the CIA," she retorted. "If your father thinks D.U. is a CIA front, you have to expect the Cubans to think the same thing. We'd end up in danger regardless of who your father is."

He shrugged. "I have the skills to evade the Cubans. I know exactly how they've been trained. It's how *I* was trained, dammit."

"The CIA can find someone else to do the job," she said implacably. She felt bad about coming across as a pushy bitch, but no way was she going to show him the true depth of her terror at the course shift his life had taken. He was heading down a path she and Dawn could not follow him down.

He huffed, sounding exasperated.

"What aren't you telling me, Alex?"

"I already accepted the assignment."

"Well, *un*accept it!"

"I can't."

"You mean you won't."

"I mean I gave my word, and I'm going to do this."

"And I'm supposed to sit at home like a good little woman and wait for you maybe not to come back? Ever?"

He shoved a hand through his hair. "Yes," he finally answered. "That's about the way of it."

"You expect me to sit around doing nothing while you sally forth to your possible death? Not a chance. If you go, I go."

"That's crazy. You're not trained for this kind of mission."

"And yet, Doctors Unlimited asked me to go on it."

"You need to stay home."

She planted her fists on her hips. "No. If you go, I'm going, too. And that's an ultimatum."

"I don't deal well with ultimatums," he snapped.

"And I don't withdraw mine," she snapped back.

They glared daggers at each other. She could be just as stubborn and pigheaded as he could. If he was determined to do this supremely stupid thing, he damned well wasn't going off by himself alone to do it and die.

A little voice in the back of her head whispered that this wasn't the way to demonstrate her trust in him. She shoved away the realization that her declaration was partly based on desperation. If he decided to leave her, there wasn't a darned thing she could do about it, right? Mentally, she knew that. But way down deep in her gut, she was forced to acknowledge that her ultimatum had as much to do with clinging to him as anything.

"What else aren't you telling me?" she demanded.

"I don't know anything more than I've told you."

"If you're dragging me off to Cuba, I have a right to know everything."

"I don't want to drag you to Cuba, dammit! I want you stay here and be safe."

"Which is exactly what I want you to do, too."

"Not happening."

"Then I'm going to Cuba, whether you take me with you or not."

He stared at her in frustration. She crossed her arms defensively and stared back. It was a long standoff, but she was a McCloud, and they were a tenacious bunch.

He finally declared, "You are the most stubborn, unreasonable female I've ever had the misfortune to know."

Hah. Capitulation. She heard it in his voice. Gracious in victory, she murmured, "And that's why you love me."

He scowled, and she didn't press the point. Instead, she asked, "Why is André going to all the trouble of infiltrating us into Cuba to hunt for something the CIA isn't even sure exists? Does this have something to do with your father?"

"Maybe," he answered candidly. "The close Cuban connection to Russia lends credence to the notion. Several of the ships that have been spotted belong to Russian front corporations, and some intelligence traffic has been tracked between Cuba and the FSB that corresponds to the appearances of the ships."

"Is that why you're so set on going on this wild-goose chase, then?"

"I'd definitely rather know what Peter's up to than be operating in the blind." He added quietly, "And so would the CIA."

"Are you ever going to give up this never-ending battle against him?"

"I will if he will."

She snorted. "Like that's gonna happen."

"Exactly."

"Cuba, huh?" she said in resignation.

"*Please* stay home," he tried one last time.

"Please stay here with me," she retorted.

"I'm sorry," he said simply. "I can't."

"There are things going on around us I don't understand, Alex, and I'm worried. My gut says something or someone's closing in on us. Whoever took that shot at me on the terrace did not do it randomly. I think it would be best if we both got out of Washington and stayed off everybody's radar for a while. Call it crazy women's intuition."

He stared at her for a long time. Secrets swirled in his turbulent, unwilling gaze. But in the end, keeping them to himself won out over talking her into staying home. She gathered, however, that he agreed with her intuition.

He released a long, unhappy sigh. "Are your parents going to be okay with keeping Dawn for a few weeks?"

"Lemme think," she drawled. "More time to spoil their adorable only grandchild rotten? Gee. I don't know."

Alex smiled briefly, but the expression didn't reach his eyes. He had some inkling of who'd taken that shot at her and why. What about that had him so freaked out? Enough to give in and let her come to Cuba with him? Was it really going to be safer for her in a hostile country where being caught meant arrest or even possible death?

Wow. Not reassuring.

CHAPTER FOUR

ALEX LEANED BACK in his uncomfortable airplane seat and pretended to sleep. Why hadn't CIA satellites picked up anything *at all* on the shooter at his condo yesterday? He'd been on the phone no more than two minutes after the shooting and André had promised the agency would take a look at its live security telemetry of the nation's capital.

The day had been sunny and clear. They should have seen *something.* A car, a figure moving away from the area on foot, a flash off a gun scope, anything. He'd given André detailed descriptions of all three of the perches a sniper could possibly use to hit that planter on his terrace. How hard could it have been to check out three lousy hides?

His gut churned alarmingly. Something was wrong. What wasn't André telling him? His instincts warned that the agency's analysts had seen something but elected not to share it with him. What? And why were they hiding it from him?

And now they were sending him to Cuba, a known swarm of Russian intelligence activity, on a flimsy excuse. *Why?* What did they think Peter was up to? Or were they just using his father's name as a hot button to get Alex to jump into Cuba?

André had been cagey when he pushed his boss for details. Fortinay had flatly refused to divulge why he and Katie specifically had to go to Cuba and what exactly they were supposed to be looking for when they got there. No way was this a random aid mission. The CIA was up to something. But André steadfastly avoided revealing even a hint of what was up.

As if that wasn't bad enough, Alex really didn't like the fact that D.U. was determined to send Katie with him. He'd tried to talk André out of it, but had failed spectacularly. He got that they wanted someone watching him, but he resented the idea that they thought they could use his civilian girlfriend that way.

This whole business of being a good guy, of playing along with their damned rules, was starting to grate on his nerves. He was half tempted to go back to the good old days when everybody hated him and he lived on the edge, tiptoeing between his enemies to stay alive.

Katie's head landed lightly on his shoulder and he shifted to make it into a more comfortable pillow for her. She gave him a purpose in life, but God, the cost of being with her and Dawn was daunting at times. He so wasn't an inside-the-box kind of guy.

And it wasn't as if he had any right to ask her to live outside the box with him in his shadow world. If Dawn weren't in the picture, maybe he would ask it of her. But the two of them had committed to raising the orphaned child, and he wasn't about to back out of that commitment any more than Katie was.

It was hard enough for him to straddle the world of espionage and the bright, shiny world where people fell in love and had families, and he had a lifetime's experience doing it. No way could Katie handle both. If only he could offer her and Dawn some kind of security for the long term.

Miami International Airport was as huge and chaotic as he remembered it. The plan was to wait out Hurricane Giselle in Florida, and then make their way to Cuba after it passed. André's contact in Cuba had flatly refused to let Alex bring any of his own equipment or supplies into the country.

The unnamed Cuban had apparently assured D.U. that plenty of emergency medical supplies were in place on the island. *Riiight.* Alex smelled a whole bunch of meatball medicine under horrendous conditions forthcoming.

He glanced over at Katie, who smiled excitedly at him, and he just shook his head. The girl had an adventurous streak a mile wide. It had gotten her in trouble before, and he had no doubt it would get her in trouble again. He was beginning to suspect it would turn out to be his fate in life to protect her from herself.

They collected their bags and found a shuttle to take them to their hotel. He had to give D.U. credit for springing for upscale lodgings. Most of the time, D.U. staffers lived in miserable field conditions—crude tents with no running water or electricity among refugees and the destitute, treating injuries and disease under grueling pressure. He had faith Cuba wouldn't be any better when they got there in the aftermath of a major hurricane.

Speaking of which, the sky overhead looked ominous. By the time they reached the hotel, the first fat drops of rain were starting to fall and the wind was picking up. Miami was forecast to get hit by peripheral rain bands but not much more.

They checked into their room with no trouble. He was amused that André had booked them one room with a king-size bed. Keeping the watcher and the watched close, much?

"How bad is the weather supposed to get here?" Katie asked as rain pounded at the big windows.

He flipped on the TV to check the latest updates. The weather channels were still showing a direct hit on Cuba. Giselle, a small but strong category-four storm and intensifying, was expected to run, literally, the length of the island. "Nothing to write home about here in Miami. But Cuba's going to get clobbered."

"Where will D.U. send us?"

"East end of the island. The mountains down its spine will weaken the storm significantly, and the west end won't get hit nearly as bad."

"So, the category five will be down to a measly category three or so when it hits Havana?" she asked wryly.

He shrugged. "They're used to hurricanes. Havana will be fine. It's the poor, isolated villages in the east that will be in trouble."

"Have you ever been to Cuba?" she asked curiously.

"Not on our list of approved conversation topics," he replied shortly.

"We still have one of those?" she asked in dismay.

"You thought having sex with me entitled you to all of my secrets?"

"Well, yes." She looked crestfallen.

He grinned and shook his head. "I swear. You're such a newb."

"If you won't tell me all, then can we at least have sex?" she asked hopefully.

His grin widened. God, she was good for his soul. He took a step toward her, but his phone rang, and he swore under his breath.

"Alex Peters," he snapped.

"Am I disturbing you?"

His father's unwelcome voice startled him, and he replied tersely, "What do you want?"

"I hear you're taking a little trip. Is there anything I can do for you while you're there? I have a few contacts who might prove useful."

Alex's jaw dropped. How in the *hell* did Peter know about their secret trip to Cuba? Obviously not so secret a trip, dammit.

Christ. Who else knew about their supposedly secret infiltration onto the island? How dangerous was this trip to Cuba going to be, after all? He glanced over at Katie in alarm. And she was out here in the line of fire with him. On the one hand, he was glad to have her close by where he could personally ensure her safety. But on the other hand, he'd promised her she'd never be in life-threatening danger again if he could help it.

Yeah, he'd bet his Russian spy father had plenty of contacts in flipping Cuba.

Why did the man feel obliged to let his son know that he was aware of this planned junket? What was his father's ploy? Was Peter worried about Alex's safety and genuinely warning him that his mission was on the Russians' radar? Or was the man putting him on notice that his every move would be watched? Or was it merely part of their long-standing pissing contest to show that FSB intelligence sources were better than the CIA's?

It was always like this with his father: circles within circles. Meanings hidden below layer upon layer of meaning. Sometimes, Alex got so damned tired of it all. Maybe that was why Katie's directness appealed to him so strongly.

Peter. How to answer Peter? He forced his mind back to the sparring at hand. His father had asked if there was anything he could do to help. Alex replied, "Actually, there is something you can do for me. I'm going to need medical supplies when I get there. Nothing fancy. Sterile needles and syringes. Clean surgical implements and antibiotics. Maybe an X-ray machine."

"It will be waiting for you when you get to Baracoa."

The air rushed out of Alex's gut like he'd been punched. How on earth did his father know exactly where in Cuba he was going? Alex himself didn't know where he was being sent yet.

Did Peter's mole at D.U. figure it out, or worse, did the information come from the Cuban government? Either way, it was a stunning display of intelligence power. Russia might be a fading empire, but its legendary spy service wasn't dead yet.

Not that it mattered at the end of the day. He and Katie would go where they were sent, treat the sick and injured until the two of them dropped from exhaustion, discover what was being smuggled and go home. He would do the job they'd asked of him, but that was it. He was damned well keeping his nose out of any other CIA *or* FSB business while he was in Cuba. He ended the call abruptly and jammed his phone in his pocket.

To hell with them all. He closed the distance between him and Katie.

KATIE STOOD BACK from the steamy mirror to inspect herself. Nobody would know she'd just screwed the living daylights out of her boyfriend…she hoped. Her cheeks were rosy and her eyes sparkling, but that could be put down to good health and excitement over the trip to come, right?

The water cut off in the shower. "Could you pass me a towel?" Alex asked.

She handed a dry towel into his outstretched hand with its long, strong fingers and dark tan. She would have expected a surgeon of his skill to have more… feminine…hands. Softer. His were anything but. They were more what she would expect of a trained killer. He even had the telltale callus at the base of his right thumb to indicate that he shot handguns. A lot. He'd developed that in the past year.

Her dad and brothers had the same shooting callus. She certainly knew how to handle a pistol—it was impossible to grow up in the McCloud house without knowing how—but she kept meaning to ask Alex to show her how to use a rifle one of these days. More specifically, a sniper rifle.

She tugged her sexy little T-shirt down to the top of her snug jeans. She might not be a doctor, but she knew how to fill out a pair of designer denims. And she could handle herself in a crisis. Compliments of more of her McCloud upbringing.

She took a quick look at the TV. The hurricane was wrapping tighter, intensifying its energy into a tight knot of monstrous strength. Its outer bands were lashing the east tip of Cuba now. By tomorrow morning, the island would be ground zero for the core of the storm. It was morbidly fascinating to wonder just how powerful the winds would get and how bad the damage would turn out to be.

"Ready?" Alex asked from behind her.

"Yup. I'm starving."

"Vigorous sex has that effect on me, too. Although I have to say you didn't do all that much work. Next time, you can do the heavy lifting and pleasure me while I sit back and relax."

She stuck her tongue out at him and he dropped a kiss on the end of her nose. "And she thinks I'm kidding," he murmured.

"I don't for a second think you're kidding. I look forward to having you at my mercy."

That sent his right eyebrow into an arch and a speculative gleam into his silver gaze. Hah. She dared him to taste his supper now. Not that she was going taste any of hers, either.

His hand landed in the small of her back in the protective, possessive way that never failed to turn her on. Oh, so that's how tonight was going to be, huh?

She leaned into him in the elevator, pressing her breast lightly against his arm as another couple entered the small space. He didn't glance down at her, but a faint smirk curved his lips.

He asked for a corner table in the darkest part of the hotel's restaurant. Pleased to see the long linen tablecloths, she immediately kicked off her heels and planted her bare foot in his lap. While she massaged his groin with her toes, he massaged her calf under the table until she was all but groaning in pleasure.

He murmured over their entrées, "So tell me, Katie. What naughty fantasy is rattling around in your head wishing to become real?"

Her steak knife fell to her plate with a loud crash as it slipped out of her fingers. Embarrassed, she picked it up and risked a peek at Alex. The smirk was firmly in place again.

Her gaze narrowed. "I rather like the idea of you on your knees. Maybe even with your hands tied behind your back."

"And then what?" His eyes glittered like shards of broken mirror.

"I would…present…various body parts for you to…"

"Make love to with my mouth?"

"Exactly."

"And if I do this for you? What will you do for me in return? Sex is, at its core, a trade, after all."

She leaned back against the banquette. "That's where you and I differ. For me, sex is a gift. Something I give freely to you. I don't necessarily expect anything back in return. Of course, I generally do get plenty back. But it's not like I think to myself, 'Okay, if I give Alex *x* amount of pleasure, then he owes me *y* amount back.'"

He asked, amused, "Are you implying that I'm a selfish male?"

"I'm just saying your mind-set is different than mine. I don't know if all men treat sex the same way you do or not." She shrugged. "Frankly, you treat everything as a bargain, not just sex."

"Do I, now?"

Interestingly enough, he didn't seem offended. Thoughtful, maybe, but not angry. They finished the meal, and Alex ordered chocolate mousse for her without having to ask if she wanted any or not. The creamy dessert was, bar none, her favorite food on earth.

He let her get well into the mousse before he commented, "Sex has always been a transaction for me. I pay a prostitute, she gives me what I want."

Katie waved her spoon at him. "You don't want them to like it, do you? You go out of your way to make sure they don't enjoy themselves." Alex arched an eyebrow at her in mild warning that she was treading on dangerous ground. But she'd had one glass of wine too many to heed his eyebrow. "I think you're taking out your anger over your mother's abandonment on those prostitutes."

Whoops. Predator Alex went still. Alert. Ready to attack. The scale of her mistake finally cut through the wine buzz to register on her.

"Are you finished?" he asked. His voice was cold. Precise. Controlled.

Crap. She trailed after him in silence to their room when he didn't slow down to wait for her. He grabbed a couple minibottles of whiskey out of the refrigerator and moved over to the big plateglass window-wall, where he sprawled in one of the armchairs there.

Was their uneasy truce over, then? She knew how much Alex hated the idea of her going with him on this trip. Almost as much as she hated the idea of him going. He'd been mature and quit fighting about it when it became clear he was going to lose the argument. But she by no means thought he'd made peace with the idea.

God knew what else was rattling around in his head and messing with his mind after the past year. She'd read enough spy novels and seen enough spy movies to have an inkling of what he'd been through.

She waited until he'd downed the whiskey and the tension had left his shoulders somewhat to go stand behind him. "I'm sorry, Alex. I didn't mean to upset you."

Nothing.

She might as well not have been in the room with him. Okay, she could deal with him being mad at her for saying something to him he really didn't want to hear, but she would not stand for him ignoring her. That was just rude. She marched around in front of his chair, wedging herself between his knees and the cold glass at her back.

She put on her best kindergarten teacher lecture voice. "Alex Peters, that is quite enough sulking out of you. It's not nice to ignore people when they speak to you. So shake out of this snit of yours, right now. Got it?"

His gaze lifted to hers. Had she not already been plastered against the window at her back, she'd have staggered back a step from the utter emptiness in his eyes. Where had her Alex gone? This man was…dead.

Remorse and fear roared through her and she fell to her knees and flung her arms around his neck. She hung on to him like a tornado was trying to tear them apart. At first, he did not respond at all. But eventually, his arms came up around her waist. He pulled her into his lap. They sat like that for a long time. Long enough for the city to grow quiet below them and the streets to empty of cars.

Without warning, he commenced tearing her clothes off her. Some he tore off figuratively. Others that didn't give way easily enough, he literally tore off her. And when she was naked, he surged to his feet and shoved her face-first against the glass. She heard a zipper rip down, and then he was slamming into her from behind. No foreplay. No words of endearment. No kisses or caresses. Just his hard, hot body invading hers.

Her breasts and right cheek mashed against the cold window. Rain struck it hard enough on the other side for her to feel the tiny impacts. The drops came so close but didn't touch her. Sort of like her trying to reach Alex's soul. An invisible but impenetrable barrier blocked her way.

If someone happened to look up at this building and zero in on this particular room, they were getting quite a show. And yet, she couldn't spare the mental energy to care. Her attention was entirely focused on the agonized man behind her. She wasn't fooled for a second by his angry outburst. This was pain, not punishment. Anguish, not rage. And if he needed to dump it into her body, she was fine with absorbing it from him.

He was being rough with her, but as always, some part of him held back just enough not to actually hurt her. Relieved that whatever barriers held the beast at bay had worked one more time, she did her best to open her body to him. To relax and not fight the aggressive invasion. To convey an unspoken sense of welcome and acceptance to him.

By arching her back and thrusting back toward him, their bodies fit perfectly. He grasped her hips to pull her back harder, and she groaned her pleasure. He growled under his breath, probably irritated that she was enjoying this. But the harder and deeper he drove, the better it felt.

Finally, as she moaned with too much pleasure to bear, he collapsed against her back, panting in her ear, crushing her against the window. His hands came up to cover hers where they pressed into the glass by her head.

"Come to bed," he eventually murmured. "You're cold."

She was frozen with fear for his soul. Did that count as cold? He tucked her under the covers gently enough, though, and then pulled on jeans and a sweater in the dark.

"You're not coming to bed?" she asked from her cocoon of warmth.

"In a while, maybe."

Translation: I'm going to be up all night, brooding. She sighed, rolled onto her side and drifted to sleep wondering what it would take to get him to shed the darkness in his soul and choose to be happy.

CHAPTER FIVE

OVERNIGHT, HURRICANE GISELLE slammed into Cuba with a vengeance. It tore the island to bits from east to west. Even in a region accustomed to tropical storms, Giselle was a monster. Death tolls were unknown, but television commentators speculated that thousands had perished. Always secretive, the Cuban government declined to share details or let any foreign journalists into the immediate aftermath to report on it. What little news did leak out painted a grim picture, however.

Alex turned off the TV. Katie was still asleep, so he used the time to get on his laptop to see if any of the feelers he'd put out on Operation Cold Intent had come back to him yet.

Bingo. An encrypted email from C¥berE¥e, perhaps the top hacker he'd ever seen operate and his anonymous mentor since his first attempts to start hacking.

Alex ran their usual decryption protocol and got gibberish. He stared at the letters and symbols in surprise. He would suspect a failed message transmission were this not from C¥berE¥e. And then it hit him. He ran a secondary decryption protocol the hacker sometimes used.

Sure enough, a short message resolved itself on his screen. He stared at it in dismay.

Blondie and ThrεεWolvεs dead. Looks like murder. What the fuck did you get them into?

He knew the forces behind Cold Intent had killed Blondie. But they'd killed her boyfriend, too? Jesus. Who was doing this? And what in the hell was Cold Intent? Why was someone killing to cover its tracks?

He messaged C¥berE¥e back, asking if the guy had any idea what Blondie and her boyfriend were killed over. Hackers had lots of enemies if they were any good, right?

The reply made him feel ill. It said that Blondie must have been looking into something within the past few days that had triggered the real-world attack. No matter how he tried to rationalize it away, Alex couldn't escape arriving at the same conclusion C¥berE¥e had. He was responsible for the hackers' deaths. He sent an email back.

Any idea if someone got their files?

The reply was immediate.

An ABC agency was making a run at them. I snagged everything and wiped the drives before the Man could get in. Some interesting shit here. Who's Cold Intent?

Aww, crap. He didn't need dead hackers all over the planet on his account. Alex typed hard, as if he could transmit his emphatic warning through the keys themselves.

Be. Careful. They'll kill you, too. And no, I don't know who "they" are. You need to leave it alone.

C¥yberE¥e's reply was succinct.

I'll find 'em. You kill 'em.

He stared at the message speculatively. He'd long suspected that C¥berE¥e was some sort of intelligence agent or at least a former one. More than once, the hacker had sent Alex timely warnings about various government agencies being close to catching up with him and some of his more adventurous online activities as a teen.

What was fascinating about that short statement was that this guy seemed to think Alex was capable of killing someone. Hackers were criminals but rarely violent ones. Who was C¥berE¥e, really? Not that it mattered at the end of the day if the guy found Cold Intent for him. Slowly, one letter at a time, Alex typed his response.

Done.

"Whatcha doin?" Katie asked from right behind him.

Alex jumped about a foot straight up in the air.

"Wow. I managed to startle the great spy, Alex Peters?" she crowed. "I win!"

He scowled at her as he stood up, sweeping her into his arms. "We'll see about that."

She laughed as he carried her back to the bed. "You always have to win, don't you?"

"Yup."

For once, their lovemaking was simple and uncomplicated, just sex. No strings attached. No deep emotional conflicts. No struggles to push past emotional blocks or physical boundaries. It felt good to him, and he was fairly certain it felt good to her.

It was nearly an hour later, and Katie had unequivocally declared him the winner in all things…loudly and passionately…before he finally collapsed to the mattress beside her. His soul felt lighter, somehow.

And that was when fear came calling, deep in his gut. This time, she had blasted past his emotional defenses so easily and smoothly he hadn't even realized she'd done it.

How she managed to take him out of his head and into a place of pure feeling and emotion, he had no idea. But he had no power to resist whatever it was she did to him. God knew, he wanted to. He hated the loss of control. His entire life was based around the concept of supreme self-discipline. Success rested upon it. Hell, survival rested upon it.

He died a little each time she broke through his mental defenses. But man, it was a good way to go. Seductive. Addictive as hell.

Still. He would give just about anything for her not to be here with him, back in harm's way. He couldn't fight them all—André, Peter and Katie herself—but his gut yelled at him that taking her to Cuba with him was a giant mistake.

"I'm hungry," Katie announced.

He had to smile. She sounded like a little kid who'd just come in from the playground, breathless and happy. "Shower, then food?" he suggested.

She leaped out of bed, laughing over her shoulder. "Last one to the shower's a rotten egg!"

How could anyone be so damned innocent? Particularly given that she was highly intelligent and by no means naive. And getting less naive by the day around him. She told him once that happiness was a choice. Was innocence a choice, as well? If so, he'd chosen long ago to forsake it. He climbed out of bed more temperately and invaded her shower.

He'd just finished dressing and she was still in the bathroom blow-drying her hair when his cell phone rang. *André.*

"Hey, boss. What's up?"

"You've got a charter flight to Inagua in two hours. From there, a boat will take you to Baracoa. My contact will meet you at the rendezvous point on shore and take you to the base camp that's being set up for you."

Baracoa. He swore under his breath. Peter had been right, after all. A sane man would tell André the Baracoa meet-up was compromised. But Alex was inclined to go ahead and show up where Peter expected him to. Maybe he could spot whatever was going on that had both the CIA and FSB so interested in Cuba all of a sudden.

"Got it," he replied to André's more detailed instructions, which he memorized in lieu of writing them down to be found by anyone else.

"Have a safe trip, Alex."

Yeah. Right. "Thanks." He hung up before more sarcasm could leak into his voice.

He looked up and spied Katie standing in the bathroom doorway. "Showtime?" she asked.

An urge to lie nearly overcame him. To take her

to the airport, put her on a plane and send her home. But not only had he promised never to lie to her, she could also sniff fibs a mile away. He sighed. "As soon as you're ready to go, we'll head out."

Into what, he had no damned idea. But one thing he knew for sure. They were headed into *something*.

KATIE WATCHED THE twin prop airplane that had been their ride lift off into the sunny blue sky, and then looked around at Great Inagua Island in dismay. She'd never seen a more barren place. It was nothing but windswept dirt and rocks. "I thought Caribbean islands were supposed to be tropical paradises."

"Not if all the tree cover is destroyed by settlers and the ecosystem collapses in response and desertifies. Then they look like this," Alex replied.

She shuddered. "It's awful. Who lives here, anyway?"

"Workers at the salt factory. About eight hundred of them."

"Are they okay after the storm?" she asked in quick concern.

"They were evacuated by the salt company. We're the only people back on the island."

"Wow. We're really all alone on a desert island, then?"

He smiled reluctantly. "Yes. We've got to make our way to the shore on foot to catch our ride. I hope you're up for a hike."

The last time he'd asked her that, they'd been fleeing with an hour-old Dawn stuffed inside her coat and a war raging behind them. "Are you kidding? Piece of cake." She just hoped no wars were about to break out around them. She had a sneaking suspicion one might, though, before this was all said and done.

Alex took off across the pale dirt. The going was easy for about three minutes. And then they reached a patch of ruined vegetation, twisted and flattened by Hurricane Giselle into a nearly impassable tangle of jagged wood, sharp-leaved foliage and hidden rocks waiting to turn the unwary ankle.

Thank God she'd been working out like a maniac since he'd left. She was panting like a dog, but so was Alex. It took them something like an hour to cover a quarter mile.

"How far do we have to go in this stuff?" she finally broke down and asked Alex.

"Just over the ridge."

Awesome. They weren't far from the crest now. Another fifteen minutes of carefully picking their way forward, and they topped the low rise.

The ocean and a blond beach stretched away in front of them. And praise the Lord, this side of the ridge was bare of vegetation until the margin of the beach below. They made their way down the hillside relatively quickly with only sharp stones and treacherous slides of gravel to avoid.

But then they got to a literal wall of destroyed scrub trees, bushes and random vegetative debris. It was easily eight feet tall and looked like a loofah sponge. "How on earth are we supposed to get through this?"

she demanded. "Even if we had a machete, it would take hours to hack through all that."

"That, grasshopper, is why man conquered fire," Alex answered.

"Isn't it too wet to burn?" she asked dubiously.

"Only one way to find out," he answered absently as he commenced laying a fire at the base of the pile. The wind was still brisk in the lee of the hurricane and the fledgling flame blew out twice before it finally caught and held.

In seconds, though, it flared from the size of her hand to waist high, and from there to well over her head. Apparently, enough of the material had been dead long enough that a single day in the sun and wind, posthurricane, had dried it out. The pile went up in a firestorm that swept down the beach at shocking speed. No fire department on earth could put that out. She and Alex scrambled back from the intense heat as the debris burned with a roar of sound.

"My God! What if there are houses down the beach?" she cried.

"No house survived two-hundred-mile-per-hour winds for fourteen hours. And if one did, it was wrecked, anyway. A stone structure might survive the hurricane, but it won't burn." Alex shrugged, pragmatic. "Burning this stuff off is how a cleanup crew will get rid of it, anyway."

She watched the fire rip down the beach in front of the stiff wind with deep misgivings. The good news was the wind was headed out toward the ocean. If they were lucky, they hadn't just set the entire island on fire. And the salt factory was on the other side of the island, well upwind of this conflagration. Still, the ease with which Alex had taken radical action without concern for peripheral damage sent up warning flags in her head.

The debris burned hard for maybe thirty minutes. Where there were decent-size tree trunks and brush, the fire continued to burn. But here and there, where the pile had been mostly small brush and dead vegetation, the fire started to blow out.

Katie spied a small shape well out on the water. "Is that a boat?"

Alex pulled out binoculars to have a look. "That's our ride," he announced. "Time to head down to the water. Keep your feet moving and your shoes won't burn as we cross over the embers."

She stared at the remnants of the fire in front of her, maybe fifteen feet wide. *Whoa, whoa, whoa.* "I don't do the walking-across-beds-of-coals thing, Alex."

"Walk lightly and quickly on your entire foot. Don't run. You'll be fine."

She scowled ferociously at him, but he only shrugged back. "Follow me."

This was how life was always going to be with him, wasn't it? He would blithely lead her into danger, and she'd follow along like a lamb for the slaughter. She sighed and walked fast across the coals, distributing her weight across her entire foot with each step.

Vague heat registered around her, but before she knew it, she was on the other side of the glowing ember field. Her heart was racing like a runaway horse, and one spot on her leather hiking boots was smoldering a bit, but otherwise, she was intact. That hadn't been so bad, after all, darn it. She hated it when he was right.

A dark-skinned man angled a crappy little fishing boat toward them. It barely looked seaworthy and was in desperate need of a barnacle scraping and paint job. He stopped about a hundred feet shy of shore and gestured for them to come out to him.

"How are we supposed to get out there?" Katie asked blankly from the edge of the beach.

"Swim. Why else do you think I made you put your gear in a waterproof bag?"

She scowled at him again. "I thought it was for rain."

"C'mon." Alex was already stripping off his shirt, pants and shoes, and stowing them in his bag.

"I don't have a bathing suit!" she cried in sudden horror.

"You have underwear. Same difference."

"Not the same, thank you very much."

"I'm sure Pedro won't mind if you want to swim out there naked. God knows, I'll enjoy the view."

Thinking terrible, murderous thoughts about him, she stripped down to her underwear and stuffed her clothes in her bag. "You're such a jerk sometimes," she muttered.

"You knew what you were getting into when you insisted on coming with me," he said stonily.

He was right. But that didn't make her any happier to be swimming out to a total stranger in lingerie, darn it. She was *so* getting even with Alex for this.

To make matters worse, the water was freaking cold. Apparently, the hurricane had stirred the ocean, pulling shallow, warm water out to sea and cold, deep water up to the surface. Her teeth were chattering like a high-speed typewriter by the time she climbed the rickety ladder into the back of the boat.

The driver's gaze raked down her nearly naked body once and then, blessedly, the man turned away to face the wheel. The boat engine started with a cough. She took the scrap of terry cloth Alex passed her.

Swear to God, the towel was covered with grease stains. But it was that or freeze to death before she got dry. She threw Alex a long-suffering look and used the disgusting towel. He was doing this on purpose, punishing her for not staying at home like he'd wanted her to.

Tough. She might not like the whole idea of him going to Cuba one bit, but if he did insist on going, no way was she letting him go alone. He was her man, and she was protective.

After a few minutes of letting the brisk breeze finish drying her skin, she shivered and shook her way back into her jeans and T-shirt. She added a sweatshirt from her bag and gradually began to feel her fingers and toes once more.

The boat bumped along over waist-high waves that Pedro assured them were wonderfully calm seas after the recent storm. She failed to convince her stomach of that, however, and ended up barfing ignominiously off the back of the boat. She felt better afterward, but the whole experience sucked.

Alex suggested she try to sleep and made her a nest in some piled fishing net, which stunk of raw fish. She was so miserable, though, that she curled up in it and managed to pass out for a couple of hours.

Pedro said something about it being about seventy miles from Inagua to Baracoa, and Alex said something about the trip taking about four or five hours. She didn't think she was ever going to get off that bobbing little boat and see solid land again. Clearly she was not Navy material like her brother, Mike.

Finally, as a spectacular sunset stained the western sky in a dizzying display of color, a black hump took shape on the horizon below the sunset.

"There it is," Alex said. "Cuba."

"How come there aren't any lights—" She broke off. Because of the hurricane. She supposed coming ashore right after the storm like this would make it a lot easier to sneak onto the island. At least, that was probably the idea.

But as the shore drew near, she saw there would be nothing easy about this at all. Giant waves pounded the rocky crags and cliffs that formed the coastline, sending up massive geysers of white spray in the twilight. If she and Alex tried to swim ashore in that they'd be torn to pieces on the rocks.

"How on earth are we getting from here to there?" she asked him.

"Wind blew us off course. The landing point's a little farther north along the coast. Pedro says there's a beach at our rendezvous point."

She sensed another swim in her near future. *Fantabulous.*

The good news was they did, indeed, motor up the coast to a stretch of shoreline without the intimidating cliffs. The bad news was Pedro refused to pull in close to the shore. Apparently, the storm surge was still way up the shoreline and the man didn't want to risk running aground on the remains of some sort of dock that had stood at this spot a few days ago.

When she slid over the edge of the boat into the water, she was startled to discover that she was only standing in chest-high water. The boat pulled away into the darkness behind her as she started the long swim to shore behind Alex.

It took forever to reach land. She was nearly as chilled as last time when they finally slogged through the wet sand to another thick wall of debris from the storm. This pile contained evidence of humans: sawed lumber, bricks and mangled sheets of rusty aluminum.

"Now what?" she murmured below the sound of the surf behind them. "Are we going to set the coast on fire and send up the mother of all here-we-are beacons?"

"Not hardly. Now we get dry, get warm and get clothed. And then we wait for our contact."

Perversely, it made her feel better to know he was cold and miserable, too. She reached for her bag of clothing, but Alex stopped her. "The fastest way for us to warm up is to share body heat. Skin to skin. Didn't you learn that in scouting or from your brothers?"

Crud. She did remember it now that he mentioned it. "I'm not thinking on all cylinders tonight."

"Symptom of encroaching hypothermia. Most people only associate it with winter cold exposure. They don't realize hypothermia is a real problem even in a mild climate like this, particularly if a person is wet like we are now."

"Thank you, professor," she replied dryly. He opened his arms and she wasted no time accepting the invitation to press herself against him from head to foot.

He wasn't any warmer than she and was also shivering, but before long, warmth built between their bodies. Still, it was taking them a long time to warm up. She muttered against his chest, "Wouldn't this go faster if we had sex? The exercise and friction would help warm us up, right?"

He chuckled into her hair. "True. But our contact could show up at any second. I didn't think you'd appreciate being discovered *in flagrante delicto*."

"Is that fancy Latin for humping like bunnies?"

"It is."

"I'm so glad I fell for a Harvard-educated genius. Life will be nothing if not educational around you."

"You have no idea," he murmured back, a distinctly sexual edge in his voice.

He had yet to show her most of the dark sexual tastes he claimed to have. One of these days, though, she was going to get him to really cut loose with her and take her there. A shiver of anticipation rattled down her spine. If only danger wasn't such sexy stuff.

"Still chilled?" he asked.

"I wasn't shivering from cold," she grumbled.

He laughed low in her ear. "Ahh, one of these days, little innocent, we'll appease your curiosity."

"Promises, promises."

His arms tightened lightly around her, pressing her a little closer to his muscular body. His hands roamed up her bare back while her hands roamed down his. His buttocks were firm and imminently gripable. They made her think of athletic sex.

"You have the best ass ever," she whispered.

"You have the best—"

A noise behind them made him shove away from her, whirling into a defensive crouch.

A motorboat was coming around an outcropping of rock at the end of the tiny beach.

"Get down," Alex bit out.

Katie threw herself down to the sand. Crap. That looked like a military patrol boat of some kind. The half dozen men on board wore military uniforms and were using binoculars to stare at the shore.

"Don't move," Alex muttered. "As long as we don't call attention to ourselves, they won't see us here in the shadows."

She made like a lump of driftwood to the best of her ability as the vessel cruised slowly, ominously, past. Was this a routine patrol? Or had these guys spotted Pedro's fishing boat on radar, maybe?

The military vessel rounded the point at the north end of the beach and disappeared from view. Alex scrambled to his feet, dressing fast. She followed suit, too terrified to pause even to brush the sand off herself. Alex eased down the beach, sticking to the shadows, and she followed close on his heels. Tension vibrated in his movements, which alarmed her mightily. Why was he so on edge after seeing that boat?

Without warning, he plunged into the pile of debris. What the heck?

She followed after him, surprised to come into a tunnel of sorts. It looked to have been hacked out by humans. It was barely wide enough for her to pass through, and in the middle she had to turn sideways to slip through. But in a few seconds, she popped out the other side.

"Now what?" she whispered at Alex.

"We're going to have to head for the alternate rendezvous point," he whispered back.

"Let me guess. More hiking."

He shrugged and gave her a hand signal to be silent followed by the signal to move out. *Oh, joy.*

They crossed what might at one time have been a paved road, but now it was a smooth drift of sand. Alex hugged the edges of the drift, sticking to the patches of exposed asphalt wherever he could for perhaps a quarter mile when he threw up a fist abruptly, signaling a halt.

She stopped, listening intently. Only the swish and crash of the nearby surf were audible at first. But then she heard voices. *Crap.*

Alex plunged into the brush at the side of the ruined road and she followed suit. Her T-shirt caught on something and she gave it frantic jerk. It tore with a sound of rending cloth, and she froze, horrified. Alex grabbed her arm with his left hand and yanked her down beside him. She mouthed a silent apology and he nodded tersely as he quickly tied a piece of dark cloth in a makeshift do-rag over her blond hair. A pistol appeared in his right hand.

Were they really in so much danger? She thought the whole point of sending him down here was that the Cubans would think he was on their side. Why was he so freaked out at the prospect of running into Cuban soldiers? Shouldn't he wave hello to them, introduce himself and let them know he was going to be rendering first aid to locals for a while?

Waiting breathlessly, she crouched a dozen feet into the tangle of brush. Who was out there? More soldiers? Locals? Looters? A line of uniformed men on foot drew even with their position, six across, all wielding automatic weapons. They looked like they were expecting trouble.

The two on the end closest to her and Alex were muttering something about footprints in the sand and she caught the fractional wince that crossed Alex's face. Was that why he'd been avoiding the smooth sand and making her stumble along on the torn-up asphalt?

Someone called out an order low in Spanish. Something about fanning out. She glanced over at Alex in panic. Shouldn't they run or something? He shook his head in the negative so infinitesimally that she nearly missed the gesture. Instead, he sank lower by extremely slow degrees. She mimicked the sinking movement until she lay flat on her belly beside him. By inches, his arm came over her shoulder blades.

Whether it was meant to protect her or hold her down if she panicked, she had no idea.

Crashing noises shockingly close to them indicated that the soldiers were pushing out into the bush. Not good. Not good at all. She tensed, and Alex's arm went iron hard across her back. The message was clear. *Don't move.*

She'd heard her brothers talk about close calls when hostiles walked right by them in the dark, but none of them had ever described the throat-paralyzing terror of it, the roaring helplessness of having to just wait and hope you weren't spotted while the bad guys crashed past your position.

A soldier passed maybe four feet from them, moving left to right. But at the exact moment when the guy had a clear sight line down to where they lay between two dead logs, a spiderweb or something similar brushed against his face. The guy sputtered and waved his right arm impatiently while he used his left hand to wipe his face. The soldier took the next step, disappeared from a direct sight line and the threat was past.

Alex held her down while the line of soldiers gradually drew away from them, moving south down the road and beating their way through the brush beside it.

After a few minutes, Alex's arm lifted away from her and he rose to a crouch beside her. She scrambled upright somewhat less quietly than he did in spite of her best efforts to be stealthy. He gave her a hand signal to hold her position, and then he rose slowly to his feet.

Her thighs were killing her before he finally held

a hand down to help her rise. He eased back down toward the road, which shocked her. Maybe it was more important for them to leave the area quickly than it was for them to remain unseen. Either way, she noted that Alex was careful to stay off the sweep of sand covering most of the roadway.

They'd been walking maybe five minutes when Alex swore low under his breath and dived for the brush again. Echoing his sentiment, she followed him again. With the exception of the chorus of insects, the night sounded completely normal to her.

She was ready to stand up and let some circulation back into her legs, but still Alex crouched there. What was he waiting for? She sent him the hand signal questioningly for moving out, and he shook his head sharply in the negative. Confused and uncomfortable, she held her position. In a few minutes, the sound of a vehicle approaching became audible.

It was a jeep picking its way slowly along the remains of the road. Four soldiers sat in the vehicle, and the passengers were scanning the shore and jungle carefully. The two in the back had automatic weapons in their laps. The two in front were armed most notably with gigantic machetes attached to their belts.

The vehicle did not stop and rumbled on by their hiding place. It retreated in the same direction the walking men had gone.

What the hell was going on? How was it the Cuban military had converged on nearly their exact position within minutes of their arriving here and appeared to be searching for them? Had Pedro turned them in? Although she disliked that idea, she disliked the alternative more. Surely, they hadn't been betrayed from within Doctors Unlimited. Or worse, the CIA.

As soon as the jeep passed out of sight, Alex eased out of the brush and continued in the direction the men and vehicle had come from. She knew it was a good thing to have slipped through the search line like they'd managed to do. But it didn't mean they'd seen the last of waves of incoming Cubans, nor did it mean the soldiers wouldn't head back this way at some point.

She followed Alex for maybe ten minutes in cautious silence before she ventured to whisper, "How did you know the jeep was coming?"

"The men on foot were talking about their district commander being headed this way."

"At this time of night? Why?"

"No idea. But given that all this activity is taking place in the exact spot, at the exact time, we arrived on the island, one has to wonder if we're the cause of it." Alex stopped and pulled out his cell phone. He fiddled with the GPS function for a moment. "Another quarter mile or so should bring us to the backup rendezvous point."

Funny, but a quarter mile of walking on sand felt like a lot farther. Her calves ached like big dogs before a roofless stone shell of a small building came into view ahead. It sat high above the road on a rocky crag overlooking the ocean.

"Gaviota hut," Alex muttered. "That's where we're headed."

"What's a gaviota hut?"

"*Gaviota* means *seagull* in Spanish. It's a ruin where only the birds hang out."

"Our contact is a seagull? Cool," she replied.

He smiled briefly and turned up a path that looked more like a washed-out gully at the moment. They wound up the hill about halfway when they reached a massive washout, maybe twenty feet across and at least as deep.

Alex screeched to a stop on its lip and she barely avoided plowing into him and pushing him over the edge. "Whoa," she gasped.

They stared down into the ravine together. A raging torrent of water rushed down the mountain. If either of them fell into that it would smash them on the rocks before washing their broken bodies down the hill.

She looked up the mountain, and the slash of the ravine was visible all the way to the top. She murmured, "Got a plan C meeting point, Captain Preparedness?"

"No. We're on our own for now."

"That doesn't sound good."

He shrugged. "I'm good at improvising. I'm going to suggest we head toward the area where the ships have been seen coming and going and scout around for ourselves."

"Where is this area exactly?"

He shrugged. "Up the coast a little ways. I've got a map and GPS on my phone. We'll find it."

"In case you hadn't noticed, this island is trashed. It's not like we can just take off hiking over hill and dale. We've got no food, no water and, worse, no bug spray!"

He arched an eyebrow at her.

"I'm serious! Think about the size of mosquitoes that are going to start breeding in this mess. In a week, they'll be carrying off small children."

"I have industrial-strength bug repellent," he replied dryly.

"You do? Hand it over."

"There aren't any insects out to speak of."

"I feel itchy," she declared.

"That's the sand in your clothes. We need to preserve the supplies we have. I have no idea what we'll find when we get to where we're going."

"Do you know exactly where that will be?" she asked in resignation.

"Nope."

He took his bearings using his cell phone, and then backtracked cautiously to a side road they'd passed a few minutes earlier. No telling if there were more military patrols out hunting for them or not. She rather thought that they would still be out here.

She stared up the narrow track that disappeared into the darkness. "You're seriously going to just head off into the jungle?" she asked in dismay.

"There are fresh tire tracks on this road. It's passable for at least a while."

Well, *that* was encouraging. This "road" of his looked like a pair of bad ruts and not much more. Her irritation, and her certainty that he was torturing her on purpose, mounted as they hiked up into the hills. The "road" did, in fact, hold up for several miles. But then, they hit a patch where, as far ahead as Alex's high-powered flashlight could reach, nothing but downed trees was visible.

"End of the road," he muttered.

"How far to wherever we're headed?"

"Far enough that it's time for us to make camp and get a little rest before we finish the hike."

Oh, God. She watched in dismay as Alex moved a ways up the hill and off into the brush. She followed glumly and helped him spread out a tarp on the ground. They spread another over a downed tree limb lying several feet above the first tarp. They laid big banana leaves in a shingle pattern over the shelter to help it shed water and then covered the whole mess with brush, no doubt to camouflage it from prying eyes.

She crawled into the tiny tent and Alex followed suit. She muttered, "Did I ever mention I hate camping?"

"I got that memo when you went looking for an electrical outlet in a cave in Zaghastan so you could blow-dry your hair."

"I did not look for an outlet! I merely complained that there wasn't one."

"I rest my case," he murmured.

"Just tell me there aren't ginormous snakes crawling around all over the place out here."

"There aren't ginormous snakes crawling around all over the place out here."

"Is that the truth?"

He snorted. "Of course not. The locals' name for the Cuban boa constrictor is the *maja*. They're native to these jungles. Not the biggest snakes on earth, but they're aggressive."

"Oh, my God."

"Get some sleep, Katie."

"You're kidding, right?"

He merely offered his arm for a pillow, and she couldn't maintain enough ire to turn him down. She was exhausted by all this Jane of the Jungle stuff.

SHE WASN'T SURE if it was the deafening cicadas outside or the steamy heat inside the tent that woke her up, but either way, she roused to bright green light and the sticky discomfort of sand and sweat on her skin. She rolled over and suppressed a groan. Her body ached from head to foot. Her Pilates instructor was going to be so disappointed. "Alex?" she called out low.

"I'm here."

She crawled out the opening in the end of their makeshift tent and sighed in relief as a stirring of cooler air caressed her. Alex was chopping up a small papaya with the same sort of machete she'd seen those men carrying last night. "Where'd you get that?" she exclaimed under her breath.

"From the tree over there. It fell over in the storm and the fruit wasn't all blown away."

"No, silly. The big dang knife."

"That road we were walking along last night used to have houses beside it. There are all sorts of household goods snagged in the rubble. I picked it up."

Personally, she'd been too absorbed in her misery to notice such things.

He passed her a dripping slice of orange papaya and she bit into it with a moan of pleasure. She'd never tasted anything so sweet and refreshing in all her life.

"I saved this for last," he announced some minutes later. He hoisted a big green, roughly triangular fruit onto a big rock and raised the machete over it.

"What's that?"

"Coconut."

"No way. They're round, brown, hairy things."

He grinned at her and took a mighty whack at it. "The brown bit is the seed. This is the entire fruit." It split open to reveal what she knew as a coconut nestled inside. He dug it out of the mushy pulp.

He gave the coconut a sharp rap with the machete and it split open. He dropped the knife and caught the two halves in his hand. "Drink the coconut water. We need the fluid."

It didn't taste bad, but it wasn't that great, either. It was wet, though, and her body craved the moisture. They scooped out the coconut flesh with their fingers and ate that, as well. She liked hers sweetened, but hey. It could be a worse meal. Alex could be asking her to eat raw fish. Or bugs.

As the morning heated up, Alex stripped off his T-shirt to reveal a glistening chest rippling with muscle. "Are you looking to get jumped, sailor?" she murmured.

"By you? Bring it, baby."

Her gaze narrowed. She did need to get naked, anyway, and shake the damned sand out of her clothes. She wiggled out of her jeans, which had dried tightly to her body. "I'm going to have to do some serious twerking to get those back on," she declared.

He grinned. "Can't wait to see the show."

Speaking of which, she stripped off her shirt slowly and made a production of reaching behind her back to unhook her bra. She brushed the sand off her breasts sensuously, enjoying the feel of her fingertips sweeping across the sensitive peaks.

Abruptly other fingers were there, pushing hers aside. They brushed the sand off her entire body, in fact, leaving her moaning and gasping with pleasure. And when she didn't think she could take any more, Alex pushed her back against a fallen tree trunk, arching her backward until her body was taut and unable to move. Once he had her immobilized and at his mercy, he finally unzipped his jeans, freed himself and plunged into her.

She cried out and he pressed his hand over her mouth fast. Good call. She never did have any restraint once he took control of her body. She arched up into him, matching him thrust for thrust sprawled across the giant log, while he took her body fast, then slow, rough, then gentle. He closed his eyes today, lost in his own pleasure. But that was fine with her. Any second now, she was going to…

She screamed against his hand. To explode. Like that. Omigosh. The orgasm had taken her by surprise, ripping through her like Giselle had gone through this end of Cuba.

Alex collapsed against her with a low, shuddering groan, pressing her buttocks uncomfortably into the rough tree bark. But nearly as quickly, he straightened, lifting her up and gently brushing off her backside. "Did we get all the sand off?" he asked wryly.

"I'm pretty sure we shook it all off," she managed to reply without panting too audibly. She pulled her clothes on with unsteady hands while he efficiently folded the tarps and stowed them in his pack.

He announced, "It's time for us to get moving. We have a ways to go before night. If you could finish packing, I'll do a little reconnaissance."

"Want me to come with you?"

"Good Lord, no!"

Whether he was concerned for her safety or for the burden she would be to him, she couldn't tell. Either way, he whirled and disappeared into the brush quickly, as if worried she might follow him, anyway.

She sighed. The man was such a loner sometimes. Darned if that wasn't part of his appeal, though. The fact that he'd chosen to let her inside his personal fortress of solitude was sexy as all get-out to her. Were they not fugitives who'd be arrested or shot on sight, and were there not boa constrictors out here, this wouldn't be a bad little spot to stay for another day or two and have lots of hot monkey sex.

But after that, she would want a hot shower in a real bathroom in a decent hotel. One day at a time, Katie. One day at a time.

CHAPTER SIX

ALEX HURRIED AWAY from their hiding spot, nervous that Katie would do something stupid like try to tail him. She'd done crazier things before.

Where had all those soldiers last night come from, and why the hell hadn't the contact met them at either the primary or secondary rendezvous points? Last night had been a setup. The Cuban army had been there with the intent to ambush the two of them.

Something was very wrong with this mission. He felt it in his bones. Of course, it was possible that the contact had been injured or killed in the storm. Or that he was tied up helping out his own family and hadn't been able to peel away to come pick up the two Americans illegally in the country.

But none of those reasons rang true with his instincts. If he was right, someone had tipped off the Cubans where to find him and Katie. He had a hard time believing his father would betray his only son…but then, maybe it wasn't so hard to believe if he stopped to think about it. His father's brand of love would follow a scorched-earth policy in the face of betrayal.

The hot sun beat down on him and he let it. In a few days, he would be tanned darkly and, with his dark hair, would blend in for the most part with the locals. Blonde Katie, however, was going to burn like a lobster, loudly announcing her non-Cuban heritage to anyone who cared to look at her. He had to get her off the main roads and tucked away somewhere safe. Soon.

Every noise was a threat to her, every snapping twig a potential disaster that could cost him the woman he loved. His nerves were frayed and they hadn't even been here a full day yet.

Baracoa sat at the eastern tip of Cuba, on the most isolated piece of the island. In fact, many people called the city the Siberia of Cuba. For decades, political dissidents had been sent there because it was so completely cut off from the rest of the island. After Giselle, the single decent road into this region was undoubtedly knocked out from both directions, cutting off the area again.

Which, of course, brought up the question of why the CIA had felt such a burning need to insert him and Katie at exactly this place on the island. What in the hell were the two of them supposed to be seeing out here?

He made his way up the hill toward a relatively clear mountaintop. If his maps weren't wrong, a decent-size village lay in the valley just beyond this ridge.

Or at least what was left of one. He topped the ridge and stopped cold as the destroyed remains of a big valley sprawled beneath him. Here and there a stone structure seemed intact. The concrete buildings more or less were standing. But the rest of the village and most of the surrounding trees were trashed. A bomb might as well have landed here. Man. The main street through the village was flooded. A woman plodded slowly through thigh-deep water, her skirt hiked up around her hips. Even from here, he could see shock and despair in the set of her shoulders.

He knew exactly what it was like to be living normal life one day and wake up the next to find everything you knew and loved totally destroyed. Except for him it hadn't been an act of nature; it had been his father's arrest for espionage against the United States and Peter's subsequent expulsion from America that imploded his world.

He watched the village through his binoculars for a long time and saw nothing to arouse his suspicion. No army patrols moved through the area. All seemed quiet.

Nonetheless, his instincts were yelling at him to pull up stakes and get the hell out of Cuba. It remained to discover, though, what Peter had to do with all of this. An unfamiliar sensation of being torn in two ripped through him. God, he hated this. His entire life had been based around becoming the best spy his father could possibly mold him into. He wasn't functioning at anything approaching full capacity. Katie was a liability to him he could not afford to continue operating within.

He and Katie would scout out the area as quickly as possible, figure out what his old man was up to and then the two of them were getting the hell out of Dodge before something bad happened to both of them.

He made his way carefully back to his and Katie's hiding spot. They ate the last of the papayas he'd salvaged from the downed tree and got ready to head out.

He did not have a good feeling about this.

KATIE WAS GLAD to see civilization again, even if it was in tatters.

It hadn't been hard to find the village's health clinic. The cinder-block building they were directed to was slightly less ruined than most, and a path had been shoveled to the door through the debris and mud. Ahead of her, Alex poked his head inside the white stucco building that was now stained with a waist-high coating of dried mud.

"Who's in charge here?" Alex asked cautiously.

"That would be me." The woman who stepped onto the porch had strands of silver in her black ponytail. She was small. Sturdy. No-nonsense. At the moment, she wore latex gloves covered in blood.

"My name is Alexei." With a glance down at the woman's hands, he did not offer to shake hands.

"I'm Sylvia Vasquez. Are you or the woman hurt?"

"We're fine. Do you by any chance need a doctor?"

"Are you kidding? If you know how to get one here, tell me!"

"I'm a surgeon. What can I do for you?"

The woman stared at Alex in shock for several long seconds. Then she shook herself a little and muttered something fast in Spanish about answered prayers. She said briskly, "This way."

Katie trailed Alex and Sylvia deeper into the building, whose back half was split into four tiny examining rooms. As Katie's eyes adjusted to the dim interior—on account of the boarded-up windows—she placed Sylvia in her early fifties. Dark eyes. Tired-looking. Like she hadn't slept in a few days.

The woman resumed stitching a nasty gash in a man's forearm in one of the rooms as she talked. "I've got a patient in the next room. Needs surgery. Beyond my abilities. Take a look."

Alex nodded and passed Katie his pack. "Come with me," he muttered.

A camp cot stood against the wall, and a man laid on it, writhing in obvious pain. Alex knelt by the injured man's side and lifted a blood-soaked pad off the man's middle.

"What have you got for medical supplies?" Alex called tersely.

Katie knew that tone of voice. The trauma surgeon was in the house.

Sylvia called back a shockingly short list of supplies and equipment.

Alex nodded and then glanced over at her. "The light's as good in here as anywhere, so we'll sterilize this room as much as possible. Katie, you'll assist me. Sylvia can keep working on the other patients."

She nodded and commenced unpacking the plastic tarps he'd brought for this purpose. Using the roll of duct tape they'd brought, she tacked clear plastic over the window frame while he sprayed the tarps, ceiling and floor with disinfectant. Makeshift operating theater in place, Alex scrubbed his hands in a bucket of water with the iodine-based soap he'd brought.

Katie cringed and joined him in washing. She knew what came next. They donned surgical gloves and masks, and he parked her next to a small tray of surgical tools he laid out. Grumbling about primitive medicine, Alex administered ether by dripping it onto a gauze pad over the man's mouth, but in a few minutes the patient was unconscious.

Surgery never failed to gross her out. But at least she didn't pass out as he dug into the man's gut to repair something or other. Alex asked for tools tersely as he worked, and she passed them to him quickly.

In maybe twenty minutes, Alex started to stitch the man up. Which was just as well. The patient started to move a little and moan as the ether wore off. At least she was getting a firsthand look at what medicine would have looked like a hundred years ago.

Alex commented, "He could use a pint of blood, but there isn't any to give him."

"I could donate a pint," Katie offered. "I'm O positive."

"That's a noble offer. But if you donated blood to everyone who needs some around here, you'd be drained dry. You need the blood more, anyway. We're going to be working long hours for a while."

Alex was not kidding. When word got out that a doctor had arrived, patients started to pour in from the surrounding area, and he worked nearly around the clock. Katie did what she could to ease his load, but there was only so much she could do to help him.

They survived on bottled water and canned food Sylvia scared up from somewhere. A hastily dug out-house behind the clinic served much of the populace, and baths consisted of sponging off over a bucket of cold water.

How Alex kept going like he did, she had no idea. He moved from lacerations to broken limbs to major surgeries without pause for twenty-four hours at a stretch. He went down for four hours' sleep, and re-peated the whole routine again.

Three days passed this way, with Katie working frantically in the background. She collected scrap wood, built a fire, put a huge kettle of water over it and spent hours dipping towels, sheets and surgical tools into buckets of boiling water. She fed children and passed out bottles of water, mopped blood off the floors and sweat off Alex's brow and forgot what it felt like to sit down and rest.

As miserable and demanding as the work was, Katie found reassurance in discovering that the Alex she'd first met and fallen in love with still existed. The doctor passionate about his work and about saving patients was still inside him. The physician was just buried beneath the spy. Now, if only the man and his feelings could be located beneath the spy, life would be perfect.

The fourth day dawned, and something dawned on Katie, too. She asked Alex over their breakfast of powdered eggs and canned tomatoes, "Isn't it about time for us to be moving on? When we were in Zaghastan, it took about three days for word to get out among the locals that we were in the area. It must work about the same here."

He nodded around a slug of water. "I'm counting on it working about the same."

That wasn't exactly an answer. She pressed. "Are we going to leave soon?"

He shook his head and picked up his trash. "Nope."

"Why not?"

"I'm timing how long it takes the Cuban army to show an interest in us."

What the heck did that mean? "They showed quite an interest in us the night we arrived. Isn't the whole point of being here avoiding those guys?" she asked.

"Someone in the intelligence service no doubt told the army to ambush our arrival point. What I'm watching is how quickly they track down reports of a foreign doctor showing up in the area."

"You're using us as bait?" she squeaked.

"More or less."

"There's no 'less' about it. You're sitting here waiting for them to come after us! And what exactly are you planning to do when they get here?"

He shrugged. "Evade them."

"Just like that?"

"Yup."

God, she hated it when he went all monosyllabic on her like this. "Isn't that just a wee bit dangerous?"

A shrug.

Great. Now he wasn't speaking at all. At least her

vocal cords were functioning normally. "This is a lousy idea, Alex. Just because your father is in bed with the Cubans doesn't mean they'll embrace you like a long-lost son."

"I've got to go," he bit out.

"You're avoiding me," she called after him as he beat a hasty retreat. "I'm not done talking about this with you!"

Apparently, he was done talking about it with her, though. He dived into the morning's line of patients with enough vigor for her to be certain he was dodging her.

Old Alex would not have taken such a risk with her around. New Alex was far too cavalier about danger for her taste.

As quickly as the deluge of patients had come, it stopped around noon that day. Sylvia told the two of them to take a few hours off. They went to her little cottage next door, which was missing part of its roof, crawled wearily into hammocks draped with mosquito netting and crashed.

It was very dark and the insects had gone quiet for the night when Katie roused to a hand shaking her awake. It was Sylvia.

"Alex, Katie, a truck just drove in with a dozen patients."

Katie groaned and rolled out of the hammock. She ached all over even though her cell phone said she'd been asleep for nearly twelve hours. She pulled on her last clean T-shirt and followed Alex and the nurse next door.

The patients were crowded into the front room of the clinic, and they looked terrible. Several were barfing into bags, while several more twitched on the floor in continuous convulsions. A few more gripped their bellies and smelled of excrement.

Alex swore under his breath. "Where have they come from?"

Sylvia collected answers to his rapid-fire questions while he started examining the worst of the bunch. It turned out they all came from a small village to the north along the coast. They had eaten enough different foods that he ruled out mass food poisoning. Cholera would have made them all explosively empty their bowels and not just a few of them, so that was thankfully off the table as a possibility.

Alex looked down throats, poked bellies and moved limbs, a frown intensifying on his brow all the while. At last, he murmured, "Sylvia, I need to know exactly where these people live and how they got here."

The nurse collected descriptions of several plantations and collective farms in a cluster along the coast.

Alex asked with chilling calm, "Find out how many have already died from this sickness."

Sylvia stared at him in alarm. "What is it? Are we looking at an epidemic?"

Katie's blood ran cold. She and Alex were vaccinated against pretty much everything known to man that had a vaccine. But this could get ugly fast if something infectious had hit the local population.

Alex merely repeated over his shoulder as he held down a convulsing woman, "How many dead?"

Sylvia asked the question.

"Taking into account that some of them may duplicate counting some of the deaths, maybe fifty. Another forty or fifty have milder symptoms, and a dozen or so were too far gone to move and are probably dead by now."

A teenage girl barfed just then, and Sylvia bent down to wipe the girl's mouth and give her a sip of water.

Katie sidled over to Alex. "What is it?" she murmured in English.

He muttered back, "Not here."

"Can you treat them?" she tried.

He looked over at Sylvia. "Comfort care. Hydrate them. Sedate the convulsers if you can spare the meds. Feed them clear liquids if they can keep them down." To Katie he muttered, "Come with me."

Alarmed, she followed him into a back room.

"Help me look for test tubes," he ordered.

She dug into the boxes of supplies beside him. "What's going on?" she breathed.

"Chemical agent."

"As in nerve gas or something like that?" she blurted in disbelief.

"Keep your voice down." He added more gently, "I can't be sure. We'll need to take samples. Get them out of the country for testing somehow."

"Does Cuba make or stockpile chemical weapons?"

"Not that anyone in the U.S. is aware of."

Ho. Lee. Cow. "Are you sure?"

He shook his head. "Can't be until we run tests."

She gestured to the doorway. “Is there anything we can do for them?”

“If I’m right, we can make them comfortable until they die.”

Her stomach dropped to the floor.

“In the morning, you and I are taking a trip,” he said grimly.

“Let me guess. Up the coast?”

“Brilliant deduction, Sherlock.”

“Should we tell somebody what you suspect?” she breathed.

He opened his mouth to answer, but Sylvia called from the other room. “Alexei!” Her voice was urgent and he bolted from the back room. Katie followed him to the doorway. He and Sylvia knelt over a thrashing patient, but they seemed to have it under control. She retreated from the gruesome scene.

Thoughtfully, she went to Alex’s backpack in the corner of the operating room and pulled out the satellite phone he stored there for emergencies. She turned it on and punched in André Fortinay’s private number. It was something like three in the morning in Washington, but he’d get over it when he heard what she had to say.

A sleepy voice answered on the second ring. “Hey, Alex. What’s up?”

“It’s Katie,” she said low. “We just got in a batch of patients. Alex thinks they’ve been exposed to some sort of chemical agent.”

Abruptly André sounded entirely alert. “Like a chemical weapon?”

"Yes."

A short pause and then, "Tell him to get me proof. At all costs, get me proof. As soon as you've got it, execute the exit protocol and get that proof back here. Understood?"

"Yes, sir."

"At all costs. You hear?"

"Got it."

She thought he might be suggesting something sinister along the lines of theft, murder and mayhem if it became necessary. But she didn't speak spy double-talk nearly as well as Alex.

"Katie!" Sylvia called.

"Gotta go," she murmured into the phone.

"Keep in touch—" She cut off her boss and stuffed the phone back in Alex's pack.

Several patients went into various stages of collapse over the next few hours, keeping her, Alex and Sylvia hopping. A man in his sixties died, and an elderly woman followed him soon after. It was, in a word, awful.

Sylvia was beside herself that whatever the patients had might be contagious and was agonizing over whether or not to shut down her little clinic and deny the locals any more care.

Finally, as the sun rose, Alex told the nurse, "Keep your clinic open for now. Katie and I will go investigate this illness further."

He sent the overwrought woman to bed for a few hours of badly needed sleep while he went looking for the man who'd driven the farm truck into the village last night. The guy was sleeping off a hangover a few huts down and roused slowly.

Alex had Katie fetch coffee from the communal eaterie the locals had set up to pool their food resources. He poured a few cups of the strong, hot brew down the man and then informed him he was taking them to the source of the sick patients. Now.

An exhausted Sylvia was roused from her nap and Alex shouldered their backpack of equipment.

The hungover driver climbed back in his truck silently. Alex slid over to the middle of the cab and Katie mashed up next to the door. The vehicle bumped out of town on the ruined road and Katie groaned under her breath. Banging around in this truck was better than walking but not by much.

The driver was taciturn. He was probably nursing a monster headache, which had to suck for him on these awful roads. Alex was equally grim, and that worried her. He was a brilliant man and a highly qualified physician. She seriously doubted his suspicions were wrong about what had sickened those poor people.

Lord, the implications of it, though. If chemical weapons were stored right in America's backyard, Uncle Sam was going to go crazy. Memory of studying the Cuban Missile Crisis in history class came to mind. Were the Russians involved this time, too?

Where else would tiny Cuba acquire the technology to make such weapons? Could the Cubans have developed the skill independently? She supposed it was possible. But why would they try, knowing how their neighbor to the north would react if such a thing were discovered? No, she was more inclined to suspect the Russians were behind this.

Given the furious set of Alex's jaw, he must surmise the same thing.

The trip was not long in distance, but it took a couple of hours to navigate the terrible roads. Twice, all three of them had to pile out of the truck and drag aside debris that had fallen or blown into the road overnight.

They crested a rise and she was surprised to glimpse the Caribbean Sea glistening like a jewel in the distance. Between them and it lay what looked like a destroyed coconut palm grove. Rows of the giant trees lay uprooted or snapped off at the base of the trunks. She hated to think about how wind could wreak such havoc. If the strong, flexible palms could not withstand it, how could anything else?

The truck turned onto a sandy path and drove to the edge of a small settlement that was still flooded. A few people waded wearily through knee-deep water. "Here we are," the man announced.

"Water-borne illness?" Katie murmured.

Alex frowned. "Most of those are caused by microbes or parasites in the water. Symptoms are typically intestinal in presentation."

"Botulism?" she suggested. "It's often fatal."

Alex shook his head. "We'd be seeing high fevers. Delirium. Those patients back at the village showed neither. They were in agony but lucid. Respiratory distress. Pinpointed pupils. Runny noses. Hemorrhaging. That's not a bug in the water or food poisoning."

He turned to the man and asked in Spanish, "Are there any more people alive in the area who are affected?"

The man nodded grimly and led them toward a cluster of makeshift tents at the far end of the tiny village. Except when they got to the crude shelters, flies swarmed everywhere outside. Inside, a dozen bodies lay in neat rows on the dirt, bloated. Stinking. Dead.

Katie staggered back, retching.

Alex pulled a surgical mask out of his pack, donned it and muttered, "Stay out here, Katie."

Oh, God. Not a problem. She turned toward the man who'd crossed the street to sit down on an overturned metal barrel. He pulled out a cigar, lit it and sat there staring blankly into space and smoking. She walked over to him. The cloud of smoke seemed to drive off the flies, and the smell of the tobacco was better than the alternative.

"Did you lose anyone in there?" she asked quietly.

He shrugged. "Wife. My brother."

"Did they die in the storm or of the sickness?"

Another shrug. She couldn't blame the guy for shutting down like this. How did one face the staggering loss of family, home and livelihood all at once? "Where are you staying now?"

"My truck."

Wow. "Food? Where are you getting that? And fresh water?"

"Around."

"Is the government passing out supplies anywhere?"

"Baracoa, maybe. I heard some boats came in."

Sharply aware of the CIA missions—both of them—hanging over her head, she asked, "Is there a port or dock anywhere around here where supply boats can tie up?"

"Yeah, sure. At the Zacara plant. But none have come yet."

"What's that?"

"Factory. They make cleaning supplies. Furniture polish. Window cleaner. That sort of stuff."

"Where is this place?"

"Couple klicks up the road." He pointed with his cigar to the north.

"Do people from this village work there?"

He nodded and took another long pull on his cigar. She coughed a little at the blue cloud of smoke he blew out.

Alex stepped out into the street and ripped off his surgical mask, breathing deeply of the fresh air. He looked shaken as he strode over to them. He asked the driver, "Did you know these people?"

A grunt around the end of the cigar.

"Can you tell me who they were or where they lived?" Alex tried.

"Yeah, sure." He rattled off a half dozen family names followed by, "They lived on the plantations north of town."

"Up by the Zacara plant?" she asked quickly.

The man glanced at her. "Yeah."

"What kind of farms were they?" Alex asked.

"Co-ops. Pigs. Chickens. Food crops—beans, plantains, vegetables."

She looked over at Alex, who was frowning. She murmured in English, which the driver didn't seem to understand a word of, "This Zacara facility is some sort of chemical factory. Makes cleaning supplies. Could the hurricane have breached storage containers of something dreadfully poisonous?"

"It's worth a look," Alex replied dubiously.

The driver had wandered away from them and into the ruined hull of a modest house. They heard some crashing as the fellow rooted around inside. He emerged onto the stoop and took a long slug out of a liquor bottle.

Alex cursed under his breath. "So much for having him drive."

Katie groaned. "We're walking again, aren't we?"

"Yup."

They headed out on foot, which probably wasn't that much slower than driving along the trashed road. Katie commented, "That guy said there haven't been any supply trucks through here yet. You'd think the government would send someone out this way in the next day or two to check on the locals. Maybe deliver some bottled water."

"You'd think."

"He also said there's a dock up by the Zacara factory. I thought maybe we could find someone who works the docks and chat him up. See if any ships are coming in at weird hours and on- or off-loading anything."

Alex nodded. "We'll have to take it slow, though. We can't afford to make anyone suspicious."

"See anything interesting in those bodies back there?"

"More evidence of some kind of chemical poisoning."

"What does it mean?" she asked in dismay.

He shook his head. "I don't even want to think about the political implications if it turns out to be a weaponized chemical."

"Could this Zacara factory have been storing some cleaning chemical that makes a horrible, evil gas when it's released? Or maybe two chemicals that aren't supposed to mix but did during the storm?"

"The operative words being *during the storm.* With two-hundred-mile-per-hour winds blowing, any deadly chemicals that were released would be swept away so fast they'd have little or no time to affect anyone in the area. If they were released in a high enough concentration to actually hurt people, we'd see a wide scatter pattern of deaths, not this tight little cluster in this one village."

"What the hell is going on, Alex?"

"That's what we're going to find out, hopefully. I'm praying the storm caused a slow leak and that a cloud of something innocent, but poisonous, built up near the factory."

They trudged onward in silence.

She spotted them first. Dead, bloated lumps in a pasture littered with tree branches. "Oh, my God, Alex. Cows."

He glanced where she pointed and swore. If there had been a fence containing the beasts at some point, it was long gone. Alex swerved into the pasture to examine the creatures. Katie had no desire to get up close and personal with any dead animals and stayed out on the road.

Alex was back quickly. “Same pathology at a glance as the people,” he announced.

Katie shuddered. They walked a little farther and spotted a child walking alone toward them.

At first, she hardly believed her eyes. And then her maternal instincts kicked in and she rushed forward to kneel before the boy. He was maybe ten years old and said his name was Oscar. He had cuts and abrasions and seemed mildly in shock.

Alex joined them, but stood back, detached and merely watched as she gave the boy a bottle of water and a couple of protein bars, which Oscar wolfed down.

“Aren’t you going to at least check him over for injuries?” she finally demanded.

Alex frowned, but stepped forward to ask the boy a few terse questions in Spanish, check his eyes, and look into his mouth. While Alex impersonally ran his hands over the boy’s limbs in search of small cuts or abrasions, the boy described his home being destroyed in the hurricane. He’d apparently been swept inland on the storm surge and was only now trying to find his way back to his family’s farm, which was somewhere nearby.

Her heart ached for what the boy was likely to find

waiting for him, but Alex didn't seem the slightest bit moved. Sometimes she really hated his detachment. Even if it was good in both of his lines of work, she couldn't stand how completely he refused to express emotions of any kind. A little simple, human kindness wouldn't kill him, would it?

Instead, Alex had a quick conversation with the child, looked at the map and checked the GPS. "I place the boy's family near where we're headed," he announced. "He can come with us."

And if Oscar's home had been in the opposite direction? Would Alex have abandoned the child and let him proceed to the ruins of his family's home alone? To discover he'd lost everything and everyone he loved by himself?

Katie took Oscar's hand and held it tightly as they continued their hike. She feared for what they would find when they reached this boy's house.

An iron gate came into view, and Oscar ran to it eagerly. But only a bare concrete slab remained beyond where the child's home had stood. He burst into tears and Katie's heart broke for him. She sat down in the middle of the road and pulled the boy into her lap to hold and console while she cried with him.

ALEX STEPPED AWAY from Katie and the child. He felt bad for the kid, but as quickly as sympathy reared its ugly head, he slammed the useless emotion shut in a drawer in his mind.

Oscar's life had just been irrevocably shattered. And the sooner the boy came to terms with that, the sooner he could pick himself up and go on. Alex knew that from personal experience. He'd been only a few years older than the kid when his own world imploded. Katie coddling him wasn't going to do him a bit of good. As much as it sucked, Oscar was going to have to grow up fast.

While Katie calmed the boy, he mentally reviewed his college chemistry for chemicals and combinations of chemicals that could be lethal. He desperately hoped Katie was right and the cleaning supplies factory was the source of the deaths in the area. But his gut told him he wasn't looking at something that simple.

Eventually, Katie extracted information from the boy that Oscar's grandmother lived in Baracoa. He wasn't surprised when Katie offered to take Oscar to the city to find her, but he really didn't have time to play fairy godfather to some kid right now. They had a crisis on their hands, and they needed to get to the bottom of it as soon as possible.

Before he could voice his objection to a Baracoa road trip, however, the boy ran toward some sort of shed behind where the house had stood and Katie followed the child. The structure looked largely intact.

Alex started when his cell phone vibrated in his pocket and pulled it out cautiously. He swore and answered in Russian, keeping his voice low. "What do you want, Peter? I'm a little busy at the moment."

"Have you found anything?" his father asked without preamble.

"Like what?" he responded cautiously.

"You tell me."

"What do you think I'm going to find out here?"

"Dead people," Peter answered promptly.

"Good guess."

A pause drew out between them. Alex finally murmured, "You're draining my battery. I'm going to hang up now—"

"Wait," Peter said sharply.

"What?"

"Have you found any…unusual deaths?"

Alex's skin crawled. Literally. It felt like a million tiny insects were clawing across his flesh. "Why do you ask?" he asked sharply.

"If you should happen to run across anything…out of the ordinary…it would behoove all of us if you… removed…any evidence of such a thing. It would be a tragedy if something…contagious…were to be loosed upon unsuspecting people."

Just which unsuspecting people was Peter talking about? Was he threatening Americans with a chemical attack if the presence of such chemicals were revealed here? Or was he merely talking about the Cuban government silencing the locals by whatever means necessary? Not that a localized massacre was that great an alternative, either.

"You're going to have to speak plainly to me, Peter. You already seem to know what I've seen out here."

"I need you to bury the evidence. All of it. Do you have any idea the international crisis that would ensue if word of what was there got out?"

"Is there more of it still in the area?" Alex demanded.

"I don't know. If you could find out and let me know, I'd be eternally grateful. You're a doctor, son. Think about the lives you will save if you do this thing for me."

"And if I fail?" he asked carefully.

"You must not fail, my son. The collateral damage in your life would be…unthinkable."

Alex stared at nothing as shock reverberated through his entire being. They would kill Katie and Dawn. If he didn't betray the United States and commit treason by burying evidence of chemical weapons in Cuba, the only people in the world he loved would die.

CHAPTER SEVEN

KATIE WAS PERPLEXED over why Alex had abruptly broken off their investigation of the Zacara factory to take Oscar to Baracoa. She didn't for a minute think he'd agreed to the trip for altruistic reasons. He'd gotten a stubborn look on his face when she first promised the boy she'd take him to his grandmother. Then, that call had come in, and Alex had abruptly changed his tune.

The shed had yielded a waterlogged moped, but Alex and the boy worked some sort of magic on it and had gotten it running again. Alex had taken apart a wheelbarrow and rigged a makeshift hitch to turn it into a towable wagon.

She and Alex rode the moped while Oscar sat in the wagon behind it. The trip to Baracoa was slow going. They were fewer than thirty miles up the coast from the city, but it took them most of the afternoon to get there.

Baracoa had fared slightly better than the villages up the coast. A number of cinder-block and concrete buildings had more or less withstood the battering of Giselle. And it had public services like police, a fire department and a hospital. It appeared that much of the populace had been recruited to clear debris and shovel mud. The highest two-thirds of the city was more or less dug out from the storm and passable, while the coastal margins of the town were still under water.

A soldier with an AK-47 slung across his back waved them to a halt as they reached the edge of the town. Katie more or less hid behind Oscar while Alex explained in fluent Spanish that they were bringing the boy to his grandmother. On cue, Oscar burst into tears. Her limited Spanish led her to believe the child was telling the soldier a fractured account of his home being washed away and his family lost.

Once Alex assured the soldier that he and Katie would be leaving Baracoa as soon as they found the boy's grandmother, the soldier let them pass.

The irony was not lost on her that Alex was doing to Oscar exactly what his father had done to him—using a child as a cover for espionage. For surely, this trip to Baracoa was about their mission in some way.

A frisson of ethical discomfort tickled her spine. She ought to object to this whole thing. Except the boy really did need to get to his family and really was too young to get there by himself. And it wasn't like they were endangering the child.

The boy tearfully directed them to a thankfully high and dry part of town. Grandma's windows were still boarded up, but the front door was open and there were signs of life.

Oscar leaped out of her lap and ran for the front door, shouting. A middle-aged woman came out and scooped the boy into her arms tightly. As the boy sobbed, the woman's face crumpled and the pair shared their grief. It was hard to look at, and Katie turned into Alex's shoulder for comfort.

His body was rigid, his face set in stone. She didn't care how tough he tried to be. He was affected. He was just conditioned to act closed off and unfeeling. His arm came up around her shoulders for a brief squeeze. Hah, she was right!

He said tersely, "Time for us to be on our way."

Oscar's grandmother barely got a chance to murmur her thanks before Alex climbed on the moped and waited impatiently for her to clamber on behind him. With just the two of them, they were able to ditch the wagon. They pulled away from the house and she wondered sadly how many more personal tragedies just like that were playing out all around them.

Alex pointed the moped toward the middle of town with purpose, like he had a destination in mind. She leaned forward to ask over the noise of the motor, "Where are we going?"

"The hospital."

She frowned. What did he want with a hospital? They couldn't just stroll in and announce their presence in Cuba to the authorities. But apparently, that was exactly what he had in mind. They parked in front of a decent-size white building that appeared to have weathered Giselle reasonably well, and Katie followed him hesitantly as he marched into the emergency room.

"Let me do the talking," he muttered low.

Ya think? She made a face at his back as he headed for a man in a white lab coat with a stethoscope around his neck. The Cuban doctor got a surprised look on his face, but in a few seconds nodded in agreement with whatever Alex was murmuring to him.

Alex returned to her side, shedding the backpack of their emergency gear as he came. “Take this and find a spot out of the way to get comfortable. This will take a while.”

“*What* will take a while?”

“I’m trading my surgical skills for the supplies we need.”

Her eyebrows lifted in surprise. “We need supplies?”

“To get clean samples,” Alex bit out. And then he was gone, turning to join the doctor who called out something about being ready behind him.

Chairs were in short supply, so she found a corner and hunkered down in it. She leaned against the backpack both for comfort and so no one could take it while she dozed. They’d gotten precious little sleep since they’d arrived on the island, and the warm, muggy waiting room knocked her out.

It was dark when she woke and the waiting room crowd had thinned considerably. The backpack was still behind her and there was no sign of Alex. She wandered the halls in fruitless search of him and eventually stumbled across the cafeteria. She took the mug of soup someone handed her and nodded her thanks. It was some sort of thin broth with canned vegetables floating in it, but it was hot and quieted the growling in her stomach.

Bored, she returned to her corner to wait for Alex.

She slept on and off through most of the night before a hand on her shoulder jerked her awake. It was Alex bending over her in surgical scrubs, looking exhausted.

"Time to go," he said low.

"Don't you want some sleep?" she mumbled, groggy.

"Later."

He doffed the scrubs, hung a light, bulky bag on the back of the backpack and passed the whole thing to her. He'd become more of an order-giver in the past year. More willing to take charge. That, in and of itself, wasn't bad, she supposed. But it could be a little irritating being ordered around. Katie had to laugh at herself a little for falling for a guy just like all the other men in her family.

How did her mother tolerate six men who were all just like this? The woman must have the patience of Job not to haul off and coldcock one of them now and then. Katie sighed and climbed to her feet, stiff and sore from sleeping on a hard, cold floor.

Since she would be sitting in back of Alex, she got to wear the backpack. The night was cool. The ocean chuckled and murmured nearby and its briny odor hung thick in the air. The moon was high overhead, a lopsided disk throwing cold light down on them. Shockingly, the moped was right where Alex had left it.

They climbed on and he pointed their ride to the north. His body was warm and vital against hers, and she snuggled close against him. His presence was reassuring like nothing else on earth to her. She probably shouldn't feel so safe given where they were, but she did. Alex could handle anything that came their way.

They ran into two military checkpoints, but the sleepy soldiers let them pass when he identified himself as a doctor heading north with medical supplies to find and treat victims of the hurricane. At the second checkpoint, the soldier opened up the bag hanging from her pack and seemed satisfied with what he saw inside. He waved them through.

The sun was rising by the time they reached the iron gate leading to Oscar's ruined home. A thin layer of fog rose from the moist earth, making the morning misty and bright.

She was surprised when Alex turned into the driveway.

"I'm beat," he muttered by way of explanation. "The shed's intact and we can use it for cover while I go down for a few hours."

Spoken like a true field operative. "I got plenty of rest yesterday. I'll take the watch while you sleep," she offered.

He nodded briefly. It took them a few minutes to carry out enough farm tools, buckets and junk to make enough room to stretch a tarp on the dirt floor for Alex. Without further ado, he handed her a loaded pistol, laid down and passed out.

She sat on the edge of the tarp inside the door for several hours, watching the day age. A few birds sang outside, and she wondered idly where they'd ridden out the storm and managed not to get blown away. Already, the area was renewing itself, recovering from the storm. If only she could find a way to do the same for Alex. There had to be a way to renew his soul. To wash away the hurts his parents had caused the boy and to heal the man.

She watched him sleep, memorizing the features of his face again. His cheeks were leaner than last year, his hair shorter and lighter and his skin darker, as if he'd spent a lot of time in the sun. His mouth spent more time compressed in a line than before, but right now it was relaxed, his lips full and kissable. Like this, he looked nearly the same as before.

But then, his eyes were closed. That was where his changes really shouted at her. His gaze now was cold and assessing, where before it had been at best sardonic and, at worst, cynical. He looked at the world now with a detachment he hadn't had before. Like everyone around him was a bug potentially to be stamped out if they made a wrong move.

For the first time since he'd come home, she allowed herself to wonder guiltily if it was her fault he'd had to endure whatever had been done to him for the past year. She'd been the one to tip the scales in his life, to force him to choose sides and accept employment in the CIA. Before she and Dawn had come into his life, he'd successfully walked a tightrope between the CIA and the FSB. He'd carved out a life for himself where everyone more or less left him alone. But no more.

She and Dawn had made him vulnerable to pressure. He'd had to give in and choose sides. She was just grateful he'd gone with the United States. Frankly, she was a little worried about the CIA having given him all the lethal training they apparently had. Even she wasn't a hundred percent sure he was fully committed to Uncle Sam. It wouldn't shock her if someday he switched sides and went to work for his father in the FSB.

It was one thing to know Alex had changed this year. It was another entirely to know she was responsible for it. She found it a whole lot harder to blame him for being like he was now.

What had Peter wanted with him yesterday, anyway? She'd heard Alex speaking, low and angry, in Russian while she comforted Oscar. And why the abrupt reversal of course to Baracoa after the call? Curiosity made her impatient for Alex to wake up so she could quiz him on what was going on. Assuming, of course, that he would tell her the truth. That might be an optimistic assumption on her part.

Something moved outside and she lurched to alertness. Gripping the pistol tightly, she eased back deeper into the shadows of the shed. As if he had radar for it even when unconscious, Alex's arm came around her from behind, startling her. Dang, he was quiet. His hand closed over hers on the pistol.

She relinquished the weapon gratefully, and he moved silently in front of her. She backed into the shed and fumbled in the pack for the other pistol and spare clips of ammunition.

She jerked violently when Alex shot fast from the doorway, two sets of double-taps one after the other so quickly she could barely count the four shots. *Holy shit.* He'd just *shot* someone.

He moved outside as fast as a snake. She yanked the spare pistol free of the rucksack and followed him out, the weapon chest-high in front of her and her heart in her throat.

"All clear," he bit out.

She lowered her pistol and watched him feel for a pulse under the neck of…*crap*...a soldier. A second motionless body in a uniform crumpled not far from the first one.

"You killed soldiers?" she wailed in dismay. Emphasis on *killed.* As in other human beings snuffed out.

"They were looters. Not military."

"How could you tell?"

"No belts. Hair too long. The one with the shotgun held it wrong."

"You shot them because they had no belts?" she demanded incredulously.

"I shot them because they weren't who they appeared to be, and they were headed for our shelter. Given the current situation, it is logical to assume they were here to loot it. Which meant they were at least casual criminals. Which meant you would be in danger from them if I didn't take them out."

"So you killed them." He wasn't showing even a hint of remorse over shooting down two men.

"So I killed them."

"Does it feel good playing Rambo?" she muttered. What the hell had happened to him? The Alex she'd known before he left was a doctor. A healer. He fought to save lives, not to casually take them. Who *was* this man?

He didn't respond to her sarcasm and merely said grimly, "Pass me that shovel behind you."

"Hiding the evidence?" she asked dryly.

"Exactly."

"My God. You're not kidding, are you?"

He glanced up from where his shovel bit into the soft earth of what had likely been a garden. "Spy Craft 101. If you kill someone, hide the body. There's no need to make your trail any easier to follow than you have to."

"You just murdered those men!" she exclaimed. She could not believe he wasn't reacting at all to that small fact.

"And last night I saved the lives of several people. Your point?" he snapped as he shoveled.

"Don't you feel anything at all?"

That made him stop shoveling long enough to look up at her. "Feelings interfere with optimal performance. If I'm going to keep you safe and get you out of here alive, I have to be on my game." He shrugged and went back to shoveling. "It was a no-brainer."

And a no-hearter, too, apparently. Color her stunned.

"Look, Katie. Killing isn't something ever to do lightly. I get that. But this is not a normal situation. We've been sent into the aftermath of a devastating storm to look for something dangerous. All the normal, everyday people have left the area. It's a good bet that most of the people who've returned to this place so quickly are not looking to rebuild their lives and practice good citizenship. This is, in effect, a war zone. The rules of engagement are different here."

She reluctantly conceded that his logic might be sound. But still, it rankled with her. She grabbed a spade and started shoveling beside him.

It took a solid hour of both of them digging to make a trench big and deep enough to lay the two bodies in. Alex searched the dead men briefly. He showed her their wallets, neither of which contained any kind of military ID.

Okay, fine. So his belt theory had turned out to be accurate. Still, it was a hell of a flimsy excuse for killing a man.

He tossed the wallets back on top of the corpses and took a pocketknife, the shotgun one of them had been carrying and a pouch full of shotgun shells. He started to shovel earth over the corpses.

She murmured a brief prayer for the dead men's souls and then picked up her spade. Covering the bodies went fast. They tamped down the dirt and Alex spread dead grass and debris on top of the spot. By the time he was done, nobody would ever guess two men were buried there.

"Satisfied?" she asked grimly.

"We're good to go. Let's see if we can find the Zacara factory and figure out what the hell's going on around here."

ALEX WISHED THEY'D been able to take the moped as they walked through the iron gate and turned onto the main road headed north. But stealth was called for over speed in approaching the factory. And if his map was accurate, the Zacara plant was only about a mile away.

He shouldered the backpack, registering with shock a faint tremor in his hands. He was a surgeon, for Christ's sake. His hands were steady under the worst of stressful conditions.

It wasn't like he'd never killed before. The CIA had taken care of that in his advanced training. But waking up to see a terrified Katie wielding a pistol…to glimpse an armed man approaching her position…a criminal who wouldn't hesitate to kill her—that had scared the living hell out of him.

He swore mentally. It was an experience he could do without repeating again. Ever.

The actual killing didn't faze him anymore. He'd long ago accepted that he was a tool. If he didn't kill a target he'd been sent to eliminate, someone else would be sent to do the job. The decision of whether or not a person lived was not his. It was, literally, above his pay grade.

If he ever attained enough rank to be in a position to give kill orders, then he could wrestle with his conscience to his heart's content. But not now. The CIA went to great lengths to make its wet ops people understand this distinction. To teach them the mantra: No guilt. Make the kill and move on.

In this particular situation, his orders were clear. Stay alive. Find out what was being smuggled in or out. Once they knew, get out. And in his best judgment, staying alive had required shooting those two men.

Was he relieved to find no military IDs in their wallets? Hell, yes. But would he still have shot them even if they'd actually been soldiers? Absolutely. They posed a threat to the mission—and, furthermore, to Katie—therefore, they must be eliminated.

Katie had accused him of not reacting to shooting the looters. She was right that he'd felt nothing much about the actual act. What she was missing was the cold, hard terror that had provoked him to kill in the first place. For her. Without thought, without hesitation.

What was this willingness to do anything for another person? Was it love? The idea exploded inside his head, filling his entire brain with disbelief.

If so, it was a hell of a way to find out you loved a person. Somehow, he doubted Katie would be thrilled. *Oh, baby, I love you so much I'll kill for you.* Nope. Not her idea of Prince Charming and happily ever after.

It damned well rocked his world, though. Had his father felt this for him? An unflinching willingness to kill for his son? Had the boy Alex just been too young and too naive to realize that, in his own way, Peter had loved him fiercely?

Katie hiked beside him for a few minutes. She broke the silence with, "Tell me again why we zoomed off to Baracoa with Oscar?"

His defenses went on full alert. Must evade this line of questioning. He answered casually, "The boy needed someone to take care of him. I know you. Had we not delivered him to his grandmother, you'd have insisted on hauling him around with us."

"And?"

He winced. She knew there was more to it than that, dammit. "And we needed supplies for properly collecting and storing samples that might come under intense international scrutiny at some point."

"What kind of supplies?"

"Sterile bags and test tubes that can be sealed in such a way that the seals must be destroyed to open the samples."

"Because if there's sarin in the samples, the United States is going to go crazy," she declared.

"Exactly."

"Why else?"

He pretended to concentrate on scanning the deserted countryside in hopes that she would get distracted and move on.

"Why else did you go to Baracoa?" she pressed.

Nope. She was not going to be distracted today. "I needed time to think," he tried.

Expectant silence came from beside him.

He sighed. "As you no doubt noticed, my father called. I don't know how, but he got wind of what we were going to find when we came up here. He called to check up on me. To see if I found any…unusual… deaths."

"How did he know about those?" Katie exclaimed.

"I assume the Cubans told him. Or he's got a mole

in the Cuban government who slipped him the information."

"Okay, so the Cubans know there was a chemical spill out here. How do they know that?"

He shrugged. "Satellite imagery, maybe. Or a local observer has reported in to Havana. Or there's a military presence in this area."

"Wouldn't the military try to evacuate the locals if there was a chemical incident?"

He answered grimly, "Not if their orders were only to protect the chemicals or to hide the evidence of their existence."

Katie stumbled a little. "If that's so, then we're in serious danger. And maybe those were real soldiers back there."

And she'd made the leap of logic he'd been hoping to avoid her taking. Dammit.

"Is *that* why you shot them?" Katie demanded abruptly. "They were doing a cleanup job and would have taken us out?"

He ground out in a moment of bald honesty, "I killed them so they wouldn't kill you." Yes, there were myriad other reasons for a preemptive strike on those two men. But at the end of the day, he'd killed to protect her.

Katie was silent. At long last, she murmured slowly, "I guess I can live with that."

He let out the breath he hadn't realized he was holding. She might not fully understand, but at least she accepted what he'd done. Sometimes, he was grateful she'd grown up in a family full of warriors. There were some things the uninitiated just didn't get about men like him or her father and brothers.

He paused and turned to face her. "I would never kill anyone if I did not deem it absolutely necessary. Can you believe me?"

She stared up at him doubtfully for a moment and then exhaled hard. "Yes. Of course I believe you."

He swept her into his arms and kissed her deeply. Her arms looped around his neck and her lithe body stretched against his deliciously. If they weren't seriously pressed for time, he would lay her down right here and now and lose himself in her body.

"God, I'm addicted to you," he groaned against her sweet mouth.

"Good thing," she murmured back. "I'm totally addicted to you, too."

Something possessive and primitive surged up inside him. He needed to make this woman his and never let her forget it. He contemplated throwing caution to the wind, stripping her clothes off her and having his way with her.

"We'd better go." She sighed regretfully. "Work first. Play later. Isn't that what you always say?"

He swore under his breath, and she laughed lightly. "Just promise me that someday you'll truly cut loose with me."

"Ahh, Katie. You know not what you ask."

"Show me?" she replied hopefully.

He didn't answer. He couldn't. His entire being was galvanized by the notion of losing all control with her. Of turning loose the beast within completely. God, it was tempting. As if his current corner of hell wasn't tortuous enough. If he destroyed her innocence, there wouldn't be a pit of fire anywhere in hell deep or hot enough for him.

The scattered ruins of farms began to cluster more tightly together, and they approached an abandoned village. It was right on the coast and they had to circle wide around the clustered houses to avoid the standing water and mud that filled the main street and hulls of buildings.

"Where did all the people go?" Katie asked reflectively.

"They had plenty of advance warning that Giselle was coming. They went across the island to stay with friends or relatives or to shelters inland."

"I thought most of Cuba inland was impassable jungle."

"The mountainous terrain is the problem. The jungle itself isn't that bad," he commented.

"You've seen it, personally?" she asked sharply.

"Not on the approved conversation list, Katie." To soften the sting of that, he added, "Any online satellite map of the island will show you what I'm talking about."

He angled their steps back to the main coastal road. The silence of the place was eerie. There were no cars, no people, no birds, nothing to disturb the quiet swish and roar of the ocean. Even the trees that normally would have rustled in the breeze were mostly destroyed.

That was why the sound of an engine in the distance made him grab Katie's arm, drag her off the road and frantically pull dead palm fronds over them.

A military jeep rumbled past with four armed soldiers seated in it. It retreated from view, and in the ensuing silence, Katie grumbled, "Fine. They had belts."

The corner of his mouth curved up slightly.

"Now what?" she murmured.

"If my map is correct, the Zacara factory should be just around that bend in the road ahead." A rocky bluff jutted out into the surf, and the coastal road wrapped around its base to disappear from sight.

"Let me guess," she said dryly. "We get to go over the hill and not around it."

"You're learning, grasshopper."

By his standards, the hike was a walk in the park. No one was hunting him, the temperature was reasonable and he only had a quarter mile or so to go. After his arctic-, desert- and jungle-combat survival and evasion training, this was child's play.

He led the way at a moderate pace, seeking the easiest route for Katie and pausing often to let her catch her breath. She'd obviously been working out hard while he was gone, for she was significantly stronger than the last time they had to hike a long distance. When they got out of Cuba, he'd love to test the limits of that new strength and endurance in bed with her.

Finally, the factory came into view below. It was a sprawling collection of big, industrial buildings with block walls. Here and there, the roofing material was peeled back to reveal steel I-beams. That was pretty sturdy construction for a simple cleaning supply facility.

The big, circular tanks he'd expected, and which no doubt held the raw chemical ingredients of the products Zacara produced, stood in rows on a big platform on the landward side of the largest building. One was tipped over, lying on the ground below the others. From here, he couldn't see if any of the other tanks were damaged. All of them appeared rusted to one degree or another. The combination of metal tanks and salt air was a sure recipe for corrosion. It lent credence to an innocent explanation for the chemical poisoning deaths he'd observed. Lord, he hoped it was as simple as an unfortunate chemical spill caused by crappy storage tanks and a hurricane.

He hunkered down to watch the plant and was surprised by the lack of movement. If this was, indeed, ground zero for a secret chemical weapons facility, he would have expected soldiers to be milling around or at least patrolling periodically.

"Looks deserted," Katie commented as the shadows lengthened around them. The ocean began to calm beyond the factory.

"It's too deserted," he replied.

"Like a trap? Why would someone set a trap way out here? Who would they expect to catch? No international aid groups are allowed near here. From what I can tell, the Cuban authorities themselves have yet to reach this area after the hurricane."

"We should wait till dark. An ounce of caution is worth a pound of cure."

"Learn that at Harvard?" she retorted.

"My father used to say it. He wasn't wrong about everything, you know."

That silenced little Miss Mom and Apple Pie. She still struggled to wrap her brain around a world where Uncle Sam wasn't only a short step down from holy. He sighed. Uncle Sam was his employer now. He supposed he was obliged to show a little loyalty to the Stars and Stripes.

Katie muttered, "We've been here all afternoon. If someone were patrolling the area, we'd have seen them by now. My guess is the soldiers or workers who would normally be here have been sent out into the countryside to help the locals. I say we go down there, get whatever samples you want and get the heck out of Dodge. It's going to get pitch-black out here and we'll miss something important if we wait any longer."

He sighed. "Fine. Pass me the bag." She did so, and he pulled out what he'd spent nearly twenty-four hours straight performing surgery in Baracoa for. A small, handheld sensor that was preprogrammed to sniff for various chemicals in the air. Civil defense agencies all over the world had them. The physician in charge of the Baracoa emergency room had been reluctant to lend this one out but hadn't been able to pass up the services of a top-notch trauma surgeon in return for it.

They had moved him from patient to patient to perform the difficult portions of a dozen surgeries, while another surgeon opened and closed for him. He'd never done so much work so fast in his life. It was assembly-line medicine at its best. However, they'd completely cleared out every surgical case in the entire hospital. He'd even performed a simple coronary bypass and repaired a hernia before it was all said and done.

The electronic sensor he'd gotten in return was of Russian make. It took him a minute to decipher the various buttons and the readout, but once he understood it, he started down the hill with the device activated.

As they neared the factory, the sensor indicated trace amounts of ammonia in the air, but not in enough quantity to pose any kind of threat. The high hurricane fence around the plant had turned out not to be so hurricane-proof, and its tangled ruins were easy to step through.

Deep silence enveloped the facility. Up close, more damage was apparent and they were able to duck into the main building through a ten-foot-tall hole in a wall. Some sort of bottling-and-labeling assembly line was trashed inside. It looked like the hull of a giant centipede.

"Sheesh, this place is creepy. I half expect a zombie to pop out of the shadows," Katie muttered.

He was too busy watching for possible threats to register such things. Something skittered in a corner, and he nearly shot a rat. He was grateful to see the rodent. It was tantamount to a canary in a mineshaft. The rat's presence meant the air was probably safe to breathe throughout the factory.

What intrigued him most was how abandoned this place looked. Had the hurricane done all this damage?

Or had the factory been decaying for a while before Giselle hit?

"This is the place with the dock, right?" he asked over his shoulder.

"That's what our driver said. He said ships come in here regularly."

Alex made his way to the ocean side of the building, and he and Katie shoved opened a big sliding door facing this supposed dock. Unlike the decrepit facility behind them, this area looked relatively well cared for. The damage from the hurricane was severe, but there was very little rust or corrosion, and the mangled equipment looked reasonably modern and maintained.

A paved road and a torn-up rail line must have been the main points of debarkation for cargo. One of each curved into the cluster of buildings behind them. But a second, smaller road seemed to pass beyond the fenced Zacara buildings. Frowning, he started to walk down it.

"Should we go ninja and be more sneaky now?" Katie breathed.

"Anyone else in the area won't expect us to be here. They won't try to mask the noise of their presence."

"So we're just going to march down that road into the unknown?"

"Pretty much." Funny how he wasn't worried about what would come around the corner. He'd been trained to handle just about any eventuality on the fly.

The chemical sensor beeped a general warning, and he stopped to run a specific analysis. The electronic face identified the airborne chemical it sensed as "Unknown." The parts per million displayed on the gauge were still very low, though, so he continued walking forward.

"Should we have gas masks or something?" Katie asked nervously.

"If the levels of unidentified gasses climb too much, we'll go back. Wind's at our backs, though, so we should be okay to proceed." In fact, a stiff breeze was picking up, blowing in to shore. Given the time of day, there must be a front of some kind moving into the area. Rain was a pain in the ass, but it did make stealthy movement easy. Not to mention it tended to keep possible pursuers indoors.

He spied a dark lump on the side of the road ahead. Intuition and many hours in emergency rooms made him murmur to Katie, "Wait here."

He moved ahead and knelt beside the dead soldier. The body looked like it had been here a few days. It was bloated and flies crawled on the exposed skin. But the signs of how this man died were still visible. Dried blood stained the corner of his mouth and had run from his nose, and the soldier's hands clutched at his own throat as if he'd choked in some way.

Alex photographed the soldier dispassionately with his cell phone before pulling out a scalpel and removing tissue samples from the inside of the man's nasal cavity, his lungs and his stomach lining. He finished by scraping dirt stained dark with blood from under the corpse into a plastic bag.

He waved Katie forward. As she drew near, averting her face, he moved on down the road with her. And he paid very close attention to the face of the gauge in his hand. The road led inland a few hundred yards uphill into thick undergrowth. It stopped in front of a low mound of weeds.

"This is it?" Katie asked, looking around in confusion.

"Bunker," he muttered, walking around to the side of the mound. Sure enough, a heavy-duty steel door was recessed into the side of the hill.

"Is this where they store the explosive furniture polish?" she asked dryly.

He smiled slightly. His gauge beeped, urgently this time. "I think we may have found the source of our chemical leak."

"And we would be leaving now, right?" Katie said, backing up already.

"Wind's blowing steadily. As long as we stay upwind of this place, we should be okay."

"Speak for yourself."

"How are you at holding your breath?" he asked, studying the steel door, which, at a closer look, appeared heavily damaged.

"Not bad. I can go around two minutes."

"I can do three. I'll go in," he announced. He started stripping off his clothes in a pile beside her.

"As much as I love sex with you, now's not exactly the time—"

He cut her off. "I don't want my clothes getting contaminated."

She threw him an alarmed look.

"Count two minutes in your head and then yell out,"

he directed her. "If I'm not out in four minutes, hold your breath, and come drag me out."

"Are you sure we should be doing this? It seems really dangerous."

"That would be the point, now, wouldn't it?" he commented as he moved forward, eyeing the door.

It looked like some sort of mudslide had come through this steep area, for the door was badly dented like boulders had slammed into it. If the mudslide had happened early in the hurricane, the later rain could have washed the evidence of it away. A big, horizontal bar that looked like part of the locking mechanism was twisted and broken. It was this he focused his attention on. He took one last deep breath and moved forward to try lifting it. It moved a little but was too heavy for him.

He backed up to her side. "I need your help, Katie."

She took a deep breath and moved forward with him. By both of them planting their shoulders under the bar and lifting with their legs, they were able to prize the bar free of a broken bracket. It thudded onto the dirt at their feet. The door behind them gapped open a little. A black abyss yawned beyond.

They both backed up and breathed again.

Alex grabbed handfuls of plastic bags and test tubes, nodded at her to begin counting and moved forward gingerly.

Katie positioned herself outside so she could point their flashlight—a high-powered, directed beam affair—into the darkness. It was enough for him to see stacks of barrels mostly filling the space. Labels in Arabic script, which he couldn't read, were visible. Next trip in here, he'd bring his phone and take pictures of those.

Careful to avoid any puddles at the bases of the barrels, he took air samples near the barrels with his plastic bags and sealed them. Katie called a two-minute warning, and he filled a couple of test tubes from the puddles on the floor before he started to see spots before his eyes. He backed out carefully and when well clear and facing into the wind, took a bunch of deep breaths.

He passed Katie the test tubes and bags. "Cover these completely with duct tape, and label them with the time, date and GPS location."

She worked on that while he pulled out his cell phone and got ready to go in again. Three more times he went inside the bunker to pull samples. The last time, he actually pried barrels open and very carefully dipped samples of the liquid contents. Modern chemical poisons were generally most lethal in an aerosolized form and inhaled. Blistering agents that relied on skin contact were harder to disseminate and less effective on a large scale, hence had gone out of fashion.

The rational part of his brain informed him in no uncertain terms that taking these samples was madness. But it was also his job. Better that he risk his life and potentially save thousands of other people from harm or death, right?

But at the cost of Katie's and Dawn's lives? He should get the hell out of here, pretend they'd never found the bunker and get on with his life like his father had told him to. He didn't for a minute doubt that

Peter would follow through on his veiled threat to kill Katie and Dawn if proof of the existence of this bunker's contents got out.

But the United States really did need to know these chemicals were here. No way would America tolerate chemical weapons in the control of a hostile foreign government so close to its own soil. God knew, there were enough chemicals in this bunker to wipe out several major metropolitan areas in their entirety.

He was deeply undecided as to how to proceed. For now, he would collect the damned samples. There was still time to destroy the evidence. If there was a way to both give the United States the evidence and to protect his family, he had yet to figure it out. He'd threaded some tricky needles in his day, but this might be the one that was too much for him.

He passed the last test tubes to Katie to seal up and label with an admonition to be careful with these ones.

When she finished, he said, "If you could pick up my clothes, I'm heading back to the beach for a bath."

"You do realize how silly you look prancing around out here buck naked, yes?"

He made a face at her. "That's me. The stark-naked spy."

She laughed and followed him down the road. He picked his way down the rocks to the water, which was brutally cold. He hoped the salt water would help neutralize any chemical residue on his skin. Katie tossed him their bar of soap, and he scrubbed his skin until he felt raw all over. After washing his hair and rinsing it out with salt water, he climbed out of the water shivering. He was just making his way up the jumble of man-size boulders when a man-made sound rose over the surf. He swore under his breath as he leaped from rock to rock.

"Run," he ordered Katie low and urgent. "Into the brush. Hide." Crap. He'd been afraid there might be some sort of alarm system in or around the bunker. He'd hoped the storm had disabled it, but apparently not. If nothing else, someone might have been watching the bunker from a satellite.

Katie dived across the road and into the scrub with him hard on her heels. A pickup truck with two soldiers in the cab and three heavily armed men in the back rumbled past.

And they didn't look like just any soldiers. These men were big, physical and carrying their weapons—AK-47s—like extensions of their arms. If they weren't special forces, he was losing his mind.

As soon as the truck rounded the bend, he turned to Katie and breathed, "When they see the bunker's been broken into, all hell's going to break loose. We need to make our way back to the moped and head south."

"To Baracoa?" she whispered.

"No! To Guantánamo. We're going to need help to get off this island, now."

"But Gitmo's on the south side of the island."

"It's under a hundred miles from here. If we can make it onto the base, it's U.S. territory. We'll be safe. If we get separated, head there on your own." He pressed the second pistol into her hand and passed her the bag of taped samples. Still naked, he shouldered the pack. "Let's go."

"You're going to get all scratched up," she protested.

He started moving, murmuring over his shoulder, "That's the least of our problems right now."

Sure enough, about three minutes into their egress, shouting became audible behind them. In another five minutes, the sound of several more trucks floated to them on the cool evening air.

He'd set a course due south over whatever terrain that offered. He modified their travel to avoid open pastures and bare mountaintops, but that was it. The moped lay to the south, and they needed a motorized escape if they were going to make it seventy or eighty miles overland across the interior of Cuba.

If he was getting scratched up by the branches and brambles, he didn't allow himself to notice it. He was too busy pushing Katie to her limits without actually killing her. It was a fine line to walk.

After maybe an hour of hard going, he paused under a giant fern and dug a bottle of water out of his pack. She drank while he, at long last, dressed. He noted vaguely that he was covered in bug bites and thin lines of blood from various scratches and small contusions. If he got out of this night without a serious infection he was going to be impressed.

He tossed down a bottle of water and a couple stim pills left over from his training. He passed Katie one of the pills as well, and she swallowed it dry.

"Ready to go?" he asked.

She nodded gamely and they rose slowly to their feet in time to hear a thwocking sound in the distance.

"Helicopter," she bit out.

He swore under his breath. If that bird had heat-seeking technology on board, they were screwed. "Find water," he ordered. "A stream or puddle. Anything."

He moved out from under the big fern and she went the other direction.

"Over here," she called out low.

A small rivulet, maybe two feet wide and no more than a foot deep, trickled past her. He raced down the hill, following the trickle as the helicopter got louder, fast. She crashed along behind him, panting.

"What are we doing, Alex?"

"Hurry." There. Below them. The trickle widened into a shallow, oblong pool. It was maybe six feet wide and twice that long, where the trickle backed up behind a cluster of small boulders that formed a natural dam.

"Into the water," he bit out.

She reached for her shirt buttons and he grabbed her hands to stop her. "Now. Just get in."

Eyes wide, she followed him as he waded into the pool and sat down in it. "Omigod, it's freezing," she squeaked under her breath.

"When I tell you, take a deep breath and lay down. All the way under the water. The pool will camouflage our heat signatures. And keep your eyes closed. There could be nasty microbes in here." She had precious little time to process that explanation, for the helicopter topped the ridge behind them just then. "Now."

He laid down under the water, his own eyes screwed tightly shut. Something touched his elbow and he jumped before realizing it was Katie's fingers. Her hand slid down his arm until she could grasp his hand.

Even fully submerged, the noise of the chopper was loud. He didn't know if such shallow water would eliminate their heat signatures or not. But it was all they had. The chopper moved past with aching slowness, which made him think the Cubans were using heat-seeking gear, after all.

Katie's hand squeezed his more tightly, and he realized they'd been under for nearly three minutes. Well beyond her stated ability to hold her breath. He sat up cautiously, letting just his mouth and nose break the surface. Katie did the same beside him. The sound of the chopper was fading now.

He sat all the way up, and Katie followed suit with alacrity.

"Well, that was fun," she muttered.

"The fun has just begun. Now we get to flee through the jungle at night in wet clothes."

They waded out of the pool and Katie frowned. "Should we check each other for leeches or something?"

"We should. But we need to get moving. The leeches can dine on our blood in the meantime."

She made a face and shuddered as he shouldered the big pack, retracing his steps up the hill to put them back on course. And that was when he heard a different kind of engine. Crap. ATVs.

Alone, he'd have had no trouble avoiding the Cubans. But with Katie in tow, the two of them didn't stand a chance when the Cuban special forces, riding all-terrain vehicles, came after them.

CHAPTER EIGHT

KATIE CROUCHED IN TERROR. Now she knew exactly what a mouse felt like when the fox came after it, or a rabbit when a hawk circled overhead.

Shadows and tangled brush pressed in on her, threatening to entangle and trap her. But she still felt naked and terribly exposed. Her instincts screamed at her to run, but her head yelled even louder not to move a muscle. The result was frozen panic and a deep desire to vomit.

"We have to split up," Alex breathed to her.

She looked around at the wild trees and looming darkness in terror.

"No!" she cried back in a bare whisper. She clutched at his arm frantically. He couldn't abandon her out here! She didn't know the first thing about jungles. She *needed* him. And she bloody well couldn't do this running around evading bad guys stuff by herself!

"It's our only chance," he explained. "I'll draw them off while you make a run for the moped. Take it and get to Guantánamo. I'll make my own way there. It may take a few days, but wait there. I'll join you."

"No—"

He grabbed her shoulders and kissed her hard, cutting off her protest. "I believe in you. I know you can do this."

"I barely speak Spanish, and I don't look remotely Cuban."

"There are blond, fair people in Cuba."

"I can't do it!"

"You must."

"It's suicide for you to engage those soldiers. They've got numbers, equipment, technology. They have every advantage. I've heard my brothers talk. You'd never survive."

"Trust me. I'm very good at what I do. But I can't do it with you here. I need you to go."

Not a chance. "But—"

He gave her a hard push that sent her stumbling, sliding and ultimately half falling down a steep slope. Muddy and covered in leaves, it was so slippery she stood no chance of stopping her descent. Some hundred feet down the slope, she turned and frantically tried to run back up it to Alex.

To no avail. She might as well be trying to climb an ice mountain. She was not getting back up that hill any time soon. Appalled, she listened as someone shouted above her. For all she knew, that was Alex *trying* to get spotted by the Cubans. Damn him!

He'd *pushed* her. The man she loved had actually shoved her down that hill. Why? Confusion rolled through her. Was he that eager to get rid of her, or was it some misguided attempt at altruism from a mind too convoluted for her to follow? She didn't know whether to be grateful or furious. Opting for the latter, she took off running through the trees. If he was going to be a giant idiot and get himself killed being a hero, far be it from her to waste the escape window he'd given her. He was insane. And stupid. And heroic. And did she already add being a giant idiot to that list?

At some point in her frantic flight, it dawned on her that tears were streaming down her face. Was she ever going to see him again? Or had he just consigned himself to a terrible death to save her?

Whether her horror or her panic spurred her harder, she couldn't say. But she ran until her legs felt like burning rubber and her lungs felt consumed by fire. And then she ran some more. It was awful beyond description.

Only the sound of the ocean on her left and the moon sliding gradually to her right kept her from running around in circles out here. The terrain was difficult during the day, but at night it was brutal. She twisted her ankles and wrenched her knees more times than she could count. She fell on her butt, and fell on her face, and ran into trees, skinned her knees and got poked in the eye. But she didn't stop. Somehow, she forced her feet to keep moving no matter what.

She tried to distract herself by thinking about Dawn and what they'd do together when she got home. But that just made her cry too hard to see where she was going.

She tried cursing out her personal trainer, which carried her for a good ten minutes. But then she had no more anger left to summon. Exhaustion set in. Her only motivation now was what she would do to Alex the next time she saw him. That, and a fierce determination to survive long enough to do it to him.

The spine of ridges she'd been crawling up and down forever finally gave way to a rolling plateau. But with the level ground came open fields. Farms. She wasn't worried about locals spotting her. There were practically none here. The soldiers looking for her and Alex—they were a different matter.

The moon wasn't quite set, either. She ended up crouching by the edge of a huge pasture for nearly a half hour while she waited for the moonlight to finally disappear. At first she was grateful for the rest. Then the vigil became a terrible fight to stay awake. She was only barely cold, damp, sore and terrified enough to keep her eyes open.

At least she was too exhausted to dwell much on the terrible truth that Alex had abandoned her. Damn him. She was not strong or smart or sneaky enough to make her way across Cuba by herself.

Wearily she pushed to a crouch and started across the open field. No one swooped down on her to arrest her, and the sky was finally quiet, the helicopters that had crisscrossed the jungle overhead for much of the night gone.

On the one hand, she was relieved as she reached a tree line and followed it around another pasture. On the other hand, she fretted that the absence of the helicopters might mean they'd found Alex. Captured him. Hauled him away for torture and interrogation until they broke him and then killed him.

She was desperate to call André or Uncle Charlie

and beg for help. For someone to come save her and Alex from this waking nightmare. But Alex had the satellite phone in his backpack. All she had was the bag of samples…which she could only pray hadn't broken in her mad flight and weren't slowly killing her already.

Where was Alex? Was he okay? How was he going to get all the way across Cuba on foot by himself? Yes, her brain knew he was a trained spy who could handle those sorts of things. But it had looked like half the Cuban army was after him back there. And she was allowed to worry about him, dammit.

The familiar iron gates leading to nothing came into view ahead as the first gray light of dawn tinged the eastern horizon. A sob escaped her throat. As tempted as she was to run for the shed, caution prompted her to kneel in the last tree line prior to the homestead. To wait and watch for signs of movement. For a trap. Alex's paranoia had obviously rubbed off on her.

As the sky turned pink and wan light washed over the farm, she finally grew too sleepy to wait anymore. She had to move or pass out.

She went to the shed cautiously, recalling that Alex had left a few surprises in place to discourage would-be looters. A glance at the garden plot behind the house, the final resting place of the last looters to pass this way, made her faintly ill.

She approached the shed door. Thank God. The trip wire was still in place. She stepped gingerly over it and opened the door an inch or so. Just enough to wiggle her fingers inside and detach the second trip wire from the latch on the inside. She eased the door the rest of the way open. The bulky tarp was still in place over the moped.

Before she wheeled the motor bike outside, she searched the shed for anything that might be of help to her. She stuffed a hand spade, an empty plastic water bottle and an old flashlight into her bag with the samples. The batteries were dead, but maybe she could find some along the way.

And then she hit the mother lode. A rusty gas can. Perhaps a gallon of gasoline was sloshing around in the bottom of it. She poured it into the moped's gas tank and prayed it would be enough to get her all the way to Gitmo.

Speaking of which, time was a'wasting. If she timed this right, she should hit Baracoa at midmorning when people were most likely to be out and around and less likely to notice her. No way could she make this trip cross-country. She was going to have to take the coastal highway around the eastern tip of the island to the south shore and the U.S. facility at Guantánamo.

People had been at work clearing and repairing the roads since they'd passed this way before with Oscar. As she neared Baracoa, she was actually able to motor along at a decent speed. She did, indeed, pass through the now-familiar city without incident. She debated trying to buy gas while she was there and decided it would call too much attention to herself. That, and she spotted a truckload of soldiers headed toward her as an operating gas station came into sight. That decided her. She kept moving.

Not far past Baracoa, the highway cut inland, due south. The condition of the road was terrible and she was forced to pick her way painstakingly around huge ruts and washouts as she headed up into the hills. Coconut plantations gave way to mango orchards and then to jungle. If Alex thought this wasn't rough jungle, she'd hate to see a bad one.

Eventually, the road came down out of the Sierra Maestra mountain range to hug the coast. Debris and the occasional sandbar slowed her progress, but the sky was blue, the ocean breezes cool and the day generally beautiful.

A hodgepodge of vehicles drove along the road—mostly military and police trucks. But a few farmers were returning to their homes in flatbed trucks piled high with kids and belongings. If the roads held up and she didn't run out of gas, she would reach Guantánamo in the late afternoon.

Of course, the roads didn't hold up, and she did run out of gas. She debated whether to push the moped along or just walk, and ended up opting for walking. Once she got to Gitmo, she wasn't planning on ever coming back to this place.

The highway, which had run due west along the south shore of the island, started to cut inland across the last peninsula prior to Guantánamo Bay. The sun was setting as she stopped in front of what looked like it had once been a major intersection. A blown-over road sign lay in the ditch with the words Naval Station Guantánamo Bay on it.

Great. Which direction would the sign have indicated she should go if it wasn't torn off its posts and lying by the side of the road? Was this even the right intersection? Or had the sign flown for miles before landing here?

This was *exactly* why she needed Alex. Or at least the GPS on his phone. Frustrated and scared, she noticed a cluster of lights in the distance. Was that the naval base? Or was that a Cuban city at the north end of the bay?

Cursing Alex, she took a deep breath and turned to the left. If she wasn't completely lost, she was heading south, toward the mouth of Guantánamo Bay. She hoped.

She'd walked no more than ten minutes when a camouflage green jeep streaked toward her, coming fast. She jumped into the ditch, but was too slow. The vehicle stopped on the road above her and a man shouted angrily at her in Spanish. Something about coming out and something else about her hands. She expected the soldier wanted her hands in the air. Oh, God. She was so dead.

CHAPTER NINE

ALEX CROUCHED IN the steamy heat of the jungle, listening to the Cuban soldiers barreling past. It was shocking how much this resembled his training last summer. The aggressors wore different uniforms, and these ones would torture and kill him for real if they caught him, but otherwise, it all was pretty much the same.

The mud he'd covered his skin with was drying and stretching his face uncomfortably tight. Katie would tell him how wonderful his pores were going to look after he washed off the mask.

His gut clenched. He'd hated with a passion sending her away from him. But it was the only reasonable course of action. He prayed, just in case there was a God, for Katie to make it to Gitmo safely.

In the meantime, he needed wheels. He didn't relish spending the next week or more making like a monkey tramping through the jungle. On top of his other problems, he was starting to feel a little feverish. If he was lucky, he'd merely picked up some sort of infection from one of his numerous lacerations. If he was unlucky, he needed serious medical care fast if he wasn't to die of sarin poisoning.

He retraced his steps carefully toward the Zacara

factory. He was counting on it being the one spot his pursuers would not expect him to go. It was the likeliest rallying point for whoever was chasing him around out here, as well. Which meant there should be vehicles. Uniforms. A cover.

He topped the ridge above the factory. Sure enough, a half dozen trucks were parked in front of one of the smaller buildings. The helicopter that had made his life a living hell last night was parked in the big open area in front of the dock. And from here, he could see three soldiers in various stages of patrolling or lounging on the grounds.

He zeroed in on the nearest soldier, a guy who was smoking a cigarette close to a hole in the fence. Smokers tended to cluster together and return to the same spots to smoke. If he was lucky, that would be the case today.

Long before he made his way to the fence line, the original smoker had wandered on. But Alex positioned himself so the corner of a building blocked the spot from the sight of most of the rest of the facility, and he hunkered down to wait.

It took about two hours, but the same soldier strolled around the corner, already shaking a cigarette out of a pack. Alex let him light up and take a long, appreciative puff. He timed his attack for when the soldier was exhaling long and slow and pounced. No air in the guy's lungs meant no warning shout was possible.

Alex jumped the guy from the back and, using the butt of his knife, clocked him in the back of the head. It was quick and quiet; however, the blow cut the guy's scalp and he began to bleed. As the soldier sagged to the ground, Alex caught him, swearing under his breath.

The guy was heavy as hell. Alex eased him to the ground and hastily stripped off the guy's shirt before it got too bloody. He went to work fast unlacing the soldier's boots from his feet. Unlike in television shows, most people had a tendency not to stay unconscious for long. By the time he was ready to strip off the guy's pants, the soldier was starting to rouse. He chopped the guy hard in the base of his skull to buy himself a few more minutes to make his escape.

Working fast, he tore a piece of cloth off his own ruined shirt and stuffed it in the guy's mouth. Out of deference to Katie, he checked the guy's nostrils to be sure they were clear and that the guy would be able to breathe while gagged.

He tore more strips off his shirt and used them to bind the soldier's wrists and ankles together. Housekeeping matters taken care of, he put on the soldier's uniform. It was a reasonably good fit. Beret jauntily cocked over his right eye, Alex dragged the guy through the fence and behind a pile of stones. He bunched driftwood over the unconscious soldier hastily, and then jumped back through the fence.

He picked up the guy's cigarette, which was just burning out. And in the nick of time, too. Another soldier poked his head around the corner and barked at Alex to get back to his post. Face downcast, he ground out the stub beneath his heel and muttered an acknowledgment.

He took a deep breath and rounded the corner. He had no idea what the soldier's post was. Rather than try to fake it, he struck out confidently across the yard, as if he'd been sent on an errand for someone.

He veered first toward the helicopter. It was an easy matter to open the cockpit door, reach under the instrument panel and yank out a big fistful of wires. He grabbed another handful and tore them out, for good measure.

After that, he made his way to the parked vehicles. His nerves were jumping all over the place, and he had to consciously force them into silence. Funny thing, fear. Once he'd learned to control it and hold it at bay, it had become more of curiosity to him than an actual force in his life.

He spotted the guy who'd yelled at him heading down toward the dock. Alex hurried his steps to reach the nearest truck before the guy could get where he was going and turn around.

Alex tested the door handle. Unlocked. He slid into the vehicle and hunted in the usual places for keys. No luck. He lay down on the seat and opened the glove compartment, and voilà. A key on a ring.

He snatched it out and tried it in the ignition. For once, the gods of luck seemed to be on his side. The key fit. Hot-wiring vehicles was Spy Craft 101, but it took a few minutes he could ill afford at the moment. Pulling on a pair of sunglasses he found on the dashboard, he started the truck, threw it into gear and pulled out of the yard.

No one yelled at him. Which meant it would take a few minutes for someone to casually ask someone else who'd just left and why. Then there'd be a few more minutes of confusion while everyone was accounted for and then questioned. He figured he would get about ten minutes' head start, worst case.

The moment he rounded the headland, he floored the truck. The ride was horrendous, but time was against him and banging his head on the ceiling was a small price to pay for his life.

The only passable road in the area was the main one back toward Baracoa, so that was the one he followed. Just north of Baracoa, a secondary road cut inland, eventually curving south to rejoin the main highway in the mountains. It was for this he headed.

The sky stayed thankfully empty of helicopters. He must have done a number on the bird back there. As he reached the south end of the flat plateau of plantations and farming co-ops, he spied a long puff of dust in the distance behind him. The good news was the vehicles were so far back he couldn't even count how many there were. The bad news was that even the cloud of dust looked pissed.

The road rose out of the long valley into the hills and he banged along, trying not to get thrown out of his seat while looking for the turnoff he wanted.

There. The intersection loomed just ahead. He careened around the corner and screeched to a stop. Leaping out of the cab, he used a big palm leaf to rub out his tire tracks hastily. It cost him precious time, but he hoped it would throw the convoy behind him off his track at least temporarily.

The quality of this road was significantly worse. More than once he tested the limits of the truck's heavy-duty suspension. He almost got stuck crossing a swollen stream, but the spinning tires caught at the last minute and hauled him up onto the slippery far bank.

He stopped again to erase his tracks from the mud and then proceeded onward. His entire world narrowed down to walls of green growth crowding him, and watching his rearview mirror. Whenever a patch of sky opened up overhead, he scanned it anxiously for helicopters. His hands ached from gripping the steering wheel, and the tops of his thighs were sore from banging into the steering wheel's bottom rim.

The afternoon passed in a green haze, and as night was falling, he finally emerged into a decent-size intersection. He'd reached the main highway again. Gratefully, he turned south. The quality of the road didn't improve much, and the tree cover was substantially less. His nerves stretched tighter and tighter.

If he was insanely lucky, the Cubans had pegged him for a simple thief and hadn't thrown their whole damned military at him. But he wasn't counting on that much luck. At some point, they would put up another helicopter and his run of luck would cut off. If only Katie was all right, he wouldn't mind having the entire Cuban Army on his tail. He'd purely hated splitting up with Katie, but it really was the only way.

Not that she was likely to forgive him for pushing her down that hill any time soon.

Not long after dark, he spotted blinking lights in the distant sky. He pulled the truck over quickly underneath a tree and hopped out to throw what downed tree limbs he could lift over it to obscure its profile. He crawled under the truck and prayed its warm engine would hide his human silhouette on any infrared radar the chopper might have.

He didn't have long to wait to find out. The helicopter, a small two-seater, landed in a field maybe a hundred feet from his position. Swearing, he rolled out from under the truck and crept away fast as a soldier disembarked from the passenger's side of the helicopter.

The terrain sucked for cover. It was open country with only small rocky outcroppings, and the grassy valley sadly lacked for bushes or tree cover. He could low-crawl on his belly through the knee-high grass without being seen, but that was about it. Staying low, he eased around behind the soldier carefully.

A bold idea struck him. It was crazy. Stupid, even. But it just might work. He waited until the soldier's full attention was lasered in on the truck. The guy had a weapon drawn and was approaching the vehicle cautiously. Alex darted behind the soldier's back, sprinting for the helicopter.

Even if the guy turned around and spotted him now, the soldier couldn't safely fire toward the 'copter and its flammable fuel tanks. Not to mention, it was the guy's ride out of here.

Alex closed the last few yards to the passenger door. Sure enough, the soldier behind him shouted. The pilot, not understanding, looked out his own door toward his colleague, who was waving his arms frantically. It was the opening Alex needed.

He threw open the passenger door and slid into the seat, pointing his pistol at the pilot. The guy lurched and shouted incoherently at him. Alex held up an imperative hand to silence the pilot.

Tersely, he explained in Spanish, "I know how to fly this. I can kill you and toss you out, or you can take me where I want to go and no one will get hurt. You have my word on it."

The pilot babbled a little bit but put his hands on the controls. Alex watched the guy like a hawk as he strapped himself into the passenger seat. The bird lifted off jerkily.

"Easy, buddy. No need to kill us both because you're panicked."

The pilot keyed the radio transmit button on the collective, but Alex swatted the guy's hand away, tsking. He reached across the guy's body and yanked the plug for the guy's headset and microphone, and then efficiently turned off all the radios, the radar identification system and the exterior lights.

The pilot's eyes widened.

"I wasn't kidding," Alex shouted over the engine noise. "I don't need you alive to fly this thing. So be cool. Okay?"

The pilot nodded, the fight gone out of him.

Dammit, Katie was a lousy influence on him. He should've killed this guy the minute he opened that door. But here he was, giving the pilot a shot at being smart and saving his own life. Still, he watched the Cuban like a hawk and his finger never left the trigger of his pistol.

"Fly south," he ordered. "Gitmo."

The pilot looked alarmed but banked the bird to the left and pushed the throttle forward. Without any navigation aids turned on, he and the pilot were going to have to find Gitmo the old-fashioned way. By looking down at the ground.

The trip was tense, but shockingly fast. In fewer than twenty minutes, the mountains fell away beneath them and the ocean came into view. It was pitch-dark below. Power was still out to most of this end of the island. But off to their right, a very faint glow lit the horizon. Alex punched up the GPS function on his cell phone to verify that Gitmo was a half dozen miles or so to the west.

"Fly that way." Alex pointed.

The pilot whined a little about getting shot down, but Alex ignored him. The Americans would let them land. A major hurricane had just turned the entire island on its head. Nothing was ops normal right now.

Following the coast, the sprawling naval facility came into sight soon. Pockets of light here and there on the base indicated where emergency generators were up and running.

"Land in the first open space you see inside the fence," Alex instructed.

Throwing him a skeptical look, the pilot did as ordered and landed in a parking lot. "Now what?"

Alex snorted. That was Katie's favorite question. "Shut down. Get out. Lie on the ground, facedown."

"You said you wouldn't kill me!"

"I'm not going to. I'll be lying down beside you, buddy."

Indeed, Alex held his gun on the Cuban until the fellow was facedown, his fingers linked behind his head. Then Alex stripped off the Cuban military shirt and beret he'd stolen and knelt beside the pilot, keeping his pistol trained on the guy until the cavalry arrived.

Which took about three minutes. Three jeep loads of heavily armed soldiers with no senses of humor whatsoever pulled up. Alex let the glare of their headlights catch him, and then he slowly popped the clip out of the pistol. He tossed the weapon one direction and the clip the other. Then, in cautious slow motion, he linked his hands behind his head and laid down on his stomach beside the pilot.

"Are you crazy, man?" the pilot demanded.

"I have been called that before," Alex commented before the soldiers started shouting at him to be quiet.

"They're going to kill us both," the pilot cried out.

"Not if you lie still and do what they say—"

The pilot panicked. He jumped to his feet and made a run for it. Whether he'd planned to head for his helicopter or the fence, Alex couldn't tell. But the guy was gunned down so hard his torso was almost cut in half by the barrage of lead. Blood sprayed all over him, hot and metallic tasting.

"You gonna try to run, too, asshole?" someone snarled at him.

CHAPTER TEN

"KATIE MCCLOUD?" a voice said out of the darkness behind the headlights. "Come with us."

Thank God. That man's English was as American as apple pie.

How on earth did he know her name, though? She had no identification on her to indicate that was her name, and she hadn't used it once while she'd been in Cuba. Regardless, they had the big-ass guns pointed at her. They won.

She stood up hesitantly.

The voice turned out to belong to a tall African-American man wearing a lot of stripes on his arm. A senior noncommissioned officer, then. He said gruffly, "Technically, we're not supposed to be out here, so if you'd get in the vehicle quickly, ma'am, we need to get back to base."

As if on cue, a radio crackled from inside the Humvee. "Return to base, Diesel. We've got Cuban forces inbound to the area. A crap-ton of 'em."

The other soldier, a whipcord-lean kid with a classic Marine-buzz haircut, took her by the arm and hustled her to the military vehicle. She hadn't even finished fastening her seat belt before the Humvee was Y-turning in the road and accelerating back in the direction it had come from.

"Shit, Diesel. Look at that radar!" the kid exclaimed.

The driver glanced at a circular green screen mounted in the dashboard. She couldn't see the display from the backseat, but the man said over his shoulder, "Who the hell are you, lady? It looks like half the Cuban army is headed this way. They comin' for you?"

She sincerely hoped not. "I'm just an aid worker. I came down here to help out after the hurricane." Best to stick to her cover story until she knew who these guys were.

In hopes of distracting her captors from who she was exactly, she leaned forward and asked, "Why aren't you technically supposed to be out here?"

"That's the deal with the Cubans," Diesel bit out. "We stay on our side of the fence. They stay on theirs."

"Did you come out looking for me, then?" she asked, curious.

Diesel started to say something, but the sound of a helicopter approaching interrupted him. It got loud fast. And then it got *really* loud.

"Fuckers are buzzing us," the younger soldier shouted over the noise. "Want me to pop a cap in their asses?"

"Keep your gun in its holster, Johnny," Diesel bit out.

It seriously sounded like the chopper was coming in for a landing on the roof of their Humvee.

"Almost there," Diesel shouted. "Radio the gate. Tell 'em we're coming in."

"Roger that."

A tall, heavily fortified fence loomed ahead, glinting silver in the starlight. The Humvee roared toward it, and at the last minute before they blasted onto U.S. soil, the helicopter peeled away from them. She could see individual rivets in its belly before it banked away and flew into the darkness.

She was no expert on helicopters, but that was a military bird. Had the Cubans somehow found out she had nearly reached Gitmo? How? Why did they care about her? Oh, God. Had they captured Alex? Had he *talked?* She shuddered to think what they must have done to him to get him to crack. Or was the 'copter just a reaction to an American military vehicle going off the U.S. reservation?

"The Cubans buzz you guys often like that?" she asked as her pulse slowed a little.

"I ain't never seen anything like it," Johnny declared. "That was awesome. But you shoulda let me shoot 'im, Sergeant Truck."

Truck? Ahh. Now the nickname Diesel made sense.

They drove onto what looked like a pretty traditional American military base. It was already cleaned up from the storm, although neatly stacked piles of firewood here and there by the side of the road looked out of place. Most of the buildings showed damage, but they were neatly boarded up or tarped.

"Where are we going?" she asked.

Diesel answered grimly, "Boss man's gonna wanna

talk with you, ma'am. You and I both know there aren't any aid workers on this island from the U.S."

ANDRÉ FORTINAY GROANED under his breath as his cell phone rang. He rolled over in bed and picked up his phone in the dark as his wife mumbled a sleepy protest. No phone call that came in at this time of night was good news. He recognized the incoming phone number with a jolt and sat up in bed. The director of the entire Cold Intent op.

"Fortinay, here. What's up?" His voice was hoarse with sleep, but there was no help for it.

No greeting. Just a clipped voice in his ear saying, "Flash traffic has come across my desk in the past few minutes that Alex Peters and Katie McCloud have been picked up at Guantánamo. They're requesting immediate transport to the United States."

"Anything else in the message?" André asked cautiously.

"A request for instructions from the Guantánamo station intel chief."

André winced. If his operatives were at Gitmo, things hadn't gone as planned in Cuba. At all.

"They were supposed to get caught by the Cubans!" his supervisor burst out. "The girl was supposed to screw up the mission. What the hell happened instead?"

André sighed. He'd never liked that part of the plan. He happened to be fond of Alex. The young doctor had a great deal of potential if he were properly developed as an asset. André got why the CIA didn't trust Alex farther than they could throw him, but personally, he thought it was a mistake. For that matter, Katie was a decent girl. Patriotic. Kind. Good for Alex.

Aloud, he replied, "I thought from the start that you people were underestimating the McCloud girl. She wasn't supposed to make it out of Zaghastan alive, and not only did she walk out of there, but she brought a newborn baby out with her."

"Alex was *supposed* to embarrass his father in Zaghastan. But that didn't happen, either. Then you people said you could break him in field ops training. But no matter what you threw at him, he didn't crack. Now this. How could Alex and the girl get out of Cuba like this? We told the Cubans exactly where they would be landing and when, for Christ's sake."

André winced. "The aftermath of the hurricane has made working conditions terrible down there. And the east end of the island is deeply isolated—"

"Be that as it may. The op is shot to hell and time is growing short. Peter Koronov's star is on the rise. Rumor has it he's on the short list to become the next director of the FSB. He's got the ear of the prime minister and the president of Russia. His enemies don't dare touch him."

And yet, Operation Cold Intent dared attempt to discredit him and destroy his career. The Americans were using the man's own son against him to bring him down, no less. If he were Koronov and ever got wind of that, he would be out for blood.

Of course, it was not his job to question the methods or ethics of this op. It was merely his job to run the operatives and keep his mouth shut. But the whole thing left a bad taste in André's mouth.

Hell, maybe when this thing was over, he'd retire from the agency and stick around Doctors Unlimited. Get it some real funding and keep the outfit going as a legitimate aid organization and not just a CIA front.

"And what's this about a possible chemical weapons spill in Cuba?" the director demanded.

"I've forwarded everything I know about it. Katie called me briefly to say that she and Alex had seen some suspicious deaths that Alex thought might be the result of exposure to something like sarin."

"Is there proof?"

"I told them to get some and bring it out with all possible speed. The fact that they're at Gitmo now makes me think they got their proof."

Of course, dealing with that would be way above the pay grade of Operation Cold Intent. He could practically hear the director's mental wheels turning over how this complication would affect the op at hand.

"If Alex brings out this proof, he'll be a hero in the West. Koronov could spin it to his advantage. 'See how brilliant and successful my son is. He learned it all from me.'"

The director's voice had taken on a bitter tone. André had long suspected that a personal vendetta lurked somewhere behind this op. After all, how often did the CIA go after one man this hard with the intent to utterly destroy him?

"Alex Peters must not get credit for this discovery. Whatever proof he's found of chemical weapons must be separated from any association with him. My team will work on creating another credible origin story for the information. In the meantime, Alex and the McCloud girl must be distanced from the intel."

André's gut rumbled a warning at him. How was that going to happen? By killing them? The question popped into his head as a rhetorical one, but as soon as it did, he knew it to be a distinct possibility.

Easier said than done, though. Not only had Alex survived his training, he'd so outperformed anyone's expectations—which had been pretty damned high to begin with—that the agency was sharply split on what to do with him. The original plan was merely to use him in Operation Cold Intent to wreck his old man. But now, a number of senior supervisors in the agency wanted to anoint him the superspy of the next generation, while another faction wanted to throw him in the deepest darkest hole the agency could find and never let him out.

The problem was that the CIA's control of Alex Peters was tenuous at best. He was a maverick at heart and didn't appreciate being jerked around. He would play nice and share his toys with the other children if, and only if, he saw a good reason for it. Fuck with Alex Peters, and he'd fuck the CIA back. Hard. And without hesitation.

Making a run at Alex and Katie to kill them could backfire spectacularly. Particularly if the girl was successfully killed and Alex survived. Which was, in his opinion, a highly likely outcome.

Casting about desperately for an alternative, André

said, "What if we separate Alex and Katie? Alex has personal feelings for the girl and we can leverage those to get him to hand over whatever proof he collected. And we can…pressure…him to go along with whatever alternate explanation for the information you folks cook up over at Langley."

Silence on the other end of the line.

He added, "It would have the side benefit of weakening Alex. He and his girlfriend are turning out to be a more effective team than anyone anticipated."

The director's response, when it came, was brief. "Do it. Break them up."

ALEX LOUNGED IN the chair as much as it was possible to lounge in an interrogation room. The man who'd just stepped through the door looked highly frustrated. Poor jarhead. The guy had so wanted to rough him up a little.

"Come with me," the Marine bit out.

Alex followed the guy down a long hall. Given that the two of them were alone, he was obviously no longer considered a hostile threat. Too bad. He'd have enjoyed knocking this guy's lights out. Sanctimonious know-it-alls had always irritated the crap out of him.

Alex was reunited with his meager personal belongings—his wallet, knife and emergency medical pack. Funny how naked he felt without the compact kit of supplies. It was as if his identity as a doctor was tied to that black bag.

"You're really a doctor?" the jarhead finally asked.

"Yeah," Alex muttered as he signed the receipt

for his stuff. "My associate—the one I told your colleagues about—is supposed to show up here with a bag of medical samples for me in the next day or two. Has she checked in with the base yet?"

"You mean the hot babe the MPs picked up outside the fence a little while ago? Cubans were right tweaked that she made it onto the reservation. Sent half the damned army after her, the way I hear it."

Praise the Lord. She'd made it to safety. His knees actually felt a little weak at the news. "Is she all right?" Alex asked sharply. "I need to see her."

"Cool your jets. She's okay. Gotta fill out some paperwork explaining what the hell she's doing down here without us knowing about it. And the MPs sent her bag over here already. Lemme go get it."

Alex was so relieved he could bust that Katie was safe. But in the next breath, suspicion over why they hadn't let her come join him blossomed.

The guy plunked the bag onto the counter hard enough that Alex's heart jolted in alarm. "Easy does it with those," he snapped.

"Who are you, anyway?"

"Just a guy doing a job," Alex answered wryly as he picked up the bag. "One last favor and then I'll get out of your hair. Can you point me to the base hospital?"

"Yeah, sure. Two-story white building. Long building. Kinda H-shaped. It overlooks the bay." He gave Alex detailed instructions on how to get there, apologized for not being able to leave his post to give him a ride. The kid seemed to have forgiven Alex for not being a bad guy he could rough up. Eager to be away from the young Marine's overblown brand of macho, he slipped out into the night.

The hospital wasn't hard to spot. The building, indeed, was snowy white with a big red cross mounted on the roof. It also had power, so the lights were on. He walked in the front door, identified himself as a doctor and followed the signs to the lab.

A technician in a white lab coat looked up from a centrifuge as he entered. "Can I help you?" the guy asked.

"Yes. Do you have a gas chromatograph here?"

"Sure do."

"I'm going to need to use it. And do you have any chemical weapons detection kits in here?"

That got a slower response. "Yesss. Why?"

"I'm going to need whatever you've got. Then I'm going to need a sealed room to work in."

"Um, who are you?"

His guy-doing-a-job line clearly wasn't going to work on this fellow. He opened up the bag. "I'm the guy who gets to test all these samples for chemical contamination. It's going to take all damned night, too. You wanna stay and help and maybe get exposed to some nasty shit?"

The tech answered hastily, "No, that's okay. We've got a reverse air-flow room back there. I'm gonna need your help moving the chromatograph back there, though. Sucker's heavy."

It took the two of them nearly a half hour to horse the equipment Alex would need back into the smaller lab. But he finally donned a disposable plastic chemical suit and went to work. He was deeply conflicted about what he hoped the tests would show. On the one hand, he'd love to be right with his diagnosis out of professional pride. But on the other hand, he'd give anything to be wrong. His life and Katie's were going to get so complicated he didn't even want to think about it if the results came back positive for sarin or some other chemical weapon.

He set up the first sample and put it in the machine. In a few seconds, the machine beeped completion of the test. He took a deep breath and looked at the readout.

CHAPTER ELEVEN

"AM I UNDER ARREST?" Katie demanded.

"No, ma'am."

"Then can I go now?"

"Where are you going to go?"

"I need to see my partner."

"The doctor? Um, your paperwork will need to be all in order. I'll have to go check on that. . . ." Her captor's voice trailed off vaguely. No matter how polite this Marine was being, he was detaining her. And as far as she could tell, the guy was doing it illegally.

"What's the holdup? I'm an American citizen here."

"This is Guantánamo. We do things differently down here—"

She cut him off. "Is this American soil?"

"Yes."

"Then I have certain rights. Look. I grew up on military bases. I know the deal. I'm going now."

"Ma'am, you can't just barge out the door and bomb around the base."

"Why not?"

"It's the middle of the night."

"What does that have to do with anything?"

The poor guy had no answer for that and merely

sputtered. She took pity on him and asked more temperately, "Who gave you the order to keep me here? Maybe I can have a little talk with him or her."

He answered reluctantly, "Base intel officer. Just a little while ago."

That startled her. The MPs had turned her over to the intelligence outfit down here? Someone must have reported their presence up the chain of command, and an order had obviously come back down to hold them here. What she didn't understand, though, was why they weren't allowing her and Alex to see each other.

She asked, "Did the intel officer also tell you not to let me see my partner?"

"Yes, ma'am." The guy sounded deeply relieved to confess that. As if she would now cooperate fully with him. She snorted mentally. Wild horses were not going to keep her away from Alex.

"Are they interrogating Alex?" she asked lightly.

"I don't think so. Last I heard, he was at the hospital."

"Is he hurt?" she demanded sharply.

"Not that I'm aware of. They killed the guy with him, but he's all right."

They who? Why did Alex come in with someone? And the Americans killed that someone? The mystery deepened. One thing was for sure. She was getting out of here and finding him as soon as she could figure out a way to do it.

She sighed in feigned resignation. "Okay, so I'm supposed to stay here until further notice. Is there anywhere I could maybe lie down for a while? It's been a rough couple of days and I'm exhausted."

"Yeah, sure. We've got a break room with a couch in it. Come on."

She followed the soldier docilely down the hall and made sure to give the guy a big yawn as she stretched out on the couch. Oh, Lord, it felt good to lie down. She suspected that were it not for the stim pill Alex had given her, she'd be unable to move right about now. As it was, real exhaustion tugged at her, coaxing her to close her eyes for just a few minutes.

The guy turned out the lights and pulled the door shut for her. She figured he would give her a little while to fall asleep before he would think about peeking in to check on her. Which meant she had to go right now.

She opened the window behind the couch and was relieved that it was properly greased and slid up silently. She had to shove out the screen and winced at the faint screech it made as she punched it out.

Feetfirst, she slid out the window and landed in a bush. It scratched the heck out of her calves and she bit her lip to keep from making any sound. She reached up to pull the window shut before she finally extricated herself from the attacking bush.

Now, to find Alex.

Hospital. Where was the base hospital? She figured it would have emergency power, so she headed for the nearest lit building at a jog. Unfortunately, it turned out to be some sort of operations center.

She picked the next nearest building with lights and headed for it.

A few jeeps passed her. She dived for cover when she had time, and when she didn't, she pretended to be out for a late-night jog and waved jauntily at the drivers. Without exception, they whistled or called back. Not many girls in these parts apparently.

The third lit building, sitting high on a hill overlooking the bay, turned out to be the hospital. The orderly at the front desk was completely unwilling to grant her access to the building, however. Unlike Alex, she was a terrible liar, and worse, she was too stupid tired to come up with a brilliant lie on the spot.

She finally retreated from the front entrance and made her way around the far side of the building to the emergency entrance. She crouched outside in the dark to ponder what illness or injury she was most likely to succeed at faking.

A police car was parked in front of the emergency room's double doors, and as she failed to think of anything halfway believable, a military cop stepped outside. Two more cops came out, hustling a fourth man along between them.

Oh, my God. Alex. And it looked like he was under arrest.

The car pulled out from under the portico and she ran after it. Of course, she couldn't keep up with the speeding vehicle, but she did see that it went back to the first lit building—the operations center.

Cursing under her breath, she jogged back that way. Now what?

ALEX STARED AT the walls of the holding cell and could scream in frustration. He'd gotten to the very end of the tests before the cops—led by the lab tech from before—barged in on him and bodily dragged him out of the lab. At least he'd managed to turn off the chromatograph and erase the results it had recorded before he powered it down. He'd swallowed the flash drive holding the only other evidence and prayed the lunging Marines didn't see him do it before they grabbed him.

Who in the hell had known what he was testing for? And why would the Americans stop him from completing the damned tests? Wouldn't they be the most eager of all to know if the Cubans were secretly storing chemical weapons smuggled out of the Middle East? It made no sense whatsoever.

Apparently, he was under arrest, too. By whom, no one had bothered to tell him. And of course, there was no mention of exactly what he'd done to merit being thrown in here and locked up in the dark.

None of this made any sense. He was an American government employee. He'd given his real name to the MPs who'd picked him up and had given the bastards André's phone number to verify his identity. Sure, an ID might have to go up through channels, but how hard could it be for an American military installation to get a yes/no answer from the CIA on whether or not Alex Peters was one of the good guys?

He felt his way around the windowless cell and located a sink, toilet and concrete bench in under a minute. He retired to the bench to make himself comfortable. God knew, he had plenty of experience with incarceration. Four years' worth in his early twenties. He'd gone on a drunken joyride with the express intent of getting himself locked up rather than taking up where his father had left off as a spy against the United States.

What were they doing to Katie? Was she locked up, too? Were they interrogating her? If he were in charge, she'd be the one he tried to break. The untrained female civilian was a much softer target than the hardened, field-experienced spy.

Unable to sit anymore, he paced the cell in the dark, swearing colorfully in a variety of languages. Not even a strip of light crept in under the door. Either it was weather-stripped or the hallway outside was darkened, as well. He suspected the sensory deprivation was intentional, meant to disorient and unnerve prisoners. He snorted. His prisoner training had included many days of blindfolds and light deprivation. Except, of course, for interrogations, which were conducted under blinding spotlights.

As time stretched on and no one came to let him out, his alarm mounted. Why hadn't the CIA given the Marines a green light to release him? Why the delay? His finely honed instinct for dealing with intelligence agencies told him something was afoot. Surely, the CIA wouldn't have spent a full year training him with the intent to throw him to the wolves on his very first mission abroad for them. And why the forced separation from Katie?

The trick, besides not panicking, was to keep an

accurate sense of time. He set a mental alarm for four hours from now and lay down to catch a nap while he waited for his captors to make their next move. He expected it would come in the wee hours of the night when his biological clock was set for sleep.

He was right. He'd been lazily dozing for less than a half hour after he'd woken from his nap when the overhead lights were thrown on. He swung his feet to the floor as his cell door banged open loudly.

"Get up! Get up! Get up!" the guard yelled aggressively.

Alex, already seated on the edge of the bed/bench, gave the guy a sardonic smile and stood up casually.

Irritated not to have surprised him, the guard grabbed Alex's arm roughly and attempted to throw him through the door. Not only was Alex expecting something passive-aggressive like that, but he'd studied martial arts basically since he could walk. It took more than a hard shove to knock him off balance. Apparently, this was not a polite visit to release the fellow American asset. What in the *hell* was the holdup with the CIA?

"Left or right?" Alex asked blandly.

"Left, asshole."

"That's Dr. Asshole to you. I'm a surgeon."

Not that he thought the guy cared, but it was good to establish a certain status with thugs like his guard. Sure enough, the guard walked a little farther behind him and didn't "accidentally" slam him against any walls as they walked down the long corridor.

The guard directed him up a flight of stairs, down

a short hall and into an interrogation room, complete with cameras and a lie-detector machine sitting on a small, rolling table in the corner.

"Are you a lie-detector tech?" Alex asked pleasantly with feigned surprise.

"No," the guard admitted, scowling.

Mission accomplished. Chasm in their status emphasized for good measure. Now to play the twerp like a violin. "It's interesting work," Alex said in a conversational tone. "Decent hours. Good pay in the civilian world. High-demand job. More and more private companies are using lie detectors on their employees or during job interviews. Which means there aren't nearly enough trained techs. It would be a good career move for you if you ever decide to go civilian."

The guard nodded thoughtfully. "Thanks, man."

Amateur. The guy had no clue that Alex had just neatly diverted him from playing bad cop for whatever interrogator was right now standing on the other side of that two-way glass. He'd bet the "good cop" knew what he'd done, though. Should come in here any second to try to regain control of the situation.

Assuming the guy wasn't working over Katie, already. He cringed to think of her undergoing a professional interrogation. Physically cringed. If he was lucky, they would make a run at him first. He could keep the bastards busy for a good long time and away from her. Long enough, hopefully, for André Fortinay to pull her out of this hell hole undamaged.

The door opened. A man in a neatly starched white shirt and pressed slacks walked into the room.

Psychologist. Alex eyed this man warily.

"Have a seat, Dr. Peters."

"And you would be?" Alex asked.

"John Doe."

"Pleasure to meet you, Dr. Doe," Alex murmured as he took his seat. He planted both feet on the floor and both palms flat on the table. It was an unnatural pose, but designed not to give the interrogator any unconscious body language signals.

Dr. Doe's mouth curved up sardonically. At a gesture from Doe, the future lie-detector tech retreated into the corner out of Alex's line of sight.

Not that it succeeded in intimidating Alex. He would hear the guy coming long before the guard could lay a finger on him. He might absorb the blow, or he might move to block it, depending on how the interrogation was proceeding. Either way, he had control of that element of the game.

"What brings you to Guantánamo, Dr. Peters?"

"I'm afraid I'm not at liberty to discuss that with you, Dr. Doe."

"Who do you work for?"

"I gave a contact number for my superiors to the MPs earlier. Feel free to call my headquarters and verify my identity for yourself."

Interestingly enough, John Doe's mouth tightened slightly. So. Doe had been in contact with the CIA already. Which meant the fuckers in Langley had told this jerk to go through with this interrogation. What the *hell?*

"What kind of tests were you running in the hospital's lab earlier?"

"I can't discuss that."

"Can't or won't?"

Alex answered politely, "Let's just say it's not on the approved list of conversation topics and call it good, shall we?" After all, there was no sense pissing this guy off more than he had to.

Doe leaned forward and planted his hands on the table to match Alex's. "Just so we're clear, you're not getting out of here until you talk. I'm a specialist. You will tell me what I want to know before I'm done with you. I'll respect your decision if you choose to resist me, but any…discomfort…you experience will be purely your choice and not mine."

This guy knew he was a spy. Knew the kind of training Alex had undergone. And Doe still thought it was possible to break him? Bastard had a big surprise coming. Alex leaned forward and stared the guy directly in the eyes. He spoke slowly, enunciating each word clearly. "Try me. I dare you."

And those were the last words he spoke. For the next hour, Doe pummeled him with questions, taunts and outright threats. For the most part, the guy disguised his growing frustration well. But Alex was better. By subtle nuances of expression, he conveyed his amusement and contempt for the man's efforts to make him talk.

Finally, Doe threw up his hands. "You leave me no choice. We're going to have to drug you." The bastard said that like he was relieved to have gotten to this point. Were those his orders all along? Put on a show for Alex that culminated in drugging away his inhibitions until he spilled his guts to this guy?

Warning bells clanged wildly in his head. Of course he hadn't told the CIA everything about himself during his simulated interrogations last year. He'd been trained from the bloody cradle to be secretive as hell. So. His employers still didn't trust him, huh? He supposed he shouldn't be surprised. But it still pissed him off.

Did they seriously think he was going to break under drugs? He was fully trained in how to resist the effects of interrogation drugs—unless they'd developed something new that they planned to try out on him. Mentally, he frowned. They usually tested new toys on enemy combatants and not their own assets.

In the meantime, he needed to deal with the asshole in front of him. He let a flash of derision over the idea of being drugged show briefly in his eyes and then resumed his deadpan expression. Doe reeled back in his chair. The guy wasn't sure what he'd just seen, but it was giving the man pause.

"Who are you?" Doe burst out.

No need to answer. His identity had already been established well before either of them set foot in this room. His ploy now was to occupy this man for as long as possible. Good Lord willing, Doe was the only interrogator on this, the nonprison side of the naval base. Keeping him occupied in here meant he wasn't messing with Katie.

Where was she, anyway? A few minutes alone with

lie-detector boy, and he'd have had the kid telling him where she was. The key would be to get rid of Dr. Doe for a while. To that end, Alex stared blandly at Doe's continuing antics and flatly refused to be provoked into any reaction whatsoever.

Finally, Doe shoved back his chair and stormed out of the room. Aware that he still had an audience, Alex didn't alter his position by a centimeter.

"Dude, you really ought to talk to him. It only gets nasty from here," the guard murmured.

Alex didn't bother to acknowledge the guy. Whether the remark was scripted or a genuine warning, he didn't know and couldn't care less. He merely closed his eyes and worked through a mental relaxation exercise.

By his reckoning, it would be dawn soon. Lie-detector guy would go off shift. If he had to guess they would replace him with a bruiser of a guard trained to hit stuff very hard. Not that it mattered. He knew how to deal with that type, too. Pain was a transient thing, blocked easily enough.

Doe stuck his head into the room and barked an order at lie-detector guy. Something about taking him upstairs to Room 10 and preparing him for medication. Going straight to the mind-altering drugs, were they? Good call. He was actually surprised, though, that Doe didn't give himself the satisfaction of watching a thug beat the crap out of him first.

Two more guards joined the first one, and the trio oversaw riding upstairs in an elevator, taking off his undershirt, laying him down on a hospital bed and strapping him down tightly.

Doe came back with a woman in surgical scrubs, who efficiently set an IV in the back of his hand and taped the needle down securely. He briefly considered resisting her, but the guards were big guys and more manpower would be nearby.

The IV drip started. For now, it was a simple saline solution. But a stainless-steel tray with several loaded syringes stood on a table beside the bed.

Doe picked up the first syringe.

Alex broke his silence to say, "I guarantee that no one in this room has the proper security clearances to hear what I have to say. Unless you want to create a severe shit storm of security violations that will land on your head, you might want to reevaluate who's in here if I start talking."

"Oh, you'll talk." And with that, Doe injected the serum into the IV line. Alex didn't feel any pain at the site of his IV. Must be one of the new-generation meds, then. A couple of the old ones burned like fire on their way into the body.

"We'll give that a few minutes to work, Dr. Peters, and then I'll be back to have a little chat with you."

Alex ignored him. He was already hard at work filling his mind with harmless images from his childhood. Soccer games on Saturday mornings. The dew had been cold and wet on the grass, a silver-gray cobweb over the soccer field. His shin guards, too big, slid down inside his tube socks and bugged him. Grass clippings stuck to the wet soccer balls. The more minute the details he filled his mind with, the better.

He registered vaguely that the guards did indeed step out into the hall when Doe came back. Alex's vision had narrowed to a brightly lit tunnel with dancing images at the end of it. Shouting kids. Harassed coaches. Matching T-shirts.

"Can you hear me, Alex?"

"Yes, Coach. I'm listening."

"Why are you in Cuba?"

"To play soccer."

"Who sent you here?"

"My father. He wants me to fit in."

"What were you testing in the lab?"

"My hands. Best part of playing goalie is getting to use them."

"We're going to give you another drug, Alex. It will amplify the effect of the CCRE."

CCRE? What was that? He'd never heard it mentioned in his training last year.

The door opened behind Doe and a nurse came in. Different nurse from before. This one was blonde. Pretty. Had big blue eyes. She looked just like someone he knew named Katie. He liked Katie—the real one. The hallucination made him smile a little. Yup, she was the reason he would fight to the bitter end. And win. He had to win this soccer game. He sank farther into his boyhood memory, wrapping it around him like a thick blanket as the second drug was injected into his IV.

His head was starting to spin pleasantly and his

body felt heavy and languid. But as quickly as that sensation registered, panic followed it. What had they done to him? How had they known to make the nurse look like a girl he liked? They were all out to get him. Was *she* part of the plot, too? It was brilliant to use her. Evil.

"Gotta win," he muttered.

"What's that?" Doe leaned down a little closer to hear him.

And that was when the nurse pulled a rock out of a wrapped towel and clobbered Doe across the back of the head with it. *Holy shit.* The interrogator fell across Alex's lap and then slid to the floor, with Katie-nurse attempting to slow the guy's fall.

That was a good ploy to get him to trust her. He watched, bemused, as the hallucination frantically unbuckled the leather straps from his wrists, neck, waist and, finally, feet.

"We've got to get out of here," she whispered. "Can you walk?"

"If I can play soccer, I can walk." And hey. If she wanted to bust him out of here as a head game to gain his trust, far be it from him to stop her. He could always get away from her later.

She ran over to the window and looked out. "Can you jump out the window? We're on the second floor. Did they teach you to drop and roll in soccer?"

"Of course," he answered indignantly. "I'm a damned goalie."

"Does your daddy know you talk like that?" she asked, amused.

"Hell, no!"

"Keep your voice down," she ordered sharply. "Help me take this guy's shirt off. It looks about your size."

"But it's white. Team colors are purple and black. Dumb colors, if you ask me."

"It's a nice shirt. It'll look good on you." She buttoned him into Doe's white shirt like he was a five-year-old. Katie knew about five-year-olds. She was a teacher.

"I pretend my mommy's a teacher sometimes."

"The fact that you have gnarly sex with me on a regular basis makes that comment wrong on too many levels to count," she retorted dryly as she eased the window open.

"I'll go first," he announced. "I'm the boy and you're only a dumb girl."

"Fine. Just get out of the way when you land. I'll be right behind you."

"'Kay."

He swung a leg over the sill and was just about to go when the woman stopped him with a hand on his arm. "No shouting on the way down. You have to jump without making any noise."

"Poopyhead," he muttered. He'd been looking forward to a good whoop as he went for a fly.

Grinning widely, she gave him a little push. "Have fun. Just be quiet about it. We'll get in huge trouble if we get caught."

"I'm really good at sneaking around," he whispered conspiratorially. He pushed off the edge and landed with a fall and roll his coach would have been proud of. He even remembered to roll again and get out of the nurse's way.

While she clambered awkwardly over the sill, he turned away and jammed his finger down his throat. He gagged but didn't vomit. He jammed his finger into his throat harder and held it there. There. He heaved and hunched over, retching.

The object he'd hoped would come up did. He picked the flash drive out of the remains of his last meal and shoved it in his pocket as the woman hit the ground beside him with an *oomph.* "Noisy girl," he complained under his breath.

"Shh. Come with me."

"Can I call you Katie?"

"Sure," the blonde replied. "Just do what I say, okay?"

They got on a bus of some kind, and he got really sleepy as it started and stopped a million times. Crap. He couldn't afford to sleep. He had to be ready to slip away from this woman when the time came.

"You can take a nap if you want," Katie told him.

Her shoulder looked soft and inviting, just like he imagined his mother's would. He laid his head down on it and closed his eyes. But he was faking. He had to stay alert. Wait for his chance to escape the woman and whatever twisted game she was playing.

His jitters mounted as the bus started and stopped over and over. Why the hell were they doing this to him? They must think he would spill his guts to this woman. Hah.

People on the bus were watching him. He felt their stares on his back, but every time he turned to check, they were already looking away. He had to get under cover. Hide where they couldn't find him. Away from the woman who was obviously leading them all to him. He had to get away from her if it was the last thing he did.

CHAPTER TWELVE

KATIE DIDN'T KNOW whether to sigh in relief or panic as Alex leaned against her side. He wasn't sleeping—he was far too tense against her shoulder for that. Worse, he was growing more tense by the minute, which panicked her, in turn. What on earth had him so badly wired? What threat did he see that she was missing?

It had been pure luck that she'd overheard a couple of Marines griping about the slowness of the shuttle bus into town while she'd been prowling through the operations center in search of Alex. She'd absconded with a stack of files from a desk and had been carrying them around as if she were delivering them somewhere. She'd also stolen the woman's purse she'd found under the desk. In addition to a wallet with a military ID in it, the purse held some cash. Thank God.

It had taken a while to walk around the building poking into offices and eavesdropping to get a bead on Alex. She'd been deeply alarmed to hear a guard talking about the batshit-crazy doctor they were about to drug upstairs. She'd known immediately that it had to be Alex.

Once she'd climbed the stairs and slipped through a locked door behind a woman dressed in medical scrubs, it had been surprisingly easy to find the break room, put on a pair of scrubs she found there and literally walk into Alex's room. Taking the doorstop from the break room, a big, gray brick, and hiding it in a towel had been a spur-of-the-moment improvisation. Funny how inspiration could strike at the exact right time, now and then.

She could use a little more inspiration at the moment. They had to get off the base somehow and hole up until Alex slept off whatever they'd given him.

But at least the two of them were back together. It was better than nothing, but she really could use Alex's input on how to proceed. She was without a clue as to what to do next. She needed him alert and operating on all cylinders as soon as possible.

And it wouldn't hurt to get a hug from him or at least a reassurance that he would take care of her. She'd had quite enough of being an independent woman sneaking around a foreign land in spylike fashion. Although she did have to admit Alex made a surprisingly cute five-year-old.

The bus passed off the naval station and she watched in minor disbelief as the huge fence retreated behind her. Surely, it couldn't be that easy. Shaking her head, she watched the countryside pass by and worried as Alex's body grew more and more taut next to hers.

Finally, she muttered, "What's wrong?"

"Nothing," he muttered back.

Bull. He felt ready to explode at any second.

The bus passed through a couple of small villages before it pulled into a decent-size town that reminded her a lot of Baracoa. "End of the line," the driver called in Spanish. "Guantánamo."

Alex was practically vibrating with tension by the time they stepped off the bus. She looked around quickly and spied a coffee shop only a few yards from the bus stop. She knew they had to get off the street and out of sight, so she headed for the café with Alex in tow.

She ordered a pot of coffee and paid for it with cash from the stolen purse.

"Where'd you get the money?" he asked suspiciously.

"I liberated a purse from its owner before I rescued you," she explained under her breath.

"Nice touch," he commented.

Huh?

"What's the plan?" he asked nervously.

She really didn't like the way his gaze was darting around in constant motion like he expected a violent attack at any moment. "Relax. You'll draw too much attention if you keep looking so uptight."

If anything, his expression got more wild, but he did stop looking around so overtly. "Are you feeling all right, Alex? What did they inject you with?"

His eyes got that shuttered, stubborn look they got when he was refusing to tell her something. "I don't feel so hot," he announced.

"You need a restroom?" she asked in quick concern. "It's down that hall."

"Got it," he said thickly. He rushed from the table

in the direction she pointed, distinctly green about the gills.

She waited a few minutes for him to return, but he didn't. Worried, she rose to her feet, moved quickly down the hall to the restroom and knocked on the door. No answer.

"Alex?" she called quietly through the panel.

Still no answer. She tested the doorknob. Locked. Crap. Had he passed out? Or worse? What the hell had they drugged him with, anyway? It was a simple lock. She fumbled in the purse, came up with a ballpoint pen and jammed its tip into the circular hole in the center of the knob. The lock clicked open. She threw the door open—

Empty. The tiny bathroom was empty! Where had he gone? She'd watched the hallway the whole time he'd been in here. No way had he slipped back out into the café without her seeing him. *The window.* It was closed but not locked. He'd bailed out on her? What the hell was going on with him? He'd separated from her back at the Zacara factory and now he'd ditched her in the middle of downtown Guantánamo?

Equal parts furious and terrified, she threw open the window and looked down the alley. No surprise, Alex was long gone. In the loose gravel of the alley, he'd left no footprints that she could see. Not that she was any kind of trained tracker, anyway.

Crap. Now what?

It wasn't as if she could go back to the Navy base and ask to be let in again. Not after she'd busted the two of them out like that. Her brain felt wrapped in cotton candy. God, she was exhausted. She tried to remember the last time she'd slept, and nothing came to mind. Alex always said never to underestimate the power of food and sleep during an undercover op.

She retreated down the hall and asked the waitress in her halting Spanish where she could find a room to stay in, nothing fancy. Just a place to sleep. The girl named a place and gave her quick directions that Katie only half-understood. But she nodded her thanks and headed out.

Belatedly, it dawned on her that Alex would tell her the last place she should go was the one the girl had named for her. Katie wandered the streets for a little while, searching fruitlessly for him until it occurred to her that there were likely soldiers out looking for her, too. Not to mention Alex would never be dumb enough to roam around in broad daylight when he was a fugitive.

Clearly, she was way too tired to make smart decisions right now. She saw a cardboard sign in the window of a tiny, cluttered convenience store advertising a room for rent. She swerved into the bodega and grabbed the sign out of the window. It turned out to be upstairs, and the proprietor wasn't thrilled about only renting it for the week. He was looking for a long-term renter. But when she plunked down a credit card and told him to charge a full month's rent for the week, he shut up quickly enough.

It wasn't fancy. A single bed against one wall. A phone-booth-size toilet and sink. A hot plate that looked like a severe fire hazard sitting on top of the lone dresser. That was it.

With a look askance at the cleanliness of the sheets, she laid down fully dressed on the bed. She could not *believe* he'd ditched her a second time! She would figure out how to escape from Cuba later, when she could think straight. One thing she knew: when she got home, she was going to find Alex and kill him. And if she couldn't accomplish the deed by herself, she would sic her brothers on him.

ALEX CROUCHED IN the ruined house, looking around in panic. They were coming for him. He could feel it. They'd turned Katie, and she was after him, too. No one could be trusted. A little voice whispered to him that paranoia wasn't healthy. But an answering voice inside his head screamed that it wasn't paranoia if people were really coming after him.

Everywhere he'd gone today, he'd felt eyes on him. Stares, boring into his back. Cell phones being muttered into, reporting sightings of him. Reporting his position. Calling in spooks to snatch him and make him disappear. He even felt Katie's fake concern reaching out to him to suck him into her trap.

Nowhere to run. Nowhere to hide. He crept into a small closet, pulled the warped door as shut as it would go and huddled in the corner, hugging his knees and rocking back and forth.

KATIE HAD NO idea how long she slept. She woke up a couple of times to go to the restroom, but that was about it. It was morning when she woke based on the sun streaming in her east-facing window. Eighteen hours' worth of sleep or so later, she finally felt human again. Alert. And pissed.

How could Alex abandon her not once but twice? If the guy didn't want to be with her, all he had to do was say so. But ditching her in a hostile country to sink or swim on her own…what total jackassery.

What in the world was *wrong* with him? The Alex she'd met in Zaghastan would never have acted like this. What had the CIA done to him? Had they destroyed the Alex she'd known and loved? Was he gone forever?

One part of her, the hopeful part, wanted to stick around and fight through the crap to find that old Alex. But another, larger part, the fearful part, wanted to cut her losses and run from the train wreck that was the inside of his head.

Either way, pain tore at her heart, ripping out big, awful chunks of it and tossing them on the ground carelessly.

Something approaching actual hatred coursed through her veins, hot and acid. Although whether it was hatred of Alex or his employer, she couldn't say. First order of business, get home. Second on her to-do list, murder Alex. Slowly and painfully. Maybe she could recruit her brothers to help. One of them must know how to torture a guy.

She took stock of the contents of her stolen purse. It held enough cash to buy food for a couple of days.

And the woman's credit cards. Although they were probably cut off by now.

Tucking most of the cash in her bra, she took the rest downstairs to the bodega. She bought a couple of big bottles of water, a few apples, a box of crackers and a can of tuna. The city's food supply was still pretty limited, but it would do.

A woman was working behind the counter this morning. Katie practiced the Spanish phrases she would need in her head and then approached the woman to ask where she could get access to a telephone with international service. The lady gave her a weird look and Katie added hastily that she could pay for the call.

The woman gestured with her head for Katie to follow and stepped behind a cloth curtain. Katie ducked into a tiny storeroom.

"Twenty dollars, U.S., for three minutes," the woman said, fishing a cell phone out of her pocket.

That was probably double the going rate, but Katie wasn't going to quibble about a little gringo gouging. "Done." She pulled a twenty out of her bra and traded it for the phone. She dialed André Fortinay's number and prayed the call would go through and not be traced by the Cuban secret police in the next three minutes.

"Doctors Unlimited," a female voice answered.

Ashley Osborne. The perky office assistant who'd sent her down here in the first place. "This is Katie McCloud. I need to speak to André."

"He's in a meeting. Can he call you back?"

"No. Interrupt him. I've got one shot at contacting him, and then I'm screwed."

"Oh. Sure, then. Hang on, I'll get him right away." At least the girl had the good grace to sound alarmed.

"Hi, Katie. What's up?" André murmured a few seconds later.

"I'm stranded in the city of Guantánamo, off base. I need to get out of Cuba ASAP, and I can't go back to the military base."

"Why not? Where's Alex?"

"Long story and I've only got about two minutes on this line. I have no idea where Alex is. He ditched me."

"You're kidding. He's nuts about you."

"Right now, he's just nuts. Can you get me an exit option, or am I hosed?"

"Where are you specifically?"

Katie stuck her head through the curtain and asked for the street address. The woman gave it to her and she relayed it to André.

"Can you call me back in an hour?" he asked her.

"I doubt it."

"Okay. Hang on, then. I'm going to use the other line to make a phone call. I promise I'll come back to this line."

Katie waited in an agony of impatience as the seconds ticked by. The woman poked her head through the curtain and announced that her three minutes were up. Katie dug out another bill, a ten this time, and handed it to the woman.

"The police, they will come looking if you stay on the line," the woman hissed.

"I'll buy you a new phone. Just let me finish this call. It's life-and-death." Katie wasn't sure the phrase *life-and-death* translated well into Spanish, but the woman backed out of the storeroom with a dubious look on her face.

"Katie? Still there?"

Thank God. André. "Yes."

"Make your way to the docks on the west side of the bay. Look for a freighter called the *Constellation Caelum.* That's spelled *C-a-e-l-u-m.* Identify yourself as the onboard nurse who's just been hired."

"But I'm not a nurse!"

"Fake it. An asset on the crew will contact you with an egress plan once the *Caelum* has left Cuban waters. The ship sails in a few hours, so you'll need to head down there immediately."

"Thanks," she murmured gratefully.

"Don't thank me until you get home," he replied wryly.

"Should I go looking for Alex and try to bring him with me?" she asked reluctantly. As livid as she was at him, it wasn't right to just abandon him the way he had abandoned her.

"Alex can take care of himself," André replied a shade tartly. "Trust me."

"I think they drugged him. He had an IV drip in his arm when I found him, and there were syringes on a table. Two of them were empty."

"I've got him covered. You just take care of yourself," André said heavily. The man sounded unhappy, and she didn't blame him. The guy had put a ton of effort into championing Alex with his superiors.

No sooner had she hung up than remorse for bailing out on Alex slammed into her. Not that he deserved an ounce of sympathy from her. Her remorse had more to do with the rightness or wrongness of her actions. As for Alex, he could go straight to hell and rot.

A tiny part of her brain recognized her anger as self-defense against the pain of being abandoned. But it was the only thing holding her together right now, the only thing letting her function. She drew the anger close around her, hanging on to it tightly.

She ducked out of the storeroom and handed the phone back to the woman with a word of thanks and the rest of her cash. She was grateful for the woman's patience. Katie took her plastic grocery bag of food and water and walked out of the store. She asked a random woman where the docks were and took off walking in the direction the lady had pointed.

It took nearly an hour to walk down to the pier. A half dozen freighters were in port, and it wasn't difficult to spot the *Caelum.* The ship was broad and long, sitting low in the water. A grain ship, maybe? She headed for the gangplank leading to a small door in the ship's hull close to the waterline.

A darkly tanned, rough-looking man lounged in front of the walkway. She'd ditched the military ID out of the woman's wallet but had kept the driver's license. She pulled that out now.

"I'm Marianne Kleck," she said expectantly. The

guy threw her an I-don't-give-a-damn look and didn't bother to answer.

"The new nurse," she tried. Then, "I've been hired on to the *Caelum.*"

"No shit?" He had a heavy accent. Maybe South African. At least he spoke English.

"Are you going to let me board or do I have to call the captain?"

"You got identification?"

She handed over the driver's license.

"Your hair's the wrong color."

"I heard blondes have more fun. Thought I'd see if it's true."

He grinned in a distinctively wolfish way that made her skin crawl as his gaze roamed boldly up and down her body. "Yeah, sure. Welcome aboard."

She paused in the hatch. "Can you direct me to the infirmary?"

"Amidship, deck three, just aft of the beam."

Whatever the heck all that meant. She ducked into a narrow, all-steel stairwell and climbed until a door with a large number three painted on it came into sight. The passageway beyond was dim and claustrophobic with exposed metal pipes crowding down from above. Randomly, she wandered down it and spotted a Red Cross painted on a door. Thank God. She opened it and slipped inside. She fumbled around on the wall until she found a light switch.

Oh, God, it was tiny. The room had a bunk bed on one wall, about two feet of floor space and a tall cabinet on the opposite wall with at least twenty drawers in it. A sink stood beside the cabinet, and a tiny desk was tucked behind the open door. Someone strode by outside and she closed the door quickly. Curious, she opened all the drawers and was alarmed to see an array of medical supplies, some of whose purposes she had only the vaguest notion of.

Beside the sink, she discovered a tiny closet with a life jacket hanging from a hook up high and a tiny refrigerator taking up the bottom half of the space. Inside the refrigerator were a half dozen glass medical bottles of serums. Crud. What were those? She read the labels and only recognized the morphine and penicillin. She had no idea what the others were. Fake it, huh? Nobody had better get hurt before she got off this boat.

Memory of the gigantic suture needles in the drawer behind her made her shudder to even think of. No way could she sew human flesh together. Yick.

The door opened. "I 'ear there's a hot sheila aboard," a big, blond man boomed in a thick Aussie drawl.

She took an instinctive step back from the burly sailor as the guy whistled under his breath. "No lie. You'll dine with me tonoight. And I'm thinkin' I'll be bunkin' in with you."

"There will be no bunking in with anyone, thank you very much," she retorted sharply.

He shrugged. "Well, if ye want the crew to gang-rape ye, that's your call."

"Gang—what?" What the hell had André gotten her into?

"I can crack the noggins of every bloke in the crew

with my bare ’ands, lass. You’d be woise to let me bunk in ’ere until I can dump ye overboard.”

“Dump me overboard?” she exclaimed.

“Well, yes. That’s what our friend André said ye wanted. As for me, if ye’ve a yen to cozy up with me for the entire cruise, I wouldn’t be sayin’ no to it.”

She sagged in relief. “No, no. That’s fine. He said you’d have the egress plan when I got here.”

“Shame. That’s quite a noice pair o’ knockers ye’re sportin’ there.”

“Uh, thanks. When exactly do you anticipate being able to drop me off?”

“If we get under way on toime, then tonoight, late. ’Ard to tell with these Cubanos, though. They do things in their own sweet toime. Sit toight in ’ere until I come fer ye.”

“Will do.”

The big Aussie backed out of the infirmary with a grin. He’d better not literally dump her overboard. But the casual way he’d mentioned it made her fear that was exactly what he had in mind.

CHAPTER THIRTEEN

As the drug-induced drowsiness wore off, sharp awareness replaced it, turning Alex's paranoia into action. As dusk fell, he stole a car and headed out. Havana was where he had knowledge that could get him out of Cuba. He had to make a quick trip to Washington, D.C., to take care of a few loose ends, and then he was going off the grid for good. He'd had it with double-crosses and backstabbing. He wasn't about to stick around and let them kill him. Or worse.

He paced the confines of the ruined house, working feeling and blood flow back into his legs. Christ, what had they shot him up with? He felt like death warmed over. His fingers were numb, and his emotions were similarly anesthetized, which was the one decent side effect of being drugged.

Now that his mind was clear, he could be properly furious that Katie had betrayed him and gone over to the enemy like that. Although, she'd never made any secret of being a dyed-in-the-wool American patriot. Logic dictated that he should feel anger toward her. Rage, even. But instead, he felt an almost robotic calm. That, and a certainty that he would kill her before he let her betray him again.

And then there were his supposed employers. He rolled his eyes. He knew better than just about anyone how dirty major governments really got their hands. Screw them all. He was done.

KATIE ATE HER snacks and hid in the infirmary for the evening. Whether the crew would actually gang-rape her or not, she had no idea. She suspected the Aussie had said it just to get into her pants. But she wasn't a hundred percent certain, hence the hibernation act.

A ship's mate of some kind had come in to meet her and ask if she was properly provisioned to sail. She'd managed to maintain a pleasant expression and meet the man's eyes when she said she was. She lied and said that a crew member had already given her a tour of the ship, too. He checked off a box on a clipboard and left quickly after that.

She napped on the bottom bunk until it was time to sail. The *Caelum* started to rumble and shake as the mighty diesel engines came to life. The sound was shockingly loud. She couldn't imagine weeks and weeks of living with that roar around her. It was maybe an hour until the ship shuddered into motion and began to rock ever so slightly. They were under way.

It was disorienting and more than a little nauseating to be tucked into this tiny, windowless cabin that rolled very faintly but continuously. She barfed into the sink and then downed a packet of antiseasickness pills she'd spotted in a drawer earlier. Too miserable to sleep, she browsed through some sort of medical reference book she found in the desk drawer. Lord, how did Alex learn all this stuff? It was dry as dust and half in Latin.

She had no idea how late it was when a quiet knock sounded on her door. She cracked it open to reveal the big Aussie. "It's toime, lassie. Oi've got the conn for the next hour."

"Um, okay."

"Grab yer loife jacket and c'mon."

Donning the bulky orange flotation device, she followed him down the passageway, which was lit only at long intervals by single lightbulbs. It was creepy as heck. He led her into the stairwell and headed up. She jogged after him and emerged onto the open deck of the ship with a gasp of surprise. It was raining. Ribbons of gray streaked downward in the glow of the ship's running lights.

"Are we meeting up with someone out here?" she asked doubtfully. It was pitch-black beyond the ship's rails. She couldn't even see where the ocean ended and the sky began. It was just blackness and more blackness stretching beyond the rusty metal deck. How on earth was another vessel going to find them and rendezvous with them in this mess?

"A ship'll be along to scoop ye up afore long. 'Ere's yer dinghy." He shoved a bulky, heavy pack into her arms.

Her *dinghy?* "What am I supposed to do with this?"

"Pull the orange tab and climb aboard. She's got a transponder. Salt water activated. Yer roide'll pick up the signal and come along."

Stunned, she let him take her by the upper arm and

lead her over to the railing at the edge of the ship. Holy crap, it was a long way down. No way was she jumping off that. There'd better be a ladder around here somewhere for her to climb down. Although even that was a daunting prospect.

"Be sure to jump well clear of the ship. 'Twould be a shame if ye got sucked into the *Caelum*'s propellers and minced to bits."

"Has anyone ever told you you've got quite a way with words?" she asked dryly.

He tied some sort of line coming from the dinghy around her waist as he replied, "Sheilas call me a silver-tongued devil all the toime."

Emphasis on devil.

"Ship's watch'll be makin' rounds soon. Off ye go, then." The Aussie grabbed her around the waist and had the gall to actually grin as he bodily hauled her to the rail.

"No! You can't do this!" She fought with all her might but was no match for the burly sailor. He picked her up off her feet and threw her out into space.

ALEX PAWNED THE solid gold bracelet operatives like him wore for emergencies just like this one. He got a fraction of its value but he wasn't concerned. A casino was open just down the street.

He walked down the Havana beachfront to the hotel and its attached casino, keeping careful watch for tails. He knew he'd been clean when he entered the city, but that didn't mean someone hadn't picked him up in the past hour. Watchers were everywhere in this town.

The all-consuming panic from before had settled down enough for him to function with caution and discretion. A lifetime's worth of training came down to this moment. He was a spy, fully in his element and at the peak of his abilities.

At the casino, he traded his meager stack of cash for chips and headed for the blackjack tables. It was the easiest game to cheat at and the fastest to accumulate winnings at. Of course, the blackjack tables were closely watched for card counting and other illegal behaviors. But he had at least an hour to play before anyone got suspicious enough to detain him. He glanced at the dealer's watch and got to work.

A HORRIBLE, GASPING scream escaped Katie on the heart-stopping fall thirty or more feet down to the water. What breath she had left was ripped out of her by the fricking freezing temperature of the water as she slammed into it.

Panic clawed at her as the black water closed over her head. Bubbles tickled her face as the life jacket did its work and carried her back up to the surface. She popped up like one of the little red-and-white plastic float balls her dad attached to her fishing line as a kid.

She heard the roar before she felt the pull of the *Caelum.* Turning in the water, she recoiled, backpedaling hard with hands and feet as the massive hull of the ship loomed shockingly close. A terrible, churning turbulence tried to suck her forward. She kicked with all her might, scared out of her mind, certain that she was about to be minced to bits, after all.

As quickly as the awful suction started, it stopped. The ocean settled into blackness around her once more, and she bobbed, tiny and helpless on the not-inconsiderable swells as the *Caelum* quickly retreated into the night. The dinghy. Where was it? Had she lost it in that damned fall?

She felt at her waist and found the line. She reeled it in and spotted the black bundle floating in the water beside her. She fumbled around on its slick surface and found what felt like a T-handle. She gave it a tug, and the damned thing practically exploded in her face. If she ever saw that Aussie again, she was going to have to hurt him.

The dinghy turned out to be a tiny little circle of black rubber tubing with a membrane suspended in the middle. And it was a pain in the butt to climb aboard. She tipped it over twice before she managed to heave herself across it far enough to grab the far side and scramble into the middle. She flopped on her face and got a mouthful of foul seawater, but managed to right herself, cursing. She didn't know whether she was more eager to kill Alex or the Aussie for getting her into this predicament.

She scouted out the tiny vessel and found a small cone made out of heavy plastic. She used it to scoop most of the water out of the bottom of the boat. Attached to a nylon cord, she found the emergency locator beacon. An orange light flashed on one end of it, so she presumed it was activated and calling in her supposed ride. The beacon turned out to have a flashlight built into it, not that the thing did her a lick of good. All it showed her was rain falling from above and scary big swells below. She turned the light off. Ignorance was bliss right about now.

She was delighted to discover some sort of waterproof cover rolled up and tied to one side of the raft. She unfurled it over herself. Wet, cold and miserable, she huddled beneath it and listened to the rain pattering off her meager protection. The thin rubber floor of the raft did little to insulate her from the heat-leeching chill of the sea beneath her, and she curled into a ball of misery on her knees in a failed effort to conserve body warmth.

She held the cone outside the tarp and caught a few ounces of rainwater at a time in it, which she drank. Up and down, up and down, the dinghy went. She barfed over the edge of the raft enough times that her stomach finally was completely empty and she only dry heaved now and then.

Once her clothes dried out, she warmed up a little. Just enough to make the mistake of peeking out from under the tarp. She was a tiny speck in the middle of a giant, yawning blackness. There was no way anyone would ever find her out here.

This was so not how she'd imagined dying. Her thoughts turned to Dawn and she grieved for the little girl who'd lost one mother at birth and now was going to lose another one to sheer stupidity. What had she been thinking to follow Alex to Cuba? Had she been so besotted with the man that she'd been willing to throw away everything, even her responsibility as a parent, for him?

She argued with herself that the purpose in going to Cuba had been to make sure Dawn had two parents to raise her. But now she saw it for the insanity it had been. Funny how, now that she was dying, so much became clear to her.

One fact stood clear of all the rest. She'd been a damned fool to love Alex Peters.

IN FORTY-FIVE MINUTES, Alex had enough chips to buy his way off the island even if he had to take less than legal means of transportation. He tossed a hefty chip to the dealer and took the rest of his stack to the cashier's window. No sense getting greedy and attracting too much attention to himself.

The hour was late, but he still caught a taxi downtown to the establishment of a jeweler who ran a lucrative side business forging international travel documents. The man was grumpy when Alex pounded on the back door at this hour, but let him in when he saw the wad of cash in Alex's fist.

It would take the forger overnight to work up a throwaway passport and fake visa, so Alex headed back to the beach to hit up a couple more casinos for the funds to pay for the documents. Prices had gone up since the last time he'd been down here.

He made drive-by hits on three casinos before he figured he had better not press his luck any further. He took his winnings and retreated to a hotel room to clean up and sleep off the past two days.

KATIE JOLTED AWAKE when something bumped the side of her dinghy. Crap. Was that a shark? She'd heard they rammed stuff they were curious about.

"Anyone home?" a voice called.

"Yes! I'm here!" She tore back the tarp and reeled back at the sight of a fat rubber bulge right in her face. A man peered over the edge of it. "Who are you?" she asked cautiously.

"The United States Navy at your service, ma'am."

"Omigod, am I glad to see you."

"Folks usually are, ma'am. If you'd give me your hand, I'll help you into our vessel."

She clambered over the edge of the bigger inflatable boat and envied the guy his wetsuit. A second man was seated in the back of the craft at the controls of an outboard motor. This fellow tossed her a wool blanket, which she eagerly wrapped around herself.

"You wanna save your dinghy?" the first guy asked.

"Not particularly." She flinched at the speed with which he whipped out a huge knife and slashed her little lifeboat to ribbons. God. Had her life depended on something so fragile? After-the-fact terror rattled through her.

As her raft disappeared into the murky depths, the rescue craft made a sharp turn and accelerated toward another vessel. A honking huge gray ship. She recognized the lines of a destroyer. Wow. André had sent the U.S. Navy after her, huh? Cool.

Not surprisingly, the crew aboard the destroyer gave her plenty of curious looks as they opened a waterline hatch and helped her aboard. She was hustled up to an infirmary not unlike the one on the *Caelum,* but many times larger. The corpsman who examined her declared her unharmed by her adventure. She was given a dark blue hoodie sweatshirt and matching sweatpants and led to a small cabin somewhere in the belly of the ship.

The sailor who escorted her to her room informed her that a helicopter would airlift her to Miami in the morning. Thank God. She was ready to be done with boats and water for a good long time. A sailor she was *not.*

ALEX GAVE A mental sigh of relief as the customs agent handed his passport and visa back to him. Normally, he would never travel on such hasty documents, but he was in a hurry to eliminate the last obstacles to a clean break with his past life.

He'd lost two days to travel: one to waiting for the passport to be made, and then another one flying south to Caracas. There were no direct flights between Cuba and the United States, which had necessitated the intermediate stop. He'd had to spend the night in Venezuela before he caught a morning flight to Miami. He would go on to Washington in a few hours.

The sharp knives of his paranoia were dulling slightly, but the certainty that he was being watched and that his watchers meant him harm remained. Soon. Soon all the loose ends would be tied up, and Alex Peters would be no more.

He supposed it was a little extreme, but what choice did he have? Until everyone stopped chasing him, he would never be safe. He dawdled in a bar until his flight was ready to board. He sat down, buckled in and closed his eyes.

Katie. How was he going to deal with Katie? His initial plan had been to kill her. But now he wasn't so sure about that. It would draw a lot of attention to him. And her brothers could be a problem if they decided to come after him. There were a lot of McCloud boys, and they were a dangerous bunch. He would hate to have to kill them all.

And what about Dawn? He could snatch her and take her with him now, but it would make establishing a cover exponentially harder with a toddler in tow. Better to run alone, set up a new life and retrieve her later.

But that left the question of Katie still looming. Katie, who had betrayed him and handed him over to the government without a second thought. She really did deserve the worst he could do to her. Not to mention it would be immensely satisfying to hurt her as deeply as she had hurt him. Which left only one burning question in need of an answer.

To kill her or not to kill her?

CHAPTER FOURTEEN

KATIE LET HERSELF into the penthouse apartment cautiously. The interior was dark and cool. Silent. She let out the breath she was holding. That was relief deflating her lungs like that, right? She was furious at him. No disappointment whatsoever, darn it.

André had been adamantly opposed to her coming back here when he'd debriefed her earlier. She still couldn't believe that Alex had turned out to be so unstable. And selfish. What a bastard. But André had regretfully informed her that the CIA assessment of him was that he had snapped. He could not be trusted. They'd declared him a rogue agent, armed and extremely dangerous.

If Alex was as crazy as they said he was, no way would he come back here. Right? It was the one place people knew to look for him. He would avoid his home like the plague.

Part of her wished he would show up here. That he would come looking for her to explain himself and to apologize. There must have been a reason he'd ditched her in Cuba not once but twice. Her initial fury had given way to grief. She'd really loved him. But he'd made his lack of return feelings crystal clear to her.

Strange how love could transform to hatred like this. She really, actively despised him for up and leaving her.

Wiped out after all the travel and long hours of debriefing in exhaustive detail with André, she crawled into the master bed.

Fortinay had been deeply disappointed when she failed to produce any proof of chemical weapons stockpiles in Cuba. But all of the samples had ended up with Alex. At this point, she expected he'd destroyed them all.

At least she was able to describe in exact detail where the bunker was located. They'd even pulled up a live satellite feed and had her zoom in on the spot. It had been creepy to look at the Zacara factory, the dirt road and that innocuous grassy mound. It was all so vivid in her mind, but it was starting to take on a dreamlike quality as it slipped into the past.

She supposed the CIA would send more operatives down to check the place out since she and Alex had failed. At least they'd brought out intel that the chemicals were there. That was something. If Alex were here, he'd call her a Pollyanna for thinking like that. The loss of him was a sharp pain in her chest.

As exhausted as she was, she tossed and turned, her thoughts churning around in her head. Maybe that was why she heard the front door locks disengaging. She rolled out of bed and to her feet in one fluid move.

No lights came on in the condo, and her internal threat sensors went on high alert. Alex or someone here innocently would have turned on the lights. Wait. It was after midnight; no one innocent was here.

A dark figure moved stealthily through the bedroom door. She slipped out of her hiding place behind the door and jammed her pistol against the man's spine. She ordered, "Freeze."

The intruder froze, and at the same moment, recognition of his height, silhouette and the scent of his aftershave registered. *Alex.* "Gotcha. I win," she said dryly.

Except she didn't win. He simultaneously dropped to his knees, spun around and surged up from below, ripping the pistol out of her hand and slamming her backward against the wall with a forearm across her neck. She glared at him disbelievingly. He'd just attacked her. *Oh, no, he didn't.*

Oh, yes, he did.

Her fury blazed and she let it. "What the hell are you doing here?" she snarled past his forearm.

"What the hell are *you* doing here?" he demanded. "This is my home."

"Not for much longer, it isn't. The entire CIA is looking for you. You're done, Alex."

He snorted. In the darkness, his teeth flashed momentarily in a hint of sardonic amusement.

She supposed he had a right to be amused. She doubted they would catch him if he didn't want to be caught, either. "What are you doing here?" she challenged.

"Taking care of a few loose ends before I disappear."

"Is that what I am? A loose end?" Her voice rose. "Why did you abandon me in Cuba?"

"They sent you down there to spy on me. And then you betrayed me."

"I never betrayed you!" she exclaimed. She reached out to activate the light switch. She wanted to look him in the eye when he spouted that crap at her. Small halogen spotlights created strategic pools of light around the room. Alex, who happened to be near one of the bright circles of light thrown down by the halogen spotlights, looked like hell. It wasn't so much that he needed a shave or that his clothes looked like he'd slept in them. It was his eyes that staggered her.

They were chock-full of barely restrained violence. He looked like his usual tight control was on the verge of failing catastrophically. He was a man on a bridge. But he wasn't there to jump. He had an Uzi and was about to start shooting everything and everyone who crossed his path. Her Alex was nowhere to be seen in the hot stare of this operative.

Funny, she'd thought his cold stare and icy focus were scary. But this volatile version of Alex was a hundred times scarier.

She ground out more unconvincingly than she'd hoped for, "I would never betray you, Alex." She would have added that she had loved him before she hated him, but there was no telling how Alex in this furious frame of mind would react.

He snorted. "That's your opinion. But I was the one interrogated and drugged. You had free rein to roam around the base and magically come to my rescue."

"There was nothing magic about it," she gasped as his arm got heavier on her neck, partially cutting off her air. "I was scared to death and had to be creative and sneaky. I climbed out a window and stole a woman's purse and had to sneak around a building crawling with Marines, thank you very much."

"You. With no training whatsoever. You want me to believe you pulled off a daring rescue at the last second before they loaded me up with scopolamine and made me spill my guts to them."

"Yes. I do." He snorted under his breath, and she added indignantly, "You're not the only resourceful, creative person on earth, you know. I happen to be able to solve problems and think outside the box, too. And if you're too big a chauvinist or have your head shoved up your ass too far to recognize that about me, then I guess you don't deserve my love."

He rolled his eyes at her grand declaration like a total jerk. "I'm neither stupid nor gullible enough to believe you miraculously rescued me. I never should have trusted you. My father always said never to let a woman past your guard. I guess he knew what he was talking about."

"Whatever the hell happened between him and your mother doesn't have to ruin your relationships with women forever, you know."

"Cut the psychobabble. I don't have time for it. And I don't have time for you. You always did slow me down." He shoved away from her and she coughed as she rubbed her throat.

Ouch. It was true that she slowed him down, but

it still hurt to hear him say it so baldly. She'd hoped he would put up with her because she loved him and he cared for her a little. Apparently not. Grief tore through her, but she brutally shoved it aside and, instead, let her fury have free rein. This was likely the last time she would ever see Alex. Her last shot at making him see he was wrong about her.

"Alex. When have I ever given you reason to believe I'm anything but totally loyal to you, first and foremost?"

"Never. Which is damned suspicious, don't you think?" He moved across the room and opened a long trunk at the foot of his bed. No surprise, it held an array of weapons in custom-made trays. He lifted them out onto the bed and surveyed the arsenal.

She spoke to his rigid back. "So, if I had acted disloyal you wouldn't have trusted me, and if I act loyal now, you distrust me even more? That makes no sense. Since when is the brilliant scholar, Alex Peters, ever illogical? Think, Alex. Get off this emotional roller coaster of yours long enough to ask yourself what's wrong with you."

He whipped around to face her. "Nothing's wrong with me. I'm exactly the creature you all made me into."

She stepped into his line of sight, forcing him to acknowledge her whether he liked it or not. "I have never tried to make you into anything. I loved you just the way you were." Past tense.

He stared at her for a moment as if he'd caught the past tense in her words. Maybe that was even a little shock passing through his silver stare. But then he whirled away and headed for his closet. Dammit. She thought she might have gotten through to him there, for a second.

If he wouldn't talk about his feelings, maybe he would at least explain to her what the hell had happened on the mission. "Why did you bail out on me in Cuba, Alex?"

He emerged from his spacious closet with a suitcase, which he opened on the bed. He began removing clothing from dresser drawers and layering the bag with weapons, ammunition and apparel. "I never bailed out on you," he eventually answered.

"You most certainly did. Twice! You made me go to Gitmo alone, and then you ditched me in that café in Guantánamo. Why?"

"It's what spies do," he snapped. "They cut their losses and run."

"Don't throw platitudes at me. I want a real answer."

"Platitudes? Coming from you, that's hilarious," he bit out.

"What are you talking about?"

"You and your entire family are a walking platitude. You believe that anything American is better than everything else in the whole damned world. You're so blinded by your loyalty to the Stars and Stripes that you can't see how your government really rolls even if its crap is stinking right under your nose. Look at me, Katie. Your precious Uncle Sam has turned me into a killer. Is that the work of a noble and honorable entity?"

She stared at him in dismay. "Knowing how to kill does not make you a killer."

"What the hell do you think I did during my training? Sit around crocheting doilies? I not only killed once, I killed multiple times. In cold blood. I snuck up on living, breathing people and murdered them at the behest of your precious government."

She reeled in shock. Is *that* what had him so messed up? No wonder he was imploding. "The way I understand it from my brothers, it's not murder if you're following a legal order."

He made a sound of disgust. "You seriously think you can split semantic hairs over killing human beings? Are you really that naive?"

"I'm not naive," she retorted hotly. "I get that killing other people is a heinous burden to bear. I've watched my dad and my brothers bear it, thank you very much. I know the toll it takes on them. So don't talk to me about being naive. We're talking about you, here. Pollyanna though it may be, I do believe that sometimes legitimate, decent, well-meaning governments have to eliminate certain threats if we're all to be safe. It's not pretty, but it's reality."

He disappeared into the bathroom and emerged with a handful of toiletry items he stuffed in around the corners of his bag.

"You know the drill as well as I do," she tried. "If you didn't do the job, somebody else would have. If I know you, Alex, you did your best to make clean kills that caused no suffering."

He didn't answer, but his jaw did ripple angrily.

"You don't have to punish yourself for doing your job. There are people you can talk to. Who can help you work out your feelings. A couple of my brothers have done it."

"I don't need counseling," he burst out.

"From where I'm standing, it looks like you do," she replied as calmly as she could muster. "It looks to me like you're going to great lengths to deny yourself happiness, to punish yourself."

"You're the one not being honest, Katie. I know who and what I am. You, on the other hand, are deluding yourself."

About him or about herself? Sadly, she asked him, "Do you hate yourself so much that you're willing to cut me out of your life rather than allow yourself to love anyone?"

He didn't bother to answer. He merely threw her a derisive look that spoke volumes.

Her spine stiffened. "You really don't deserve me, do you?"

For an instant, something like pain crossed through Alex's cold stare. But then the shutters closed again.

Something snapped inside her. He was being an idiot, plain and simple. She battered against his internal barriers without much hope of breaking through, but she had to try. "You're so convinced that any show of emotion is a sign of weakness that you can't let yourself experience the most basic and simple of human emotions. I see a pitiful, broken human being when I look at you, Alex Peters, not some tough-as-nails superspy. You're nothing more than a scared little boy running around trying to convince everyone else of how terrible you are. And you're failing. Do you hear me? You've failed."

Waves of icy rage poured off him but she was too infuriated to care at this point. How dare he walk out on her like this?

"Here you go, running away from home again. This is the cowardly act of a child, Alex."

He zipped the suitcase closed and set it on the floor by the door. He whirled so fast that she recoiled in spite of herself, and snarled right in her face. "You are an anchor around my neck, and furthermore, you betrayed me. I do not trust you. You do not deserve my love. I'm *finished* with you."

He grabbed the suitcase and stormed out of the bedroom, leaving her to stare at the empty doorway and struggling to draw her next breath. He was gone. Really, truly gone. It was as if the earth had fallen out from under her feet and she was plunging downward into a bottomless abyss that would never end.

It was so tempting to let her knees buckle. To fall to the floor and curl up in a little ball and never uncurl. Blackness closed in around her heart, so dark and thick she didn't think she would ever find her way out of it. But from somewhere deep, deep inside her a kernel of determination remained.

Dammit, she was a McCloud. A fighter. She might have lost the man, but she wasn't about to let him leave thinking she'd betrayed him. She would never betray a friend, let alone the man she had loved. He bloody well did *not* get to have the last word this time.

She ran after him, but he'd already left the apartment. Crap, he was fast. She threw open the front door. The elevator was on its way downstairs already. She headed for the stairwell and flew down it, taking huge chunks of steps with every bound. This was her last chance to have her say. Once he left the building, she would never find him again.

She tore out into the lobby with the intent to head for the driveway to block his car from leaving the parking garage. But as she raced outside, she spotted his silhouette striding down the street. He was on foot. She tore after him.

"Alex Peters! I have one more thing to say to you!" she shouted.

She heard the gunshot, a sharp clear sound piercing the silent night. Felt something hot slam into her chest. Was aware of being spun around and thrown into the door at her back. Registered the sound of shattering glass and remembered the pavement rising up to meet her.

But then everything started to fade, gray heading toward black. And truth be told, she was kind of glad for that. She probably couldn't have watched Alex walk out of her life for good, anyway. Poor Dawn. Poor Alex. Who would love either one of them now?

CHAPTER FIFTEEN

AT THE SOUND of the gunshot, Alex spun down behind a car and whipped out his pistol. Sonofabitch. He'd been so furious with Katie he'd barged out here right into the damned line of fire. Of course, the CIA had sharpshooters out here to take him down.

He scanned the rooftops looking for sniper perches. Where were the sight lines to him? Too many. He had to move to better cover. He spied a vestibule to the building next to his about twelve feet away. He could make it. He gathered himself, sprang forward and dived low, rolling into the deep doorway.

Huh. No gunshot. Why hadn't the sniper taken the shot? Surely the guy'd had time to get a bead on him and knew Alex would head for better cover quickly.

He eased forward, staying in the shadows, but close enough to the street to scan the area. If there was a shooter out there, the guy was hidden too well for him to spot. Deep, waiting silence settled over the street.

Into the night, he heard a faint sound. A moan.

He was not a trauma surgeon for nothing. He'd heard that sound a thousand times. A semiconscious person in severe pain. Who in the hell was moaning out here…?

Knowing exploded across his brain with the force of the gunshot. *Katie.* The shooter had taken out Katie. The bastard was using her as bait to draw him out.

He should walk away from here. Let her bleed out. He owed her nothing. He wasn't a gullible amateur to fall for such a thing. And yet, he checked out a route back to his building's entrance that would give him maximum cover. *What the hell.* The act of moving back toward her should cause the sniper to take another shot at him and reveal his position.

He darted from the safety of the doorway to the side of a parked car. No shot. Hmm. The sniper must be off to the side and not have a clear shot yet. Alex moved behind a steel trash can built around a tree trunk. He had significantly less cover here. The shooter should be able to get a bead on him from most of the street now. He braced for the hit, covering his head with his arms to prevent an outright kill shot.

Still no shot. What was up with that?

He looked around and spied Katie lying facedown in a spray of broken glass. Blood was spreading from underneath her, a river of red among the crystalline shards.

Frowning, he moved away from the trash can toward her prone form. Why was the shooter waiting? Surely there was a sanction out on him by now, a kill-on-sight order. Even if the order was just to bring him in, they had to know he was armed and dangerous. At a minimum, any half-decent sniper would want to wing him. To drop him and take him out of commission. And yet, no shot was forthcoming. Had the sniper fled already?

Why in the world would the sniper shoot Katie and then leave the area without shooting him, too? Unless…

Oh, holy God. No. Swearing violently, Alex moved over to Katie fast and rolled her over. She was bleeding from a wound in the upper left quadrant of her chest.

He worked quickly, his movements practiced as he ripped away her shirt to expose what turned out to be two wounds—an entry and an exit wound. He used the torn cloth to fashion makeshift pressure pads. Pressing down hard on the wounds and making her moan more loudly, he used his left hand to pull his necktie free. He bound the pressure pads in place rapidly, and then grabbed her arms and hoisted her over his back in a fireman's carry.

He took off jogging down the street toward a major thoroughfare. When he reached it, he started watching for a taxi and urgently hailed the first one he saw.

The cabbie slowed and rolled down his window to yell, "Hey, buddy. I've got a fare, but I'll radio for another cab to head over here!"

Alex nodded his thanks and kept moving. Mustn't stop. Mustn't make himself and Katie any easier targets than they already were. God, he felt naked out here like this. Every cell in his body screamed for him to take cover. To go into full stealth mode. But Katie was shot and unconscious, and he had no choice but to run along a damned city street for all the world to see.

That fucker had shot at Katie.

Why in bloody hell was *she* the target and not him?

As desperate as he was to get the hell away from her, his gut told him it was vital to answer that question before he disappeared. *Goddammit.*

KATIE WOKE UP SLOWLY. Her left shoulder felt like it had been smashed with a baseball bat. It throbbed horribly and felt stiff and swollen. She reached for it but her right hand encountered tape....

Her eyes flew open and she craned to look down at herself. *A bandage?*

She looked around. She was lying in a double bed in a plainly furnished room. It didn't look like a hotel room or a hospital. Someone moved beyond the doorway and she sat up carefully. Crap. The room spun around her for several unpleasant seconds. It finally settled down and she stood up cautiously. No more whirligig, thank God.

She felt strangely weak and light-headed as she shuffled to the doorway and peered out. A plain living room furnished with only a sofa, coffee table and television on a stand unfolded before her. There was no carpet on the dirty wood floor, and plastic roller blinds on the windows were pulled down.

Off to one side a small, dingy kitchen was visible. She caught movement in there and headed for it.

Alex looked up from a glass of orange juice he'd just poured. "How do you feel?" he asked emotionlessly. Professionally. Like a doctor talking to a patient.

"Like crap."

"Drink this. You lost a fair bit of blood."

"What happened?"

"Sniper took a shot at you. An inch lower and he'd have killed you. Must've been a long-range shot for him to have missed. You should be dead."

That last sentence was delivered with all the sympathy of a robot. Which was almost more upsetting than the news that she'd been shot. She'd almost died, apparently, and even that wasn't enough to break through the damned walls Alex had thrown up against her. He really was lost to her, after all. The grief of it hurt almost worse than her wounds. She took the juice and downed it all.

"More?" he asked.

"Yes, please."

"How's the pain on a scale of one to ten? Can you function?"

Seriously? He could make polite doctor conversation with her like he wasn't shattering her world with every unemotional, detached word he uttered? She forced herself to consider his question. "A six. It hurts a lot, but if I had to walk or run, I probably could for a little ways. Where are we?"

"Safe house."

"Still in Washington?"

"Close by."

"You have a safe house in Washington in addition to your fortress of a condo?" she asked, startled.

"Never can be too careful."

"Or paranoid."

"It's not paranoia if people are really shooting at you."

She rolled her eyes at him.

"Speaking of which, who's shooting at you?" He turned fully to face her and met her gaze directly for the first time.

"They were shooting at me?" she echoed blankly.

He nodded once, tersely. "I gave the bastard a clear shot at me and he didn't take it. The sniper was definitely targeting you. Probably thinks he killed you, too."

"Um, that's good?" she tried.

"It is good. Gives us a window to figure out who in the hell sent someone to kill you before they come after you again."

"They'll come after me again?" she squeaked.

He made a "don't be stupid" face at her. Okay, she deserved that. If she were under orders to kill someone and realized she had failed, she would go back to finish the job off. She sighed. "Unlike you, I don't have a long list of enemies eager to do me in."

"Do you have any enemies at all?" he asked a shade derisively.

"Actually, no. I mean, there were a couple bitches in high school who hated my guts for no apparent reason, but I highly doubt any ex-hormonal teens are climbing on rooftops and taking potshots at me after all this time."

"This is serious," he snapped.

"I am being serious," she snapped back. "Kindergarten teachers don't run around making mortal enemies."

"Apparently, you do."

"This isn't about Dawn again, is it?"

"Doubtful. I called your dad while you were sleeping. He said there's been no unusual activity up their way. He had a couple of your brothers come over to the house to beef up security around Dawn for now."

Wow. That was actually pretty thoughtful of him. So unlike him in his current asshole-ish frame of mind. "Uh, thanks," she mumbled.

He shrugged.

"Don't attempt to use your left arm or move it. The bullet passed through just above your left lung and below the shoulder joint. You were lucky the guy didn't use a hollow point round. The exit wound in your back is only a few millimeters larger than the entry wound, so I'm guessing he went with a Teflon-tip bullet. Which means we're looking at a pro. Snipers prefer hard-tip shells—they fly truer."

She truly did not care what type of bullet had nearly killed her. At the moment she was less interested in his spy self than his doctor self. "What did you do to fix my shoulder?" she asked.

"Cleaned the wound mostly. Had to cauterize a small artery and then stitch it all up. You really were incredibly lucky."

Yeah. Incredibly lucky that a trauma surgeon with tons of experience treating gunshot wounds happened to be a few yards away from her when she got shot. Incredibly lucky that he had actually turned around and came back to help her. Incredibly lucky that he kept a crash pad nearby and usually traveled with a wide array of medical gear in his luggage.

"Thanks for saving me, Alex."

His answer was quick. Sharp. "Don't thank me. I only came back because I thought the sniper was using you as bait. I needed him to take another shot so I could get a position fix on him."

Jerk. But after her reflexive reaction, she paused to actually consider what he'd said, tilting her head to study him. Was he being honest, or was he just covering up the fact that he'd cared enough about her to come back for her?

God, he was harder to read than ever. She was really getting tired of that cold shell the real Alex was hiding behind. Assuming this robot of a man wasn't the real Alex nowadays.

"Now what?" she asked.

One corner of his mouth turned up reluctantly. She supposed it was just like old times for her to be asking him that.

He answered, "Now I do some poking around. Figure out who wants you dead."

"What kind of poking around?"

"Computer poking to start with." To that end, he moved past her, being careful to avoid physical contact. Was he being considerate of her injured shoulder, or was he just loath to touch her?

Frowning, she followed him into the living room. He sat down on the sofa, propped his feet on the coffee table and cranked up a laptop computer.

"Can I help poke?" she asked reluctantly. She was still furious with him, but the guy had saved her life. It was hard to hate him after that.

He shook his head absently, already typing away. Truth be told, he probably did know just about every important detail of her life already. Her life was pretty simple, and she'd always been an open book to him.

She picked up the TV remote off the coffee table and channel-surfed, bored. Every now and then a sharp pain knifed through her shoulder, but she suffered in silence. She'd be damned if she'd whine to Alex Peters. Sometimes, having the McCloud stubborn streak truly sucked.

In between dealing with the bouts of pain, she fretted over Alex's earlier accusations back at the condo. She was an anchor around his neck? He'd been wrong to trust her? She'd betrayed him? She didn't have the first idea how to convince him he was wrong, now that he'd fixed the ideas in his head as fact.

Personally, she didn't think she'd performed too badly in Cuba. Things had gotten pretty dicey there for a while, and she'd followed his instructions and pulled her weight while they were together. She had managed to make her way to Guantánamo all by herself, too, which was no small feat. And then there was his rescue. Although it was probably an unrepeatable, minor miracle that she'd pulled it off, still, she'd pulled it off.

Now that she stopped to think about it, she hadn't done half-bad for being just a kindergarten teacher. A trained field operative couldn't have done much better. "Tell me, Alex. How could I have performed any better than a trained spy in Cuba? I stayed alive, I didn't get you killed and, furthermore, I managed to rescue you. What else did you want from me?"

He stared at her silently, a stubborn look on his face. She would take that as tacit admission that she had a point.

As for the rest of it, the not trusting her and believing so easily that she would betray him—those accusations concerned her more. They spoke to his core distrust of all women. She was more convinced than ever that she *had* to find his mother and unravel that mystery if she was ever to salvage him from the morass of his broken soul. Of course, he would tell her to forget trying. To let him stew in his own private corner of hell.

It was tempting to walk away from him. His problems loomed larger than she felt like she could conquer. And his verbal attack earlier at the condo had been almost more than she could absorb. She might have been strong enough to save his life in Cuba, but she doubted she was strong enough to save his soul.

But then he had to go and save her life. To come back for her after she was shot. The McCloud men took owing someone their life pretty seriously. And no surprise, it turned out she felt the exact same way. Even if Alex was doing his best to deny the debt she owed him.

How could one man send so damned many mixed messages in so short a time? She fell asleep fretting about it on her end of the sofa and without finding any answers.

WHEN SHE WOKE UP, the apartment was silent and dark, lit only by the flickering light of the television. Alex was nowhere in sight. Alarmed, she bolted to her feet and raced for the bedroom.

She skidded to a stop in the doorway, her shoulder screaming in protest. He was sprawled across the bed, his naked, muscular back as beautiful as a statue in the peachy streetlight coming in the window. An alarm clock beside the bed said it was a little before 6:00 a.m.

Restless and uncomfortable, she gave up on sleeping and pulled on a turtleneck shirt she found in Alex's backpack. It was big on her and she had to roll up the sleeves. But it fit over her bulky bandages. She found a notebook and tore out a piece of paper. She laid it on the tile kitchen counter to write a note to Alex. That way, an impression of her note wouldn't be left in the notebook.

"I'm going out to take care of something important. I'll talk with you about it when I get back. Please be here." She underlined the *please* and signed the note with a *K*.

She took her purse from the kitchen counter where Alex had left it. It must have been in the front pocket of her sweatshirt when she bolted from the condo last night. She crept out of the apartment quietly. Where was she? Thankfully, her cell phone, which had been in her jeans pocket, had a mapping application. It placed her in northern Virginia. She wandered a couple of blocks until she found a bus stop. It took studying the map inside the shelter to figure out how to get to Langley using public transportation, but in about an hour, she stepped off a bus a few blocks from CIA headquarters.

She called Uncle Charlie's cell phone, which he didn't answer, and left a brief message naming the coffee shop she was sitting in. A sparse early morning crowd stared at computer screens or read newspapers while they waited for paper cups of caffeine alertness to kick in. She finished with, "We need to talk. Off campus."

Her uncle surprised her by striding into the café not even a half hour later. Wow. That was fast. He wore a suit and tie beneath his dressy wool overcoat, too. Either she'd caught him on his way out the door to work, or else he'd rushed like a big dog to get over here to meet her.

He slid into a chair across from her at a tiny table. "What's up, Katie-kins?"

She noted that his lips barely moved. Was he worried that someone was watching them on a security camera? She did her best to emulate him, murmuring from behind a frozen half smile, "You tell me."

"What do you mean?"

She spoke low in deference to their public location. "I got shot last night. Was it your guy?"

He jolted at that. "No!" If that wasn't genuine surprise, he was a fantastic actor. "Are you okay, Katie?"

"I'm fine only because a trauma surgeon was there to take care of my injury."

"Mmm. Lucky," was Charlie's noncommittal answer.

"Alex said it was a pro. Used some sort of Teflon-tipped round preferred by snipers to shoot me."

"Christ, Katie. What's that all about? How are you, really?"

"I've been better, but I've been worse. Good news is I'll live. As for what it's about, that's what I'm hoping you can tell me."

"Thank God you're safe." He reached across the table to squeeze her hand in what she took as a real gesture of concern. Then he asked casually, "How was your trip?"

"Interesting. Did André tell you what we found?"

He frowned slightly. "No. Should he have?"

She lowered her voice further, even though no one was sitting near them. "I have no idea what your chain of command is. We found sarin. A lot of it. With Arabic labels. In a bunker."

Charlie went still and visibly paled before her eyes. He leaned forward to mutter low, "What proof is there?"

"None. We lost it on the way out. But we have pictures of victims and the barrels it's stored in. A whole bunker full of barrels, by the way. And Alex examined dozens of dead victims."

"And you told Fortinay about this?"

"Yes. We told him nearly a week ago."

Charlie's gaze went hard and angry. So. André, or André's boss, had kept that little bombshell under wraps, huh? Maybe they were waiting for the proof to come out of Cuba before they blew the lid off it. Or maybe the White House was using the time to prepare for the coming showdown with Cuba and big brother Russia. It was all way, way above her pay grade.

"Where's Alex now?"

"Safe house."

"Any idea at all who might have shot you?"

"None. I'm a kindergarten teacher, Uncle Charlie. I thought *you* might know."

His eyes, so like her mother's, were troubled.

Katie leaned forward across the tiny bistro table. "What can you tell me about something called Cold Intent?"

"Where on earth did you hear that?" he blurted.

"I read it. Alex doodled the words."

"Katie-kins, I'm urging you in the strongest possible terms to drop that line of inquiry. Do you hear me?"

"Y-yeah, sure," she stammered. "Consider it dropped."

Charlie exhaled in relief.

"Can I ask about Alex's mother and if you've turned up anything on her?"

Charlie's shoulders went rigid once more and he painted on a ghastly imitation of a smile. Whoa. What was up with Alex's mother that had him so freaked out?

He spoke so quietly she had to strain to hear him. "Claudia Kane. That was her name. She was American."

"Was? Is she dead?"

"Her file is closed."

God, she wished she knew how to interpret that. If only Alex were here to dig through the innuendo and doublespeak. She made careful note of Charlie's body language to describe to Alex later. Her uncle swallowed convulsively and wiggled an uncomfortable shoulder.

"How did she get to Moscow to meet Peter? Was she one of yours? Surely, she was. Civilian Americans didn't get into Russia easily at that time."

"Leave it alone, Katie."

"Why?"

"Because I'm asking you to."

"I'm sorry. That's not enough. Alex is falling apart, and he needs answers."

"Falling apart?" Charlie echoed in quick alarm.

She sighed. "Something happened to him at Gitmo. He was drugged, and he's been a little crazy ever since."

"What did they give him?" Charlie demanded.

"I don't know. The syringes I saw were filled with a pale yellow serum."

Her uncle frowned. "I've seen all the standard interrogation meds. Scopolamine and the other standard medications are colorless. Describe how he's crazy? Is he violent? Psychotic?"

"Nooo," she answered slowly. "I'd describe him as paranoid. Defensive. Angry. Maybe even a little schizophrenic."

"Those are not typical symptoms of truth serums. They're designed to lower inhibitions, not raise false ones. Sounds like they hit him with a mind-altering substance of some kind."

"They who?" she demanded low and urgent. "And why?"

Charlie opened his mouth to answer. Snapped it shut. *He knew.* But he wasn't going to tell her.

"Can you at least tell me how long the effects will last?" she pleaded.

"Stuff like that usually runs its course in about a week. Maybe two at the outside. Of course, it's possible for residual effects to persist for years or permanently."

"Don't tell me that," she groaned under her breath.

He shrugged apologetically.

"What more can you tell me about his mother, this Claudia Kane?"

"Nothing."

His eyes were wary. Guarded. He *so* knew more about Alex's mother than he was telling her. The woman was a CIA operative, or else her uncle was the tooth fairy.

"Was she a sparrow? Was she sent to Moscow to seduce Peter, or was that an unplanned side excursion in her mission?"

"You know I can't answer that, Katie."

But his gaze had flickered down and to the left evasively. She'd guessed correctly. Claudia had been a sparrow—an agent who used sex to compromise targets and to gather intelligence via pillow talk.

Charlie lifted his gaze, spearing her with an intense stare. "I'm telling you. Leave it alone, Katie. You have no idea who or what you're messing with."

She frowned, staring back questioningly. If she wasn't mistaken, he'd just warned her off more than Alex's mother. He'd warned her off all of it.

He gathered his hat and newspaper. "You'll send me those pictures, yes?"

That was an abrupt shift of topic. "Yes. Of course," she mumbled.

"We'll have to do this more often. It's delightful to see you again, Katie-kins." He startled her by leaning down to kiss her cheek affectionately.

"Be careful or people will think you're having an affair with a younger woman," she muttered.

He chuckled, put on his hat and turned to leave.

She stayed a few more minutes, finishing her coffee so it didn't look like they'd just come in here for an information trade. She'd picked up a few things from Alex, after all.

THE MAN IN the corner of the café with his nose buried in the business news glanced up briefly as Katie finally left the café and hurried away. He pulled out his cell phone and placed a phone call.

"Tell Reggie he missed last night." And knowing the sniper, the guy was going to get right tweaked about it, too.

The voice on the other end betrayed no hint of dismay, or any emotion at all, for that matter. "That's a shame. Where's the target now?"

"Moving east from here. On foot."

"Roger. Will acquire the target momentarily. No need to follow."

"Great," the man replied brightly. Frankly, he was surprised he wasn't receiving orders to follow the girl and clean up Reggie's mistake.

"Come in now. We need to revise the strategy."

"Ya think?" he retorted jokingly. "Okay, I'm outta here. I'll see you in a few." He picked up his gym bag. A metallic clank and its unusual weight were the only hint as to its lethal contents.

CHAPTER SIXTEEN

ALEX WAS FURIOUS. He'd risked his damn neck to save Katie and she'd pulled a runner on him? Her note notwithstanding, he had no faith she'd return.

He was so done with her. He was done with all of them and their damned head games. His computer beeped to indicate incoming email, and he opened the first one of two that caught his attention. It was a file from Blondie. She must have sent it before she died. It had a gigantic attachment. Had she sent him… He opened the email that went with it eagerly.

Cold Intent is some serious shit, dude. I think you need this hacking algorithm more than I do. You're gonna have to dig all the way to the bottom of the CIA cesspool to find what you're looking for. I got too spooked at what I was finding to keep going and backed out. Sorry, but you're gonna have to finish this research project on your own.

Swearing under his breath, he opened the second message, from C¥berE¥e, and decrypted it impatiently.

It was short. *You want me to sit on what you sent me? Are you shitting me? It's not dynamite. It's a fucking nuclear bomb.*

He sat down to type and encrypt his reply.

Our deal remains in place. If you don't hear from me for a week, send everything to every major newspaper on the planet. I'm sorry to drag you into this, but I needed somewhere fast and secure to send the data. I only need you to sit on it a few more days, until I don't need a dead man's switch anymore. Then you can destroy it all.

He hit the send button and leaned back, frowning at the blank screen. He ought to destroy the flash drive and its evidence of chemical weapons in Cuba right now. If it fell into American hands, a global crisis on the scale of the Cuban Missile Crisis would explode. And personally, he had little faith in today's politicians to get a solution right like Kennedy and Khrushchev had.

He stood up to go tear apart the flash drive and flush its pieces, but the doorknob rattled and he whirled and pulled his pistol instead. He waited tautly, his finger starting to squeeze through the trigger.

"Alex? It's me. Let me in."

Swearing under his breath, he moved to the door and threw the lock. He stepped off to one side, pistol at the ready in case she was not alone and being coerced.

Katie stepped through the door and started to close the panel behind her. He spun out of hiding and she jumped violently. "Holy crap. You scared the heck out of me, Alex!"

He straightened and lowered the gun. "Where were you?"

"I went to see my uncle."

Stunned, he burst out, “Why on God’s green earth would you go to Langley and lead the CIA right back here to me?”

“I was really careful to make sure I wasn’t tailed. I rode buses all over northern Virginia to be sure I was clean.”

“They don’t need to tail you on foot. The CIA has satellites and security cameras to do the job. We’ve got to get out of here immediately.”

She threw up her hands. “I have nothing but the clothes on my back. I’m packed and ready to go.”

He grabbed his backpack and tossed his computer into it. “C’mon. They’ll be here any second.”

She sucked in sharp breaths of pain between her teeth as he raced down the stairwell. Tough. It was her fault they had to flee this place. He ducked into the alley behind the building and used the skeleton key he’d made for the restaurant’s delivery door a few yards down the alley to open it. Katie slipped under his arm just as a whistling sound split the air. Sonofabitch. He shoved her inside and threw himself on top of her frantically.

A big explosion shook the building and stuff rattled on the shelves around them, raining down dust, but this building hadn’t been in the direct line of fire.

“Oww!” she complained beneath him. “And what was that?”

He pressed up onto his elbows and stared down at her. He registered her body’s welcoming softness and the way she fit him perfectly. He answered tightly,

"That was a rocket-propelled grenade. My safe house is probably a smoking hole right about now."

"Oh, my God. I'm so sorry—"

"Later." He pushed up and away from her. Damn, she'd felt good underneath him. Evil seductress—"Let's go." He dragged her to her feet by her good arm and peeked out of the storeroom into the restaurant kitchen. Empty. They wound through the place, unlocked the front door from inside and strolled out onto the street.

He did have to admit that she made for a good cover. Anyone who looked at her saw a perfectly normal young woman who wasn't the slightest bit suspicious or scary. If she ever decided to become a field operative, she'd make a good one. By association, she made him fit in with the normal world around them.

"Now what?" she asked on cue as they turned the corner and headed away from the mess of his life behind them. Sirens screamed in the distance. They had to be well clear of this area before it was crawling with cops and fire trucks.

"Now, we keep on walking. And we don't look back."

As darkness fell on a long, harrowing day, Alex finished searching a cheap motel room in Delaware for surveillance devices and sat down on the bed to think. He hadn't planned to disappear with Katie. He'd assumed she would choose to stay with Dawn if it came down to a choice between the two of them. He could respect that. The baby needed her more than he did.

Although sometimes he wondered about who was neediest—

He cut off the thought before it could finish forming in his head. He did not need relationships. He did *not* need her. Katie was a liability. End of discussion. Which meant he had to get rid of her, and sooner rather than later.

"Uncle Charlie told me your mother's name this morning."

He lurched around to face her and stared at her in shock. How in the hell had she pulled that off? He'd had the best hackers on the planet digging for years for information on his mysterious mother, and Katie had…what? Just waltzed into CIA headquarters and *asked?* Tension stretched his vocal cords taut. "Tell me."

"Her name is Claudia Kane. Charlie hinted that she's dead but wouldn't say so outright."

"Why would he tell you her name and not tell me?" Alex demanded.

"Have you ever just asked the CIA for her identity?"

He frowned and answered evasively, "She came up during my training. But they never told me anything about her." His mother had been the focus of a particularly nasty interrogation session involving car batteries and some of his rather tender body parts. The bastards had known he had no information whatsoever about her, but they'd tortured him, anyway, just to be sure he wasn't holding anything back.

She shrugged. “Before we left for Cuba, I asked Charlie to research her for me. For you.”

He had to give Katie credit for being honest. She hadn’t ducked the fact that she’d visited her uncle this morning, or that she’d been asking about his mother. One thing he had never doubted about her was her honesty. She had always been straight up with him, sometimes to her own detriment. Still, this news had him reeling. His mother, that faceless ghost who’d hovered over him his entire life, had a *name?* Was she coming forward? Was this a first step by her to approach him? Eagerness and desperate need raged in his stomach at the idea of finally filling that gaping hole in his life. The emotions were too turbulent, too powerful, to shut away in a mental drawer. He tried, and failed to contain the glee and terror.

Appalled at his loss of control, he forced his mind back to the business at hand by sheer dint of will. Katie had asked about his mother before Cuba, huh? He blurted, “Did you inquire about her before or after that gunman took a potshot at you on the roof of the condo?”

“Before.” Katie threw him a wide-eyed look. “Do you think the attempts on my life are related to my asking about her?”

It was possible. Had the attacks not been about Cold Intent at all? Had they been purely about his mother? Which begged the question of why an inquiry about his mother had sent an assassin into action against Katie. It was hard to believe that Uncle Charlie would set up his own niece to be sanctioned for a hit.

His mother was alive and had a name. God, he wanted to talk to her. To get the answers that had taunted him with their absence for all these years. Why did she leave him? Did she love his father? *Did she love him?*

Alex ordered Katie, "Start at the beginning and don't leave out anything about your conversations with your uncle, no matter how small."

He listened intently as she described her two meetings with Charlie, the one before Cuba and the one this morning. Alex's first impulse was to be suspicious of the information. Why would the CIA cough it up to her, when they'd refused for all this time to tell him?

This was probably part of the grand manipulation of Alex Peters the CIA seemed to delight in playing at. Or maybe Uncle Charlie genuinely wanted to please his niece. It was possible, of course, that the information was caught up in some sort of internal power struggle within the agency. The CIA made a habit of hiring wolves, who in turn made a habit of fighting over turf. Was his mother just another bone being snarled and scrapped over within the wolf pack? Or was *he* the bone?

The questions swirled around him so thick and fast he hardly knew where to turn his attention. He felt out of control. Buffeted by hurricane-force confusion. Why were they doing this to him? Or was this about him at all? God, and he'd thought his CIA field training had been a mind-fuck. This was a thousand times worse. Who to trust? What to think? What to feel?

More agitated than he could ever remember being,

he pulled out his laptop and initiated a deep web search for information on one Claudia Kane. As he'd expected, there was nothing. As in *nothing.* Which was, in its own way, informative. In this day and age, nobody left absolutely zero trail of their existence. Not unless that trail had been professionally swept clean. Interesting.

If Katie's information was correct and his mother had been an American intelligence operative, the non-trail would make sense. Hell, Claudia Kane probably wasn't even her real name. He would have to dig into the CIA's computers if he wanted more. Or, of course, he could always ask Peter....

His train of thought derailed. Actually, that wasn't a half-bad idea. His father had never spoken of his mother. But then, Alex had never asked about her, either. It had always been understood between him and Peter that she was an off-limits topic of conversation.

Thoughtfully, he activated one of the burner phones in his pack and dialed his father's personal cell phone number.

"Son. To what do I owe this pleasure?" The connection was scratchy, but he could make out his father's voice, speaking in English. He replied in Russian. They were both cautious of wagging ears around them apparently.

"Tell me about my mother."

There was a long pause filled only with quiet static. Then, "Why?"

"Because I'm asking."

Peter's voice was heavy. "What do you want to know?"

"Was her name Claudia Kane?"

He thought he heard his father inhale sharply, but it was hard to tell over the poor connection. His father's answer was wooden. "That was a name connected to her, yes."

"Was she an American operative? A sparrow?"

"Yes and yes."

"Did she target you specifically?"

"I have always believed so, but I have no proof."

"So she didn't attempt to blackmail you or turn you?"

"No," Peter answered firmly. Okay, his father sounded like that was the truth. He never could be one hundred percent certain with Peter, but that was as close to sounding as if he was telling the truth as his old man ever got.

Alex asked reluctantly, "Did you have feelings for her, or was I a…business transaction?"

"I loved her. Never doubt that, my son."

"What about her?" Alex asked heavily. "Did she have feelings for you? Or were you just a job?"

"You would have to ask her."

"She's still alive, then?"

"As far as I know."

"C'mon, Father. That's the sort of thing you'd use your position to be certain of. I deserve to know the truth." When Peter did not reply, he added reluctantly, "My life may depend on knowing the truth."

"What's this?" his father burst out.

"Is she alive or not?"

"You'll tell me what's going on?" Peter challenged.

Alex closed his eyes tightly. That was all the answer he needed. His mother was alive. And a casual inquiry about her from Katie had elicited two sniper attacks. Not only was Claudia Kane still alive, she was still an active operative. And apparently, she or her superiors didn't appreciate somebody poking around into her existence.

"Do you know her real name?" Alex asked quietly.

"I do not know that she has a real name. She has moved from legend to legend over the years, and never retains any one identity for long."

"Do you know where she is now? What she's doing?"

"I'm sorry. I do not. Last I heard, she was directing an operation called Cold something. Our source only captured the first word of the name."

"Cold Intent?" Alex blurted. "I'd bet my life that's it. Hell, I *am* betting my life on it."

His *mother* was part of Cold Intent? He reeled in shock. What the hell was she doing with that bunch? Why would the woman who gave birth to him be out to kill his girlfriend? Surely, this Claudia Kane wasn't trying to keep other women from moving in on her son. He highly doubted the woman felt the slightest inkling of maternal protectiveness toward him. Otherwise, she never would have abandoned him with his father all those years ago.

"What's going on?" Peter asked urgently. "Tell me. I can help. You're my son. If you're in trouble, let me pull you out. I'll even bring out the girlfriend and the baby safely. You have my word on it."

"Thanks. But we're good for now. Anything you can find out about Claudia Kane or Operation Cold Intent would be helpful."

"Consider it done."

Alex sagged against the cheap headboard at his back. His old man might be an ass, but blood was thicker than water. When his son was in trouble, Peter could be counted on to come through for him. Yes, there would be strings attached to the help, and they would get tugged on later. But for now, his father would do his best to help him. But against what?

Peter was speaking again. "…about that other thing. I gather your abrupt exit from Cuba means you were able to bury anything…incriminating?"

Alex wasn't willing to give up that bargaining chip just yet. He trusted his father a little, but not *that* much.

Huh. And here he was right back up on that tightrope, teetering between his father and the CIA. Again. And this time a third factor was pushing and pulling at him. His flipping mother, of all people. How did he keep ending up caught in the middle like everyone's favorite tug toy?

He shook his head to clear it. He faked making a few static noises into the receiver and disconnected the call. Jerkily, he turned the phone over, pulled the battery and SIM card out and flushed the pieces down the toilet individually.

"Well?" Katie demanded impatiently.

"Get some sleep. I need to think."

She frowned unhappily, but disappeared into the bathroom. The toilet flushed and he heard the sounds of toothbrushing. She emerged wearing one of his T-shirts. Her legs were long and sleek, and the curves of her breasts soft and inviting under the cotton fabric.

"I've been honest with you, Alex, and now I need you to be honest with me."

Aw, hell. She wanted to talk about feelings again. It was a good interrogation tactic. Catch him when he was emotionally and mentally off balance. Drop a bombshell on him that his mother was alive and then move in for the kill when his defenses were down. His warning antennae wiggled wildly. He muttered cautiously, "You need me to be honest about what?"

"Guantánamo. What happened to you there?"

He swore mentally. It figured that she would want to dredge up all that crap. It was where he'd gone off the carefully prepared script the CIA had laid out for the two of them. He answered tersely, "I was drugged. You pulled me out. We each egressed the country."

"What drug did that doctor give you?"

He frowned. Actually, that was a good question. Dr. Doe had called one of the medications CCRE. He'd forgotten about it until now.

Quickly, he powered up his laptop and typed in the four letters. It took a little searching but finally a Department of Defense paper came up on the screen. Concentrated Cannabis Resin Extract.

"What's that?" Katie startled him by asking from over his shoulder. "Cannabis? They gave you *pot?*"

He scanned the medical paper quickly. "CCRE is

a highly concentrated and refined derivative of cannabis resin."

"Why on earth would they want to get you really, really stoned?"

He grinned in a flash of unwilling amusement. But his humor faded as he caught sight of the extract's main symptom.

Ever perceptive, Katie asked quickly, "What is it?"

He leaned back, staring at the screen. "CCRE is designed to provoke paranoid schizophrenic episodes."

"In English, please?"

"Put in lay terms, it's a mind-altering substance that makes a person fearful and distrustful of others. Makes them think someone's out to hurt or kill them."

"But I thought they were questioning you. Wouldn't they want you uninhibited and trusting so you'd tell them everything?"

"If that were the case, they'd have shot me up with scopolamine or some other truth serum–style drug."

"Why did they treat you like a criminal and not me?" she asked. "You're the government employee, after all. I'm the one they should have been really suspicious of. Was it because I'm a girl and you're a big, strong, dangerous man?"

She was as perceptive as always. He frowned thoughtfully at her. She'd asked a hell of a good question. Why hadn't they interrogated her? The obvious answer was that she was in on the scam.

But if that was the case, why would she point it out like this? A feint within a feint to throw him off her trail? Was she actually that subtle? Was he a gullible fool to have taken her at face value for all this time? Was she a great deal more than a civilian kindergarten teacher who loved him and was willing to lay her heart on the line for him openly and honestly?

God, he didn't know who to believe anymore. The maelstrom whirled around him more violently than ever. His mother. The CIA. Katie. His father. Cold Intent. Who else wanted a piece of his soul?

An urge to scream rose in his throat. Appalled, he bit it back. *Focus, Alex. Guantánamo. Follow Katie's line of reasoning and see where she's trying to lead you.*

There had been plenty of time for John Doe, his interrogator, to get instructions from Washington. John Doe couldn't possibly have had the rank or authority to decide to dope a U.S. intelligence operative for grins and giggles. The decision to drug him *had* to have come from Langley.

Why had the CIA been out to mess with him and not with Katie? Particularly since it seemed that someone within Langley pretty seriously wanted to see her dead. His suspicions from before roared to the fore once more. Was this all an elaborate head game designed to throw him violently off balance and off guard? But to what end? What did they want from him?

He looked up sharply as the computer lifted off his lap. Katie tossed a leg across his hips and straddled his lap. "What the hell are you doing?" he blurted.

"Getting your undivided attention." She pulled at his belt buckle, and it gave way under her fingers.

She was really raising the stakes now. What was her gambit? He braced to resist her sexual advances. He'd been trained in how to handle situations like this, but the hookers in his training hadn't been Katie. She was the one and only woman who'd ever managed to get inside his head.

He swore at himself. This was his fault. He'd let her past his guard. He'd set himself up for this. Was this what his mother had done to his father? No wonder Peter had fallen prey to her. Christ. He was lucky his old man even spoke to him, let alone raised him after this mind-fuck.

Katie wiggled suggestively, demanding his attention. He yanked his thoughts back to the woman stripping while she sat on his crotch. "So," he commented. "You're a sparrow, after all. I have to compliment you on your extraordinary acting talent."

She replied tartly, "I'm not a sparrow, and you, of all people, know it. You know how little sexual experience I had before I met you. No sparrow would be sent out in the field to use sex as a weapon with barely any knowledge of it."

He examined her logic as calmly as he could with her hands on his zipper. Reluctantly, he had to admit she had a point. He asked desperately, "Why is the CIA trying to kill you, but not the slightest bit interested in questioning you? Do you know something they don't want revealed?"

She sat back on his thighs, staring at him thoughtfully. "I do know *you* better than anyone else."

"Why would that alarm the CIA?" he asked reflexively.

"Is somebody trying to hide your real motives for joining Doctors Unlimited?" she asked slowly. "Or is this internal CIA politics? I've heard Charlie gripe about those before. Is someone engaging in a slam campaign against you that you're not aware of? Maybe someone's spreading lies about you and doesn't want me to tell the truth?"

"The CIA is not a high school lunchroom."

"No, but it is made up of human beings subject to human flaws and weaknesses," she retorted.

He knew he'd become a source of controversy in the agency after his training had finished. Some people saw him as a threat, and others saw him as an exciting weapon. Was all of this the two factions infighting over him? He mumbled under his breath, "How in hell am I supposed to know who's my friend and who's my enemy?"

"I am not the enemy, Alex." His zipper slid down and his fly melted back under her hands.

He ought to stop her.

"I'm not out to hurt you in any way," she murmured. "I only want to help you. I'm loyal to you. Only you."

If only. At least she was a known enemy. He could deal with that.

Her clever fingers dipped inside the waistband of his underwear and grasped his member in a warm fist. Blood rushed to the site and his hips flexed of their own volition. Dammit.

"Do you hear me?" she demanded. "I'm on your side."

He had to keep his head clear. He couldn't afford to get lost in her body or sucked into the emotional vortex she always managed to create around him when they had sex.

"They gave you drugs to make you suspicious of me. But you know, don't you, that I would never hurt you." Her fingers tightened around his rapidly hardening erection, and a groan escaped his throat before he could pull it back. His mental swearing grew more violent as her fist slid up and down his shaft. Damn, that felt good.

"Say it, Alex. Tell me you know I would never hurt you."

He surged up beneath her, capturing her around the waist with his arm while he used his free hand to yank her hand off him. He ground out, "You think you can use sex as a weapon against *me?*"

"Go ahead, Alex. Show me how you really feel."

She was courageous to taunt him like that. With a growl, he sprawled on his back, carrying her down on top of him, then rolled over, until she splayed beneath him. He pinned her to the lumpy mattress with his bigger, stronger body, and she didn't struggle. He shoved the T-shirt up her naked body, not stopping until the gray cotton completely covered her face. She wouldn't have any trouble breathing through it, but he had to shut her up. She was pushing him beyond his ability to control himself.

He ought to kill her. Any spy worth his salt would

eliminate the threat she posed without a second thought.

He only kicked partially free of his jeans before he rammed into her. She bucked against him, driving him deeper inside her. He groaned in spite of himself, and just like that, her body softened and opened, welcoming him home. Dammit, she made it impossible to use sex as a weapon against her when she surrendered unconditionally to him like this!

Swearing violently inside his head, he paused to strip off his clothes. And then he sank into her again. As always, her complete welcome and acceptance undid him, unraveling his rage as easily as a piece of knitting.

The probability that this was the last time he would ever have sex with her slammed into his awareness and he involuntarily slowed down to savor the moment and imprint it upon his memory forever.

He couldn't look her in the face. It would be too painful for him to see the deceit there. This one last time, lost in the depths of his desperation, he needed to pretend she really loved him. He planted his hands on either side of the T-shirt fabric and pinned it lightly over her face in place in hopes that it would help distance her from him, but it didn't. Everything he'd loved about her—her generosity, honesty, innocence and joy in life—wrapped around him, embracing his heart and bathing him in love until he couldn't fight it off anymore.

She was better at her job than he could have ever

imagined any sparrow being. Was it possible she was telling the truth—

No. Impossible. She was in on the conspiracy. She *had* to be.

As an orgasm built fast in his belly, a mirroring explosion of emotion built in his chest. She arched up into him, her body sucking him down effortlessly into the whirlpool of everything he'd tried so hard to avoid. Feelings broke over him, drowning him in gratitude and regret, affection and reluctant acceptance. Of being lovable and loved.

For just a breath of time, he didn't care if she was working against him or not. She owned his heart. He could not believe he was going to have to turn his back on this. On her. It was going to feel like ripping his heart out of his chest to leave her and Dawn behind forever.

Their lovemaking reached an exquisite peak and his body clenched around his release. He couldn't hold back a muffled shout as the orgasm tore free of his control and exploded from the depth of his being.

Stunned at the power of it, he stared down at the sweet contours of Katie's covered face. As he watched, a small circle of wetness appeared in the center of Katie's forehead, darkening the gray cotton. Swearing, he pushed away from her and rolled out of bed, swiping at his eyes. He did not cry. Not for her. Not for himself. Not ever.

He stormed into the bathroom and ran himself a steaming hot shower. It pounded his flesh into gelatin but did nothing to soothe the fury tearing apart his heart. Nothing could soothe it.

When he came out of the bathroom, Katie was dressed and curled up in a chair, going through the motions of reading a book on her cell phone.

Devastated at how easily she'd apparently disengaged from the overwhelming emotional power of their lovemaking, he pulled out his laptop and read up some more on the drug he'd been given. So much about the end of his Cuba mission made sense now. The fog of terror, the extreme measures he'd taken to hide and to escape Katie—he'd been flailing in an artificially induced paranoid state. He hadn't been losing his mind, after all.

Small comfort, that.

Thing was, the CCRE was well clear of his system by now. Any paranoia or suspicion he was experiencing currently was wholly his own. His doubts about Katie were not drug induced. None of it was drug induced.

Absently, he fiddled with the flash drive he'd brought out of Cuba. The one holding all the evidence of the chemical weapons secretly stored in Cuba.

"Oh, my God!" Katie exclaimed without warning. "Is that what I think it is?"

He jammed the drive back in his pocket. "Depends on what you think it is."

"Is that your pictures from Cuba? Did you manage to run the samples we got from that bunker? Are the results on that drive, too?"

"It's nothing," he lied. "Just some personal information I'll need to set up a new identity."

"Bull," she retorted bluntly. "That's the evidence of the sarin."

He didn't bother denying it. She knew him too well for him to successfully lie to her.

She demanded, "Why do you still have it? Weren't you going to hand that over to André?" She paused, but then continued in a breathless rush, "Are you using that as insurance to make your escape?" She didn't even stop for him to answer. "How could you? We were supposed to give that to André. It's vitally important to America's national security that he get it!"

"Are you done?" he snapped.

"No, I'm not. No wonder everyone and their uncle is running around trying to catch or kill us. You need to send that to André immediately. He can clear up this whole mess if you let him. Do your job. Show you're a good agent and can be relied upon. I'm sure that's all it will take for the dogs to be called off."

"Hah," he retorted. "For all we know, the only reason the dogs haven't already killed us is because of this flash drive. If I hand it over, they may blow us to smithereens."

"You told André you'd get him the proof," she accused.

"No, you told him that."

She opened her mouth, but shut it again as it obviously dawned on her that he was right.

"There's actually a good argument to be made for destroying this evidence," he said thoughtfully.

"That sounds like your father talking."

"I've said it before, and I'll say it again. My father is not always wrong. If what's on this drive were to come to light, a massive international crisis on the scale of the Cuban Missile Crisis would follow. Do you trust your government to do the reasonable thing and save the world this time around?"

She got a stubborn look on her face.

He added, "Even if you do trust your own government, do you trust the Russian government to get it right? Do you see the current regime backing down meekly and removing the chemicals from Cuba?"

That made her wince.

"My point exactly. I think the best thing to do is destroy the drive."

She tilted her head questioningly. "Then why haven't you already destroyed it? I think part of you does want to hand it over to the Americans. I think you do want to prove to the CIA that they can trust you and that you'll be a good operative for them."

"Bah!" he scoffed.

"You accuse me of lying to you, but don't lie to yourself, Alex. I *know* you."

Damn her, she did.

She pressed her own point home. "If you truly were the rogue agent you claim to be, you'd have let me bleed to death on that sidewalk. Even if you didn't have a single feeling for me, and even if you weren't first and foremost a doctor at heart, you'd have looked out for yourself first. But you didn't. You're not a bad person, no matter what you try to tell yourself."

"Lord, you're such a Goody Two-shoes."

"Yup, and I wear rose-colored glasses, too," she replied cheerfully. "I'm not apologetic for having a positive outlook on life. You could use a little more of that, by the way."

He rolled his eyes and didn't deign to answer. She seemed to think she'd gotten the last word and buried her nose in her book once more.

Irritated, he stared down at his computer screen. Thanks to Blondie, who'd given her life for him without knowing that was what she'd done, he had the means to get into the CIA's mainframe. And thanks to Katie and whatever political games her uncle was playing, he now had both a name and an operation to investigate. His father said Claudia Kane was running Operation Cold Intent. What in the hell was she doing with it?

Did he dare break into the CIA's secure server to search for an answer? Alex put his hands on the keyboard. He would have to move fast. He might have two, maybe three minutes once he got in. Better to stick with a two-minute time limit. He set up a stopwatch on his cell phone and started typing.

Blondie's algorithm was subtle. It did not take a sledgehammer approach to getting past the CIA's firewalls. Rather it wormed its way in through tiny code gaps and by taking a massively circuitous, randomized route into the mainframe. Each time the hacking program was used, it would take a different route into its target, which meant it would be nearly impossible to create countermeasures to stop it. It was reusable, in other words.

The algorithm ran for nearly a half hour, but his patience was rewarded when a CIA search screen popped up. He started the timer and typed in his mother's name and the Cold Intent name.

A minute passed.

A minute and a half. Crap. The information was buried too deep. He would never find it in the limited amount of time he could afford to stick around waiting.

All of a sudden, his screen lit up. A list of file names associated with the search parameters "Cold Intent and Claudia Kane" scrolled down his screen.

Startled, he typed as fast as he could, attempting to download them, wholesale. No go. They were write-protected. It would take a whole other decryption algorithm to bust the protections preventing them from being copied.

In desperation, he clicked on the most recently dated file.

It opened to reveal an innocuous-looking document. He scanned it fast. An intel report on… His jaw dropped.

On Peter Koronov and his father's odds of becoming the next director of the FSB. The analysis deemed Peter far too effective a spy and charismatic a leader to be allowed into the position. The report speculated that, under his capable direction, the FSB could be rejuvenated into a formidable intelligence apparatus.

His phone beeped that his two minutes were up.

He swore and clicked to the end of the report quickly. The conclusion was too damned wordy to read in its entirety, but he scanned it fast. The report concluded with verbiage having to do with agreeing with the director on the optimal plan for taking Koronov out of the running for the post of FSB chief.

His computer beeped an incoming query warning, and he slammed the escape key. He powered the computer completely off and unplugged it from the wall.

Operation Cold Intent was an op to take down his father? He could see his mother being involved with that. It certainly answered the question of how Mommy Dearest had felt about his father. Why would a working group with that goal go after Katie, then? What key piece to the puzzle was he missing? How did Katie McCloud, kindergarten teacher extraordinaire, fit into all of this? He'd seen her reflex reactions in life-threatening situations before; he knew without a shadow of a doubt that Katie was *not* a trained field operative. A sparrow, maybe. But not a spy.

He turned over possibilities in his head for some time. He eventually noticed her nodding off in her chair and he muttered, "Go to bed."

She jolted upright. "That's okay. I'll stay up."

It hit him suddenly what she was doing. She was standing a flight watch on him. Terrified he was going to sneak out and leave her again, was she? Katie was trying to stay awake and keep an eagle eye on him. It would be cute if he could trust her even a little.

"I'm not going to leave until I figure out why the Cold Intent team is trying to kill you, Katie."

She stared at him long and hard. "Promise?"

"I give you my word of honor." She sagged abruptly in the chair, and he smiled sardonically. "Go to bed. I'll be here when you wake up. Or, if I've stepped out, I'll be back momentarily."

She stood up, but instead of climbing into bed, she came over to stand in front of him. "You do know that I would never betray you, right?"

He stared up at her. He might accept that the drug they'd fed him had messed with his head, but his heart was another matter. He'd been betrayed so badly in his past it was hard for him to trust anyone the way she was asking him to. It was as if the cannabis extract had flipped on a paranoia switch in his brain, and he had no idea how to turn it off.

Maybe the paranoia had been there all along. And now that it was exposed to his conscious mind, he couldn't put it back in the unconscious box it had come from.

Paranoia or no, his gut was telling him to stay in spy mode. Not to let her seduce him out of that cold, detached place in his mind where life and death were merely two decisions among many.

She sighed. "I'll find a way to prove to you that I wouldn't turn on you, Alex. That's my promise to you."

He had no frame of reference to know how to answer a statement like that. Everybody turned on everyone else eventually. It was why relationships were so dangerous.

He picked up the pad of notebook paper lying on

the room's desk and started writing notes and drawing lines between them, looking for connections he'd missed before. And when he gave up for the night, he burned the entire pad and flushed the ashes down the toilet.

One thing he knew for sure. He was being used by somebody. And whether it was Katie or his parents or someone else altogether, he didn't like it. He was not going to play ball and be a good little spy. Not by a long shot.

CHAPTER SEVENTEEN

KATIE WOKE WITH a jolt. Crap. There was some reason she wasn't supposed to sleep. No, wait. Alex had promised he wouldn't run out on her and abandon her again. She sagged back to the mattress in relief. Except something was still wrong. But what?

Alex was curled on his side facing her, sleeping quietly. Lord, he was handsome with his hair tousled and his face mashed against a pillow. Even in sleep, though, he radiated pain. She'd give anything to lift it away from him. For his mother to be a lovely woman who had desperately missed her son over the years and adored him in absentia. But Alex seemed to think she was somehow tied in to their current predicament. He was so suspicious of everyone and everything. She thought she'd gotten past that with him, but at the moment, she seemed to be included in his lengthy list of people not to be trusted.

It was dark outside. She checked her cell phone. A little after 4:00 a.m. Restless, she slid out of bed and padded over to the window. She lurked beside the curtains like she'd seen Alex do before and peeked sideways around them without disturbing the hanging drapery.

A car was just pulling into the motel parking lot. Weird hour for that. Even weirder as it turned the corner that its headlights were off. It parked beside another car of identical make. It must have been the noise of the first car pulling in that woke her up. A warning vibration erupted in her gut.

"Alex," she called low.

He lurched awake and was out of bed in a single catlike lunge. Talk about reflexes. Dang. Remind her not to startle him out of a hard sleep when she was within arm's length of him.

He stopped in the middle of the room just long enough to see what she was doing and then he slid over to the other side of the window. It took him about two seconds to announce, "Get dressed and head into the bathroom. Lie down in the bathtub."

"What are you going to do?"

He ignored her question and ordered, "Call 9-1-1 on your cell phone and tell them there's a shootout in progress."

"But there isn't any shooting—"

Alex lifted the pistol he'd been holding down by his side. "There's about to be."

Where… He must have been sleeping with it under his pillow. *Paranoid, much?* "Who's out there?" she asked in quick alarm.

"Go, Katie."

She grabbed her clothes, closed the bathroom door and felt her way to the tiny bathtub in the dark. It wasn't long enough to stretch out in, so she curled on her side in it. Extremely awkwardly and with copious mental swearing, she managed to pull on her clothes. But they were all crooked and pulling at her in weird places. She finally gave up and stood up to adjust the darned things.

A tremendous explosion of sound erupted from the living room and she instinctively dropped like a rock into the cold, hard tub. Holy mackerel! Sometimes she forgot just how loud gunshots were, particularly in a confined space. A dramatic fusillade of return fire from the parking lot finished deafening her. That was at least three weapons firing back at Alex, maybe more.

"Alex!" she shouted. "Are you okay?"

Another round of gunfire exploded from the living room. She would assume that his shooting back at whoever was outside constituted proof that he was still alive. Abruptly, the bathroom door flung splinters of wood every which way. She yanked the shower curtain shut, not that it would do a lick of good, and covered her head with her arms. Something metallic and fast moving pinged off the cast-iron bathtub, and his order to climb in here suddenly made sense.

The bathroom door burst open and she jumped violently.

"Get up, Katie. We've got to go."

"Out there?" she squeaked.

"Window," he grunted. "Hurry. I've set a timed charge in the front room."

Omigosh. She leaped to her feet and jumped up on the toilet seat as he disappeared out the open window.

She dived after him, and he caught her under the armpits, pulling her legs through and setting her upright.

She opened her mouth out of habit to thank him, and he held an urgent finger to his lips. Stealth. Got it. She nodded and followed him as he eased into the light woods behind the motel.

Another round of gunfire erupted from behind them, and on cue, a tremendous explosion lit the night around them. The ground shook and Katie staggered as Alex steadied her and dragged her onward.

The tree line turned out to be thin and gave way to a farm. The place was pitch-dark. Old-fashioned. Alex crept to the big, red barn and carefully slid open a huge door a few feet.

He disappeared inside after signaling for her to wait here. She fretted for about one minute and then stared in shock as he led out a giant horse. The chestnut had on a bridle but was otherwise bare of tack.

"Give me your leg," Alex breathed.

"You want me to get on that monster?"

"Trust me. It's better than running all night."

She was no horsewoman! Stunned and terrified, she let him hoist her onto the broad back of the beast, who shifted under her weight and stamped a foot. *Ohgod, ohgod.*

"Easy, boy," Alex murmured. He led the clopping beast over to an unpainted, wooden fence, handed the reins up to her, then climbed the fence and eased onto the horse behind her.

The animal's back was warm and wide and alive. Scared to death, she wrapped her hands in the horse's thick, flaxen mane and hung on for dear life. Alex's arms came around her and he pried the reins out of her panicked fists. She felt his legs tighten around the animal's girth behind her and the horse moved out, his hooves quiet on the grass.

At least Alex didn't spur the beast into a mad gallop. Although, in her panic to get away from whoever was shooting at them, she almost wished he would send the horse on a mad dash to safety.

Alex breathed in her ear, "We'll draw less attention moving quietly. And this is a draft horse. He's designed to go all day at a slow pace, but he couldn't run a mile without being totally winded."

He guided the horse across the road in front of the farm and into another patch of woods. The animal found some sort of path and turned onto it of his own accord. Alex gave the animal free rein and let the horse plod along in the dark.

"Where are we going?" she finally ventured whispering.

"Away from the motel. As for what awaits us ahead, I have no idea. We'll adapt when we get there."

The horse walked for maybe twenty minutes at a steady but surprisingly ground-eating pace. All of a sudden, a clearing opened up in front of them. A simple, one-story building stood in the middle of it.

"That's a one-room schoolhouse!" she exclaimed quietly. "Was that farm Amish?"

"Mennonite, I think," Alex answered. "I saw a tractor in the barn."

The horse strode up to a hitching post with a watering trough beside it and shoved his nose into the black water. After that, no matter what Alex tried shy of beating the beast, the horse refused to budge. Period.

Finally, Alex gave up, slid off the animal and helped her down. She watched as Alex slipped the bridle off the horse and gave it a sharp swat on the rump. The horse threw up its head, startled, and turned to trot back down the path it had come from.

"If I know horses, that guy'll go right back to his barn and maybe even back into his stall. If we're lucky, the farmer won't report his stolen bridle to the police."

To that end, Alex hung the bridle on the end of the hitching post, where it didn't look at all out of place. "We're on foot from here."

Except before they could take a dozen steps, they heard something rattling toward them. Katie dived for cover behind the trees on the far side of the clearing and waited pensively for what would emerge from the dirt road beyond the schoolhouse.

A black, boxy carriage rocked into sight, pulled by a lean, dark horse, shambling along casually. A woman climbed down from the carriage and tied the horse to the hitching post before disappearing inside the building. In a few seconds, a soft, yellow glow illuminated one of the windows.

"How early do Mennonite kids start school, anyway?" she whispered to Alex.

"They're early risers as a group. C'mon."

"Are we going to steal a buggy now?" she asked in jest.

He nodded and indicated that she should climb up

into the black conveyance. Stunned, she clambered between the narrow wheels awkwardly. The thing rocked and squeaked a little as she settled onto the seat. Alex threaded the reins inside the carriage, and as she held the ends, he leaped in considerably more gracefully than she had.

With a quiet slap of the reins on the horse's rump, he guided the beast back into the night. Whether or not the teacher inside the school heard them or ran out to give chase, Katie had no idea. The grassy meadow and sandy dirt of the carriage path muffled sound tremendously well. If they were lucky, they'd gotten away cleanly.

The genius of Alex's theft became apparent as the path gave way to a paved road. "Pull the curtains down and tie them in place," he told her.

The entire interior of the carriage was shrouded in black fabric in a few seconds. Even the front window was covered, with only a narrow slit at eye height for Alex to see through to steer.

And when they approached a parked police car blocking the next intersection, the cop nodded respectfully and waved them past without stopping the buggy.

"Sonofagun," Katie murmured.

"The Mennonites are peaceful people. Good citizens. In return, they ask that their religious customs be honored. *Meidung* is one of them. It's a German term referring to social avoidance. Some Mennonites don't like to interact with outsiders. A shrouded buggy is indicative of occupants practicing *meidung*."

"Which means what for us?"

"Local authorities won't screw with us. We should be able to pass any cops undisturbed."

"Nice. So we're making our big getaway in a horse-drawn carriage, huh?" She leaned back against the black leather cushions. The vehicle was actually kind of cozy in a coffinlike way. Which was somehow entirely appropriate to this fiasco.

Alex murmured, "We should be able to trade this rig for a motorized vehicle in the next town. Some Mennonites do drive cars. And this is a good horse and a brand-new carriage."

Perplexed, she watched him drive with quiet confidence. "When did you learn how to ride horses and steer carriages? Was this part of your CIA training?"

He commented dryly, "I'm a man of many talents."

"I'll say." Silence fell inside the carriage. She reflected on their flight for a few minutes, but then curiosity got the best of her. She couldn't resist asking, "Who was that back at the motel?"

"Cold Intent. That was my fault. I broke into the CIA's mainframe last night and stayed online too long. They must have traced me. Or maybe they think it was you in that room."

"Why does this Cold Intent bunch want to kill me—or us—so badly?" she demanded.

"I wish I knew," he answered grimly.

Hey. A sign of human emotion out of him. He wasn't a robot, after all! She was worried about him. He'd just been through a gigantic shootout, and for all she knew, he'd killed a few guys back at the motel. Heck, he'd blown up a whole motel room without a backward glance. Shouldn't he show at least a little reaction after the fact? Instead, he'd dropped into that cold, emotionless fugue state she was rapidly coming to hate.

It dawned on her abruptly that, as soon as he knew why Cold Intent was after her, he would probably leave her. Forever.

So…what? She should wish for him never to solve the mystery and for her life to be in mortal danger permanently? Ugh. This sucked. Be safe, lose the love of her life. Stay in danger, keep the guy, but probably die. And maybe break through his emotional walls someday. *Maybe.* What kind of choice was that?

Was she willing to settle for whatever scraps of affection he deigned to toss her way? Did she realistically stand any chance at all of getting through to him, or was she deluding herself? Maybe she should just cut her losses and run.

"What do you know about this Cold Intent operation, Alex? Did you learn anything last night?" When he hesitated, she added, "I think I have a right to know why somebody's so set on killing me, don't you?"

He exhaled hard. "I found out that they're out to discredit my father."

"By killing me?" she exclaimed.

"Yeah, I'm stumped by that one, too."

She stared at his tense profile. What the heck?

They bumped along on country roads for several hours. The sun rose, and other vehicles, both motorized and horse-drawn, began to share the road with them. A small town came into sight through the slit in the window covering, and Alex found some sort of farmer's market and feed store.

He duly bartered the horse and carriage for an ancient, black land yacht of a car, all of whose chrome trim had been painted a flat, ugly black. But it ran. And the bearded owner threw in a tank of gas and a paper bag full of the most delicious pastry-wrapped sausages that Katie had ever tasted.

THEY MADE WILMINGTON by noon, ditched the car, which would look out of place if they strayed too much farther from Amish country, and caught a train from there bound for New York. As Philadelphia and then New Jersey sped by outside, Katie finally breathed a sigh of relief. They'd escaped yet again. She had no idea how many of his lucky nine lives Alex had left, but she was starting to feel like she'd burned through a few of hers recently.

"Are we safe?" she murmured as Alex leaned back in his seat and seemed to relax.

"There's no such thing as safe in this world. The sooner you accept that, the better a chance you have of surviving it."

She stared at him. "Do you really mean that?"

"Safety is an illusion. Bad guys are all around us all the time. Be they petty criminals who want your purse or terrorists who want your life, they're everywhere. I've seen the shadow world, that other place the dark ones live in, and it's closer to this world than you know."

"You sound like an advertisement for a horror movie."

He shrugged. "My world is the real one. It's where life and death live." He gestured to the suburban sprawl speeding by outside the train. "This happy, shiny world of strip malls and middle-class America is the movie. It's carefully crafted by the media, big business and the government."

"Well, that's…cynical."

He lifted an eyebrow as if to say, *When have I ever been anything else?*

"So my whole life to date has been what? A lie? A dream?"

He shrugged. "You've asked me more than once to strip away your innocence. That's what I'm doing now. If you want to run in my world, you have to grow up and let go of childish ideas, Katie."

In other words, agree with him that the world was a deadly place populated with unseen threats, or walk away from him and never look back. She looked up at him, and he was staring at her expectantly.

"I need to think about this," she mumbled, staggered. She didn't know whether to be overjoyed that he was opening a tiny window for her to stay with him or horrified that he wanted her to step into the shadows with him and his madness.

"Think fast, Katie. My world will come calling soon. And then your time will be up."

Or more likely, he would reconsider his offer and withdraw it. She subsided against the worn seat cushions, terrified like she'd never been terrified before.

She was less worried about him when he doubted himself and his view of the world. But when he was like this, so sure that his perceptions were absolute fact, she had to believe he was slipping into some sort of delusional insanity. It probably had a fancy Latin name—that he would know, of course. Did she love him enough to abandon reality and live in his delusion with him?

God, how had he messed with her head enough for her to even consider that?

His paranoia was getting the best of him. She was losing him.

CHAPTER EIGHTEEN

THE TRAIN STOPPED somewhere in northern New Jersey, and Alex startled Katie by murmuring, "Let's go."

"We're not going into New York City?" she asked.

He shook his head. "Way too much surveillance and security there. We're more anonymous here."

Alarmed, she slid out of her seat and followed him off the train. In short order, he'd obtained a crappy motel room for them using a fake ID and its matching credit card. And then he announced, "I need to find a computer. Do you want to stay here or come with me?"

"You seriously have to ask?" she retorted.

He smiled a little, sardonically. "I'm not going to disappear until I figure this out. I don't want it pursuing me into my new life."

His new life. The exclusion of her from that future hurt bad enough to steal her breath away. What had happened to him? He'd acknowledged that he'd been drugged into chemically induced paranoia and that she hadn't betrayed him like he originally thought. Why was he still thinking in terms of leaving her behind?

"You know I would never force myself upon you, right, Alex?"

"I beg your pardon?" He stared at her blankly.

"And you do know that no matter how much I hate you, I still love you, right?"

"How am I supposed to respond to that?"

His coldness in response to her bald honesty was a blade straight to her heart. Although her heart felt so shredded by now that one more cut shouldn't matter. And yet, it did.

Along with pain, she felt sorrow. Sorrow for the lost little boy, sorrow for the lonely, isolated man. Sorrow for what they could've had but which he'd thrown away.

He'd completely withdrawn from her emotionally. He was firmly entrenched in being the icy, analytical spy in his fantasy high-threat scenario.

Oh, sure, she accepted that they were in a certain amount of actual danger. After all, the wound in her shoulder was entirely real. But she was equally convinced it was all a big misunderstanding. If Alex would just hand over that flash drive and the evidence of chemical weapons in Cuba, the CIA would be happy and leave them alone.

She'd planned to tell him that she loved him enough to place his happiness before hers and that she would seriously consider his implied offer to go with him. But he was obviously in no mood to hear anything she had to say right now. Instead, she sighed. "Now what?" she asked in resignation.

"I'm going to the library. Are you coming?"

"Sure. Why not?" Maybe she could check out a book on abnormal psychology and gain some tiny insight into Alex and his thoroughly screwed-up head.

The anonymous, slightly decaying urban landscape around her was oddly comforting. She was rapidly picking up Alex's aversion to being noticeable. The local library was a dingy beige building, mostly deserted inside. Alex sat down at a carrel with a computer in it, and she pulled up a chair beside him to watch him work his magic.

"What are you going to do?" she asked curiously.

"I'm going back in for more information on Cold Intent."

"Are you crazy?" she exclaimed under her breath.

"Do you have any better ideas?"

"We could talk to Uncle Charlie."

"He told you to stay away from it. He knows what the operation is all about, and somehow the two of us pose a threat to it."

"Is there any way you can figure out who gave the order to have you—" she dropped her voice to a whisper "—drugged?"

"I gave the MPs in Gitmo André's phone number. It came through that chain of command."

Katie frowned. "At first, the Marines were nice to you, right? They gave you the samples from me and let you go to the hospital on your own."

He leaned back to stare at her. "Follow that train of thought. See where it takes you."

"After they let you go, they called André. He told them something that made them go to the hospital, arrest you, interrogate you and drug you. And that something made them hold me and not let me join you."

"Go on."

"André likes you. He must have called his boss and was relaying the boss's orders. So, why did the boss want the cops to go after you? You had information the CIA desperately wanted. Why not bring you in with all possible speed?"

Alex stared at her, his gaze dark.

She continued. "The boss had to have told them I was not a threat, but that you were. And the two of us were to be separated. I presumably knew as much as you did about what we found in Cuba, so I was as big a threat as you to whatever's going on. Since they didn't formally detain me, I have to rule out the information about the chemical weapons as the cause of your arrest."

Alex looked startled at that. *Shock. She'd actually outthought the genius for once?*

She continued more enthusiastically. "Why separate us specifically? What's the big deal about the two of us being together?"

Alex frowned. "The CIA thinks you're keeping me in line. That I won't go off the reservation if you're around."

"Then why would they take me away from you?" A nasty connection dropped into place. She spoke slowly, feeling her way through the logic. "Alex. Not only did they take me away from you, but they gave you drugs to make you paranoid. What if they made you suspicious of me intentionally?"

He tilted his head, considering. "It's a bit of a stretch, but it is plausible."

"What do I bring to you that you can't do for yourself?" she asked.

"That's easy. Stability. Predictability. And control over my more dangerous impulses."

"How's that?"

"I am known to have feelings for you and Dawn. Threaten the two of you, and I'm forced to stay in line and behave myself."

She was dismayed that he thought she was such a big vulnerability. "I'm so sorry."

He shrugged. "It was my choice to get involved with you. My fault."

Fault? She was a fault in his life? She'd been a mistake for him right from the beginning. He'd tried to warn her, but she'd ignored him and thrust a relationship and even a daughter on him whether he liked it or not.

The two of them could never make it as a couple if all he saw when he looked at her was a potentially lethal error in judgment. The last thing she wanted to be to him was a fatal vulnerability. He was right to leave her. A sob escaped her throat, and she bit back its sibling as it bubbled up in her chest.

"As soon as this is over, Alex, I'll let you go. I get it now. If my being with you puts you at so much risk, then we can't ever be together. I'll walk away and never look back. I love you too much to be the cause of your injury or death."

For just an instant, his gaze raged with some turbulent, unnamed emotion. And then, as usual, all expression drained from his eyes. His face went smooth and still, completely unreadable. Lord, she wished she knew how to do that, too.

Her vision swam in tears and she looked away from him hastily. The computer screen was the only nearby target for her unseeing stare. "Let's finish this," she said fiercely. "The sooner, the better. Every day we're together puts you at risk."

He made a tiny sound that might be a laugh half-formed, or maybe something else…like pain. Either way, he placed his hands on the keyboard and started to type. He played the machine like a virtuoso, and she couldn't begin to understand the lines of code that flashed across the screen almost too fast to read. But she did recognize the Central Intelligence Agency seal when it briefly flashed up on the monitor.

"When I tell you to, start counting the time," he muttered as he plugged a flash drive into a port in the side of the monitor.

"Okay." She pulled out her cell phone and set up a stopwatch app.

"Go," he murmured. She started the counter.

A list of files came up on the screen quickly enough. He didn't mess with them, though. Instead, he pulled up another window and appeared to commence running another program. "What are you doing?" she asked.

"Trying to break the write protection on those files so I can download them."

He typed frantically for another few seconds and then stopped. "Okay. That's it. Now we have to let the program run and see if the algorithm can break through the copy protection protocols on those files before we're kicked out of the mainframe."

"That's two minutes elapsed," she murmured.

He nodded tersely. They stared at the monitor in silence as his decryption program did its work.

"Three minutes."

His jaw muscles rippled like he was clenching his teeth, but he didn't acknowledge her minute-by-minute count in any other way.

"Are you going to give up?" she asked.

He shrugged. "As long as their security guys don't kick me out, I may as well sit tight and see if I can capture those files. I've got nothing to lose by trying, and I won't get another shot at this. It's now or never."

"Eight minutes." Every second crawled past, taking an eternity. The code in his second window continued to scroll past too fast to read. She counted all the way to fifteen minutes without anything appearing to happen. And then, all of a sudden, a download progress bar started to turn from white to blue across the bottom of the monitor.

"You did it," she breathed.

"We're not out of the woods yet," he warned. The bar had almost turned most of the way white when all hell broke loose on the screen. A new window opened of its own volition and code started scrolling down the monitor. Alex jumped and started typing, his nimble fingers flying across the keyboard. He muttered unintelligibly to himself, and Katie sat frozen beside him, not wanting to distract him.

"Pull out the flash drive," he ordered suddenly. "Now!"

She reached up and yanked the drive out of the port. The screen went black. "Did we get the files?"

"We've got to get out of here," he said by way of an answer. He stood up fast and strode toward the exit with her half running beside him.

"Well?" she demanded as they burst out into the street.

"I won't know until I open that drive and see what made its way onto it before the agency's countermeasures kicked in. But first, we have to get away from this location."

Her shoulder gave a warning shout but she ignored the flash of pain. She asked nervously, "It'll take them a while to track down that computer terminal, right? We've got plenty of time to get away."

"Not how it works," he bit out. "These are the big boys we're messing with. They have resources you can't even begin to imagine."

They'd walked briskly several blocks back toward their motel when Alex swore under his breath.

"Let me guess," she muttered in dismay. "We've got company."

"That would be correct. Don't look back."

But how? They'd been in the library a grand total of maybe twenty minutes. Unless the agency had figured out the two of them were on that train, and the CIA had sent agents into this general area already to search for them.

"There's a cab over there," she suggested. "Across

the street just beyond the next intersection." It was the only cab she'd seen in this dilapidated and mostly residential part of town. Finally. A piece of luck had broken their way.

"Stay with me," Alex ordered absently as his eyes roved in all directions. "We'll cross over to it in the middle of the intersection."

She didn't reply. He was obviously busy formulating plans and evaluating various contingencies.

She did sneak a peek behind them as they approached a stoplight. Darned if she could spot anyone following them. Was the tail real? Or was this all part of Alex's elaborate paranoid delusion about how dangerous the world was and how people in it were out to get him?

They reached the stoplight and he didn't pause. He plunged into the oncoming traffic, and she squeaked in alarm as cars swerved and honked their horns angrily. Scared to death, she dodged along with him, practically climbing on his heels.

They somehow reached the safety of the far curb, and Alex broke into a run. She kept up with him, but barely, gritting her teeth against the pain in her shoulder as she jarred it pounding on the concrete sidewalk. He hailed the cab and opened the door for her to slide into the backseat. He jumped in after her and gave the cabbie the name of their motel.

She started to turn around to look behind them for pursuit, but Alex bit out, "Don't look. Assume they're following us."

Too late. She'd caught a glimpse of a man in a beige

raincoat leaping into the passenger's side of a big, dark SUV way too frantically to be a regular civilian just going about his business.

God almighty. Alex wasn't entirely wrong about his world colliding with hers at a moment's notice. It was as if the curtain separating the two in her mind had suddenly become tissue thin. In times like this, she almost could believe Alex wasn't crazy. Almost.

The taxi rolled for about five minutes, and then suddenly, Alex leaned forward and said sharply, "This isn't the way to the motel."

"There's construction," the cabbie replied. "I'm going around it. I'll knock a chunk off the fare if you want."

Alex subsided, frowning slightly. When he worried, she worried. He not only had a great deal of training she didn't have, but he also had an incredible instinct for sensing trouble. It was no doubt part of what made him a great spy.

Abruptly, the taxi left the surface street and swerved onto a highway entrance ramp, accelerating quickly.

"Hey!" she exclaimed. This was definitely *not* the way back to the motel. She reached for her cell phone to call 9-1-1.

But Alex reached out to grip her forearm and forestall her. He shook his head infinitesimally in the negative. Crap. He was right. They couldn't call the police. If they did, they'd be found by the CIA. Alex would be hauled in and drugged again if he was lucky, and killed as a rogue operative if he was not lucky. As for her, she would just get dead. The two of them were on their own with this lunatic and his cab.

She looked forward toward the driver and froze in horror. The small black bore of a pistol was pointed back at her.

She looked over at Alex in panic. What was happening? Were they being *kidnapped?*

CHAPTER NINETEEN

KATIE STARTED TO open her mouth to ask that very question, but Alex shook his head the tiniest bit at her again. That look had entered his eyes. The one they'd had the first night he'd gotten home. The look of a killer. Absolutely chilling calm rolled off him. Oddly enough, it comforted her. Spy Alex was in the house. And she trusted that version of him with her life.

Why didn't Alex shoot the driver? Although there *was* the whole business of the taxi traveling at seventy miles per hour. If Alex shot the guy, the vehicle would crash spectacularly. Still. They might have a better shot of surviving a crash than whatever their kidnapper had in store for them.

She sat back and tried to memorize the roads, to keep her sense of direction and to stay oriented as to where they were. And above all, she tried not to panic. But it was hard not to. A man had a freaking gun pointed at her. On cue, her shoulder throbbed fiercely, a pointed reminder of how real a threat that weapon posed.

Worse, a sick realization that Alex was not crazy at all twisted and turned in her gut. The darkness did lurk just below the surface of what she knew as the normal world. Just like he'd said it did. And she'd just been too naive and stupid to see it. Or maybe too stubborn.

It wasn't as if she'd never heard her brothers and dad talking about it. She had willfully chosen to ignore the warning signs of its existence with them, and she'd done the exact same thing with Alex. No wonder he was fed up with her and counting the seconds until he could ditch her forever.

God, she'd been a fool. Only now, when it was far too late, did she finally let go of *her* delusions long enough to realize Alex had had it right all along. And they were both going to die because of her stubbornness and stupidity.

"I'm so sorry, Alex," she mumbled.

His gaze flickered toward her long enough for her to be sure he'd heard her, but he didn't acknowledge her apology in any other way. He looked too busy observing the driver and thinking about something. Hopefully, he was devising a brilliant escape plan.

But she bloody well didn't see a way out of this mess. She had a sinking feeling that this time they would not miraculously elude disaster.

Her entire body started to shake at the idea of dying. It was one thing to consider being in danger in the abstract, from a distance. It was an entirely different animal altogether to be staring death in the face.

Something really, really bad was going to happen to them, and it was all her fault.

The cab drove south for maybe fifteen minutes on the highway and then exited onto a country road headed west, inland and away from the Atlantic coast. The vehicle slowed barely enough to squeal around the corner at the top of the exit ramp, and then it accelerated immediately down a deserted, two-lane road. The driver must be worried about them making a jump for it out the back doors. Not that she would try it at these speeds. She was no trained stuntwoman.

Outside was a mixture of farmland and forest, and human dwellings were becoming sparse. The driver was taking them out in the middle of freaking nowhere. This could not be good.

Who was this guy? And how had he known where to be conveniently available for her and Alex to jump in his cab? He must have been working with whoever had tailed them after they left the library. Which spoke of coordination and communication on a scale that only a bunch like the CIA could pull off on short notice.

The sophistication of this kidnapping was daunting, to say the least. But which one of them was the target, her or Alex? The people who'd been shooting at her obviously wanted her dead, not kidnapped. Did that mean this elaborate assault was directed at Alex?

The obvious culprit was the CIA. They had shown deep distrust of Alex from the beginning and it had only intensified recently. But she supposed this could just as easily be his father attempting to snatch him from the clutches of the CIA. Man, Alex's life was complicated. She didn't envy him the pushes and pulls coming at him from all directions. And now his mother was somehow part of the tug-of-war over him. That had to be messing with his head big-time.

The cab slowed abruptly and careered onto a narrow gravel road. The tires skidded and the car fishtailed, taking the slippery surface far too fast for safety. She braced herself and did her best not to become motion sick at the violent ride.

The car turned off the dirt road and onto a barely passable driveway, hardly even a path through the weeds. Crap. Nobody would ever find them out here in the boonies.

The cab stopped in a sunny, weed-clogged clearing in the bottom of a swale. On the rising slopes around them, thin trees cast dappled shade over the undergrowth. No sooner had the vehicle stopped than the barrel of the pistol aimed straight at Katie from the driver's seat.

"Get out," the man ordered them. "Slowly. The girl first."

If she wasn't mistaken a hint of triumph flashed in Alex's eyes for an instant, as if to say the driver had just made a fatal error. She didn't see it, though. She couldn't seem to peel her gaze away from that tiny, deadly black hole gaping at her face.

"Out!" the driver barked.

She looked over at Alex, and he nodded in encouragement. She fumbled at the door handle and pushed the door open.

"Go out, and move forward," Alex murmured in Zaghastani. It was a rare dialect spoken only in one tiny region of central Asia. When they'd gone on a mission to Zaghastan last year, Alex had picked up a little of the language, in which she was fluent.

She did as he instructed and stepped out of the cab. She circled wide of the door and moved toward the front of the vehicle. The cabbie tracked her with his pistol, aiming it at her through the driver's side window, which he'd opened.

"Now you," the driver snapped at Alex. "No funny business, or I kill the girl."

What was she supposed to do? Dive for the front of the cab and use the engine for cover? Stand here like the guy'd told her to? Run? Poised on her toes and ready to bolt, she waited and watched for a signal, any signal, from Alex.

He stepped out of the car slowly. But then he moved so fast she barely saw the blur of motion. Alex lunged forward, grabbed the pistol by the barrel and twisted it violently free of the man's hand all in one lightning-fast attack.

"Get down, Katie!" Alex bit out. The driver's door started to open, and in the next millisecond, the pistol fired deafeningly, a single shot. A spray of blood coated the inside of the windshield.

"Get in the backseat," he ordered, already pulling the driver's door open. He dragged the driver's body out of the vehicle by the feet as she darted past, leaving a wide smear of blood in the grass. Alex slid behind the wheel and started the engine as she dived into the backseat.

He'd barely thrown the car into gear when a fusillade of gunshots erupted around them. Screaming a little, she threw her arms over her head and plastered herself flat against the vinyl upholstery. Alex swore from the front seat and returned fire.

"These guys are pros, Katie. They'll kill the car. We're sitting ducks in here. When I say go, kick open the door you just crawled in and run like hell for the woods. Zigzag. It makes you harder to hit. I'll cover you."

"Pass me the driver's pistol," she responded in a trembling voice. "Then I can cover you while you join me."

A hand came over the back of the front seat and she took the weapon from it. All those years of shooting tin cans with her dad and brothers were finally going to come in handy apparently. She couldn't actually believe she was about to run out into a firefight. But she and Alex were in life-threatening danger. He was outnumbered, which meant he was also outgunned. If she didn't help him, he would die. They would both die. Determination temporarily overrode her panic. She reached back, staying low to unlatch the door.

"I'm ready," she reported.

"On my mark. Three. Two. One. Go!" Alex popped up from the front seat and sprayed gunfire at whoever was out there.

She kicked the door open, rolled out onto the ground and to her feet in one motion and then ran like she'd never run before in her life. She dodged randomly from side to side as she went, but it barely slowed her headlong flight. She ran into the trees and dived behind the first good-size fallen log she came across.

Propping the pistol on the log, she trained it on the clearing and searched frantically for a glimpse of the shooters or at least their positions. There. A muzzle flash from across the little valley. And another one from beyond the bullet-riddled cab. That guy would have a better angle to shoot at Alex, so she trained her weapon on him. Disbelief that she was engaging in a gunfight briefly passed through her mind, but she shoved it aside. Alex needed her.

The cab's front door flew open, and she shot at the assailant behind the cab. She saw a movement there like someone diving for cover, and she shifted her aim to the second shooter. She squeezed off two rounds at that guy until he ducked, as well. She swung back to the first shooter and sent another round in his direction for good measure.

Alex raced from the car much as she had and almost landed on top of her as he dived across the log. She rolled aside at the last minute to avoid being summarily crushed.

The swale went quiet. Carefully, she ejected her clip and counted bullets fast. Seven rounds left. One would already be in the chamber. Eight shots to live or die.

Alex jerked his head at her to follow him and rose to a crouch. She mimicked him and was not surprised when he took off running up the hill. High ground was a sniper's friend. They reached the top of the rise and Alex paused his headlong dash to crouch between two table-size boulders.

She knew from games in the woods with her brothers that stealth was vital now. Alex leaned close to murmur low and urgent. “This is as defensible a position as we’re likely to find. You’re going to have to cover one direction while I take the other. We have limited ammo, so wait until you’ve got a decent shot to fire. Understood?”

“Yes.” She couldn’t resist adding in a rush, “I’m so sorry I didn’t believe you. You were right. It’s all real. You’re not crazy.”

“Uh…thanks. Now concentrate. Slow your breathing and focus.”

A strange calm overcame her. Adrenaline was screaming through her blood, and she felt light and weightless. But her mind was crystal clear. Every leaf, every blade of grass, was vividly outlined as she peered out of the narrow gap in the boulders.

Time seemed elongated, each second stretching out around her as she waited. Alex’s presence was warm and steady at her back. They could do this.

“Incoming,” he murmured. “One’s circling to my left. Should come into your line of fire in a few seconds. I’ve got the second guy.”

Her pulse increased even more, and it was already leaping in her veins like rushing rapids. She concentrated on the forest to her right, alert for the slightest movement. Any second now. She braced her shooting elbow on her upraised knee and used the two-handed grip on the pistol that her father had taught her for maximum stability.

There. Was that a shadow in the trees? So jumpy

with nerves that she could hardly sit still, she waited a few more heartbeats to be sure. Alex had said not to waste ammo.

Could she do it? Could she pull the trigger and kill another human being? The words she'd heard so many times in her youth held entirely new meaning for her: *kill or be killed.* Her brothers and her dad hadn't seemed to think it was a difficult choice at all.

An image of sweet baby Dawn's face flashed through her head. The little girl deserved to have parents. She'd already lost so much in her short life. Katie's fist tightened around the butt of the pistol. She and Alex had no choice at all. They had to do whatever was necessary to stay alive out here.

The shadow glided forward, moving away from her and slightly right to left. She would have to time it carefully for when the attacker was between trees. She picked a gap ahead of the guy and waited for him to reach it. She drew in a slow, deep breath the way her dad had drilled into her, and held it as the black-clad man stepped into the gap. She squeezed the trigger. The pistol leaped in her hand, startling her. The man fell or dived to the ground—she couldn't tell which—but from above him on the hill like this, she still had a small sight line to target him.

Alex shot twice behind her, quickly. After her shot, his target must have taken off running.

She'd been a pretty good shot over the years. Assuming this weapon was sighted reasonably true, she could make the shot. She exhaled, held her diaphragm perfectly still, lined up the sight on the black, leather-clad lump and took the shot.

A grunting cry from her target signaled a hit.

Should she shoot him again or save her bullets for someone else? God, she wished she had more training.

"Incoming, your left," Alex bit out.

She swung her attention and her knee to the left, setting up for another shot. A man burst out of the trees no more than a dozen feet from her, scaring the hell out of her. She fired twice, fast, almost instinctively. The guy slammed backward to the ground, but rolled over. She dived behind the rock as he fired back at her.

She could hear him breathing in ragged gasps. She'd hit him for sure. Making a mental picture of the spot she'd seen him go down and using the gurgling rattle of his breathing as a guide, she rolled out from behind the boulders. She'd expected a small target, like the top of his head, and that was about all the guy gave her. Nonetheless, the shot was at a range of about fifteen feet, and her father had trained his kids thoroughly.

Katie didn't miss. The top of the man's head exploded in a grisly eruption of red gore. She glimpsed a palm-size chunk of the guy's skull fly up into the air, twirling end over end in macabre flight.

She looked back to her right. Crap! The lump of the first guy was gone. "Splash number two," she bit out. "Number one's hit but on the move."

"Got it," Alex replied tersely. He switched to Zaghastani. "When I say go, do it. You will use your tool."

His vocabulary was rough, but she got the idea. They were going to break out of this position and she should expect to shoot her way out. She backed deeper into the crevice until her back touched his, keeping her vision trained on the slice of forest still visible beyond the boulder. Alex eased away from her and she slid backward again until she connected with his back once more.

She felt his body gather in preparation to leap, and she did the same. Without warning, he jumped up.

A man shouted from what could not have been more than twenty feet away. She spun low out of the crack just in time to see Alex double-tap the attacker in the face, rendering the guy no longer human.

Another man roared over the top of the boulder from behind them, practically on top of Katie. Terrified beyond any ability to think, she reacted instinctively, whipped up the barrel of her weapon and fired as fast as she could pull the trigger. The weapon jumped hard in her hand three times, but the fourth time it merely clicked. Empty. Crap. Those had been her last three shots.

Her target yelled and crashed on top of her, knocking her down hard as his weight slammed into her. She grunted, her breath knocked out of her, and shoved in panic at the man. He was bleeding profusely from a neck wound, soaking her with hot, metallic-smelling blood. He twitched convulsively and then was still on top of her. She heaved for all she was worth and managed to pull her legs free of the corpse. Gasping for air, she scooped the pistol out of the guy's hand as Alex gestured urgently from a dozen yards away for her to get moving.

She leaped to her feet and ran for him. His weapon rose fast to point at her and she swerved hard out of his line of fire as he opened fire at someone behind her.

Jeez! How many guys were out here, anyway?

Alex moved out walking, but fast, placing his feet with catlike lightness. She tried to mimic him but it was damned hard work, and she was still trying to catch her breath. They half ran through the trees for maybe five minutes in silence. Well, *he* was silent. She panted like a hot dog and crackled leaves far too often for safety. Had they eliminated all the bad guys or not?

The longer they went without being shot at, the more her heart rate dropped to something commensurate merely with strenuous exercise. But then her hands started to shake. And then her whole body started to shake.

She popped out the clip of this weapon—a *Russian* make of pistol. What did *that* mean? *Were these attackers freaking Russians?* She yanked her attention back to the gun in her hand. Mike had brought a similar model of weapon home from a mission a few years ago. All her brothers had tried shooting it, and not to be left out, she'd insisted on trying it out, as well.

She was relieved to count eleven bullets in the clip. Alex had to be getting low in his weapon by now, too. On cue, he ejected a clip and rammed a new one into place. She rested against a tree and took several blessedly deep breaths while he extracted the two remaining bullets from the first clip and pocketed them.

She knew from experience that he usually had at least two spare clips on his person whenever he was packing a weapon. They were back in business for a little while, at least. Thank God for his paranoia and his associated obsession with preparedness.

Hopefully, they would not need their remaining firepower.

And…she was wrong.

Alex froze abruptly in front of her. She peered over his shoulder and saw a man in a black leather jacket poised beside an SUV, wielding a sawed-off AK-47 alertly.

The guy spoke aloud into a wireless earphone device and her jaw dropped as she identified the language he spoke to be Russian. Alex frowned faintly beside her, but she dared not break the silence to ask what the man had said.

Alex backed up a dozen feet, placing the crest of the ridge between them and the man below. Alex eased down quietly behind a thicket of weeds and brambles, and she joined him. He lifted away a few leaves to reveal wet, black earth. In the soil, he drew a crude car. He pointed at his own chest and then drew an arc to the left. He pointed at Katie and then drew another arc to the right. He then drew two lines from the stick figures from him and her toward the man.

He mouthed the words, "Field of fire," and she nodded immediately. By flanking the shooter below, the two of them had to be careful not to end up shooting each other. Alex was lucky she'd grown up in a military family and knew about such things!

"Shoot when I do," he breathed. Without any further ado, Alex moved away from her. Lord, she felt naked out here without him beside her. Every tiny sound made her jump, and she felt as twitchy as a marionette on a string.

When she deemed that she'd reached the position Alex had drawn for her, she inched forward toward the top of the ridge on her belly, pistol at the ready. Using the largest tree she could find, she stood up and peered out from behind the trunk.

The shooter was looking off toward Alex's position intently. Focused. Had he seen or heard Alex out there? The guy's AK-47 swung up from his hip to a shooting position as she planted her forearm against the tree trunk to steady it, blew out her breath and lined up the sight on the front tip of her gun barrel with the sights mounted above the trigger. Oh, he was so not getting off a shot at *her* man.

Screw Alex's signal. Without hesitating, she went ahead and fired. She was sure she'd hit the bastard. Although he staggered, he didn't go down. The man swung his weapon toward her and raked the hillside with a barrage of automatic fire as she dived behind the tree.

Was the guy wearing a Kevlar vest under that bulky jacket?

Alex opened fire from across the ridge, and the sweeping gunfire swung away sharply from her and toward Alex's position. She wasted no time stepping out from behind the tree far enough to take aim and fire again, this time at the man's head.

She missed twice and was forced to duck back behind the tree as he sprinted toward the back of the SUV. She only waited a fraction of a second before swinging out from behind the tree again. The shooter was going to take cover behind the vehicle and possibly take to the woods beyond it. Their lives would be immeasurably more difficult with this jerk and his vastly superior firepower roaming around in the forest hunting them.

Alex shouted something in Russian and the man shouted back as she took careful aim one more time on the guy's head. She held her breath and squeezed off the shot.

The man's legs crumpled and he dropped to the ground. She held her position and scanned back into the woods in the direction she and Alex had come from. She heard Alex crashing out of the tree behind her. She turned in time to see him running fast and low, zigzagging as swift and nimble as a cheetah, toward the downed man.

"Come down!" Alex called out in Zaghastani.

She stepped out of the woods fully in time to see Alex extend an arm straight out from his body at a downward angle and fire two shots into the prone man's head. It was brutal. Cold-blooded, even. She could shoot at an armed attacker who could shoot back at her, but she severely doubted she could've taken those shots. Alex had just *executed* that man. Shock and horror roared through her.

He crouched, patting down the dead man's pockets. He straightened, a car ignition fob in hand as she reached his side. "Did you have to kill him like that?" she demanded, appalled to her core.

"Get in the car. I'll drive."

She piled into the SUV as Alex punched the ignition button. The big engine roared to life. He steered the vehicle toward the fresh tracks in the grass at the edge of the clearing and they bumped down a rough driveway of sorts.

"Buckle your seat belt," he ordered without taking his eyes off the path ahead of them. How could he sound so damned calm? Didn't he care in the slightest that he'd just murdered that man?

As she clicked the seat belt across her body, she asked incredulously, "Aren't you the slightest bit upset that you just executed a helpless man like an animal for the slaughter?"

He glanced over long enough for her to reel away from the cold calculation in his eyes. "I never claimed to be a Girl Scout. You knew who I am, what I do, when you signed up for this. Deal with it or leave."

Just like that? "It's not that simple—" she started.

He cut her off sharply. "Yes. It is. This is my life. If you want to be part of it, don't ask me to change. I can't be someone else and survive. I have no choice."

She subsided against the cushions. Was it really that simple?

"Check the back for weapons," he bit out.

She clambered between the front seats and into the back. She leaned over the bench seat, reaching into the far back to pull up a canvas tarp and peek beneath it. "Two AK-47s, a wooden ammo box and two pistols. I think they're Makarovs."

Without waiting for him to tell her, she dragged all the weapons forward to the backseat. The ammo box was heavy and gave her more trouble, but she horsed it into the seat, as well. She rejoined Alex, panting.

"Who were those men back there?" she finally asked as the SUV burst out onto the main road and Alex stomped on the accelerator. "Russian weapons. The shooter was speaking in Russian. Did your father order this hit on us?"

Grimly, Alex fished out his cell phone and punched in a number, one-handed, as he drove. He jammed the phone to his ear and snarled, "I know it's the middle of the damned night in Moscow. Did you order a hit on me?"

It was as angry as she'd ever heard Alex. He listened in silence for a few seconds and then swore under his breath. "Check it out and let me know," he snapped.

"He denied being behind this, didn't he?" Katie asked grimly.

"Bingo."

"Do you believe him?"

Alex shrugged. "I think he believes he can still convince me to work for him. If that's true, he wouldn't kill me."

"Would he have some thugs fake a hit on you to give you credibility with the CIA?"

One corner of Alex's mouth turned up briefly.

"There may be hope for you yet. You're learning to think like a spy."

If that meant she was learning to be suspicious of everyone and not take anything at face value, she supposed he was right. "Could it have been someone else in the FSB?" she asked.

Alex frowned. "I fail to see how they could have picked up our trail from that library so quickly. I could see the CIA picking us up that fast, however, particularly if they were already looking for us in the New Jersey area. But not the Russians. They only have a certain number of resources on short-notice call in the States, and Russian wet teams aren't just cruising around New Jersey for grins and giggles."

"Why would the CIA send a team to kill you?"

He was silent long enough she thought he wasn't going to answer. But then he said grimly, "I am controversial within the agency. I have many detractors."

"Yes, but a hit team masquerading as Russians?" she challenged. "That seems like an awful lot of trouble to go to. I mean, they even spoke Russian to one another."

Alex frowned and did not answer. She gathered she'd asked the right question, then. He steered the SUV out onto the highway, pointing it to the north.

"Now what?" she asked.

He smiled slightly at her trademark question. "New York City for the moment."

As it became clear they hadn't been tailed, she relaxed and took a look around the SUV for clues as to who their kidnapper and assailants had been. She opened the storage console between the front seats and peeked down inside.

"Hey, look what I found," she exclaimed. She reached down into the compartment and pulled out a cell phone. It was a high-end model like someone might own for personal use, not a cheap burner phone.

Alex grinned wolfishly. "Well, well, well. The kindergarten teacher hits the mother lode." He added more seriously, "Speaking of which, that was some nice shooting back there. You're a hell of a marks-woman."

"For an amateur?" she added wryly.

"You saved my hide a couple times. That's as much as I could ask of any pro."

She sat back, shocked by the compliment. "Thanks," she mumbled.

"We make a good team," Alex commented off-handedly.

Whoa. She wasn't anywhere close to being in his league and never would be when it came to being a spy. But it was the first time he'd ever acknowledged that she wasn't always a dead weight on his back. She liked being able to hold her own beside him… at least a little.

Silence fell between them as he found the New Jersey Turnpike and navigated the increasingly heavy traffic.

Eventually, she asked, "What are you going to do with that phone?"

"Strip it of all the information it'll give us and form a plan based on what we find."

"Should we ditch this vehicle?" she asked.

"If we didn't kill all of our attackers, it'll take any survivors a while to figure out we've fled in their car and to report in. In the meantime, it'll throw off whoever's tracking this SUV on GPS when they see it moving. They'll assume the mission was accomplished."

"This car's being tracked?" she squeaked. God, would they never escape the constant surveillance? She was beginning to think they were living in a high-tech police state. Oh, Lord. And now he had her thinking just like him about the United States government being Big Brother.

He said casually, "I figure we've got another hour in this car before it's burned. But we'll be in New York City by then."

"Then what?"

"I'm sick and tired of sitting back waiting for these assholes to come after us. It's time for us to go on the offense."

CHAPTER TWENTY

KATIE WAS ALARMED when they ditched the SUV in front of the FBI headquarters in New York City. But since Alex pointed out that no one would think the government plates were out of place, it made sense to her. If someone was tracking the vehicle, they could easily assume the occupants had needed some sort of official assistance of one kind or another.

Alex ducked into the first drugstore they came across with her in tow. They bought hats, scarves and cheap raincoats they pulled over their clothing. Appearances changed, they emerged back on the street.

She opened her mouth, but Alex held up a hand to forestall her. "I know," he murmured. "Now what?"

She grinned up at him from under her Yankees baseball cap.

He answered his own question. "Now, a crowded, public place."

"Central Park crowded, or subway-at-rush-hour crowded?" she queried.

"Subway. Good idea."

Stunned that he liked any idea she suggested, she followed him down the steps into a subway station. They caught a train headed northbound out of Lower

Manhattan, and managed to snag a pair of seats. She kibitzed with him as he pulled out the stolen cell phone and took a brief look at it. Although, was it still stolen if its owner was dead?

Alex pulled out his own cell phone and initiated some sort of internet search. “What are you doing?”

“Reverse phone book. Getting a name for the owner of this phone.” His phone dinged an incoming message. “Voilà. The guy’s name was Brian Remolatto. Now. We do a quick search on him.”

“Why?”

“Looking for addresses and birth dates.”

“Because…”

“I need his numeric password for his phone.”

“Ahh.” She held her hand out. “Give me your phone. I’ll suggest numbers while you type.” He passed her his phone and she started rattling off old addresses, and the names and birth dates of various people associated with Brian Remolatto.

Alex made a sound of satisfaction and then muttered sarcastically, “How sweet. The guy used his mother’s birthday as his passcode.”

He started scrolling quickly, then cruising the dead man’s phone for useful information. He announced under his breath, “Huh. Here’s the mission tasking to eliminate us with extreme prejudice.”

“Both of us?” she asked, shocked.

“Looks that way.”

“Who sent it?” she demanded, aghast.

“An excellent question. Sadly, it looks like a numbered ISP address.”

"What's that?"

"Without waxing technical, it's an anonymous internet location that will be untraceable."

"What about his contact list? Have you checked that out?" she asked over his shoulder.

"Well, lookee here," Alex crooned. "A contact labeled Boss."

She chuckled. "That's either his CIA supervisor or his wife."

"Given the number of women in his contact list, and the number of X-rated texts in his message folder, I'm going to postulate that young Brian was single."

The train stopped, and they climbed the stairs into Grand Central Station. The place was mobbed with commuters striding in every direction across the cavernous space. "This crowded enough for you?" she asked under the din.

Alex nodded and unwrapped his headphones from around his cell phone. He put one earbud into his ear and passed her the second one. She huddled close to him to listen as he dialed the phone number of Remolatto's boss.

A male voice answered. "Go ahead, Remolatto."

Alex replied easily, "This isn't Brian. It's Alex Peters."

"Peters?" the man exclaimed. "What the hell?"

"Hey, I need to get in touch with the director of the op. Something's come up and I need to have a face-to-face conversation with the top brass."

"Christ, Peters. I had no idea you were read-in on the op. I thought you were a blind asset."

"Obviously not. Brian said you could hook me up, though."

"Kane left the office about an hour ago. She's on her way home if I had to guess."

Katie's jaw dropped. As in Claudia Kane? An icy chill passed over her. Alex's mother was the director of the entire Cold Intent operation? Even Alex seemed staggered. He physically shook himself, swallowed convulsively and then said more lightly than she'd have been able to pull off, "I guess I'll just have to call her there. How long will it take her to get home?"

"Well, she's got to get all the way out to Fairfax. I'd give her an hour. Traffic's a bitch at this time of year. Damned tourists flock to Washington and clog up all the roads."

"No kidding. Can't get a parking spot or restaurant reservation to save your life," Alex griped.

The guy at the other end snorted in commiseration.

"Okay, well, thanks, anyway, dude. Brian and I will take it from here." Alex disconnected the phone. He passed her his earbud, and she wound the thin wire around her hand while Alex deftly pulled out the phone's battery and SIM card.

"Killing it so they can't track us with it?" she murmured.

"Yup." He stowed the pieces in his pocket. "C'mon. We need to get to Washington."

"Crud. Do we have to go back into the bad guys' sandbox?"

"It's my sandbox, too," he replied grimly.

They spent the next hour getting to a car rental

agency and using one of Alex's seemingly endless supply of fake IDs to rent a car. They headed out of the city at a snail's pace as rush hour ripened into a full-blown mess.

Finally, as they inched forward, she said, "Did you have any idea your *mother* was in charge of Cold Intent?"

"My father said as much. But I didn't have confirmation until just now. It makes sense, though. The op is centered around screwing over my father."

"So this has all been a feud between your parents? Are you kidding me?"

Alex rolled his eyes at her. "I suspect there's more to it than that."

"Well, yeah. They're trying to destroy each other. And they're freaking spies. That could get pretty violent." She added wryly, "Divorce, CIA style. How special."

Alex just looked grim.

God, that had to suck for him. Sympathy for him having to grow up in his screwed-up family coursed through her. His parents had really done a number on his head. Fierce protectiveness for the child Alex flooded her. Despite her misgivings about him going on the offense against his own family, she couldn't bail out on him now. Not when he most needed her.

They drove late into the night and stopped somewhere in Pennsylvania to sleep for a few hours. Katie could seriously have used a cuddle and some comforting after the previous day's trauma, and she expected Alex could use a little TLC after finding out his mother was behind his troubles. But no sooner had she climbed under the covers than Alex stretched out on the floor beside the bed.

"What on earth are you doing down there?" she demanded over the side of the bed.

"If you busted into this room looking for a shoot-out, would you expect someone to be down here?"

"Well, no. But won't you be uncomfortable?"

"Hmm. Comfortable or dead," he said by way of an answer.

Well, hell. She sighed. "Do I need to sleep down there, too?"

"If you want."

"Yippee," she muttered. She dragged her pillow and a blanket down on the hard, drafty floor beside him. "The things I do for love," she grumbled.

"Your choice," he murmured, already half-asleep.

She was sleeping on the floor of a motel room with a perfectly good bed right beside her. It was a fitting metaphor for her life. She really liked normal. She liked waking up in the morning and feeling comfortable and safe…in her own bed. Was she really up for this lifestyle, forever? Her idea of roughing it was a Holiday Inn instead of a Marriott. Who was she trying to kid? She wasn't cut out for the *floor* of the freaking Motel 6.

Deeply conflicted, she wrestled with her choice until she passed out sometime before dawn. She woke up aching from head to foot and half-frozen. Alex was already gone from beside her. The shower cut off as she rolled over and sat up, groaning.

Alex spun out of the bathroom naked and wielding a pistol. She lurched, alarmed. "What's wrong?" she gasped.

"I heard you moan."

"I wasn't in trouble," she explained hastily. "I'm just sore from the floor."

He made a disgusted face and retreated into the bathroom. She heard the faint scraping of a razor. Huh. He hadn't shaved in several days. She'd figured he was using the dark beard stubble on his face by way of a disguise. Why the careful toilette today? Did he want to look nice for meeting his mother, perchance?

God, how weird must that be? Today, for the first time, he could meet the woman who'd given birth to him. She would be a wreck in the same situation.

Once Alex finished in the bathroom, she took his place and grabbed a deliciously hot and all too short shower. Funny how for granted she took the act of bathing until she couldn't do it. When she emerged from the steam room she'd turned the bathroom into, Alex was distracted and uncommunicative. Obviously, his brain was in overdrive. She left him alone as they headed downstairs to the front desk.

It was almost laughable how easily Alex charmed the motel's desk manager into letting him use her computer terminal. Katie took a seat in the lobby to wait for him, but he wasn't online long.

She stood when he rejoined her with a terse nod. He said merely, "I got an address."

THEY HIT THE ROAD, arriving in the rural outskirts of Fairfax, Virginia, in the early afternoon.

"So what are you going to do," she asked. "Walk right up to her front door, knock and say, 'Hi, Mom. It's me. I'm home'?"

"I'm treating her as a hostile until indicated otherwise. We'll set up a surveillance and information collection detail and see what we learn. Then we'll formulate a plan from there."

"Won't she be pretty good at spotting surveillance?" Katie asked dubiously.

"Undoubtedly. We'll just have to be better."

Katie gulped. Suddenly she felt a great deal like a minnow swimming with a pack of sharks. Sharks who wouldn't hesitate to turn on one another and attack in cold blood. She didn't belong in the company of these experienced operatives jockeying against one another.

"What do you suppose she looks like?" Katie asked.

"We'll find out soon enough."

He guided the car to an address on a country road. A modest, two-story farmhouse stood well back from the road. It was white clapboard and traditional, with a broad covered front porch and a red barn behind it. A pair of horses and a dozen beef cattle grazed in a pasture around the place. Several mature shade trees cozied up to the house. It was all very placid and normal looking.

Alex drove on past without slowing down and continued several more miles along the road before turning, going a mile or so to the west and then turning back to the north on a parallel farm road to place them behind his mother's house.

Seeing what he was doing, Katie grumbled, "We're going to have to hike again, aren't we?"

He smiled over at her a little.

"You're a sadist, Alex Peters."

"You have no idea."

"Someday, you're going to quit talking the talk and walk the walk," she retorted.

He glanced over at her in surprise. "Haven't you figured it out yet? It's really about keeping a woman off balance. I don't have to cause women any pain, or do anything at all for that matter, as long as they don't know what's coming next. The fear and anticipation does all the work for me."

Her eyebrows disappeared into her hairline. "Are you actually giving away your trade secrets to me? Since when?"

He pulled the car off the road and parked it behind an abandoned barn that looked like the next strong wind would blow it over. He half turned in the seat to face her. "Since you killed a man. There's blood on your hands now. And it won't ever wash off. Whether you planned it or not, you've crossed a line into my world. You can't go back now. I figured I might as well throw you a few survival tips."

And with that, he opened the door and got out of the car.

Gee. That was…humanitarian…of him. Jerk. Except in the next breath, she had to admit she could use all the survival tips she could get. She was a literal babe in the woods out here, running around playing spy.

She stared at his back as he dug around in the trunk of the car in the bags of supplies he'd picked up at a Walmart somewhere in rural Maryland earlier. Was he right? Was she irrevocably consigned to his world?

Dismay and terror tore through her. No! She didn't want this! She wanted to settle down with him in some small, quiet town. To raise their adopted daughter together and have a few kids of their own. She wanted rocking chairs on a porch and big family get-togethers on holidays.

A sob rattled silently through her chest as it dawned on her that the men she and Alex had killed would never get that with their families. She wasn't a murderer.

She wasn't! She was a good person. Kind. Considerate of others. Moral. A role model to little kids, for God's sake.

And yet, the facts shouted otherwise. She was no better than Alex.

The thought froze her in her tracks. Had she really thought herself better than him all this time? Had she subconsciously been judging him? And knowing him and his brilliant perception, he must have sensed it, or even recognized it outright.

God, no wonder he wouldn't commit to a relationship with her. She was no better than any of the other women in his life. They'd all judged him and condemned him. Just like she had.

Well, at least that problem was solved. She'd gotten down in the emotional muck of his shadow world and rolled around it shamelessly. She was every bit as dirty as him now.

What had she done to her life? To all of their lives?

CHAPTER TWENTY-ONE

ALEX MIGHT HAVE spent the past eight hours more or less motionless, observing a quiet farmhouse, but he felt like he'd run a damned marathon. The strain of knowing his mother was inside that building was almost more than he could stand.

He'd imagined her incessantly for pretty much his whole life. He'd dreamed about her. Had pretend conversations with her. Imagined her hugging him goodnight and tucking him into bed. He'd even answered the hard questions for her in his own mind. Why did you leave me behind when you left my father? Did you want me? Did you *love* me? Why didn't you come back for me, or at least contact me?

He wasn't even sure he wanted to hear the real answers. She'd been an insubstantial ghost hovering over him for so long, he was apprehensive of giving her an actual face or a voice.

"How late do you plan to wait before you approach her?" Katie murmured into his earpiece. She was positioned behind the house to watch for movement there.

Truthfully, they could probably go in now. It was almost 10:00 p.m. The local civilian populace would be in bed and safely out of the way, leaving the night to his kind of people.

"Getting cold?" he asked her through the microphone mounted on his earpiece wire.

"A little," she admitted.

"Any sign of movement over that way?" He already knew the answer. She'd been faithfully reporting rabbit and squirrel sightings for the past eight hours, whether out of boredom or nerves, he couldn't tell.

"Nope. All's quiet on the western front."

"We'll give it a little while longer. Once a few more lights go out in the house, I'll head in."

"What's this 'I' stuff?" she demanded in quick alarm. "I'm going with you."

"Um, no. You're not. You're my backup. If things go wrong, I'll need you to call in the cavalry."

"How will I know if anything goes wrong unless I'm with you?"

"You'll know," he replied dryly. Spies didn't usually go down quietly or without a fight.

She huffed in his ear.

They sat in their respective hides for maybe another fifteen minutes. The silence between them was actually kind of companionable. It was nice having company on a boring surveillance mission. One of the things he appreciated most about Katie was her ability to be with him without feeling a need to fill in the silences with meaningless chatter.

Without warning, though, the woods around the farmhouse erupted with movement. All of a sudden, men were moving through the woods fast. They swept the area like a Special Forces team, spaced evenly, big-ass weapons at the ready. Night vision goggles and throat-mikes identified them as pros.

Stunned, Alex ducked behind the beef steer that had wandered over to his position some time ago and been grazing quietly nearby. What the hell?

The bastards didn't even bother to be quiet. They shouted back and forth, coordinating their search and reporting possible targets to one another. He didn't even dare whisper instructions to Katie. There were too many men and they were too damned close. She was on her own.

And then he heard a sound that made his blood run cold. A woman's voice raised in fear. Katie's voice. The entire search team rushed toward the back of the house.

Panic roared through him. He was responsible for her. He'd dragged her out here, put her in harm's way. His entire body tensed with a need to rush over to her position and rescue her.

He watched from underneath the steer as a pair of big men hauled Katie up the front steps of the house. The door opened and light spilled out into the night. A tall, slender, blonde woman stood in the doorway.

It was her.

His body went hot and cold at the same time, and he could not stop himself from staring hungrily at her face. He hadn't gotten her far wrong in his mind. She was beautiful. And even from here, she looked cold. Her expression was harder than diamonds as she gestured to the men to bring Katie inside.

Why hadn't the bastards shot her in the woods where they'd found her? These guys had to be Cold Intent's core operatives. The same people who'd been shooting at Katie for the past few weeks. Why not just kill her now?

Of course, the answer was obvious. Claudia Kane had a few questions for Katie about her son. And *then* they would kill her. Knowing Katie, she would hold out against questioning as long as she could. And God knew, the McClouds were a stubborn bunch.

But Claudia would break her. Katie was no professional operative. The good news was that after the sweep netted Katie, the team of men had all trooped back into the house behind her. The bad news was he had maybe an hour to rescue her from his mother. At most.

KATIE STARED AT the woman who'd given birth to Alex. Claudia Kane was as elegant and cold as she'd expected the woman would be. Tall, thin, blonde, silver-eyed, and wearing her middle years with hard grace. A bit of a dominatrix vibe came from her. Or maybe that was just the severe wool suit and black patent leather stilettos talking. Any mother who could abandon her newborn baby to the clutches of a spymaster like Peter Koronov couldn't have much of a heart.

Claudia, seated in a big wingback chair across the elegantly furnished living room, studied her closely, as well.

The men who'd dragged Katie up off the ground and into the house had released her arms and now stood quietly in the corners, weapons still drawn, alert and wary. It was clear they were waiting for Alex to make a move to rescue her. She was bait. *Sit tight, Alex,* she thought desperately. *It's a trap.*

Claudia finally broke the silence. "Tell me about my son."

"He has your eyes," Katie blurted. Although Claudia's might contain a tiny bit more blue than Alex's gray eyes, both sets of eyes were sharply intelligent and observant.

"Where is he?"

"I have no idea."

"Don't lie to me. You're not any good at it."

"But I really don't know." Technically, she didn't. He could still be in the pasture in front of the house, or he could have fled somewhere else entirely in his efforts to avoid Claudia's men.

"What are you doing here?" the woman demanded. Her voice lashed at Katie's waning courage, shredding what little she had left.

"Sitting, at the moment." As irritation flashed through Claudia's eyes in the exact same way it did Alex's, Katie added less confrontationally, "I'm curious actually. I'm wondering why you chose to surface now. Why you thought you could use your son to destroy your ex-lover, and why you would hold such a grudge against Peter Koronov after all these years."

Not by so much as a flicker of an eyelash did the woman react to Katie's accusations. Cool customer. Had Katie not dealt with the woman's equally cool son for so long, she'd have been scared to death of this woman. But Katie *had* dealt with Alex, and she *did* know how to read his moods and tempers. Katie sat back patiently in the wooden chair they'd hauled in here from the kitchen. She could wait out the mother the same way she waited out the son.

"How did you meet Alex?" Claudia threw out.

Katie knew the technique. She did it with her kindergartners. Get them talking about something, anything, innocuous, and then shift the conversation to the thing she really wanted the child to talk about once they were already gregariously chatting. She replied, "I suspect you already know that. How long have you been watching Alex? A few years? His whole life, perhaps?"

"I'm asking the questions here," Claudia snapped.

She could ask all she wanted. It didn't mean Katie was going to answer. She wasn't about to spill Alex's innermost feelings to this woman.

"Why did the two of you go to Cuba?"

Katie frowned. "You don't know? I would have assumed you were of sufficient rank in the CIA to have been briefed on his activities. If nothing else, I would have thought you'd know what the primary operative in your operation was doing. Yet, here you are, asking me? Interesting."

Claudia's pale stare narrowed. It actually was interesting seeing Alex's eyes in a blond, fair head instead of contrasting with Alex's dark hair and bronze skin. "You're in too much trouble to be flippant with me, young lady."

"How am I in trouble? Call the police and accuse

me of trespassing if you'd like. I haven't done anything else wrong." A flash of the dead bodies she and Alex had left in a forest in New Jersey zinged through her mind's eye. But she pushed the grisly images away.

"You've interfered with a secret, high-level government operation."

Katie jumped on that one, replying casually, "You mean Cold Intent? Sheesh. That's no secret. A ton of people know about that."

Even the guys in the corners lurched at that salvo.

"Who knows?" Claudia bit out.

"Well, there are Alex's hacker friends. I don't know how many of them helped him with the research on Cold Intent. Could be dozens. Oh, and there's Alex's boss at Doctors Unlimited. But you already knew that, didn't you? You're the one who had André relay your orders to have Alex and me separated and Alex drugged at Guantánamo, aren't you?"

Claudia's eyelids flickered slightly. *Hah.* Katie's stab in the dark had struck true.

She continued. "I imagine André has told some of his staff about it by now. And then there's my uncle, Charlie McCloud. You might know him? He's the deputy director of Plans for the CIA. And then there's my brother Mike. He's Navy intelligence. And my other brother in the FBI. And my dad, of course. He's a retired Green Beret and an ex-cop. And then my other brother—"

"Enough."

The guys in the corners looked restless. They were watching Claudia with something akin to concern.

Like maybe their boss was losing control of the situation. Katie pressed her advantage.

"What do you think, Claudia? Do you suppose Alex has told Peter about it yet?"

"You tell me."

Katie shrugged. "You'd have to ask him."

"Oh, I will."

"You can ask. I doubt he'll answer. You made a mistake, you know, leaving him with Peter. His father trained him superbly over the years. Alex is way too smart to fall for your machinations."

"I hope for your sake you're wrong," Claudia retorted.

"What? You think this transparent little trap is going to catch Alex off guard? You really don't know your son, do you?"

She probably shouldn't have pointed out to Claudia that using her as bait wasn't going to work. It made her useless to Claudia. The good news was she doubted Claudia would let the men shoot her in this pristine house. They would haul her outside to execute her. Good Lord willing, that would give Alex a window to do something miraculous to save her.

"Tell me something, Ms. Kane. Why did you leave your infant son behind when you left?"

Claudia leaned back and crossed one elegant leg over the other. Katie didn't honestly expect the woman to answer, so she was surprised when Claudia said, "It wasn't my choice, really. I had to get out fast before Peter had me arrested or killed. My escape route relied on stealth and speed. It wouldn't accommodate a squalling newborn."

"And yet," Katie replied softly, "Alex and I managed to escape Zaghastan with a squalling newborn. You could have taken your son with you had you really wanted to. You'd have found a way. But you chose not to."

For an instant, Claudia looked stricken. As if the woman had actually believed her own excuse all these years. But then, her eyes shuttered the exact same way Alex's did. Katie had scored a direct hit with that one.

After a long, thoughtful pause, Claudia commented, "I may have underestimated you, Miss McCloud."

Katie nodded sympathetically. "Everyone does. I think it's the kindergarten teacher thing that throws people off."

An unwilling smile tugged at the corner of the woman's mouth. God, that was just like Alex. It was a little freaky looking at a blonde, female version of him like this.

A need to keep this woman talking, to buy Alex time to figure out a rescue plan or to call in the cavalry, pressed in on Katie. She murmured, "Peter must have been very angry when he discovered you were a spy. He told Alex he loved you."

"He was furious." Claudia shrugged. "As for having feelings for me, who knows? It's complicated with spies."

"Tell me about it," Katie agreed fervently. "It's all layers piled on top of layers, meaning buried within meaning, nothing straightforward, nothing black or white. It's all shades of gray."

"Said like a woman in love with my son."

"Oh, I've never made any secret of my feelings for Alex. But as for how he feels about me…that's anyone's guess. You did quite a number on his head, Claudia. He doesn't trust any woman farther than he can throw her."

"For your sake, you had better hope he cares enough about you to reveal himself to me."

Katie gulped. She honestly didn't know if he would put himself on the line for her at this juncture. He'd been willing to play house with her and Dawn a year ago. He'd even pushed past his personal demons far enough to invite her to live with him.

But now? After his mother had turned on him? After the CIA had finished turning him into a killer? After the drugs in Guantánamo had unleashed his subconscious paranoia? After his mother had dived into the ongoing game of manipulating and controlling him? After she, herself, had refused to believe him when he'd tried to show her how dangerous the world really was? Who could he trust, really?

Tragically, she suspected the answer to that was no one. Absolutely no one at all.

CHAPTER TWENTY-TWO

COMMON SENSE TOLD him to back away from his mother's house very slowly. To melt into the night and disappear. To leave behind everyone and everything he'd ever known and never look back.

Alex's head felt like it was going to explode as he watched the only two women who'd ever been important in his life through the window of that house. He was so full of conflicted feelings and thoughts he couldn't make sense of any of it. What the hell was he supposed to do now? Was Claudia dangling Katie as bait to suck him inside, or was there more to their stilted conversation? Was it all an act? Had the two of them been working together all along?

Think. Work through the logic. Except logic refused to come. Instead, feelings bombarded him from every direction. Voices. His father's voice. André's voice. Katie's. Dawn's. His mother's. The voices of the people he'd killed. Those he had yet to kill. The cacophony deafened him.

He mashed his hands against his ears, but nothing would silence the mad chorus. All of them pushing and pulling at him, tugging him one way and then another. Back and forth like a rag doll. God, they were tearing him to pieces.

He squinted at the house, brightly lit from within, barely able to make it out as everything spun wildly around him. Something warm brushed past him. He threw a hand out to steady himself and his fingers sank into thick, coarse hair. The damned cow was back, looking for food.

He clung to its back for balance, for sanity, until it shifted away from him uncomfortably. But the animal had done its job, given him something concrete to focus on. Given him a second to find himself.

Slowly, laboriously, Alex pushed every thought out of his mind. Every sensation. He took a breath. Held it. Exhaled slowly. Again.

When all else failed, he returned to the beginning. To the most basic act of existence. Breathing. Cold air filled his lungs but was hot in his nostrils when he blew it out.

Better. He stretched his senses to include the night sky above him. Black. Pinpricks of light peppering it. Stable. Motionless for the moment. He moved on to including the darkness around him. The frost-crusted grass crunching beneath his feet. The rough warmth of the cow a few feet away, its earthy smell.

House. Barn. Trees. Light. One by one, he added the objects around him to his awareness. Cautiously, very cautiously, he added thought. Katie was inside. His mother's men had snatched her. Bait. They were holding her to lure him out.

Decision. He had to make one. Leave Katie to her own devices. Or rescue her.

He loosed the reins on his mind enough to let it evaluate the threat. Not great odds of success if he went in. Better to make them bring her out.

The exercise of forcing his mind into a semblance of discipline was exhausting. More so than he'd expected. Faint surprise registered. Was this what it felt like to go mad? He'd wondered a few times in the past if he'd been losing it. He'd been wrong before. *This* was what total loss of mental and emotional control felt like. The scientist within him greedily registered and cataloged sensations and observations.

He started when abrupt movement filled the living room window. Two men, previously not visible to him, stepped out of the corners of the room to take Katie by the arm. They would take her out back, to the barn. That was where he would execute a prisoner. Out of sight. Sound muffled.

Except the men headed for the front of the house. Pushed her out onto the porch. Ahh. Getting frustrated with her little fishing expedition, his mother was. Tired of this game, she was. Claudia was going to force the issue. Maybe have her guys shoot Katie in the kneecaps.

His odd detachment retreated a little. The idea of Katie in pain burned away some of the haze shrouding his brain. Was that haze actually shock? Was this shock from the inside looking out?

Now what? Katie's trademark question floated through his mind. If he wasn't going to let them kill her, he probably shouldn't let them maim her. It would be a useless waste of her body.

But something stubborn deep within him, some part of him determined to survive, and furthermore to win, rebelled against meekly surrendering to those bastards. He spied the tall, slender form of his mother rising from her seat to follow Katie outside.

Now.

His body went into motion of its own volition, propelling him at a silent sprint toward the back of the house. His instincts had spotted the opening before his conscious mind had. His body had started exploiting it before his thoughts even began to catch up to his training. Peter might be a bastard, but he'd trained a hell of an operative.

And what his father hadn't accomplished, his mother and her cronies at the CIA had finished off.

He was a creature of the night. Of shadows and stealth. Of cunning and violence. He was exactly the son his parents had raised him to be. For the first time in his life, he embraced what he was with a certain measure of peace. They'd both wanted a killer for their separate reasons—and they'd gotten one. He was better than either of them could even begin to dream of.

He raced up the back steps to the kitchen door. The lock was so old and simple he didn't even need a second lock pick to throw the tumblers. One did the job. He was inside in a few seconds. He padded across the marble tiles of the kitchen floor and glided down a short hallway. The front door was straight ahead.

Katie was visible on the porch, as were the restraining arms of her captors on either side of her. Alex waited, perfectly still, part of the shadows themselves. His mother stepped in front of the door, back a few feet from the opening.

"Go ahead, Katie," Claudia ordered. "Call for him to come out. Feel free to tell him that my men are going to shoot you very painfully if he doesn't."

Katie whimpered a little and then shouted, "It's a trap, Alex! Run!"

One of the men backhanded her viciously. Blood flew from her mouth in an arc that splatted on the white porch column as Alex lunged. In one blindingly fast move, he was at his mother's back. His left arm went around her throat, and his right hand jammed a pistol to her neck, under her ear.

He growled, "Hi, Mom. I'm home."

The men on the porch whirled and their weapons came to bear on him.

In his mother's ear, he murmured, "You might want to explain to your thugs that my pistol has a hair trigger. Tell them how the impact of a bullet slamming into my skull will cause an involuntary reflex that makes my fists clench. Your brain will be sprayed all over the house along with mine. Shall we die together, Mother?"

Even he heard the acid in his voice when he said the word.

The woman in his arms went deceptively relaxed and then lurched violently, attempting to tear free of his grasp.

As if he hadn't seen that one coming from a mile

away. He tapped her almost gently in the temple with the barrel of his pistol. Just enough to daze her but not enough to knock her out cold.

"Tsk, tsk," he chided. In the moment it had taken for him to subdue Claudia, Katie had managed to get herself turned around in her guards' arms to face him. The voices were clamoring again in his head. He had a gun to his mother's head. How fucked up was that?

Katie looked equal parts relieved and chagrined to see him. "I told you to run. To save yourself."

"My mother. My problem."

She stared at him closely. Worry blossomed in her big blue eyes. Dammit, she knew him too well. She saw how hard he was having to fight to hold it together. She spoke slowly, carefully, as if willing him to hear her. "She's not worth it, Alex."

His mother stirred in his arms, rousing to full awareness once more.

He ordered grimly, "Call off the dogs, Claudia. I'd hate to have to kill this batch, too."

"It was a tactical mistake to call my ops center, Alexei," Claudia said calmly. "It was obvious that you would make a run at me like this. You didn't seriously think I would not take precautions to protect myself, did you?"

As if on cue, a half dozen weapons safeties disengaged behind Alex. *Sonofabitch.* She'd had an entire backup team just sitting in the woods, waiting for him to show himself. Bastards had probably had him in their sights all along.

"Disarm him if you please, gentlemen," Claudia said pleasantly.

Hard hands grabbed him, yanked the pistol out of his hands and searched him roughly and rudely. He was manhandled back into the living room, along with Katie.

"Found this, ma'am," one of the heavily body-armored men announced. Alex spied the flash drive of chemical weapons evidence in the guy's palm.

"I'll take that," Claudia announced triumphantly. She moved over to the rolltop secretary's desk in the corner and opened a laptop computer. The tableau of armed men and prisoners froze in time as the computer turned on and booted up. His mother plugged the flash drive into the computer and quickly opened the contents.

Photographs, the gas chromatograph readouts and his own case notes flashed onto the screen. "I'll be quite the hero for bringing in this evidence," Claudia purred.

"Other people in the agency will know where it came from and who obtained it."

"Of course they will. The loving son shared it with his thankful mother just before an unfortunate accident claimed his life and that of his girlfriend. So many enemies my poor son had. One of them finally caught up with him."

He watched dispassionately as she typed out a quick email, attached the contents of the flash drive to it and hit the send button with a flourish.

"Was Cold Intent really only about revenge against

my father?" he asked curiously. "Did you love him so much, then?"

"Love—" She burst out laughing. "I hated his guts."

He shrugged. "In my experience, love and hate are the two sides of the same coin. The opposite of love is apathy, Mother, not hate. If you actively hate Peter, you still have powerful feelings for him."

He felt everyone in the room gaping at him. Of all the stares, the one he chose to meet was Katie's. She was the only person here who would truly understand what he was saying. After all, she'd both loved and hated him.

Sure enough, she smiled wistfully at him just a little. Then she mouthed the words, *I love you.*

"I love you, too," he murmured back aloud. His gaze swung to his mother. "Thank you for that, Claudia. You may have been a complete failure as a parent, and I may have been raised in hate, but at least I have the satisfaction of knowing I was conceived in love."

"Love?" she screeched. "I despised Peter Koronov!"

"He never got over you, either," Alex said calmly in response to her enraged outburst.

His simple words deflated her like a balloon. She collapsed into the same chair she'd been sitting in earlier. All of a sudden, she looked every year of her age and more.

She stared at a spot on the carpet for a minute, or maybe even a little longer. And then looked up and said simply, "Kill them both."

Katie let out a cry of distress.

Alex laughed.

Claudia looked up at him sharply. “You think this is a joke? That I won’t do it?”

“I think you’re a fool for underestimating your own son, Mother.”

Claudia raised a hand to forestall the thugs from dragging him and Katie from the room.

“You asked me if I thought you wouldn’t see my approach to you coming. Let me ask you a question. Did you seriously think I would barge in here without a backup plan of my own?”

“You’re bluffing,” she scoffed. “I have access to every operational deployment order in the CIA. No team was sent out here to save you.”

He threw back his head and laughed richly at that.

“What?” she demanded.

“You thought I would call the CIA for help, knowing that you have the agency in your back pocket? That was a stupid miscalculation on your part. I guess we know which side of the family my brains come from, now, don’t we?”

Katie gasped. Smart girl. She’d figured out what he’d done.

Claudia half rose from the chair. “What have you done?” she demanded.

“What else, Mother dearest? I called Father dearest.”

The phrase *Father dearest* was the prearranged signal. Alex had just enough time to dive for Katie and knock her flat on the floor beneath him before every window in the house burst inward in an explosion of shattered glass, as a Spetsnaz team poured in, their AK-47s spitting death.

CIA men leaped every which way for cover, firing back as all hell broke loose. Dozens of razor-sharp cuts from flying glass sliced his arms, back and face as he covered Katie as best he could.

The lights went out, and the chaos was complete as muzzle flashes exploded from every direction. Something hot slammed into his left leg, and he grunted involuntarily in pain. It took a little maneuvering to roll on his side and tend to the wound, but he managed to tear off a length of his undershirt and tie off the gunshot wound without getting hit again.

"Can you move?" he yelled in Katie's ear.

"Yes!" she shouted back.

He paused long enough to peel off one of the two cloth patches taped to the shoulders of his sweater and to slap it on Katie's shoulder. The infrared marker cloth would identify her to his father's men as a friend in the firefight and not a foe. His remaining shoulder patch would do the same for him. "Stay low and follow me!" he ordered as the worst of the gunfire moved outside the house.

"Ya think?" she retorted.

Grinning, he belly crawled toward the front door. Claudia's men had made for the exits and were scattering to the woods as he looked on. Good call. The Spetsnaz team had superior numbers and the element of surprise on their side. The last thing the CIA team needed was to be pinned down in the confines of a house with wooden walls, entirely permeable to high-caliber gunfire. He'd have bugged out, too, if he were caught in the same situation.

Black figures chased other black figures into the woods, and sporadic muzzle flashes were accompanied by increasingly distant sounds of gunshots. He sat up cautiously on the porch, leaning back against the wall of the house. Katie did the same beside him. He didn't know if she was even aware of huddling tightly against his side.

"Um, what was all of that?" she asked in a small voice.

"The cavalry."

"Holy cow. That was impressive."

"My old man comes through in a pinch."

"He really loves you, you know."

"Yeah. He's got a funny way of showing it, though."

"Those are some parents you've got," she commented dryly. "They're going to make the world's worst in-laws."

He chuckled, and then it grew into a laugh, and then into uproarious hilarity. She joined him, laughing until tears ran down her face. They'd done it. They'd survived his first meeting with his mother.

A black Hummer rolled up the driveway as their humor subsided.

"Now what?" Katie muttered in disgust. "Do we have to run again?"

"I'm shot in the leg. I couldn't run if I wanted to," he commented.

"What?" She jumped away from him in panic. "Where? How bad is it?"

"Bullet passed through my calf. It's not life-threatening." He jerked his chin at the man climbing out of the Hummer. "Besides, we've got company."

He recognized the bulldog silhouette of André Fortinay. Alex sighed. Time to face the music for this little stunt of his. "Help me to my feet," he murmured to Katie.

She leaped up and bent down to help hoist him upright. His leg hurt like hell, but that was a good sign. The nerves were operational. He tested the limb, and it held his weight without any new pain or numbness. Bone wasn't broken, then.

Fortinay strode right up the porch steps, not stopping until he was face-to-face with Alex and Katie, who'd wrapped her arm tightly around his waist. Protective little thing, she was.

"What in the hell have you done, Alex?" André demanded.

He shrugged. "I took what measures I deemed necessary to protect myself when I approached an armed and hostile target."

"That *target* was your mother. A high-level intelligence asset in the U.S. government in charge of an extremely important and classified mission that you have blown to hell and back."

"That asset tried to kill me and Katie."

"Speaking of which, where is Claudia? I have orders to bring her in for debriefing."

Katie piped up fervently, "Please tell me she's in huge trouble for trying to kill her son."

André shrugged. "I'm just following orders. I have no idea what will happen to her."

Alex looked around the front yard and pasture. "She didn't come out this door. She must have gone out the back."

"Or she's still inside," Katie added. "Did she get caught in that initial burst of gunfire?"

Alex hobbled inside quickly, alarmed. He didn't pause long to examine his feelings. For operational purposes, he hoped she'd been immobilized if not taken down outright. But in his heart, his feelings weren't so simple. He'd loved the idea of her for so long it was hard to separate the reality of the woman from the fantasy of her.

Katie wrapped her arm around his waist again, restraining him when he would have hopped over to the stairs to clear the upper floor of the house. "Let André's men do it," she murmured.

"Clear!" someone shouted from upstairs. "There's no sign of Claudia Kane, Mr. Fortinay."

André swore under his breath. Alex shared the sentiment. And yet…a breath of relief whispered down his spine.

They waited almost another hour while André's men did cleanup duty in the woods around the house. The Spetsnaz team disappeared as suddenly as it had arrived. If any of the Russians had been injured or killed in the firefight, they'd carried out the casualties when they left.

As for Claudia's team, a number sported gunshot wounds around the high-tech body armor they'd all worn. One man had been killed by a head shot between the eyes. His body was loaded in the second Hummer that had arrived not long after André's, and the vehicle drove away.

Finally, the cleanup team reassembled at the house. A big, gruff man reported in to André. "There's no sign of Ms. Kane, sir. She's gone."

Alex snorted. Now there was an understatement. He had no doubt the Claudia Kane identity was dead. His mother would disappear to who-knew-where and not emerge again until she'd built a new legend, a new face, a new life. Just like he would have. His mother was back to being a nameless, faceless ghost who might or might not ever reappear in his life.

And maybe that was as it should be. She'd been a ghost in his mind for so long he almost couldn't conceive of a flesh-and-blood woman taking its place.

In the meantime, Katie's body was warm and vibrant against his side. Real and alive. Here and now. She was no ghost at all. She had substance and form. He could wrap his arms around her, hang on to her, tell her his fears and dreams, pour his love into her, and she would return all of it.

Finally, at long last, the ghost of his mother had released its hold on his heart. He was tired of her cold comfort. Cold Intent had been well-named, after all. It had been all about her rage and desire for revenge.

But Katie had banished all of that from his heart. Instead, she filled him with laughter and the heat of real love. A real relationship. As reluctant as he was to admit it, he might just need a relationship in his life. With a woman who loved him unconditionally.

He pulled her into his arms and kissed her long and deeply. She melted into him the way she always did, and for once, he didn't fight the feelings she aroused in him. He embraced her heat, letting its promise burn away all the icy pain locked in his soul.

"Let's go home, Katie. To our daughter. Our family."

"Oh, Alex," she breathed against his lips. "I love the sound of that."

"I love you."

"I know that, silly. I've always known it."

And that pretty much said it all. She'd known him better than he'd known himself, all this time. And she loved him, anyway.

"I don't deserve you," he muttered as he tucked her under his arm and led her outside.

A sleek, black limousine was just turning into the long driveway.

"Yikes," Katie exclaimed softly. "Now what?"

"More like, now who?" André mumbled.

The vehicle stopped and the driver jumped out to open the passenger door. A tall, portly, gray-haired man wearing an expensive wool coat stepped out of the limo.

"Sonofabitch," André breathed.

Smiling, Alex started forward, dragging Katie with him. He spoke in polite Russian. "Ambassador Deryevnan. To what do we owe this honor?"

"Alexei. Your father sends his greetings to you."

He bowed his head respectfully. "Thank you, sir. What can I do for you this cold evening?"

"Cold? This?" The Russian ambassador chuckled. "We must send you back to Moscow in January for a visit if you think this is cold."

"No, thank you, sir. I'm afraid I've become a soft, coddled American."

The Russian ambassador to the United States looked around at the assortment of armed and alert men lounging deceptively around the yard. "The way I hear it, you are as tough and smart as your father. A great credit to Peter."

"Thank you, sir."

"So. You nearly start a war this night. You have put many good Russian men at risk. What are we to do with you?"

Frowning, he braced himself mentally. What in the hell was someone of this rank doing out here in person to clean up his mess? He answered carefully, "I gather by your presence here that you have something in mind, Ambassador."

The big man threw his head back and laughed. "Ahh, you are so much like him. I do, indeed, have a proposal for you."

And the guy was prepared to lay it out to him in front of his CIA handler? What the hell? Alex glanced over at André, who was listening in closely on the exchange as if he understood Russian fluently.

"What might that be?" Alex asked cautiously.

"Your mother. She works for CIA. Your father. He works for FSB. How are you to choose sides, then?

And who will trust you? Neither, I am thinking." The ambassador added shrewdly, "Or both."

"How's that?"

"From time to time, our countries need to exchange information. To share certain…sensitive…pieces of knowledge with each other. Discreet channels for such transfer of information are difficult to come by. We propose that you and your companion consider continuing your employment with Doctors Unlimited."

The Russian paused for a moment, and then continued carefully. "And we propose that you two also join the employ of a similar Russian aid organization. Doctors of such skill as yourself and your indispensable assistant—" the man glanced in Katie's direction "—are few and far between. Surely the Americans will not mind sharing your talent with others. After all, your mission as a doctor is to help all patients, no matter what their nationality."

Alex's jaw dropped. They wanted him and Katie to work for both the CIA and FSB…with the full knowledge and approval of *both* agencies? "I've never heard of such a thing," he blurted.

"I think we can all agree that your situation is unique, can we not?"

André interjected, "We most certainly can."

Katie muttered urgently, "What's he saying?"

Alex answered quickly, "He wants me to work for both the CIA and the FSB and act as an information conduit from time to time."

Her jaw dropped in shock. He knew the feeling.

"Are you going to do it?" she breathed.

Alex looked down at her. "What do *you* think? We're in this together, after all."

"Really?" she asked in a tiny, hopeful voice.

"Really," he answered firmly. "Not only do I love you, I think I *need* you."

Her jaw went slack for a moment. Then she gathered herself. "Well, in that case, I'd say the two of us will make a heck of a tightrope-walking act together. And I'm all for open lines of communication between our countries."

Alex looked up at the ambassador and André, who were both staring back expectantly. "The lady has spoken. We'll do it. Together."

* * * * *

New York Times bestselling author

Susan Andersen

proves that some mistakes are worth repeating...

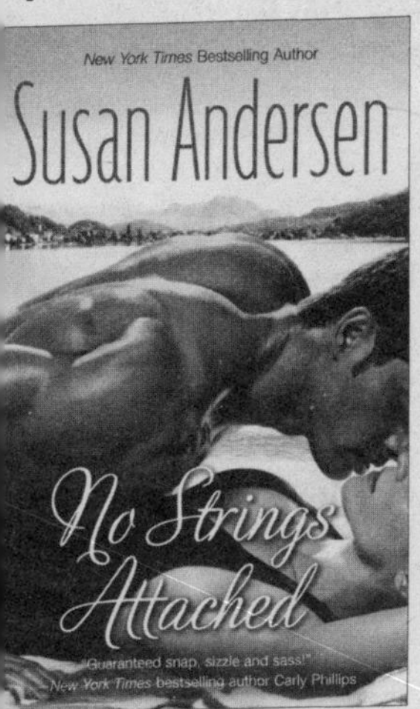

Tasha Riordan's one night with Luc Bradshaw was the best of her life. The following two—when he left her to be thrown into a Bahamian jail on bogus charges—were her worst. Now, seven years later, the undercover DEA agent is back. Invading her town. Her restaurant. Her *fantasies*. She can't trust a man who lied to her. Yet neither can she trust herself—not when their chemistry burns even hotter than before.

Learning he has two half brothers shocks Luc. Discovering they live in the same town as Tasha—that's a different kind of thrill. Their mutual st is still off the charts, but he can't get her to listen to his side of hat happened on that long-ago night. Good thing he's got powers f persuasion that go deeper than words. Because nothing has ever lt this right....

Available now wherever books are sold!

Be sure to connect with us at:

Harlequin.com/Newsletters

Facebook.com/HarlequinBooks

Twitter.com/HarlequinBooks

PHSA887

***New York Times* Bestselling Author**

JULIE KENNER

Bookstore owner Veronica Archer is eager to oblige when sexy detective Jack Parker shows up at her shop, seeking help on the stalking case he's working. Verses from Victorian erotica are being left for the victims, and Jack needs to interpret the clues—before someone gets hurt. Thankfully, Ronnie's an expert on naughty turn-of-the-century prose, but if she's going to play teacher, Jack will have to be a dedicated student....

With her own love life stuck in Neutral, Ronnie's sensual studies have piqued her curiosity, and she wonders if reality can be as stimulating as fiction. She agrees to help Jack with his case if he'll satisfy her wildest, most scandalous desires—a request Jack has no problem accommodating. But the closer they get to each other, the closer the stalker circles in, leaving Jack to question if Ronnie is merely a very skilled scholar—or the key to something far more sinister....

Available now wherever books are sold!

Be sure to connect with us at:

Harlequin.com/Newsletters

Facebook.com/HarlequinBooks

Twitter.com/HarlequinBooks

PHJK

ANOUSKA KNIGHT

How do you learn to love again?

In one tragic moment, Holly Jefferson's life as she knew it changed forever. Now—to the external world, at least—she's finally getting back on her feet, running her bakery. But inside, she's still going through the motions befitting a twenty-seven-year-old widow.

Then she meets Ciaran Argyll. His privileged and charmed life feels a million miles from her own. However, there's more to Ciaran than the superficial world that surrounds him, and he, too, is wrestling with his own ghosts. Will Holly find the missing ingredient that allows her to live again—and embrace an unknown and unexpected tomorrow?

Available now wherever books are sold.

Be sure to connect with us at:

Harlequin.com/Newsletters
Facebook.com/HarlequinBooks
Twitter.com/HarlequinBooks

PHAK928

***New York Times* Bestselling Author**

DIANA PALMER

He's everything she fears...and everything she wants.

Mercenary by name and by nature, Carson is a Lakota Sioux who stays to himself and never keeps women around long enough for anything emotional to develop. But working with his friend Cash Grier on a complex murder investigation provides Carson with another kind of fun—shocking Cash's sweet-but-traditional secretary, Carlie Blair, with tales of his latest conquests.

Then Carlie lands in deep trouble. She saw something she shouldn't have, and now the face of a criminal is stored permanently in her photographic memory…and Carlie is the key piece of evidence that could implicate a popular politician in the murder case.

Her only protection is Carson—the man she once despised. But when he learns that Carson is more than just a tough guy, Carlie realizes she's ndangered herself further. Because now her only chance to live means osing her heart to the most dangerous kind of man….

Available now wherever books are sold!

Be sure to connect with us at:

Harlequin.com/Newsletters

Facebook.com/HarlequinBooks

Twitter.com/HarlequinBooks

PHDP880